Haddad scanne[illegible]
as they left the [illegible] crossed the bridges spanning the Havel river, and turned into Gatow Strasse. Kathy watched him from the corner of her eye. She remembered the editor of *Soldier and Fortune* who had recommended Haddad saying of him: "This man's good, he's very good—one of the best there is—only trouble is he doesn't give a shit for anyone . . ."

"There it is," Kathy said.

Haddad looked up and saw it, a great red-brick fortress with massive austere towers and ramparts and small barred windows, looming over the surrounding buildings. Spandau.

Also by Daniel Carney

THE WILD GEESE

and published by Corgi Books

Daniel Carney

The Wild Geese II

(originally published as The Square Circle)

CORGI BOOKS

THE WILD GEESE II

A CORGI BOOK 0 552 11831 1

First publication in Great Britain

PRINTING HISTORY
Corgi edition published 1982 (as The Square Circle)
Corgi edition reissued 1985

This book is set in 9½ on 10 Plantin.

Corgi Books are published by Transworld Publishers Ltd.,
Century House, 61–63 Uxbridge Road, Ealing, London, W5 5SA

Printed and bound in Great Britain by
Hunt Barnard Printing Ltd., Aylesbury, Bucks.

Dedicated with love
to Sally

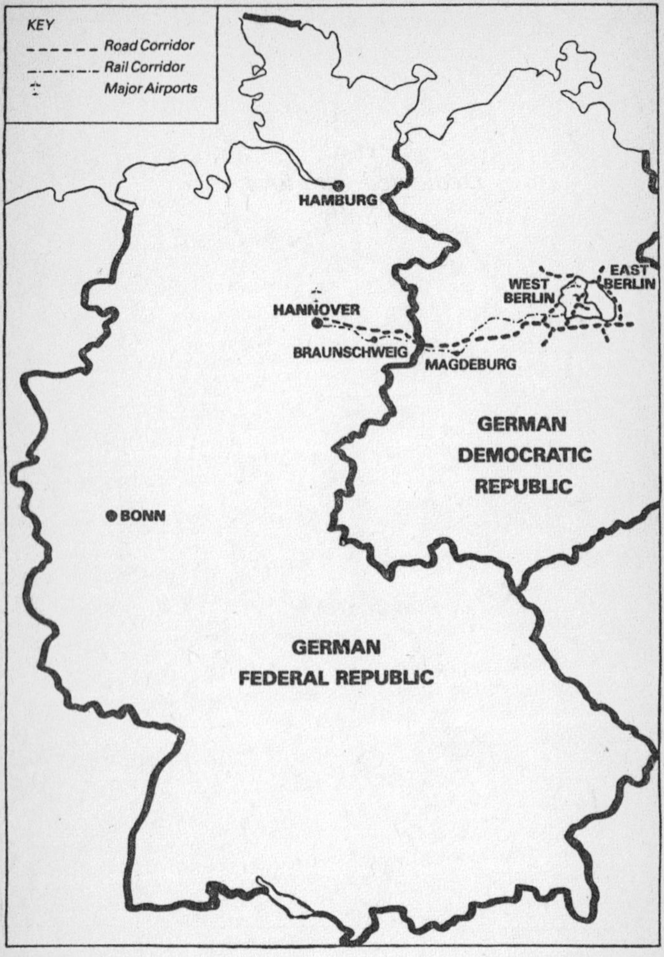

The German Federal and Democratic Republics, showing road and rail corridors from West Berlin to the West.

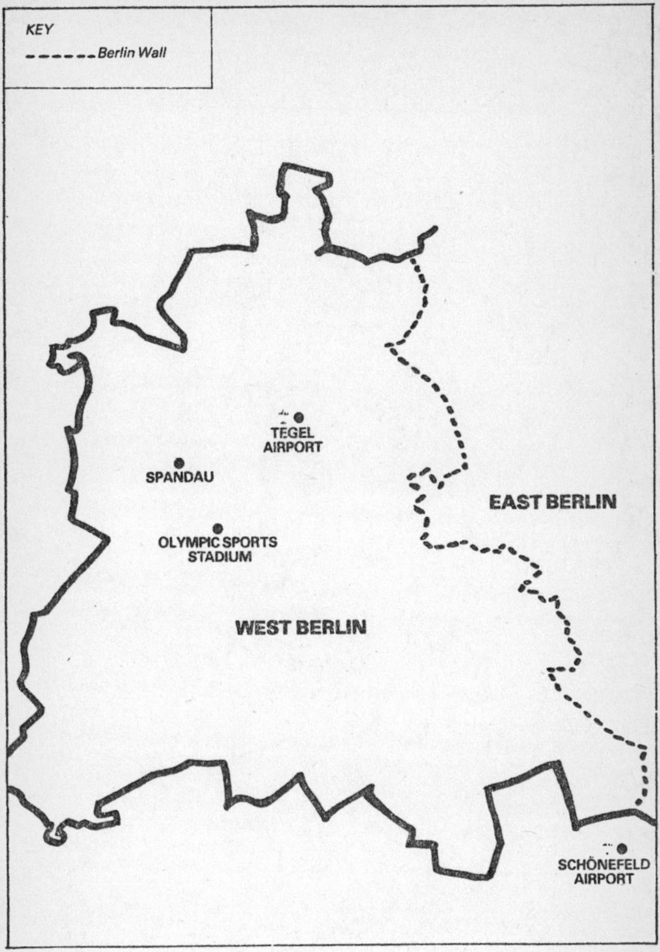
KEY
Berlin Wall
TEGEL
AIRPORT
SPANDAU
EAST BERLIN
OLYMPIC SPORTS
STADIUM
WEST BERLIN
SCHÖNEFELD
AIRPORT

West Berlin.

PROLOGUE

BERLIN- AUTUMN, 1980

A British military police convoy escorting two ambulances turned through the gates of Spandau prison fortress and drew up in the enclosed courtyard. Representatives from the four military powers controlling Spandau were waiting on the steps.

A medical orderly helped the prisoner out of one of the ambulances. He was in his eighties—a small wizened man, with sunken dark eyes. He tried to draw himself up straight, but he suffered from the shoulder stoop that often afflicts habitually erect military men in their old age. His eyes, though, as he looked about, were alert and intense.

"We saw a suspicious-looking vehicle parked across the road from the main gate, sir," the convoy commander reported.

"It's alright. We've spotted it," the duty governor replied. "It belongs to an American news team. We've decided to take no action. They'd only use it to gain publicity for themselves."

The governor signed for the prisoner and a British warder, a man in his late fifties, fell in at the head of the prisoner's escort. "I hear you're malingering again, No. 7," he whispered to the prisoner. "The B.M.H. have given you a clean bill of health." The old man did not reply. He was concentrating on climbing the ten steps ahead of him.

The guards drew up at a second massive set of doors and then entered the main cell block. On the right were the governor's offices and warders' rooms. No. 7 ignored them and shuffled on down a long, dimly-lit passage. A small procession of warders had fallen in behind him, their footsteps echoing through the empty building. They passed rows of vacant cells. At the end of the passage on the left was the old man's cell. One of the warders took the keys from his belt and unlocked the heavy wooden door. He pushed it open.

"Welcome home, No. 7," the governor said, standing back as the old man, weakened by age and self-denial, shuffled painfully inside. His cell was small and narrow, furnished with an iron bed, a small desk and a wooden chair. These three articles took up nearly all the space. The old man waited for the reassuring sound of the heavy door to slam on him, the bolts to slide home.

Alone at last, he moved slowly across the cramped cell to a barred window. He gazed up, watching the black Russian rooks wheeling and turning in the little patch of sky that showed above the outer prison wall. The old man squeezed his hand through the bars and tapped on the glass to tell the birds he was back. He wondered who had been feeding them in his absence. The footsteps of the warders receded and the fortress fell silent.

This was no ordinary prisoner. The soldiers with their machine-guns manning the guard towers on the walls, the governors and warders drawn from each of the four powers, the whole massive neo-Gothic fortress with its six hundred empty cells, all were there for him alone. His name was Rudolf Hess. He was the last man in Spandau and he had occupied that cell for nearly forty years....

HARVARD, MASSACHUSETTS, U.S.A. – WINTER, 1980

A television set flickered in a softly-lit bedroom overlooking the Charles river. A tall slim woman in her late twenties came in from the shower, untying her dark hair and shaking it loose over her shoulders. As she passed the screen she recognised the features of a well-known announcer and turned the volume up.

The woman's name was Kathy Lakas: she was a lecturer in social anthropology at Harvard University. As she sat at her dressing-table, brushing her hair with strong swift strokes, she watched a map orientating West Berlin to the rest of Germany flash up on the screen. Shots of the Berlin Wall...then the image changed to that of a documentary programme's anchor man. He was standing on a city street corner.

"As you can see from the warning notice on my right," he said, pointing to it with a gloved hand, "this is a protected area. The taking of photographs here is strictly forbidden, which is why I am carrying no microphone and the camera crew are concealed in a van across the street. I am in the British military controlled sector of West Berlin. Behind me, looming up against the leaden sky, is the grim prison fortress of Spandau.

"This fortress occupies a unique place in West Berlin's

postwar history; it is controlled by the city's occupying powers, America, Russia, Great Britain and France. All four countries provide a permanent staff of warders and each country's military take it in turns to guard the fortress one month in four. The effort in time and manpower and the cost expended is enormous, estimated to be well in excess of three million dollars a year. Half the Third World is starving, and yet all this for just one man. A solitary prisoner now in his eighty-fourth year.

"You ask yourself if this can be happening in what is supposed to be one of the most civilised societies the world has seen. Well, we have heard that the prisoner is being returned today from the British Military Hospital in West Berlin where he has been undergoing a physical check-up. We hope to be able to show him to you."

Kathy's attention had become firmly fixed on the screen, her hairbrush resting unused on her lap. A convoy of military police Landrovers escorting two ambulances appeared. They swung around the corner past the reporter, the great gates of the fortress opened and the vehicles swept inside. The camera panned forward trying to focus through the gates into the courtyard but the gates closed, shutting them out. The reporter appeared on the screen and shrugged his shoulders ruefully. "I guess they were too quick for us, but then we couldn't really expect to bring you a picture of the prisoner. He's a man who has been stripped of all identity, known and referred to only as No. 7, and just about no-one on the outside has had any contact with him for thirty-nine years. Impossible, you say, not even Alcatraz was as tough as that."

The reporter crossed the street, walking towards the camera.

"May, 1941," he went on. "In the second year of the Second World War, Rudolf Hess, the only man Hitler ever trusted and one-time deputy Fuehrer of Nazi Germany, now prisoner of Spandau, flew to England in an unarmed plane and offered himself as what amounted to a hostage for peace...can this man truly be a criminal or is he, and has he always been, a political prisoner who has been subjected to the harshest and most inhuman punishment? The whole story of Rudolf Hess is shrouded in secrecy, but tonight, in the 60 Minutes Programme, we're going to try to find some answers."

A thunderous knocking at the door broke her concentration.

"Come on, Kathy," a man's voice yelled. "We're late."

She rose and pulled back the lock. An attractive man with greying hair stood in the doorway. His eyes took in the outline of Kathy's figure through her thin robe and the hairbrush in her hand.

"The wine is flowing and the celebrating's started," he said, "and we wondered what had happened to you."

"I'm sorry," Kathy answered distractedly. "Something's come up on the television I really want to see."

"What is it?"

"60 Minutes are doing a programme on Hess."

"Hess!" Her visitor sounded surprised. "God, I thought he was dead."

"He's alive," Kathy replied. "If you call being in a cell for thirty-nine years, alive. Look, you go on ahead, I'll catch up with you in a while. . . ."

* * *

Kathy let herself back into her apartment late that night. She sat on her bed. An idea that had been stimulated in the opening minutes of the programme on Hess had been taking shape in her mind all evening. She checked the scheme through again and again, feeling the tension grow in her stomach as she realised that she'd stumbled onto something important. Time was of the essence: she would need two, possibly three, weeks to take care of the initial research, but she could just make it. She reached for the phone by her side and made two calls. The first was to her brother in Paris, the second to a colleague in New York.

"Matt," she said as his voice came on the line, "did you watch the 60 Minutes Programme tonight?"

"Yes," Matt replied. "I couldn't believe that stuff they dug up about Hess."

"Can you call a meeting of the committee?" Kathy asked urgently. "Make it for three weeks from today. I'll come down to New York. I think we've found the answer we've been looking for."

CHAPTER ONE

It was that time of year in New York when the onset of winter can no longer be ignored, when the cold and the damp bite into the bone and the early evening darkness presses down through the canyon-like spaces between the buildings onto wet black pavements. Kathy Lakas hurried up the steps of the School of International Affairs on the Colombia University campus and on along the corridor past the Frank Altchual auditorium. Matt lectured at the S.I.A. and out of hours the committee used one of his classrooms for their meetings.

Matt was waiting by the door as Kathy opened it. He took her coat and she could see behind him the six men in the room already seated around a long wooden table. Kathy knew them all. They were contemporaries of hers, men who in the heady years of the late sixties and early seventies had joined her in the forefront of student-inspired social upheavals that changed the face of university campuses and helped to alter American politics. After graduation several had followed academic careers like herself. Others had been sucked into business or the professions, but they had all kept to their liberal commitment, joining together in the mid-seventies to form a pressure group known as the Committee for the Preservation of Human Rights.

"Hi, Harry," Kathy said as a short, paunchy, ginger-haired law professor rose to greet her. "Welcome, Kathy," he answered. He was chairing the meeting and he waved her to a seat at the head of the table. Kathy nodded to the other men around her, Don, Aaron, John, Blake, Paul. Matt drew up a chair close to hers and she knew him for her ally, in spite of his reservations concerning the project.

Harry tapped one of the briefing sheets which Kathy had prepared for them. "Let me begin by thanking you for providing us with this really good report. I can't fault your research in the time you've had available to you, but I have one question which puzzles me and I think all of us here. To wish to rescue a man from persecution, well," Harry shrugged, "that's what we're here for. But Kathy, why Hess? What craziness is this? For a start most of us here are Jews, what do we want with an old Nazi?"

Kathy felt the attention of the men in the room fasten on her. She disciplined her mind to think and speak clearly, knowing that this was going to be one of the most difficult questions she would have to answer that night.

"We are being criticised, and it's partly justified," Kathy said, "that our concern for human rights has centred mainly on political dissidents who are academics like ourselves, held in the East, most of them happen to be Jews. We are in danger of being considered an extension of Israeli policy and this would be very damaging to our cause. For our work to be effective, we must be clearly seen to support all men who are the subject of injustice, regardless of race or creed. True, Hess was an enemy of the Jews, but he flew to England during the early years of the war, trying to make peace, and after thirty-nine years of living death alone in a cell no-one pretends he is still paying for any crimes he once committed. He has become a political pawn and therefore part of our concern. Our committee was founded to monitor the General Assembly's Declaration of Human Rights, part of which was written into the Helsinki Agreement of 1978. Thirty-five nations were signatories to that agreement, among them the two superpowers, Russia and America, and then Great Britain and France. It is these last four countries who are responsible for holding Hess in Spandau.

"We have been searching for a cause to bring to the forefront of public notice the failure of these powers to abide by that agreement. What better example can there be than Hess?"

"You can look upon Hess as a cause?" Aaron asked incredulously from the end of the table.

Kathy looked towards him. She had grey-blue eyes and she possessed a disconcertingly direct gaze. Matt recognised the determined set to her mouth and chin. They had been lovers briefly, long ago, when she was a wild, unkempt girl driven by a sense of purpose greater than he could match, and they had criss-crossed the country, speaking from any platform they could find. The years had matured her into a very attractive woman, still with a driving sense of purpose, but with a depth in her eyes now that showed her for a thinking, caring person.

"It sounds harsh," Kathy admitted. "But we need a cause. Since '77 we've been losing ground steadily. A liberal pressure group such as ourselves can no longer count upon public support because as the promises made at Helsinki are conveniently being forgotten, the governments, particularly those based in Eastern Europe, feel they now no longer have to listen to us. We can campaign and petition and canvass in utter frustration, but we can no longer deliver. You know as well as I do, Aaron," she went on, "that without some major success our friends' support and our funds will dry up, and within two years this committee—which in the past has been so successful—will cease to exist. We either hit back or go under."

The men in that room were silent, knowing that she spoke no less than the truth. They were also uncomfortably aware that the death in exile of Kathy's father had left her with a greater commitment to the human rights cause than any of them held.

"I don't need to remind you," Kathy pressed home her argument, "that the reason behind Hess's incarceration in Spandau has evoked a great deal of interest. He has attracted a constant stream of publicity over the past thirty-nine years and as you know he was recently the subject of a major American television documentary. Attempts have been made, particularly in Europe, to have Hess released since the early 1960s. You will even find a note in Winston Churchill's memoirs disclaiming any responsibility for the way in which Hess has been treated. So we have a popular cause. One which will draw to us a storm of controversy and publicity and which strikes across the board at the powers who signed the Helsinki Agreement. With this one act," Kathy urged, "we can reach from Europe to Russia and America; the governments of three-quarters of a billion people are involved and we put ourselves right back on the map."

Kathy sensed that this was the time to strike. "Therefore I suggest," she continued calmly, "that we take a lesson from the more successful terrorist organisations. I am not proposing that we follow their actions directly, but they have understood the value of one major violent act to draw world attention to their cause. I have thought this through and come to the conclusion that we have to use their methods, which have proven very successful, but I will not ask you to undertake this rescue if we cannot be sure of using the minimum of violence."

"Who would you propose to get to help us on this?" Harry asked incredulously. "A terror group? Because none of us here are equipped to do it."

"No, I thought of that," Kathy replied. "Any contact with a terror group would only weaken our cause with the public and the media. I propose that we use a mercenary."

The reaction was much as she had expected.

"My God!" Harry sounded shocked. "You've got to be crazy!"

"To use such a man," Aaron said quietly, angry, "is out of the question. It is a totally immoral suggestion and I will have nothing to do with it."

"Would you prefer to consider a terrorist group?" Kathy asked them drily. "Do you think a group of hotheads like that will be more acceptable to your consciences...?"

Matt cut in from across the table. "We agreed to this meeting. Now let's listen to what she has to say," he demanded.

"We have no choice," Kathy told them. "We need a professional who is as trained and experienced in this field as we are not. We want a man who will work solely for money. We have the brain—all we need is to buy his muscle and control him. We could not hope to control a terror group in the same way, they might well substitute our cause for their own, which is a risk we cannot take."

"Well," Matt said, catching Kathy's eye as he leant back in his chair, "no-one likes them, but we've achieved nothing through talking and if it comes to a war, then you need soldiers."

The others were silent, still uncommitted.

"I don't like it," Aaron protested, "we'd be getting way out of our depth. We're not equipped for this."

"Aaron, will you shut up and listen," Blake spoke from beside him. He was a professor at Colombia and his field was sociology. "This is the first time I've heard anything I can get excited about since I joined this committee. When I think of the frustration that we've faced over the past two years, I think she could have something."

"Well, Kathy," Harry silenced them, "who is going to find us this mercenary?"

Kathy was silent for a moment. She realised that no-one there was going to volunteer. "I will," she said.

"Have you a man in mind?" Blake asked.

"No," Kathy admitted. "If the committee give me their approval, I guess I'll have to find one."

One of the men who had remained silent all through the meeting was Paul. He lectured in political science at U.C.L.A. Tall and aesthetic-looking, he had once been one of the most radical men in California.

"Kathy," he asked, "if we do get Hess out of Spandau,

what are we going to do with him? He's eighty-four years old and he's been alone in a cell since the Second World War. He's probably insane by now."

"No," Kathy said, "I've checked on that. He is still sane. Very withdrawn, but sane. I've heard that he's even kept a somewhat sardonic sense of humour all these years. As to what we're going to do with Hess, well, I don't know how much to expect until we can get close enough to talk to him," she admitted. "But through the medium of press conferences and television we can take a man who has spent thirty-nine years in a cell right into people's homes. You and I know what ten years in a jail can do to a man, well, let the public see what thirty-nine years can do. At the same time we'll use him to draw as much attention as we can to the other political prisoners held in psychiatric wards and labour camps, then we'll send the old man of Spandau home to his wife. She has never remarried and she's prepared to look after him. I'm certain he'll be left to die in peace there, because once Hess has found his freedom, Western public opinion will be so inflamed that the four powers won't dare to bring him back."

Harry glanced at the men on either side of the table. "Kathy, would you give us a couple of minutes to talk this over amongst ourselves?" he asked.

They called her back after twenty minutes.

"O.K. Kathy," Harry said unwillingly. "A few of us here have very strong reservations but we'll go along with you. At least far enough to find out if this idea is feasible."

The meeting broke up.

"Where are you staying?" Matt asked.

"With my aunt."

"I'll give you a lift," he offered, "I'm going that way. Mary's waiting dinner for me with friends. Do you want to come?"

Kathy shook her head. "I'm expected home. Thanks for your help back there," Kathy said as they reached his car.

"That's O.K."

"How far do you think they'll go?" Kathy asked as they drove.

"Well, they'd really like all that publicity for their committee, so they'll go along with you, but if things look too dangerous they'll drop you. Times have changed—don't expect those men back there to be as committed as they used to be. Like me," he explained lamely, "they've got wives and kids."

The car drew up at some traffic lights. Matt looked across

at Kathy, but she hadn't heard him, she was deep in thought.

"Matt," she asked, "you're a man of the world. Where the hell do I find a mercenary? I don't even know where to start?"

"Have you heard of *Soldier and Fortune* magazine?"

"No."

"It deals with all the pornography of the trade of killing. In the classified columns at the back the mercenaries advertise their services. It's in most bookstores," Matt said. "You can make a start there."

CHAPTER TWO

A tall dark-eyed man with a strong, slightly cruel face made his way through the Harvard yard and down a long corridor to one of the lecture rooms. He pushed open the door and squeezed inside. The old-fashioned room was filled to capacity with the students at the back standing on their chairs.

Kathy Lakas was at the podium. The subject of her lecture: "The persecution of the individual in present-day society". She was known across the campus for the strength of her view on this subject, and she spoke with a biting brilliance that won her a grudging hero-worship from her students.

Kathy made an important point, her gaze travelled over the students packed in the lecture room. Then she spotted the dark man by the door. There was a chilling presence about him that made him stand out clearly from the students. He was alert, dangerous; one could sense a violence in him that lay just below the surface. Kathy brought her lecture to a quick conclusion. She waited until the last of the students had left, brushing aside the ones who wanted to linger and talk to her, and made her way over to the stranger.

"Is your name John Haddad?" she asked abruptly.

The man nodded.

"I thought I told you to wait for me outside," Kathy said. She was nervous of the mercenary and she used an abrasive manner to hide it.

The man didn't bother to reply.

Kathy led the way out through the gates to where she had parked her car. The grey afternoon was drawing into night; a chill wind blew that carried with it the scent of more snow. He climbed into the car beside her. In different circumstances Kathy would have found his unusual and slightly battered face highly attractive.

"Where are we going?" he asked. She noticed he spoke his American-learned English with a slight French accent.

"To my apartment," Kathy answered. "I am the person you'll be working with, the others just want to look you over." Kathy shot him a glance out of the corner of her eye, trying to gauge his reaction at working for a woman, but the mercenary had long ago learned to hide his feelings and she could gain nothing from his expression.

"How did you get my name?" he asked as they drove. He didn't look at her but watched the road ahead.

"*Soldier and Fortune* magazine. An editor there recommended you. He said you were a top man and that you had done a lot of work in the Middle East for Israel."

Kathy parked her car outside an attractive old building overlooking the Charles river. They climbed the creaking stairway to her apartment on the third floor. Kathy opened the door.

"Gentlemen," she announced to the men assembled in the room, "this is John Haddad, occupation mercenary, whatever that means."

"I guess it means he'll do whatever we pay him to do," Aaron commented. He had all the intellectual's distaste for a man whose trade was violence. His dislike for the mercenary was coming through clearly in his voice.

"Steady, Aaron," Harry cautioned nervously. "Come in, Mr Haddad, take a seat here, will you."

The mercenary was shown to a small hard-backed chair which was placed directly beneath a standard lamp. As his eyes grew accustomed to the glare of the light, Haddad made out the faces of six men gathered in a semi-circle around him, in a room that was small and warm, overfilled with Kathy's books and possessions. He guessed that most of the men there were academics, they had a protected, intelligent, unworldly look about them. They didn't offer him their names.

"Do you know anything about a man called Hess?" their ginger-haired, paunchy spokesman asked.

"Isn't he in jail in Eastern Europe?"

"That's correct. Mr Haddad, let me tell you a little about us," the spokesman said. "This committee or pressure group, call it what you will, was formed to fight for the human rights guaranteed to all men by the General Assembly and the Helsinki Agreement. Over the last two years we have been less and less successful, we recognise the need now to make a major impact on world attention and Rudolf Hess has become of particular interest to us; not only because of the controversy surrounding his imprisonment, and the publicity he could bring our cause, but even the geographical position of his prison has importance. Spandau is in West Berlin, a tiny island of the West situated two hundred kilometres within East Germany which operates the most oppressive anti-human rights government in the Soviet bloc. If we were successful in rescuing Hess, we would automatically focus world attention just where we want it. However, we are ill-equipped to stage such a rescue, so we looked for a man who was qualified. You will have realised by now the reason we brought you here, Mr Haddad, is because we want you to get Hess out of Spandau for us."

Haddad thought back through all he could remember about Hess and his grim jail in Spandau.

"I don't think you understand what you are asking of me," the mercenary told them. "Hess must be one of the most closely guarded men in the world. Have you discovered some way I could get him out?"

"No," the spokesman admitted, "but the guarding of a fortress containing one eighty-four-year-old man must be largely a matter of ceremony between the four powers by now. We believe that with enough help from the outside there must be a way. We don't have any experience with which to find it, that's your job."

Haddad was amazed at the naïvety of these assembled men, and he hid his scorn for those who felt able to flaunt their theories on human rights and liberty from the comfort and safety of a wealthy university. What did they know of his world? Haddad looked into their smug faces. He liked them no more than they liked him; he knew at best it would be an uneasy partnership and he suspected that few of the group harboured any real belief that he would be successful. An unsuccessful attempt would serve just as well to publicise their movement and Haddad, of course, was expendable. But, for very pressing reasons, he badly needed this work.

"I'll go and look," Haddad told them, "but I do not promise you anything, and if I come up with a way of getting this man out you'll have to pay me my contract price, and that price, gentlemen, could be very stiff." The mercenary stood up, signifying that his interview was over.

"Kathy Lakas will brief you," the spokesman said. "She's fortunate enough to have a research grant that allows her to travel. She'll be going with you to Berlin. I want to make it clear she'll be representing this committee; you will make your reports to her."

Kathy Lakas followed the mercenary down the stairs and into the street. She thought she knew what was going on in his mind and she warned him: "Don't underestimate those men. They are among some of the finest minds in their discipline in the country, and the committee we've formed has more authority than you'd think." They climbed into her car and she handed him a large bulky envelope.

"This contains all the information which we've been able to compile on Hess."

The mercenary switched on the interior light and as the car pulled away from the kerb, he tore open the envelope. Inside were photographs, several sketch plans of the prison and a sheaf of typewritten notes. "Where does this information come from?" the mercenery asked suspiciously.

"My brother researched the press-cuttings agencies in London and Paris."

"Was he able to find out how Hess was guarded?"

"No. But I have a contact who is a major in the American military in Berlin and I may be able to get his help on that. I've put an air ticket to Berlin in there," Kathy nodded to the envelope, "and money for expenses. It's not that generous, but then we haven't got the sort of money I suppose you people like to splash about. And another thing," she continued, "your job is just to go in and find a weak spot, see with your trained eyes if it can be done. That's all. I'll be there to make sure you don't go killing anyone, understand?"

She had meant to define clearly the terms of their relationship, but the mercenary still unnerved her and without meaning to, she knew she was sounding abrasive again. It was a bad start.

Haddad made no comment. If he had taken offence at her jibe, he didn't show it. He was not what Kathy had imagined a mercenary to be like, there was none of the bravado, the macho flamboyance she had been prepared to resent. He dressed well and conservatively; his clothes did not hide the grace of his powerful, very fit body. Nevertheless he carried the stamp of a born leader's authority, a dangerous aura, and she knew she would have to handle him carefully.

Kathy drew her car up outside the Holiday Inn.

"O.K. I've booked you in here tonight. I'll see you tomorrow if there's any last things need clearing up and maybe drive you to the airport."

"There's no need," the mercenary answered. "I have a few things left to do. I'll make my own way to Berlin. Leave me a number where I can contact you." He got out of the car and walked a few paces, then he turned and came back to Kathy's window.

"Miss Lakas," he spoke quietly, making it clear that he didn't want what he knew to be a headstrong, politically motivated woman getting in his way. "I accept that your committee are paying me and I will work for you to the best of my ability, but it is best that I work alone because I warn you, the world that you and your friends live in can have no understanding of the risks that are taken in mine. If you insist on working with me in Berlin, then you will learn, because you will have to enter my world."

Haddad's dark eyes seemed to challenge hers through the open car window, but Kathy had been prepared for this move.

"I'll be in Berlin in twenty-four hours," she said determinedly. "Make sure you contact me."

CHAPTER THREE

The PanAm 727 descended on flightpath along the Berlin air corridor, sinking through the low cloud that threatened a dark, flat land, flashing over fields and trees, stark and wet and smattered with snow. The 727 flew on over the wall with the cleared, mined killing ground beside it that ran like an open wound around the city. Banking steeply the plane came back again into the West, passing over emergency stockpiles of coal, flaps down, engines screaming, on final approach for Tegel airport.

John Haddad collected his bag and handed in the French passport he was travelling on at Gate No. 12. A heavy-set Customs Polizei placed the passport face-down over a lighted panel on his desk. He opened it at page one, then flicked on through pages two and three. Haddad studied the photographs of wanted terrorists hanging on the cubicle wall as he waited. The passport was a good forgery and the Polizei seemed satisfied. He snapped the passport closed and handed it back.

A bus dropped Haddad at the terminal. He bought a large street-map of Berlin and found a cheap hotel in one of the side roads behind the Kurfürstendamm. He was shown to a small room on the third floor overlooking the street; it was sparsely furnished, with a narrow bed, a table and chair, and a small half-cupboard built into the wall. The anonymity of the place suited him well.

As soon as the concierge had left, he sellotaped the map of Berlin onto the wall above his bed and then began to trace the major arteries and suburbs of the city, imprinting the harsh, unfamiliar-sounding street names in his mind. He memorised the situation of the British barracks and the side streets surrounding Spandau until, at least on paper, he could find his way around like a native.

Darkness fell and he stood at the window, the reflection of the blue neon lights across the road flashing in his face. He opened the window a little and smelt the icy breath of the wet city streets, watched the prostitutes and the pimps, the scurrying mass of people silhouetted in the glare of car lights.

He stood immobile for a long time, breathing in the sounds and the smell of the city, feeling its pulse, watching and listening.

In the morning Haddad rose very early and for a full hour put himself through a gruelling routine of physical exercise. He phoned Kathy Lakas and arranged a meeting, then showered, dressed and then walked through the Kurfürstendamm area with its nightclubs, cinemas and shops. Kathy had been in Berlin a week. She had hired a little VW Golf and was waiting for him by the entrance to the Zoo Garden. He crossed the street and slid into the car beside her.

The darkness was giving way to a grey winter's daylight, the temperature well below freezing.

"Welcome to Berlin," Kathy greeted him wryly, wincing at the blast of icy air that entered the car from the open door. Haddad nodded briefly in reply.

"Did you make contact with the American major?" he asked as they drove.

"Yes."

"What unit is he in?"

Kathy was concentrating on the rush-hour traffic. "He's just some ordinary joe working in his general's staff, but he's proving very helpful."

"What have you got?"

"I didn't know what you'd be looking for," Kathy said, "so I've made notes of all the information I could lay my hands on." She drew up at some lights and nodded to the folder in the dashboard shelf. "It's in there."

Haddad scanned the contents of the folder as they left the city centre, crossed the bridges spanning the Havel river, and turned into Gatow Strasse. Kathy watched him from the corner of her eye. She remembered the editor of *Soldier and Fortune* who had recommended Haddad saying of him: "This man's good, he's very good—one of the best there is—only trouble is he doesn't give a shit for anyone. . . ."

"There it is," Kathy said.

Haddad looked up and saw it, a great red-brick fortress with massive austere towers and ramparts and small barred windows, looming over the surrounding buildings. Spandau. It lay stark and grey under a scudding sky, cold, menacing and impenetrable.

"O.K.," Haddad said as Kathy parked the car, "leave me here."

"No," Kathy answered him stubbornly, "I'm working with you on this." She had persuaded the committee to risk their money and their reputation on this mercenary and whatever happened, she was staying with him.

Haddad did not argue with her, he shrugged his shoulders and got out of the car. Kathy followed him down the street. Haddad did not waste time with the front entrance, he'd already guessed that it would be the most protected part of the fortress. Instead, he continued on down Wilhelm Strasse where the red brick walls of the barracks, built by the old German Kaiser in the 1870s and now used by the British army, joined onto those of the prison fortress.

He paused by a boom that was blocking access through the barrack gates and a sign saying "Smuts Barracks". Beside it were two flagpoles, one flying the Black Bear of Berlin and the other flag belonging to the British squadron in residence at the same time. The boom lifted and a small convoy of camouflaged trucks rolled out through the main gates onto the street. The soldiers on the barrier noticed Kathy and Haddad and they moved away, returning to the car to escape from the cold. He didn't talk and she felt conscious of being in his way. Haddad was trying to picture in his mind the area around the fortress. The west and south sides were either set back but clearly visible from the street, or protected by the British barracks. That left the east side. . . .

"Come on," he said impatiently.

They found their way around to a small strip of waste ground that led to the east side. To the right lay a row of wooden and brick shacks, each surrounded by a postage-stamp sized plot of ground where the Berliners would camp during the summer weekends and get away from it all by working in their miniature allotments. On the left was a broad strip of dead ground between the double four-metre-high wire fence and the main wall of the prison. At the top of the wall, spaced at regular intervals were modern concrete and glass "goon" towers. Overcoated and helmeted sentries armed with automatic weapons were watching in each tower.

On the north side there was just the single line of fence, but the goon towers had less area to cover.

They waited until dark, then came back and picked the lock of one of the small shacks. Inside were deckchairs, lilos and umbrellas packed away for the winter.

"Make yourself comfortable," Haddad advised Kathy tersely. "We're going to be here for the night."

Spandau loomed above the gleam of searchlights. Viewed from a crack in the shutter, it was a huge and grim fortress, the walls surrounding it so impenetrable that Kathy was forced to realise the sheer impossibility of the target she had chosen. How were they ever to get an 84-year-old man out of there? She had no answer. She was beginning to feel hopelessly out of her depth in Berlin. Her only hope of success now lay with the mercenary—she was forced to rely on him.

The day had been long and the ceaseless walking against an icy wind had tired her out. At first she had relished all the tension and excitement of action; but now there was a fear in her, a feeling of great vulnerability at spending the night alone in a shack with this unknown man whose declared trade was violence. She wondered for a moment if she were completely crazy, then consoled herself with the thought that a professional like the mercenary worked for money, and without her he would receive no payment.

To her relief, Haddad ignored her. From a crack in the shutter he watched the east wall: he knew that the fence itself would be no problem. The five-metre-high wall could be scaled, but the goon towers were so positioned that even a half-witted sentry could pick a man off as he came over. There was a hundred metres of dead ground on this side, and he was pretty sure there would be another hundred metres of cleared killing ground on the other. Without going closer it was impossible to spot trip wires or other more sophisticated alarms.

Kathy found some foam mattresses stacked on the floor at the end of the shack. She gave one to Haddad and wrapped the other around her as best she could.

"Let me help you," she offered after a while.

"Later," Haddad answered impatiently, not turning from the crack in the shutter. "It only needs one of us to watch at a time." He checked the times of the sentry changes and watched their searchlight beams running out along the tops of the walls and over the fence. He picked up the glow of a half-hidden cigarette from time to time, as a sentry walked along the platform braving the moaning, freezing wind that whistled all the way from the Russian steppes. They could not afford to risk the smallest spark of light. Added to that Haddad resented any unnecessary movement that could spoil his concentration or give him away.

Kathy's watch was not luminous and she sensed the hours dragging by; the cold in the shack was almost unbearable. She felt her feet and her toes and her body grow numb, and she had to bite her tongue to stop her teeth from chattering. When Haddad had curtly rejected her offer of help, she suspected that he had brought her there for the night as a way to shake her off him. She refused to give him the satisfaction of hearing her complain, but as the cold wracked her more and more, she resented him, crouching there, ever still in the darkness by the shutter.

In what seemed like the middle of the night, Haddad reached out and shook Kathy. "You can take over now," he said. "Call me in an hour."

Kathy watched as Haddad lay back in the darkness, assessing the information on Spandau that she had given him. The fortress lay in the British sector of Berlin, but by treaty it was administered jointly by the four occupying powers, each power providing a unit of fifty soldiers to guard the prisoner for a period of one month. This guard rotated so that the British, American, French and Russian armies occupied the fortress one month in four. A governor from each power was appointed to command the fortress, but he was really only in evidence when it was his army's turn to be guard. It was the warders, one chief warder and one subordinate, who remained constant, and they were the ones who had contact with the prisoner. In normal times the soldiers did not enter the cell block beyond the warders' rooms.

By morning both Haddad and Kathy were stiff and chilled to the marrow of their bones. They ate breakfast at a nearby café and warmed themselves over pint-sized mugs of steaming coffee.

"Well," Kathy spoke bitterly, suspecting that it had been a total waste of time, "apart from freezing our butts off last night, what else did we achieve?"

"We know, for the rest of this month anyway, the routine of the guards on the north and east walls," Haddad told her. "Miss Lakas," he said quietly, after long moments of silence, knowing what her concern had been, "you can see you're getting your money's worth, there's no point in the two of us freezing through another night. I know what I'm looking for and I haven't the time or the inclination to train you, so I'll look from the outside and you try to find out what's going on inside. I need to know what Hess's routine is, if they move him from cell to cell, if a warder is permanently stationed in the passage outside his door . . ." He was offering her an honourable means of retreat, and Kathy was forced to accept the sense in his proposal. "O.K.," she said, "I'm not sure how much longer I can work on Major Dade without outstaying my welcome, but I'll try. Contact me every second day, or sooner if you're onto something."

Haddad watched her leave, then he walked the area surrounding Spandau again, familiarising himself with the main road and side streets. Within half a kilometre of the fortress were two more British barracks, Brooke and Wavell, both occupied by crack British units. Haddad worked with the inbred caution of his trade, but he failed to spot a car turning innocently at the end of the road or the passenger in the back who photographed him through a 500 mm zoom lens.

Haddad returned to his room at the hotel and lay on his bed, hands behind his head, staring up at the map of Berlin. In his mind he fixed the position of the three British barracks that surrounded Spandau and tried to estimate the number of soldiers who would come pouring through those barracks gates if the alarm were given at the prison. Many hours later he sat up and began to sketch a rough plan of Spandau. As he drew the western wall, the one that formed a common boundary with Smuts barracks, he remembered seeing in the distance a low slate roof that reached from within the barracks almost to the prison wall.

Haddad drove to a street market that he had noticed earlier and bought himself some worker's clothes. Early next morning he watched the construction labourers flashing their passes to the soldiers in the guardroom as they made their way to work on a modern, multi-storeyed block that was being built within the barracks. Haddad clutched his lunchbox and walked along with the men. When they flashed their i.d. cards at the soldiers in the guardroom, he held up his driving licence. He was almost at the back and no-one took any notice of him.

The workmen moved off to the building which was diagonally across from the guardroom. Haddad carried on until he reached a crossroads. Ahead of him were the tanks and scout car parks. A narrow road to the right led in the general direction of Spandau fortress and the building he was trying to find. A number of soldiers passed him, but he walked on as if he knew where he was going and no-one called him back. He followed the road through an area of red brick neo-Gothic buildings. Beyond an Engineers Squadron Headquarters he branched left and found himself in a disused part of the barracks, facing what must once have been the old stable blocks. These were beautiful examples of Germanic architecture, slate-roofed, double-storeyed, craftsmen-built with exquisite brickwork patterns. They had been abandoned for some time and were becoming derelict.

Each stable block was about one hundred metres long and the end of the last block seemed to run right up against the

Spandau fortress wall. It would have been impossible to walk in the open along the stable walls without being seen by someone in the barracks or the fortress guards, but there was just a chance that a man moving carefully could make it to the fortress wall if he went through the stables.

The great stable doors were closed but one of them, under Haddad's coaxing, creaked open on rusty hinges. On either side, stretching to the distance, were endless stalls, now filled with debris. The place was silent, the wind whining through broken window panes. Haddad paused, allowing his eyes to grow accustomed to the gloom. On the right were what must have been the feed and tack rooms and beside them six flights of worn steps led to the attic, which ran the length of the stables. Haddad climbed the steps, trying to keep his footfalls from echoing through the empty building.

Weak shafts of grey, wintry light filtered through the skylights; the rest of each barrack lay almost in darkness. Haddad passed through two stable blocks; the third, he knew, would take him to the wall. These barracks were darker, more derelict than the others; the light barely showed through the partially snow-covered skylights. He made his way towards a glimmer of light that showed through a doorway some forty metres further down. He moved slowly and carefully, alert to possible danger ahead, certain that they must have rigged up some kind of alarm in a building that lay so close to the prison wall.

The door opened into a small end room. There was a window fastened with a rusted latch: several of the top panes were broken, the rest were covered with the dirt and dust of years. Carefully, very carefully, so that his face remained in the dark, Haddad drew himself level with the broken window panes. He found himself looking down over the main wall of Spandau and into the prison grounds directly opposite the main cell block. Like the stables, the old fortress had been allowed to grow derelict: many of the windows of the cells on the top three storeys were broken and no-one had bothered to repair them.

Haddad felt a surge of excitement. The prison authorities had failed to secure the stable blocks which were thought safe within the barracks. He knew that this was the closest that anyone could get to Hess without actually being inside the prison. He had found the weak spot, a place where there were no fences, no area of dead ground to cross under the glare of searchlights. A trained man could jump from this window to the top of the wall. Haddad leaned further forward to improve his field of vision. Then, from the corner of his eye, he caught a movement and ducked below the window ledge, cursing his stupidity. He had been so intent on memorising the ground that lay before the central cell block that he had not actually spotted the sentry when he stirred, but his eye had caught the outline of his rifle.

Haddad waited for the alarm to be given. When he heard nothing he cautiously raised his head again. The goon tower that he had failed so completely to notice was immediately below his line of vision to the left of him. The sentry had walked out of the shadow and was standing with his back to Haddad, staring down into the prison grounds. Haddad checked carefully—there was just the one man. His mind was racing. One sentry could be silenced. From there a group of men could make their way over the wall and through the grounds to the barred window of Hess's cell, but then Haddad knew that his problems would just be starting. How did he get a frail eighty-four-year-old man out of his cell and then back over a five-metre wall and away through a British barracks without someone giving the alarm? It was getting late. He crawled back through the attic and joined the workmen who streamed past the barracks guardroom at the end of the day.

Late that night Haddad lay stretched out on his bed, his brain exhausted from poring over his notes and sketches. It was not just a question of getting Hess out of Spandau, but then out of Berlin and across the East German border before the alarm could be given. It was problem enough that the old man was held in a fortress and that, being the only prisoner, he was watched constantly. But Berlin was surrounded by a wall and checkpoints; in effect, everyone in that city shared a cell. It seemed an impossible project. Haddad told himself it was no good trying to work any more, he was too tired. What he needed now was sleep, and yet sleep would not come.

The neon lights on the opposite side of the street flashed through the net curtains and coloured the wall and his face and hands with a cold blue radiance. Haddad's mind wandered back to memories that were better left undisturbed: to the village near the peak of the Sannine where his parents had their summer home. He remembered terraced hillsides, the rivers of his native land of Lebanon and the flat where he had lived in the suburb of Septieh, on the slopes of the mountains in East Beirut.

Haddad had a wife and child then—they were dead now. He tried to picture them, tried to bring them back into his mind, but there was a wall deep inside him, a great barrrier of pain that closed everything out.

He came staring awake later that night from a sweat-stained nightmare. He could or would not remember the dream, but he remembered some of the fighting, the city burning, looted shops, debris all over the streets, the ash-filled polluted air. Where the fighting was taking place, the people could not leave their houses to queue for bread to feed their children, and some of them died from starvation rather than risk the senseless killing in the streets. He remembered the priest, old Father Joseph. He was more than a priest, he was one of the oldest friends of his family. Now he was saying to Haddad as though he were in the same room, "John, John, I've just heard what they have done. Come into my church, my son, we will pray for your wife and child." The priest put his hand out to guide him, but the man who now possessed John's face and body turned and walked away.

"Where are you going?" the priest called after him.

"To the streets."

"And what do you think you are going to do there?"

"Survive," John said. He looked up at the smoke and ash rising over the desolated areas of the city. "There is no God, Father," he said, "only the Kalashnikov."

CHAPTER FOUR

Haddad woke early in the morning, switched on the light and stared unseeingly at the wall. At first he felt drained and alone, the emptiness in him left over from the nightmare welling up like the aftertaste of vomit. Then his eyes found the map and he had something to focus his mind and his will on again. He was almost grateful to the old man in Spandau for that.

Today he decided to visit the checkpoints in the wall between East and West Berlin. He wanted to familiarise himself with the routine at these border posts. In the back of his mind was the knowledge that if he was successful in getting Hess out of Spandau, then the road, air and rail corridors were too obvious a route for moving him to the West, could too easily be closed. Perhaps there was some opportunity available in the East.

He left the car and took the u-bahn. It was easier to use the underground than try to navigate the narrow back streets leading to the checkpoints. He came out of the underground at the corner of Simmer and Friedrich Strasse. Checkpoint Charlie, with its empty shops and bullet-scarred buildings, was just down the street. He walked past the Nissen huts housing the British, French and American military police, climbed the wooden observation tower and looked down into the no-man's-land that divided the East from the West.

In the immediate area of the crossing the road zig-zagged between crash barriers of concrete blocks and boom gates with chains hanging down. In the middle was a tall East German observation tower. On either side, stretching far into the distance, lay an area of ground that had been almost completely sanitised against human crossing: it seethed with tank traps, anti-personnel mines, barriers, ditches, searchlights, guard dogs and trip wires designed to set off lethal explosive charges.

Haddad moved on into the area of freedom bridge which the West and the East still used as a place to exchange prisoners. The checkpoint and the sanitised zone behind the wall were much the same. Even in the areas where the border ran in the middle of the canals, great barricades of razor-hooked metal spikes had been placed deep in the water. Years of development had made this wall and the killing ground behind it virtually impossible to cross. Haddad saw the small memorials along the wall to the East Germans who had died in the attempt and he knew that the only way for him to get Hess across to the East had to be with forged papers through one of the checkpoints.

Haddad was walking back towards the u-bahn station when he realised that he was being followed. He picked up just one man at first. When he tried to shake him off he spotted the second tag. They had been working him in a pincer movement. When the tags realised that they had been flushed they didn't bother to hide themselves any more. One followed about forty metres behind, the other walked some seventy metres in front. He knew there would be a third in a car and that if they weren't bothering to hide themselves any longer, they must be getting ready to pick him up. Haddad found a telephone kiosk on a crowded corner, dropped in a coin and dialled a number. As he waited for a reply he wondered who employed the men who were following him. He was a man who had made enemies, but he had not expected them to find him in Berlin. At last someone lifted the receiver at the other end and cut through his train of thought.

"Hello. Pierre Helou."

He recognised the voice. "This is Haddad," he said.

"John!" The voice at the other end was warm with delight. "Where the hell are you?"

"I'm in Berlin, there's no time to talk now. I'm in trouble. Will you help me?"

"Of course," Pierre said instantly.

"There are men following me," Haddad said quietly into the mouthpiece. "I don't know the city, tell me some place I can go to shake them off, somewhere I can get to without going onto the streets again. I think they're getting ready to pick me up."

"Where are you now?"

"Near a u-bahn."

"Good," Pierre said, his voice immediately efficient. "Take the u-bahn, Line 1, to Nollendorf Platz, get out there and go up the steps. There is an elevated section of the station that used to run into East Berlin. When the wall cut it off they turned the carriages which were blocked in there into flea market stalls. At this time of the evening it will be very crowded. Now listen carefully. At the far end of the platforms there are two exits, one on each side leading down to the street. They'll be watching those so don't try to get out that way. Instead, on the left-hand platform, half-way down, there's a door that leads to a fire exit. That's the way you must go."

"They'll be watching my hotel," Haddad said. "If I can shake them off, can I spend the night with you?" He knew he was endangering Pierre and his family. He hadn't wanted to involve them, but he had nowhere else to go. It was typical of Pierre that he agreed at once.

"I live in the Turkish quarter," he said. "If you don't shake them off in Nollendorf Platz, you'll certainly shake them off here. The u-bahn will take you on to Kottbusser Tor. My son—do you remember him? He's eight years now—he'll be wating on the station, don't say anything, just follow him. He'll take you through an arcade into the streets behind. When it's safe, call out his name and he'll know to take you home."

"Is René there?"

"Don't worry, René will be expecting you. We'll have a celebration."

Haddad rang off. The tags were all around him. One of them, a stocky young man in a lumber jacket with long greasy yellow hair and a three-day beard, was leaning contemptuously against the opposite wall. Haddad had been so easily tagged that somehow it spoilt their enjoyment of the chase. Sooner or later they would force him up onto the street and then pick him up. That was, of course, if they wanted to pick him up.

Haddad slipped out of the booth and mingled with the small knots of people who were making their way down to the platform. He kept his back against the wall, well away from the rails, while he waited for the train. And he kept his hands in his overcoat pockets, hoping they'd think he was armed. He had no gun: he hadn't wanted to advertise his presence in Berlin by carrying one through Customs and he was regretting it now.

The underground station was clean and well-lit. A bright yellow futuristic-looking train came gliding in, doors opening, people spilling out. Haddad waited until the last moment, quickly crossed the platform and took a seat by the window. Two men got into the same carriage and sat by either door. The train stopped at station after station. Haddad made himself relax, half-closed his eyes, pretending to be dozing.. His followers grew bored of watching him and stared out of the window, waiting for him to make a move. At Hallesches Tor he changed trains with the tags crowding him. Soon they would send a message to their control that he was not coming up and then they would try something else. Haddad counted three stations from Hallesches Tor. The fourth would be Nollendorf Platz.

As the train glided to a stop, he rose, forced his way past the people at the door and ran up the stairs, gaining a good fifty-metre start on his startled tags. He reached the ticket office at street level and saw the sign pointing up left to the flea market. There were now crowds of people milling around and he pushed past them up the steep flight of steps. His superior fitness was telling and he was gaining all the time on his pursuers. Finally he reached the top of the steps.

Bright yellow railway carriages, two abreast, with light spilling out from their windows occupied all the space between the platforms. They were filled with every kind of article from junk china to jewellery, toys, old clothes and antiques. The place was packed with people. There was no room in some of the carriages for the purchasers to move; the wares were spilling out onto the platforms, chairs hanging from the roof and pots and vases underfoot.

Haddad made slow progress through the crowd; in places it was just too dense for him to push through. He saw the exits at the end of the narrow, enclosed station. One of the tags was pushing his way along the right-hand platform, the other following Haddad behind on the left—they expected to head him off at the end. But Haddad was nearing the fire exit in the middle of the left-hand platform. There was only one tag to shake off, the other would not be able to cross the platform in time. Haddad stopped forcing his way through and let himself go slack. Changing his profile, hunching his head and shoulders, he drifted along with the crowd for a few paces as he edged towards the door. He glanced back and saw the tag pulling himself up onto one of the carriages, looking for him above the heads of the tourists.

Haddad showed himself for a moment: the tag leapt down and plunged through the crowd after him. In the split second that the tag jumped from the carriage and was unable to see what his quarry was doing, Haddad opened the door of the fire exit and slipped through. He came down the metal stairway fast, his feet only just touching the rungs. He jumped the last few steps and the hard tarmac came rushing up to meet the soles of his feet. He picked himself up. There was sleet in the wind and it stung his face, but he was safe for a moment, protected from the street lights by a patch of shadow below the stairway.

Few people would be out on a night like this and Haddad did not want to remain exposed on the streets any longer than he could help. He began to make his way around the side of the raised station. He felt the headlights on his back first, then the roar of a car engine above the sound of his hurrying footsteps. The tags must have been in radio contact with their control. The car came right up onto the pavement after him, the back and front passenger doors opening as it drew level, pinning him up against the wall.

The pain of a blow to his groin brought his head down against the car roof, then he was dragged half-unconscious inside. It was over in seconds. The big Mercedes came smoothly off the empty pavements and turned back into the traffic.

Haddad was forced onto the floor, his head pinned down by a heavy boot pressing hard against his neck. As a further inducement for him to remain still, the cold muzzle of a gun was rammed against his temple. The pressure on his neck was choking him, the blood from a cut on his cheek streamed into his eyes and the lower half of his body was still rigid with pain from the blow to his testicles. These people were professionals, they understood the use of pain in tranquillising a victim and not for one moment had Haddad been able to give thought to resisting them. His arms were wrenched back and he felt handcuffs close over his wrists, pinching the bone. Manacles were fastened around his ankles. Then the pressure came off his neck and he was lifted up onto the seat where he was squeezed between two big, overcoated men. Haddad let his head loll forward. One of the men began to slap his face, cursing when he realised that he was splashing the blood from the cut onto his coat.

"Hans, don't hit him any more," a quiet voice ordered. "You'll knock him out."

From the passenger seat beside the driver a man turned around; his gloved hand reached out and lifted Haddad's head.

"That's better," he said, as he saw Haddad's eyes open. "You don't want Hans hitting you any more, do you?"

The man in the passenger seat could have been in his forties or much older, it was difficult to tell. A hat was pulled down over his forehead. A scarf concealed his throat and chin, but not the thin cracked lips which resembled a livid scar. The transparently pale skin was stretched so tightly over the bones of his face that, in the dim light of the car, Haddad felt he was staring at a skull. Only the frightening sunken eyes had any life in them, and they glittered coldly with a zealot's fervour. Haddad had seen men with wasted bodies and hollow eyes like this when he worked in the American University Hospital in Beirut. He knew that this man was losing the fight against cancer or some equally terminal disease, and that he had not much longer to live.

The man let Haddad study his face so that he would know better than to expect mercy. Then he asked, "Mr Haddad, what brings you to Berlin?"

"How did you know my name?" Haddad countered.

The man shrugged. "This is our city. We like to know what goes on here."

"Who are you?"

"I ask the questions, Mr Haddad. Now, what brings you here? Tell me, Mr Haddad," the man said patiently, "you will tell me in the end, you know."

The car was turning through the back streets away from the main city centre. Haddad was silent. The pain had eased enough now for him to begin quietly testing the grip of the handcuffs around his wrists and the manacles on his ankles. The man in the passenger seat watched him and understood—he'd had years of experience in interrogation. He nodded to one of the men beside Haddad.

Haddad's mouth was forced open and a gag was fitted between his jaws so that he couldn't close them. Then a plastic bag was pulled down over his face and fastened tightly around his neck. Haddad tried to hold his breath and shook his head violently from side to side, struggling to brush the bag off, but the men on either side held him up and away from them. The bag was completely airtight. When he had to breathe, the plastic sucked against his mouth. He tried to control himself but he felt panic coming on. He attempted to bite through the gag so that he could chew through the plastic, but it was impossible. His lungs screamed for air and he knew the absolute terror of suffocating. He was throwing himself around the back of the car with maniacal force, beating his head against anything he could find, trying to tear the bag from his face. Then he felt himself fainting, his limbs giving way, his head lolling down. The fight went out of him and he collapsed onto the floor of the car.

One of the captors leaned down and pulled off the bag. The man in the front seat looked at his watch. "Nearly two minutes. He's very fit," he observed. "Wake him up."

Haddad came to with the memory that his last conscious moment had been spent trying to breathe. He knew what they were going to do to him now. Already he felt the first flickering of terror of the plastic bag. It was nonchalantly held up in front of him.

"Mr Haddad," the man began again, "tell us why a man who makes his living as a mercenary should wish to come to Berlin? What did you think you would find here?"

"If you've been following me then you'll know what I'm doing here," Haddad said. He tried to gain control of his fear, tried to stall the moment when they would put that plastic bag over his head again, but the man in front would give him no time.

"Mr Haddad," he said sharply and glanced at the bag, "answer my question."

Haddad was silent and the bag was pulled down over his face. This time he forced himself not to fight it. He sat still, shrouded in tight claustrophobic darkness. A silence descended inside the car; they waited for him to break. He heard only the hum of the engine and the tyres licking over the wet streets. Somewhere in the distance a car horn sounded. The car drew up at some traffic lights—it was the first time they had stopped. Haddad threw himself blindly to one side, trying to crash through the window. The man beside him blocked him with his shoulder. Haddad's head smashed against the door. The shock of pain used the last of the air in his lungs, the plastic sucked against his mouth. He screamed silently to himself, then his limbs gave way and he collapsed unconscious onto the floor again.

It took them longer to bring him round this time. Haddad's face was a mask of blood and sweat.

"Mr Haddad," the man in the front seat said coldly, "this will go on until you tell us—you must know from your own experience of these matters that eventually you will tell us. You were seen in the vicinity of Spandau prison. What brought you there? We think we already know, Mr Haddad, we'd just like you to confirm it. You are interested in Hess," the man in the front seat prompted. "Is that right?" Haddad nodded. They knew what he was doing, there was no point in hiding it from them any more. Besides, he was pretty sure he would have to report that it was impossible to rescue Hess.

"Who gave you the contract, Mr Haddad?"

Perhaps they still didn't know about Kathy Lakas. "Some people in America," Haddad hedged, "nobody special. Just some pressure group of liberal academics."

"And you were to try and rescue Hess?"

"I was to see if it could be done."

"And can it?"

Haddad shook his head. "No."

The man in the front seat seemed to lose interest in him. "Mr Haddad," he said contemptuously, "you are an amateur and the people who employed you are amateurs. Many people have studied ways to rescue Hess and no one has yet come up with anything remotely practicable. This city is already a battleground between East and West, we don't want mercenaries who can be bought and sold entering the fray. And in your case, Mr Haddad, we've discovered that by the time you left Beirut you had inflicted so much damage on the Palestinian P.F.L.P. commando units that they were driven to put a price on your head. These people have been good friends of ours in the past and we are anxious to render them a favour in return. That is why we are going to kill you, Mr Haddad."

The car was turning into one of the big autobahns, the windscreen wipers were flicking away the lightly falling snow. The temperature had dropped well below freezing and patches of black ice had formed on the road. The overhead lane guidance lights were showing three green and two red, indicating three lanes open to vehicles coming out of the city, two going in. There were no embankments or chains dividing the lanes, just a great wet stretch of tarmac along which cars and lorries raced at breakneck pace. One of Haddad's captors was forcing his feet into the bottom of a large hessian sack. They doubled him over and closed the sack around his head, tying the top tightly with wire. The car slowed for a moment and one of the back doors opened.

"Goodbye, Mr Haddad," the man in the front seat said. "We don't want mercenaries in our town. The manner of your death will be an example to the others who might wish to work here."

Haddad was pushed violently from the car. He couldn't use his arms or legs to protect himself, but he buried his chin in his chest, trying to roll as he hit the tarmac, to take some of the shock out of the impact. As it was, the black ice saved him—he hit it on his side and slid for about twenty metres. He heard the deep note from the Mercedes exhaust as it accelerated into the traffic.

For a moment there was silence. Then he heard the roar of one of the great trans-continental diesel trucks approaching him at speed, twenty tons on sixteen wheels hurtling down at him. He couldn't tell which way to move, the sounds seemed to be coming from all around him. Yet he knew that if he didn't move the driver high up in his cab would mistake him for a sack of rubbish, and rather than change lanes in the heavy traffic would run straight over him.

Haddad brought his knees up under his chin, rocked backwards and forwards to gain momentum and then threw himself over so that he balanced on his forehead and his knees. He rolled over again and repeated the procedure, trying desperately not to move into the way of what he thought was an oncoming stream of cars.

Then the truck was on him, a great roaring diesel, the wheels half as high as a man, hooter blaring angrily as it passed him with inches to spare, the sudden blast of air and exhaust fumes from its passing sucking him in and pitching him over. He could hear cars passing him now. He could not see, he could hardly breathe; the sack was his tomb, there was no time to try and get out of it. He thought the only way to survive was to attempt to roll across the lanes to the side of the autobahn. A blind three-legged dog stood a better chance. The traffic was heavy and although the cars were prepared to move lanes rather than run over a stricken object, the big trucks, especially the ones towing trailers, would have no option but to go over him.

There were two of them now, one truck just behind the other across two lanes. He could hear the thunder of their diesel engines above the more subdued roar of the other traffic. The beat of so many wheels confused him: he couldn't tell which way to move so he lay still, curled up in the sack, trying to take up as little room in the road as possible. The trucks bore down on him, the whine of the great wheels on the road growing louder and louder until they were on him. One of the truck drivers must have seen him. Haddad heard the sudden squeal as a foot stamped on the air brakes but there was no way the truck could have stopped in time. The driver did the next best thing and lined the sack up between his wheels. The freighter hurtled over Haddad, first the engine cab and then the trailer. The noise was unbearable. The shock absorbers and the massive wheels must have passed inches from his face. Haddad could stand no more, he was near to fainting.

The driver of the pantechnicon pulled over onto a layby and made his way to where he had seen the sack. He had noticed it move and thought that someone must have trussed up a big dog in there. A gang of youths had done that to one of his neighbours' Alsatians once. Haddad felt someone pulling at the neck of the sack and he cried out.

* * *

Haddad regained consciousness some time later in hospital with his face, arms and head in bandages. A policeman was sitting by his bedside and a doctor was bending over him, examining the extensive bruising on his thighs.

"You're a very lucky man," the doctor said. "There's nothing seriously wrong with you. Your chances of survival on the autobahn last night must have been less than ten per cent. No one else would have stopped for a sack—you have a dog lover to thank. Now," he continued, standing up, "when you have rested the police would like a statement."

Haddad told them nothing.

The following morning, when he was due to be released, a British Intelligence officer came to see him.

"You were in our sector of Berlin when you were found," he said making his visit appear casual. "Strange business. I thought I'd pop over and see what had happened." He was a shy, almost diffident man of similar age and height to Haddad, but with a small-boned body and ginger hair growing thin on top. He drew up a chair beside the bed.

"My name is Major Reed-Henry." He didn't offer to shake hands. Haddad noticed that he wore mittens to protect the angry red chilblains on his fingers. "The cold plays havoc with me," Reed-Henry confided, "school was the worst time, they never let me wear any warm clothes and the classrooms were always unheated. We Scots were supposed to be tough, you see, but of course I wasn't." He looked up with a gleam of amused self-deprecation in his eyes. "Now," he said, "just for the records, Mr Haddad, we know who you are and where you're from. Would you like to tell us what you're doing here?"

Haddad had been warming to the diffident Scot and he was caught off-guard. It took him a moment to recover.

"I told the police—I was a visitor here and somebody hit me over the head from behind."

"And then they tied you up in a bag and dropped you in the middle of the autobahn," Reed-Henry nodded sympathetically. "Well, then, Mr Haddad, do you have any idea who did this to you? I know," he said before Haddad could speak, "you didn't see anything. However," Reed-Henry reached painfully into the pocket of his overcoat and pulled out an envelope of photographs, "would you just have a glance through these and see if you can recognise anybody? It would save you having to come down to headquarters," he added.

The implied threat had its effect and Haddad began to go through the photographs. They were all shots of men either extracted from police files or, more often, taken clandestinely when the subject was unaware. One of the first photographs he came to was that of the man who had given the orders from the front seat of the car. The picture had been taken in summer and he did not look so wasted and ill then.

"That's Heinrich Stroebling," Reed-Henry said. "He's an old Gehlen Organisation man, used to be right-wing but everyone's forgotten that, now he works for the communists. Stroebling specialises mainly among European urban terror groups, re-organising their cell structure and trying to get them to achieve more than just speeches about revolution. I chose pictures of his group because they are the most active here at the moment. The East Germans, as far as we can ascertain, have placed sums amounting to four hundred thousand dollars at his disposal in the last two years."

Reed-Henry leaned forward. "Recognise anybody?"

Haddad shook his head and turned over the rest of the photographs. Someone had done a good job. Shots of the tags and the bodyguards in the car were all there.

"It would be very dangerous to cross these people," Reed-Henry remarked. "Will you be staying in Berlin much longer?"

"I don't think so."

"Well then," Reed-Henry said almost genially, "you'll be needing this," and handed Haddad back his passport. "I imagine the French would be a little concerned if they knew what good forgeries people are making of their documents these days."

Haddad discharged himself from hospital. He went to a post office on the Kaiserdamm and called Kathy Lakas.

"Haddad here," he said as she answered.

"Where the hell have you been?" Kathy asked worriedly. "I've been expecting you to get back to me before now."

"Listen," Haddad said, making it brief. "I can't do it, I can't find a way to get him out. The contract is off."

Haddad hurt as he said that. He hated to recognise any kind of defeat, but this was a professional decision.

"Hold it," he heard Kathy shouting as he lowered the receiver. He lifted it to his ear again.

"Let's meet somewhere," Kathy urged desperately. "You can't just drop out on me like this."

"I have to get out of Berlin."

"Are you in trouble?"

"Yes."

Kathy thought quickly. The PanAm flights along the air corridor were routed through Frankfurt and he still had some mileage left on his ticket.

"O.K." she said. "Meet me in Frankfurt in a couple of days. Phone me and I'll give you my flight number."

Forty-eight hours later Haddad met Kathy off the PanAm flight into Frankfurt.

"I've only got a couple of hours stopover here," she said. "I'm going back to New York tonight."

They made their way out of the airport buildings and along the road between the taxi ranks and the car park.

"Oh God, I'm sorry about what happened to you," Kathy said, seeing his bruises. "The papers used a different name but I guessed it was you. Why didn't you tell us you had a P.F.L.P. price on your head?" she accused.

"Would you have done so if you were me?" Haddad answered. "It's not something that one would willingly advertise."

"Goddammit," Kathy said bitterly, "do you know the damage this will cause us with the committee? They're bound to hear what happened to you in Berlin and they sure as hell won't want to get involved in some Middle Eastern feud. They're running scared as it is and I'm having trouble keeping them together."

"You have no reason to try any more," Haddad told her. "As I said, there's no contract."

Kathy walked a few paces in silence. She stopped and turned to him. Her candid grey-blue eyes seemed to change with the light.

"Mr Haddad," she spoke determinedly, "I'm not ready to give up yet. I believe you can do it. I want you to go back to Berlin for one last try. There *has* to be a weak link, something you haven't seen."

"Let me explain the problem to you," Haddad said as they walked on. "First there's Spandau. I think it might be possible to get him out of there but then there's the wall and the checkpoints around West Berlin. Everything's controlled: the traffic, the railways, the airlines—they all have to cross a two-hundred-kilometre corridor through East Germany to the West. That's the problem, to gain sufficient time, with no one giving the alarm, to get Hess to the West. I just can't see how it can be done. Believe me, Miss Lakas, I don't like to fail any more than you do."

"Look," Kathy said, "in two world wars men escaped from prison camps worse than Spandau and without any help from the outside. They made their way on foot across hundreds of miles of enemy territory, some of them even walked clean out of Germany. And that was in the middle of wartime. I don't believe it's impossible. Give it just one last try."

They turned to walk back towards the airport buildings.

"Why should you risk so much to rescue an old Nazi?" Haddad asked curiously. "I imagine that your colleagues are beginning to understand, after what happened in Berlin, how dangerous it is to deal outside the protection of the law. Do you realise what you may be risking?"

"I believe that the world needs a new creed of human rights," Kathy said, always the fighter. "If we can only get people to understand that human dignity and freedom is their right and their security, then that creed can have just as powerful an influence on mankind's development now as that of capitalism or communism at the turn of the century. We need to do something massive to gain attention. Get Hess out for me and I'll hold his name up and brandish it to the world like a banner," Kathy promised. "I'll build a movement round him."

The tannoy was calling her flight. "Will you do that?" she asked.

"Miss Lakas, your committee may not like. . . ."

"To hell with the committee," Kathy interrupted brusquely. "I'm asking you."

Haddad stared unblinkingly at her. Tall, attractive, the sheer force of her personality was impossible to ignore.

"All right," Haddad said. "I'll go back, but first I need to get myself some protection. I'm not going in there unarmed again. Secondly, I want to know and read everything there is documented about Hess."

"That's easy," Kathy said. "Go see my brother in Paris. He did most of the research on Hess in the first place and he's still got all the papers."

Kathy Lakas turned just before Passport Control. She seemed less tense. "Hey, call me Kathy," she shouted to Haddad and disappeared through the barrier.

CHAPTER FIVE

HARVARD, U.S.A.

Kathy Lakas humped her suitcase up the stairs, opened the door to her apartment and found five out of the seven committee members waiting for her in her living room.

"I hope you don't mind, Kathy," Harry apologised. "It was urgent that we meet and your landlady let us in."

Kathy shrugged. "Make yourselves at home, what's the problem?"

"We asked you to call off that mercenary. Instead, we discover that you have persuaded him to go back to Berlin."

"That's true," Kathy admitted. "There's still a chance he'll find a way to rescue Hess. Matt," she accused, "you've been influencing them."

Matt nodded. "They share in our responsibility, they had a right to know."

"After what's happened in Berlin," Harry cut in, "we don't want the responsibility for the mercenary's death—nor do we want the responsibility for anyone he might kill. We reconciled ourselves to a minimum of violence to achieve what we believe is an important social objective. But in using this man, Haddad, we're already too far out of our depth. I told you before and now the committee is instructing you: call him off, tell him there's no contract. If he's in Berlin, get him out of there as fast as possible."

"What happens to the committee then?" Kathy asked. "Do we just rot?"

"No, Kathy, of course not," Aaron protested. "We haven't abandoned Hess. It's just that we're backing off from direct action. We'll still petition and canvass and put pressure where we can. We'll campaign for human rights harder than ever before—but peacefully."

"Peacefully—you're going to get a man like Hess out of Spandau peacefully! That's bullshit and you know it," Kathy exploded angrily. "People have been trying to free him peacefully for twenty years." She felt betrayed by her colleagues.

"We've just got started on the only course left open to us and already you're running scared," she said bitterly. "We've been all over the morality of what we're doing—I thought you felt deeply enough about this, that you cared enough to take the risks."

"Kathy, spare us your scorn," Harry said. "We care, sure we care, that's why we formed this committee, but we've had our wars. We're no longer students—we've got our careers and our families on the line. It's clear to us all now that we should never have let you talk this committee into taking direct action."

"And Hess and all that bullshit we believed about finding a new direction, a new catalyst to unite liberal consciousness," Kathy asked, "what do we do with that now?"

"I'm not saying your way won't work," Aaron answered her from across the room. "I'm not even arguing the morality of using a mercenary. I'm just saying that in the sixties I was prepared to go out and get bloody, but now it's the eighties and I'm getting too old, too secure in my career, my family, call it what you will," he blustered, "but call that contract off."

"O.K.," Kathy said, despising them, knowing that Haddad had read them right all along and almost preferring the mercenary's morality to theirs. "I'll do it alone."

"You can't be serious!" Matt exclaimed, startled. "You can't go without us. Where will you find the money to pay him?"

"I'll find it," Kathy replied obstinately. "When I started this I meant to see it through. And if Haddad finds a way to get Hess out of Spandau, I'll back him. I'll resign from the committee and I'll take full responsibility for what happens."

Kathy opened the door. The committee members filed silently from the room. Aaron stopped in front of Kathy. "You're a very stubborn woman," he said, "but let me tell you, when you mix with killers, whatever your good reasons, the violence has a way of coming home."

Matt stayed behind.

"Get out of here, Matt," Kathy said.

"No, not until you see sense," Matt replied. "You can't possibly employ a mercenary and go against a place like Spandau on your own."

"I'm not on my own, I've got my brother with me on this and if there's a way, we're going to do it." Kathy collapsed tiredly into a chair. "Oh God, Matt," she said, her resolution faltering for a moment, "we were part of a generation that brought down a president when he tried to change the course of American society, what's happened to us? Whatever happened to our courage?"

"That was a long time ago now," Matt answered her gently. "You heard Harry; we've made our statements, paid our dues.

We've rejoined society with all the responsibility that entails. You're fighting still and you've got all the courage it takes, but you don't have as much as us to lose."

* * *

Haddad dropped out of sight for a week, letting his trail cool, then he made his way to Paris. A taxi set him down on the Rue St Louis en L'île before a narrow doorway with a number almost obliterated by age. The door was open; he checked the names on a row of mail boxes and climbed the steep stairway to the fourth floor. Across the landing was a shabby green door. He knocked. After a few moments a stocky, bespectacled, bearded man opened the door.

"You must be Haddad," he said. "My name is Michael Lakas." He was a few years older than Kathy and possessed the same direct manner. "My sister called, I've been expecting you, come in."

Haddad followed Michael Lakas into a small but very comfortably furnished apartment.

"Do I continue with this contract," Haddad asked immediately, wanting to know where he stood, "or have your committee decided to abandon it?"

"Well, we're still picking up your expenses," Michael replied, "and I've got a message for you from Kathy. She needs to know how much a rescue, if it's possible, could cost."

"Tell her I have no possible way of knowing at this stage," Haddad answered, "but if it can be done, then she can advise her committee that it is unlikely to cost less than two hundred and fifty thousand U.S. dollars."

"That's a hell of a lot of money," Michael protested, polishing his glasses nervously.

"In Spandau you have chosen a very tough target," Haddad observed unsympathetically.

Michael replaced his glasses and tried to read Haddad's face. It would be no good attempting to appeal to his sympathy or concern for human rights. Haddad's dark eyes were empty of all expression like a bottomless ocean. The mercenary was obviously unreachable and very dangerous.

"Kathy said you wanted to see all the documents." Michael led the way into a small dining alcove. "I've laid all the books and press cuttings out on the table for you," he said, "you can go through them here, it's private and it will save hotel bills." More than ever, now that he had met him, Michael had no intention of sharing his apartment with Haddad—he found the chilling presence of the man unnerving. "I'll move in with my wife—we're cited—until you're finished."

Haddad nodded.

"There's food in the kitchen, make yourself at home."

Haddad turned on the lamp which cast a pool of light over the table, then he pulled up a chair and drew a file towards him. He was not sure precisely what he was looking for, but he knew that amongst that mass of clippings there would be something about Hess he could use, some weak spot perhaps in the guard system.

Michael had packed a bag and was heading for the door when Haddad stopped him.

"Tell me, because I do not understand," the mercenary asked, "what is so special about this man that they should keep him in a closely guarded fortress all these years?"

"Well," Michael replied, "it would seem that it's the Russians who are holding on to him, but we believe that the Allies are not interested in pressing them too hard on this matter. There's a lot in Hess's past, the real reason that he fled to England, that we do not understand and perhaps we will never know.

"Our research shows that the Russians always suspected that Hess brought with him to England some secret offer of a treaty, which would explain why he flew there in an unarmed plane in the early years of the war. England was alone at that time and beaten to her knees, and yet within six weeks from the date Hess landed, Germany committed suicide by opening a second front and attacking the Russians, and as you know, the pressure on England was relieved. I don't think any of this can be proved because so many of Hess's papers have been stolen or made secret. In any event, our concern is with the present."

After Michael left, Haddad worked until the early hours of the morning, then dozed on the sofa for a while. He worked again for the rest of that day. When his eyes became too tired to follow the print he stood at the window and looked down at the street.

On the afternoon of the second day he left the apartment and made his way to a house on the Rue Paul Valéry in the fashionable 16th arrondissement just off the Champs Élysées. The house was a bordello, the best in Paris, once owned, so the story went, by the famous Madame Billy. She had received police protection since the Second World War when an integral part of the Resistance Movement was run from her establishment. She had sheltered Jews and Allied airmen alike from the Nazis, and old men handed her phone number on to their sons. Times had changed. Madame Billy had retired and the new owner, Madame Paul, had made her reputation and fortune in Beirut before the Civil War.

Haddad was shown into the ground floor reception area. There was a small, well-appointed bar and beyond that a hall, lit by chandeliers, with a stairway leading from it to the bedrooms above. It was just after three in the afternoon, the time when French businessmen liked to relax after lunch. Madame Paul was behind the bar. She was a stocky fifty-year-old woman, expensively dressed, with a round face that showed her age in spite of her carefully applied make-up. Pretty girls were reporting for work dressed in Levis and jerseys, nodding to Madame Paul as they passed and then reappearing in chic evening dresses.

Madame realised Haddad was a stranger and poured him a drink. "Chéri," she said, looking him over, "I am glad you have come here. The girls on the Rue St Denis know what you want but I, Madame Paul, know what you need."

All the windows of the building were shuttered, closing out the dark grey of the winter afternoon. The lights around the bar were subdued.

"Can I talk with you privately?" Haddad asked.

Madame Paul thought he was shy and led him to a side room with long curtains and antique chairs. She took twelve or so photographs which showed her girls in poses that were sensual, erotic, but not vulgar, and tossed them down in front of him with the confidence of a hustler dealing a stacked deck.

Haddad shook his head and gave her back the photographs. "I was in Beirut," he said quietly, "you would have known my uncle then." He gave the recognition code used in the Civil War. Madame Paul's eyes narrowed as she sensed trouble. "What was your name again?" she asked.

"Haddad. John Haddad."

The name rang alarm bells in her mind and instinctively she moved away from them. She had left the war behind her; she wanted no part of it here.

"You can tell me where Maroun is," Haddad said. "I need to find him. I have information that he's working with you again. He's nearby, I know that."

"Who told you about me?" Madame Paul asked softly. "The French?"

"It doesn't matter. Where's Maroun?"

"There will be trouble," Madame Paul warned.

"No," Haddad said, "there will be no trouble. I can handle Maroun."

She looked into his face and believed him. She knew all about Haddad's part in the war. "The building opposite this one," Madame Paul said quickly, "the third floor in the front." She got up. "Now please leave here."

Haddad walked across the street. The building was let as apartments and there was a sign up announcing that it was shortly to be demolished to make way for the new Peruvian Embassy. He opened the door and crossed the stone-flagged hall. A creaking, old-fashioned lift took him up to the third floor. He stood on the landing, allowing his eyes to grow accustomed to the gloomy rays of light that penetrated from a single dirty window. There were three doors off the landing. Haddad chose the one that opened into the street-facing apartment. It was unlocked. He quietly let himself in. The occupants had moved out already: the hall was dark, light fittings wrenched out and strips of paper torn from the walls.

Haddad stepped over some cardboard boxes and a cracked lavatory cistern. From one side he heard the noise of a tap dripping into the bath. He went down the passage. The shutters across the window of the front room had been closed and only the barest glimmer of light filtered into the apartment. Haddad walked softly, but even so his footsteps creaked on the old boards. He checked the bedrooms, the handleless doors swinging open to his touch. Then he came back along the passage and stood in the doorway of the living-room. He knew Maroun had to be there, and he waited.

A low chuckle came from the darkness of one corner, a movement which was the clicking of a flint, and then the gas flame of a lighter flared. A face appeared streaked with tiger stripes of dark camouflage cream, only the paler parts visible in the light. It was a night ambush's face, perfected in the streetfighting days of the Civil War in the Lebanon. The man wore a gold earring and a headband torn from a piece of red material. His blonde hair fell below his shoulders. He had lean features with a full moustache that drooped over the corners of his mouth, and tawny, hooded eyes that flickered with a mad light. He lifted his rifle so that Haddad could see it was pointing at his stomach.

"John, my brother," Maroun said and there was almost a childish pride in his voice, "you didn't get past me. I saw you long ago in the street, you could have been dead any time." Haddad ignored the rifle and walked into the room.

Maroun let him come. He was seated by a tall window; there was no glass in the pane. He pulled the metal lever beside him and the shutter opened an inch or two, letting some light into the room. There was a sleeping-bag rolled out on a piece of cloth, a folded blanket in front of the window where he could rest his arms, a tiny campus gas stove on which he could heat his food and a bucket in which he could defaecate. He had been in that room for days, and the place smelt of urine and damp and unwashed bodies.

"How long have you been here?" Haddad asked.

Maroun glanced up at the wall where he had scratched the days. "Eleven. He will come the next three or four days. I can feel him coming. Just like the old days," he said. "Remember, I would wait and wait and sure enough they would walk right into my sights. You can get anybody if you wait long enough."

He reached into his pocket, shook out a couple of pills and swallowed them dry.

"You take many of those things?"

"Sure," Maroun replied. "When I'm high I can look down to the street at night and pick out a face with my naked eye, just like I'm looking at it through a starlight scope."

He rolled onto his stomach, cradled his rifle and quickly checked the street.

"Who are you waiting for?" Haddad asked.

"Hussein Farawaz, he has a girl-friend at Madame Paul's. Whenever he gets into town he comes to see her. You remember that mean bastard who gave us so much trouble in Kantari?" Haddad remembered Farawaz: he was a Mourabitoun, a thug of a street-gang leader who had fought his way to political power with Syrian backing.

"Who's paying you?" Haddad asked. "The Israelis or the French?"

"I don't know," Maroun said. "I don't care. I just take the money and kill who I'm paid to kill."

Maroun had been born in America of Lebanese parents and he had returned to Beirut at the start of the Civil War. He had been the only survivor when his unit was wiped out in an ambush. He had survived again when he feigned death under the bodies of his comrades in the basement of the Holiday Inn Hotel, while the Mourabitoun walked around looting the possessions from the bodies of his friends and cutting their throats to make sure. He survived so many times that people tried to stay with him, thinking that some of his luck would rub off on them, but Maroun preferred to work alone as an assassin.

He would choose his targets, hole up and wait for them to walk into his sights. With the heavy Dragunov sniper's rifle he used, he could pick off a man at nine hundred metres. The war and the pills he took by the handful kept him on a constant high. When the ceasefire came he tried to join Haddad. "I just can't make it in the real world," he said....

"You want some coffee?" Maroun asked.

Haddad shook his head.

"I need someone to protect me," he said. "I've got a contract, but I need someone to keep the P.F.L.P. off my back."

"Why me?"

"You are the best I know."

"It's true." Maroun turned back to the street. "You know," he went on, mostly to himself, "I don't care too much who I kill. Sometimes I just lie here sticking this rifle out of the window leading on people and cars as they pass by and the rest of me is dead man, the only feeling I have is in the tip of this finger." He held up his trigger finger and smiled.

"Tell me where I can find you," he said. "I'll be along in a little while."

* * *

Kathy Lakas made her way through the crowded New York streets to the Cooper-Hewitt Museum. She had made an appointment with one of the directors and she was ushered into his office.

"Ah, Miss Lakas." Ben Enderbry rose from behind his desk to greet her. He was a distinguished-looking man in his late fifties with silver hair swept back off his forehead. "You have come to see the altar candlestick." He reached for his keys and led Kathy through the museum to the section housing their collection of Chinese ceramics.

They stopped before an armour-plated glass wall. Spotlighted on the shelf behind, in pride of place in the collection, was the altar candlestick. The label described it as early Ming c. 1400–1450, perfectly potted and beautifully decorated in underglaze blue.

"Magnificent, isn't it," the director commented over her shoulder, "and of course so very rare. As you know, the only other one like it is in the Peking museum. Your father was a very fortunate man to have owned this."

"He brought it out of China with him in '46," Kathy said.

"It was the only possession he was able to salvage after half a lifetime's work and four years in a Japanese prisoner-of-war camp. At that time not even he knew how rare it was."

"Would you like me to open the glass?" the director offered. To hold such a rare ceramic was an honour he reserved only for the very privileged. Kathy shook her head.

"I've really come to ask you for a valuation. How much could we expect if my brother and I decide to sell it?"

The smile left the director's face. "Since your father left it with us, we have always felt that it was meant to be part of our collection."

"No," Kathy said firmly. "His will was quite clear. The altar candlestick was left to my brother, Michael, and me."

"I think we'd better discuss this in my office," the director said. He turned abruptly on his heel and left Kathy to follow him. By the time he reached his desk, Enderbry had been able to recover some of his composure. "Well now, Miss Lakas," he said, "I suppose technically the candlestick does belong to you, but if you took it away from us, it would leave an unfillable gap in our collection. I am sure your father would not have wanted that," he said shrewdly, but he missed his mark with Kathy.

She fixed him with her very direct gaze. "You still haven't told me how much the candlestick is worth," she prompted.

"A piece as rare as this is impossible to value," Enderbry shrugged resignedly. "The only way to find out would be to auction it and then of course there is the great risk of it passing into a private collection."

"I don't want your museum to lose it," Kathy told him, "but my brother and I may need to raise three hundred thousand dollars. Would you pay that much for it?"

Enderbry knew that the price she was asking was more than fair. "I'd have to put it to my trustees," he said. "How urgently do you need an answer?"

"I'm leaving New York at the end of the week. Could you let me know by then?"

Before she left the museum, Kathy stopped again for a last look at the candlestick. Its value to her and Michael lay in that it had always represented an important link with their father. She felt guilty at the thought of selling it, but consoled herself with the memory of her father telling her as a child that no one person should be able to own such an ancient and exquisite piece. Kathy's father was a man who shared the same idealistic beliefs as his daughter and she was certain that he would approve of the use the money would be put to.

CHAPTER SIX

Michael met Kathy's plane at Orly. The weather had cleared during the flight and they made their way into Paris with the wintry afternoon sun glowing soft gold on the domes and spires of the city.

"I'd forgotten how much I feel at home in this place," Kathy said.

"All this tension seems to suit you," Michael observed. "You're looking good. So," he added as he drove, "the committee has dumped us."

"They'll come back."

"How did it go at the museum?"

"They're not happy about it, but they'll pay our price." Kathy glanced into her brother's face: he was looking tired and strained. "Do you have regrets about selling?"

"No," Michael answered, "I don't know about you, Kathy, but I've never felt I owned that altar candlestick. I'm with you on this all the way."

"Thanks," Kathy said, grateful for her brother's support. "When the time comes to make the sale, will you handle it?"

"Sure, I've already arranged with Haddad where and how he wants to be paid."

"How's he doing?"

"I haven't seen him much," Michael admitted. "That kind of man is right outside the limits of my experience. He really scares me. Is he good at his work? I mean, he didn't start out too well back there in Berlin."

"I don't know how good he is," Kathy replied. She thought back to their time together in Berlin. "But there's something about that man that makes me respect him."

Michael drove onto the Left Bank and along the Boulevard St Germain. "Where are we going?" Kathy asked.

"I'm taking you for a great 'welcome back to Paris' lunch," Michael said. He parked the car and they walked to a small bistro off the Plas St Sulpice.

"Remember this place?" he asked as the aproned owner settled them at a table. Kathy nodded. It had been a favourite of hers and it was considerate of Michael to remember it.

"Isn't Marie-France joining us?"

"No, she's tied up," Michael said. "Anyway," he added

lightly, glossing over her absence, "it's been a long time and it will give us a chance to talk."

"How is it with Marie-France?" Kathy asked, sensing trouble.

Michael shrugged resignedly. "I used Haddad taking over my apartment as an excuse to try and get back with her," he admitted, "but it's not working out. It seems we get on fine as long as we don't try to live together."

Kathy watched her brother fumble his glasses off and begin to polish them. She recognised it as one of his nervous gestures. Michael had an expressive, strong, ugly-attractive face that showed all his emotions. He tried to hide behind his beard, but Kathy could see the hurt in him as he spoke of his wife. He was a warm, sensitive man who for many years had been almost totally absorbed in his field of psychology, which he taught at the Sorbonne. In all these traits he closely resembled his father; there was an inner strength in Michael, he had his own kind of courage, but he lacked the decisiveness and drive of Kathy. Their parents had died in the last four years, one soon after the other, drawing brother and sister closer.

"Do you still love her?"

"Yes, very much, the silly bitch, she hasn't a brain in her head—but you've got to admit she's beautiful."

Kathy felt sorry for her brother. "It's been a bad year," she said. Michael didn't want his younger sister to think he was appealing for sympathy. He looked up and grinned warmly at her. "It'll get better," he said firmly. "We'll work things out. Anyway, researching Hess came in time to save my sanity. At least it's given me something to think about other than my vanishing relationship with my wife. How long are you staying in Paris?"

"As long as I can. My research grant expires at the end of this year. I've been contributing to an enquiry into the effects of long-term prison sentences on the families of the prisoners and I've arranged to finish my work here, that's if I don't get fired first." Kathy shrugged. "The thought doesn't worry me unduly. I'm in a rut at Harvard and I've been planning on settling back in Paris for a while."

"Have you got somewhere to stay?" Michael asked. "I'd offer you a bed, but mine's taken," he grimaced, "and Marie-France is not very good company at the moment."

"I'm O.K. I've phoned Simone, she's going on vacation and she's letting me use her apartment."

Michael glanced at his watch. "I've got to get back to

work," he said. "What are you going to do now?"

"I guess I'll go check on Haddad."

"I have to go to London from the middle of this week until the end of next, to deliver a series of lectures," Michael apologised. "It's a long-standing date and I can't break it. Will you be able to handle Haddad?"

Kathy reassured him, but Michael was very concerned. "Kathy, be careful of that guy," he warned as they left the restaurant, knowing how headstrong she was. "He's a totally different breed to us. And don't take risks, that's his job. Remember, he's equipped for it, we're not."

* * *

Kathy was in the apartment when Haddad returned. He came in quietly and startled her. She saw him standing by the door, cool, watchful, alert, as though he had been expecting someone else.

"I was just checking to see if everything was alright," she said, glad it was him, showing him Michael's key and at the same time feeling angry with herself. Why should she apologise for being in her brother's apartment?

"I heard you were coming," Haddad said. "Michael tells me your pressure group are no longer backing us."

"That's a temporary situation," Kathy replied. "If we're successful, they'll fall over themselves trying to give us their support. In the meantime, we're backing you. Michael has the details. We're guaranteeing you all your expenses, so when can you return to Berlin?"

"I'm waiting for someone to contact me," Haddad said.

"How long?" Kathy demanded impatiently.

"I don't know," Haddad answered impassively. "He doesn't keep to a schedule."

Kathy glanced across the table and saw it strewn with open files. "What are you looking for? Maybe I can help speed it up?"

"I'm searching for something to give me a lead," Haddad said. "Anything about conditions in jail, his routine. I see amongst his papers it's claimed that Himmler had the real Hess killed and planted a substitute to make the flight to England. Do you think the man held in Spandau all these years could be an impostor?"

"No," Kathy replied briefly. "I'm convinced he's the real Hess. There are nearly forty years' worth of clippings here. Michael sent me copies. I'd go through the files and photostats from the London *Daily Telegraph* first, they're the best." She made some coffee and brought it to the table. Haddad nodded and took no further notice of her.

Kathy felt a flash of pique, but she brought up another reading-lamp and worked with him for the rest of the evening. They sat across the table with the files open, each silhouetted in their own pool of light. Michael's apartment was very small, a narrow hall with a single bedroom on the one side and a tiny kitchen and bathroom on the other, opening out onto this larger living area. He had given a lot of thought to its decoration, mixing the old with the new, the spotlights from the brown walls illuminating modern paintings, antique figures and leather-bound books, a chess set by the slate-lined fireplace and more books occupying what space remained.

It was a good room, Kathy reflected, a place to think and listen to music and be at peace above the bustling streets. They spoke little, and as they worked she took the opportunity to study Haddad. It had been a long time since she had been so physically aware of a man. Certainly he was good-looking, but she couldn't believe that she was attracted to him. He was too ungiving, too male-arrogant and icily self-controlled.

She came back the next evening after setting up her own research in the main library of the Sorbonne. She caught herself checking her appearance before knocking on the apartment door and shrugged it off, irritated, telling herself that without the committee's support she would have to work closer with Haddad now than in Berlin. She was beginning to wonder just how far she could handle him.

"You know Paris?" she asked warily when they broke from work to eat a snack he had prepared.

Haddad shook his head. She was surprised, knowing the extent of French influence in the Lebanon. He gave her a rare smile and she sensed an unexpected spark of warmth in him. "Until two years ago, I had rarely left Beirut," he admitted.

"What did you do?"

"First I worked on buildings, in the docks, anything, and then I was a student." He knew she thought him too old for a student and he went on: "We were poor, my wife and I saved for a long time for the money to put me through university."

"What did you study?"

"Medicine."

"Did you qualify?"

He shook his head. "I left in my fifth year." He pushed

his plate away and stood up. She knew he didn't want to answer any more questions.

They went back to work. Occasionally Haddad would get up and put another log on the fire. His domesticity was strangely reassuring. Kathy found it good to have a man doing that again in her life, and in the mellow atmosphere of the room she began to relax with him.

She found a cutting that she thought would interest him. "The more you read about Hess, the more you cannot help but feel for the old man of Spandau," she said. "This is a letter he wrote to his wife after he had been in jail for some twenty years and thought he might be released. He wrote every month, you know, and in this one he told her: 'After so many years in jail, I will never keep a bird in a cage, now I understand why the Chinese or the Japanese, when fate has been particularly kind to them, go to the market to buy captive birds and set them free. I too will do that one day.'"

"Find me articles about what goes on inside the prison," Haddad said. He was resisting any emotional involvement with Hess.

"They don't write too much about that," Kathy replied. "Have you heard from this guy you're waiting for?" She knew they were just marking time. "Not yet."

The next morning she came early to the apartment. "It's the weekend," she said, "and we've been cooped up here for days now. Let's give it a break." Kathy went to the window. She grimaced at the weather then grew thoughtful. "The sun isn't exactly shining, but at least it isn't sleeting. Why don't I show you something of Paris?" she asked.

Haddad stood up from the table. His eyes were tired and his head felt muggy. "Why not?" he said.

"What do you want to see?"

"I don't know."

"Do you want to see the tourist spots?"

"Not necessarily. Show me the Paris you know."

"O.K.," she agreed happily. "I'll take you on a childhood walk. I spent most of the first eighteen years of my life here. Some afternoons," she said as they clattered down the narrow stairs, "Dad would come and pick me up from school and we would visit the places Michael and I grew up in."

Once outside, Kathy took charge. She hardly seemed American now, she was streetwise and at ease in Paris. She had a sharp tongue and a quick answer for anyone who jostled her. They took the Métro to the Boulevard deClichy and walked along the cobbled streets packed with porn shops and neon signs. "This isn't what I brought you to see," she said. They turned left into the Rue de Steinkerque, wending their way through the colourful street market and on towards the dome of Sacré Coeur. They took a rest from walking, huddled up in their coats, on a bench in the stark tree-lined square opposite the old Théâtre Trois Frères.

"You O.K.?" She smiled happily at him, looking radiant and full of well-being, glad to be out on the streets of Paris again. Haddad nodded. Now that they were relaxing together, away from a purely working relationship, he began to really notice Kathy. She was almost as tall as him and though she dressed stylishly it was for comfort rather than effect; but still he was aware that beneath her coat was a lithe, full-breasted body, her tight blue jeans tucked into her boots. Her face was strikingly formed with high cheekbones and a small upturned nose, and there were times when he was almost dazzled by the fire in her eyes. He thought her beautiful now, her face happy and animated. He already knew of her courage; he was beginning to enjoy her directness and warmth. They strolled on through an area of attractive bohemian buildings with tall shuttered windows looking down over small cobbled squares. As they walked she told him about Paris and, because of the route they took, about herself.

"My father was an anthropologist," she said. "He spent most of his early career in China before the Second World War and he did some important work on the discovery of Peking man. He was fascinated with China and became involved with the growth of their communist movement. The Japanese put him in a concentration camp after Pearl Harbor. When he came home to America at the end of the war, he expected his work to be recognised. Instead, because he was a communist, and not ashamed of it, his work was suppressed and many of the men he thought were his friends took the honours he should have had and abandoned him. All he could find to support us was the odd teaching job at some small-town university, then, when the McCarthy era really swept the country, even though he had proved all over again that he was a truly brilliant man, he could not find a job at all and had to leave America.

"We settled over here in the fifties," she continued, "this was one of the few places where they would let him teach. My father and mother were tired and it was hard to make another start. It was O.K. for Michael and me. At least, it was better for me, Michael was older and got deeply hurt by it. But Dad never really could settle down, he was an American and he missed America. He never did go back though, he died here. Michael felt that Dad had been persecuted and that made him very bitter, he really loved my father."

Watching her, Haddad knew she was speaking for herself.

"Is that why you have become so involved in the human rights cause?"

Kathy nodded. "After what happened to my father, I've always hated any kind of injustice. Michael stayed over here but I went back to fight. I got involved in the campus disturbances and a couple of times I came unstuck, but don't get me wrong, Mr Haddad, Michael and I are stubborn and serious about Hess. If you can possibly find a way to free that man, we'll back you."

They walked up the Rue de Ravignan, climbing the steep cobbled streets towards Montmartre.

"Did you ever marry?" Haddad asked.

"No, but I lived with a man for nearly four years." Haddad's silence seemed to draw her out. What the hell if he knows, she thought, and she told him: "It seemed as close a relationship as any marriage could be, but it didn't work out. I know now that he was a vain, weak man but, God, at the time I loved him so completely, I nearly let him destroy me." Kathy had taught herself to strive against failure and she tried to keep from Haddad how inadequate the break-up of that relationship had made her feel. She was aware that she had made more of a success of her academic and political career than her personal life, and the giving of herself to a deep relationship brought a sharper sense of loneliness when it ended. Haddad could see this vulnerability in her, and from time to time a flash of her former wariness.

They came out into Montmartre and, for all its touristry, to Haddad it was a place that still held much of its magic. As they walked the narrow streets he smelt hot bread and good cooking, and the door of some bar opening brought gusts of warmth into the freezing cold air. Kathy took him into the church of St Pierre just off the artists' square. On one side was the confessional and small altar with a few people singing Mass, their voices in soft, beautiful harmony. The massive columns held up the arched roof as if lifting the weight of the world off the people inside.

"I warned you," she said wryly, as they came out into the gloom of the winter's afternoon, "I was going back into my past." The abrasiveness in her was gone. Haddad was seeing a different side to her character now.

"There was a time when I belonged here," she said. "As

kids we played in these streets above Pigalle. Some of the other kids were really tough, but it never affected us. Michael and I used to protect each other. If we got into trouble we used a special mountain call and Dad would come rushing out to rescue us."

Kathy showed Haddad the small back streets and alleys and bars of Montmartre, where the flaking old buildings nearly touched each other across the cobbles. She was proud of her adopted city and she tried to make Haddad imagine what the old Montmartre of Toulouse-Lautrec and Renoir must have been like.

"Renoir used to live here," she said, pointing at a house that was now a museum. Haddad stared at it. It was almost dark and he realised that she must have lost all track of time.

"I preferred the bars," he said, stamping his feet. "It's warmer in there." He was teasing her, feeling warm with her after a good day, but their relationship was still too new for Kathy to understand his dry sense of humour.

"I don't know why I'm telling you all this," she flared angrily, suddenly trying to back off, feeling that she was making a fool of herself, getting too involved. Haddad shrugged, retreating as well, but they had left it too late to withdraw. They were awkward with each other after that, like strangers again, conscious of not being entirely in control of things. They stayed together wandering all over Paris that wet weekend, using the excuse that they needed a break from the files.

On the Sunday evening, tired and cold from walking all day, they brought food back to the apartment. Neither of them knew when or how it happened, or to what lengths they would go to preserve or deepen what was between them, but after they had eaten, when it was time to leave, she asked him hesitantly though with her now familiar directness: "Listen, can I stay here tonight?"

Haddad reached out, his strong hard hands touched her face with surprising gentleness, then he drew her to him. She promised herself that this was just going to be an affair, and that was all, but she had already begun to fall in love with him.

CHAPTER SEVEN

Kathy woke with a sense of something wrong. Immediately she put her arm out of the covers to feel for Haddad; he wasn't there. She heard a noise from the living-room. Quietly she climbed out of bed and opened the door a crack. Haddad had cleared a space amongst the furniture and was working out, but this was no ordinary form of exercise, he was punishing his body, testing each muscle to its limit. It was as though he were taking a masochistic pleasure in the pain he was inflicting upon himself. In spite of the intense cold, his face and body were streaked with sweat.

Kathy wanted to stop him, but silently went back to bed. She remembered as she lay there the surging physical power of Haddad's body against hers, his flat stomach, hard muscular thighs and back, and yet he had been gentle with her, considerate. She remembered the clean smell of his skin, the strong grip of his hands. Their love-making had been good for her, she hoped it had been for him too.

There was silence from the next room. She waited a few minutes then went into the living-room. Haddad was sitting with his back against the wall, breathing evenly, relaxing.

"Good morning," he said, and smiled at her. "I was coming to wake you."

"Why do you do that to yourself?" Kathy asked.

"It's one of the hazards of my profession," Haddad explained. "I don't smoke, I drink very little, I need to keep a fit, well-disciplined body if I am to survive."

"You wouldn't work for anyone you don't want to, would you?" Kathy enquired. "I mean you wouldn't just kill anyone?" Haddad raised his head and looked at her. His eyes went empty and dark. "If you mean by that, do I have a conscience, the answer is no."

But Kathy didn't believe him; she preferred to rely on her instincts. "I'll run you a bath," she said.

She cooked up some eggs in the kitchen. It was still dark outside and raining. "Monday," she said to herself and wrinkled up her nose. "Listen," she shouted through the open door, "shall I take the day off and help you?"

Haddad was dressing. "That sounds good," he said. "But

are you sure there won't be any trouble?"

"No, I'm just winding up my research and I'm right up to date with my work. I'll phone the library, it'll be O.K."

By mid-morning Haddad had finished sorting through the last of the files. Kathy was right, there was a lot about the man but very little information about Hess's life in prison. Haddad had not made much progress, except for a glimmer, a tiny germ of an idea that was beginning to form in the back of his mind.

"Do you want me to try and find you anything else on Hess?" Kathy asked.

"No," Haddad answered. "I think our best chance is for me to contact your friend, Dade, when I get to Berlin."

They had lunch out and returned in the afternoon. Kathy went up the stairs first, up to her eyes in parcels. Fumbling blindly with the lock, she got the door open and then backed in, noticing that the living-room was in pitch darkness. She didn't remember drawing the blinds. She went up the step, making her way across the room to pull them back, when a voice said from the darkness: "Hello, lady." She heard the metallic click of a gun being cocked. The voice spoke again: it had a husky, sensuous quality. "Strip." A reading-lamp flared in the corner and she saw a gun and then the face, a droopy moustache, high cheek-bones and the tawny hooded eyes with madness in them. She noticed the heavy sweet smell of hashish. "Strip," the man commanded her again. "Start with the skirt." He motioned with his gun and his finger tightened on the trigger.

Half-paralysed with fear, Kathy began to lift her skirt.

"That's good," the maniac said approvingly as her skirt rose over her thighs. "That's very good."

Kathy heard Haddad at the door. The lights came on and she broke and ran crying out to him. Haddad held her. When he made no move to take cover she looked around and saw that the maniac was watching them.

"Sorry," he said amiably to Haddad, "I didn't know she was your lady. Man," he added approvingly, "she's got nice legs."

"Do you know him?" Kathy asked aghast.

Haddad nodded, glad that at least Maroun had washed off his night ambush's face and cleaned himself up. "He's the one I was waiting for."

Maroun got up from the corner where he had been crouching and came towards Kathy. He tossed his hair and his gold earring flashed. He was no more than twenty-eight and looked much younger. Tall, lean, loose-limbed, Maroun had a tennis player's physique and a classically sculptured face.

"Lady," he said and grinned like a naughty child, "I'm sorry if I scared you."

Kathy's heartbeat began to slow down. Maroun's good looks and easy charm soothed her.

"You read too many cowboy books," she said cuttingly.

"That's right," Maroun agreed earnestly, thinking she understood him. "That's right, they are the only books I read." Maroun saw the grocery bags. "No cooking," he said. "I'm taking you both out to dinner. Where do you want to go?" he asked Kathy. "Think of somewhere nice."

* * *

Kathy chose the little restaurant run by a married couple where she had often been before. The owners had been good to her and now she wanted to return with her custom. The husband acted as head waiter and he greeted her warmly as they entered.

"I can remember a time when you came here by yourself and sat in a corner with a book," he teased her. "And now you come escorted by not one, but two men."

Kathy felt good. She liked being in male company again, and Maroun was so strikingly good-looking that she could feel every woman in the room turn and stare after them as they walked to their table. The owner took their order. Kathy excused herself and made her way to the ladies room.

While she was away, Maroun leaned across the table to Haddad. "Is it finished?" Haddad asked.

"Yes," Maroun replied.

His hand went up and his right index finger, the one he used on the trigger, began to massage his temple. The stress had gone out of him, he was very relaxed, at peace, like a man after making love.

"You know," he said, "you get to feel the man, people say they are just targets, that's not true. If you are a professional each hit is exquisite. You wait and wait, you suffer cramps and cold and you hardly eat. You can't close your eyes in case you miss him and you are alone with your mind high up in some empty place. All you think about is the man you're going to kill, what he's doing, who he's with, and you come so close mentally to him that you get in his bones and then when he is coming you can feel it, five days away you can feel it. Then suddenly he's in front of your sights and after all the waiting you are with him, and when you kill him something in you goes out with him." Maroun's trigger finger had closed. "I can't explain, you've got to feel it to understand. Man, you think I'm crazy," Maroun said, and laughed his crazy laugh. "But you're lucky I never came after you; there's a good price on your head, you know that."

"That's why I'm here," Haddad said, watching him, knowing that Maroun was growing more and more unstable, that he was more dangerous now than he had ever been. "I need your help."

"Yes, I remember," Maroun nodded. "You told me. John," he said almost pleadingly, "you're my brother, we saved each other's lives back there in the war. I love you, you know that I'd never do anyting to hurt you."

Kathy was making her way back to the table when the owner stopped her. "You're looking lovely," he said. "So fresh, so radiant, like a summer flower. Why haven't I seen you like this before?"

Kathy shrugged happily. The owner nodded towards the table. "Those men," he asked quietly, "where are they from?"

"They are Lebanese," Kathy replied.

"Marionites?" the owner enquired.

"I don't know," Kathy said. "I think so."

"These are the people descended from the ancient Phoenicians; they may look European," the owner warned her, "but be careful, child, they are Arab underneath."

"I will be careful," Kathy promised.

"What are you two talking about?" she asked gaily as she sat down.

"The war," Maroun said. He nodded to Haddad. "Did he ever tell you about the war?"

"No," Kathy said. "He's told me hardly anything."

"Well," Maroun said, pouring her wine, "when the war came, for a long time John and I would not get involved. They killed his father and he still didn't do anything and then some sniper killed his wife and kid and John came out onto the streets. Man," Maroun said, remembering, "did he ever come onto those streets! He was good, he was very good and in next to no time he was leading the men in our area. We all had street names then. They called me 'Sundance' after the film, but John here, even the Moslems called him 'Captain Angry'.

"Some of our men were holed up in a cellar about to get overrun and I saw John coming down the street with a relief force and I swear to God he was firing a 60-mm mortar off his hip, I swear to God I saw it," Maroun said. "One man was carrying the bombs and John had the tube, he would run a few paces then stop and brace the mortar plate against his thigh and send off a bomb. He had bombs falling around the ears of those Mourabitouns who were pressing an attack. Man, they'd never seen anything like it and they fled."

"What was the war all about?" Kathy asked. "I'm sorry, I don't know. We were still all of us here tied up with Vietnam."

"It was a civil war," Haddad said. "A stupid civil war that no-one could win. It was a time of madness for the Arab and Christian people in the Middle East, it's best forgotten."

"What happened to your wife and child?" Kathy enquired and then she knew she shouldn't have asked.

Haddad didn't answer her, and she would have said something else to change the subject, but Maroun spoke.

"Haddad was finishing medical school, the Moslems kidnapped him during the fighting because they wanted him to look after their wounded. His father was already dead. He left his mother, his wife and his child back in their flat. It was six days before he could find his way home. It was just a tiny flat, one bedroom, with a living-room and dining-room leading off the kitchen. Some sniper had got into the block opposite them and for sheer pleasure he held them pinned down in one room. They couldn't get to the bathroom and they couldn't get to the kitchen for food and water.

"John here figured that after a couple of days his mother tried to make it to the kitchen for food and water for the child. As she got to the fridge the sniper put a bullet through her head. Later his wife tried to get to the body of her mother-in-law and the sniper killed her too. He killed the child last. She was a little girl, no more than six years old. We never knew exactly who did it. Some said it was an ex-French Foreign Legionnaire working for the Palestinian Rejection Front, all I know is we killed a lot of people trying to find out. Didn't we, John?" he said.

Haddad was very pale; he could not bear to look at either of them. He got to his feet and pushed the table away.

"You two can make your own way home, I need some air," he snapped, and before Kathy could stop him he had left the restaurant.

"I knew how to get back at those Moslems," Maroun said, staring after Haddad. "But John never much liked me for being a sniper."

* * *

Haddad wandered the wet night streets of Paris trying to walk out the pain, make his mind too tired for the nightmares that would come if he slept. He walked the wide neon-lit streets and the people pushed past him on the pavement, and he walked the silent alleyways with only the sound of his footsteps following him. He let himself back into the apartment in the early hours of the morning.

Maroun was sitting in the living-room, staring out of the window. He just nodded as Haddad came in. Kathy felt him undress in the dark and lower himself into bed. Her hand went out and touched him, he was freezing cold, shivering. Gently she began to stroke him, running her hands soothingly over his back, moving her body closer to his to warm him. She rubbed his temples, his neck, his arms, she massaged his fingers and warmed his feet with hers.

"I thought you weren't coming back," she whispered.

"So did I."

"I know you must have loved your wife very much," Kathy said, reassured in a way that he was human, that he had loved someone.

"I should have moved them to a safe place when the war came to our district." Haddad sounded weary. "My father was Christian, my mother a Palestinian refugee from the Israeli occupation. My family had been wealthy but my father was a gambler and lost it all in 1963. I'd never thought much about working but then suddenly I faced the prospect of being poor all my life. To be single and poor isn't too bad but to be married and poor in the Middle East is terrible for a man, you cannot provide for your wife or children.

"I suddenly became aware that I didn't want to be like the other men on the building sites. I had known comfort and respectability, I wanted to find it again. I decided to study medicine, it wasn't too late to get a place at university if we had the money. My wife backed me all the way and for five years we slaved, praying each time I took an exam because we didn't have the money for me to take it again if I failed. The war came and we tried to ignore it; the rich used their money to leave the country but what could the poor do?

"One day my father and mother were on a bus that was stopped at a Moslem checkpoint. Because my father had 'Christian' marked as his religion on his identity card they dragged him along with several others behind the cemetery walls at Bashoura and shot him. My mother, though she was a Palestinian, couldn't save him; she wanted to die with him but they wouldn't let her. That should have warned me but I still thought somehow I could avoid the war. My wife and I both felt that I should finish my studies, we just didn't have the energy to start all over again. It was my fault, I should have moved her away to somewhere safe."

"Why don't you finish your studies?" Kathy asked him.

"What for?" Haddad spoke bitterly. "I couldn't start to study again now, besides, I received a better training in the streets than I could have ever got at the university and I can sell my talents for a great deal more money. Like Maroun out there, I've left it too late and I've got nothing to go back for."

* * *

Haddad was busy the next morning and Maroun went shopping with Kathy. She found him a good companion, he laughed easily and carried her parcels uncomplainingly. He walked with a relaxed hip-swinging grace, wearing a battered old windcheater and faded jeans. The fact that his clothes probably concealed a gun made it all that much more unreal. Kathy stopped taking him seriously and began to enjoy herself, flattered by his attention.

They met up with Haddad at lunch-time in the snack-bar of Au Printemps, the fashion department store on the Boulevard Haussmann. Some of Kathy's happiness was brushing off on Haddad, he seemed at ease, enjoying being with her.

"Oh, God," Kathy exclaimed, running her hands along a rail of dresses. "Will you look at these clothes?"

"Do you want it?" Haddad asked as she lifted out a dress.

"Oh, no," Kathy said. "I was just looking."

Haddad persuaded her to try it on.

Kathy came out of the cubicle. Passers-by stopped to admire her. She knew she looked sensational in that dress and Haddad was proud of her. Another man caught her eye: it was Maroun, standing back by the lifts. He looked first at the dress and then at her and nodded his approval and appreciation. Haddad bought the dress for her. Kathy was radiant: in the company of these two men she felt very feminine and very beautiful.

They started down the escalators, making for the ground floor, and now Maroun began to stalk Kathy. He would suddenly appear at the bottom of an escalator, or across a counter, or at the head of the stairs, delighting in surprising her and then disappearing again. She realised that he was flirting with her, showing off his skill as a hunter, and a sophisticated game of hide and seek developed.

She and Haddad would leave Maroun on the stairs and take a lift but somehow, when the doors opened at the bottom, Maroun would be there—then he would toss his head, his gold earring would flash and he would be gone. It was as though he could just melt into his background, become invisible as and when he chose.

They carried the game onto the streets and as Kathy crossed the road with Haddad she would find Maroun waiting for her, leaning nonchalantly against a lamp-post. When she thought he was ahead he would come out of a side street behind them. In the end she was completely confused and could not tell which direction he would appear from.

"I never see him," Kathy complained.

"If you did," Haddad answered, "he'd be no good at his job."

They made their way back to the apartment. Maroun came bursting in a short while later and threw himself exhaustedly down in a chair, scattering parcels on the floor.

"That lady of yours thinks I'm a pack animal," he groaned.

Haddad went into the kitchen where Kathy was making coffee. "Be careful of Maroun," he warned. "I've known him a long time—war changes many people and it changed him most of all."

Haddad seemed always to be down on Maroun.

"Leave him alone," Kathy said defensively. "He's O.K."

"He's very dangerous." Haddad realised she could have no idea of the kind of man Maroun was. "He may not ever mean it, but one day if you caught him the wrong way he could hurt you."

Kathy and Haddad went to the corner bistro that night; Maroun would not join them. When they returned, Kathy found him sitting by the window, the big Dragunov sniper's rifle cradled in his arms. He was leading on the people passing below in the street, pulling the trigger as they came into the sights, dry-firing, willing them dead.

"Look at all those bastards down there," he said. "What gives them the right to live?"

"He's coming down off a high," Haddad told her quietly. "His nerves are beginning to jump. It's time we left. . . . Berlin could be very dangerous for us now," he said. "I don't want you to come."

Kathy tried to protest but they had been over this ground before, and Haddad remained firm.

"O.K. I'll stay here with Michael. Contact me as soon as you can."

The next morning he said to Maroun, "We're leaving for Berlin, can you get me a weapon?"

"Sure." Maroun was excited at the prospect of action. "No trouble, just tell me what you want. I know a man who'll sell us anything."

CHAPTER EIGHT

The train pulled into West Berlin's Central Zoo Station at 6.20 p.m. on a dark winter's evening. The coaches, which had been sealed during the long crossing of the East German corridor, now opened their doors and disgorged a crowd of travel-weary passengers, most of them Turkish Gastarbeiters. Affluent West Berlin's guest-workers, swarthy, dark-haired, dark-eyed men in workmen's clothes, they clutched their belongings to them in cheap cardboard suitcases.

Haddad and Maroun mingled with these men as they passed the East German officials who still administered this part of the German railway system. At the end of a passage, beyond the DDR officials, waited the West German Customs Police in great-coats and peaked caps. They stopped Maroun and searched him.

"Hey man," he said to them, his tawny eyes flashing dangerously, as the other passengers swept on past him, "why is it always me?"

Haddad walked on through the seedy station building, a desolate skid row for junkies and alcoholics. On the street the Arctic wind cut through him like a knife. He hurried after a nondescript man who had travelled in their compartment and tapped him on the shoulder.

"I think there has been a mistake over our suitcases," he said.

"Of course," the man replied promptly. "I apologise."

Haddad gave him an envelope. The little man quickly checked the contents and was well pleased. He had beard-stubble on his cheeks and bright, foxy eyes. He slipped the money into his pocket.

"If you find that you should need friends in this city," he said, "contact me here in Kreuzberg, the Turkish quarter." He picked up Haddad's suitcase and walked on.

Maroun came ambling up as Haddad opened the case in a sheltered spot by a wall.

"It's cool," he said. "There's no one following. Man," he added bitterly, the wind blowing his long, blonde hair around, "those bastards really shook me down."

"You are inclined to attract attention to yourself," Haddad replied drily.

He took out two airways bags and handed the larger, bulkier one to Maroun. Maroun undid the zip, checked his weapons, took out a small two-way radio and put it in his pocket.

"There's something else," he said as he slung the bag over his shoulder.

Haddad rummaged around in the case. "This?" He lifted out a small package.

"Yeah."

"What is it?" Haddad asked, tossing it to Maroun.

"Lebanese gold, the best, you want some?"

"You know I don't smoke it. Find us some places to use as safe houses," Haddad said, closing the case and standing up. "Then drop way out of sight and watch my back, O.K.?"

"Don't worry, John," Maroun promised. "Each way you turn I'll be there, I will keep you alive."

He said it lightly, almost as though he were teasing him. But there was something in Maroun's eyes that worried Haddad. He watched Maroun turn and stride away until his lean figure was swallowed up in the darkness.

Haddad made his way to another small hotel in the back streets behind the Kurfürstendamm. He knew that area of West Berlin now and he took a room where he could see down into the street. He unpacked the weapon that Maroun had secured for him. It was a Walther 9 mm automatic, a well-balanced gun with a good stopping power, shaped after the style of the old German Luger. He raised his arm a few times, dry-firing the automatic, refreshing his knowledge of its balance. It had a big magazine and the butt fitted comfortably into the palm of his hand.

He stripped the weapon and laid the parts out neatly on the bed, oiled and cleaned them, reassembled them and stripped it again and again, getting the feel of it, getting to know the gun so well that he could strip it, clear a jammed bullet from the chamber and reassemble it in the dark if he needed to. Automatics, no matter how well designed, were more prone to jams than revolvers and he didn't want this one to fail him.

He shrugged on the soft leather shoulder holster, adjusting it until the automatic lay flat against his side. He looked at himself in the mirror, satisfied that the outline of the weapon hardly showed in his jacket. Then he stood at the window, the room behind him in darkness, and looked down over the street. He coudln't spot a tag but he knew it wouldn't take them long to get on to him.

Nights like this, alone in hotel rooms, were the worst times for Haddad. He watched the people moving below him. He tried to clear his mind, to think of the contract; instead he kept seeing Kathy and he knew that was dangerous. It was safest for him to have no future beyond surviving each day. The moment he cared about someone, hoped for something, he became vulnerable.

The next morning he phoned the American Army officer who had helped Kathy when she was here. A deep voice boomed back at him over the receiver and they made a date to meet that evening.

The British Officers' Club was an attractive two-storeyed building, surrounded by lawns, with a large swimming-pool and tennis courts, some of them protected from the weather by air-filled plastic canopies. Haddad climbed the stairs to the bar. There were several people drinking quietly in there but he picked out the man he was to meet immediately. He was heavily built, with a strong face and short, curly hair. He seemed to fill the bar, bursting with vitality and warmth. Kathy's description fitted him exactly.

"Major Tom Dade?" Haddad said and the major swung round.

"Dammit," he said in a deep voice. "It's good to see you, any friend of Kathy's is a friend of mine. Sit down, have a drink. What can I get you?" He signalled the bartender. "Three whiskies," he ordered. "Another man's joining us," he said to Haddad. "I hope you don't mind. . . . Kathy is some girl," he remarked. "I chased her clear across Berlin for the two weeks she was here and never got as far as first base, but I liked her," he shook his large head wistfully. "I really did like that girl. She something special to you?" He glanced up shrewdly and Haddad shrugged.

Haddad felt, rather than saw, someone slip into the seat beside him.

"Major Reed-Henry," the American said.

Reed-Henry raised the whisky that awaited him. "We know each other," he said. "Welcome back."

"Wall, I'm damned." The American feigned surprise at the coincidence, but Haddad knew he had been set up.

"You want to know why I drink here and not my own club?" Tom Dade asked, trying to take the edge off the atmosphere. "It's because of my general, the man's made a refugee out of me. He's a fitness fanatic, you see, and he doesn't like his officers to smoke or drink or even consort with women because he claims it weakens the mind and the Russians will get you, so I'm forced to drink here. I shout a lot and talk loud but the British don't really mind, do you?" He turned to Reed-Henry who smiled.

"It's when you don't pay your bills that we worry," he replied. "Other than that we manage to ignore most Americans here."

They were obviously old friends and they made a strangely assorted pair, one large and assured with a booming voice, the other small-boned and diffident.

"You ready?" the American said, sliding off his seat. "Come along, we'll show you the town."

Haddad followed them to Reed-Henry's car.

"Climb aboard," the American said. "What do you want to see, the cultural life in this town or the vulgar side?"

"I'll go along with anything you suggest," Haddad replied.

"Take the vulgar side," Reed-Henry urged. "Tom Dade knows the best, he's never seen the cultural side, only heard about it from his general."

"You leave my general out of this," Dade growled. "I hate to even think of that man."

They visited a good number of the gaudy, neon-lit transvestite bars and strip joints on the Kurfürstendamm and around two o'clock in the morning Tom Dade, who had been drinking heavily, said, "O.K., it's time for Salambos."

He led the way to a club at the top end of the Ku-damm. They stood in the foyer while Reed-Henry argued with a dwarf in the ticket-office over the admission prices.

"We are British," he insisted. "Special discount for Scottish officers."

"It's no good," Tom Dade said, spilling out a handful of Deutsche marks. "These Krauts can spot an American a mile away, pay the man."

A woman, completely naked but for a gold chain around her ankle, had come up quietly to stand by Haddad and was fixing her hair in the mirror.

"That's what I like about Berlin," Tom Dade said. "None of your arty-crafty sassiness of Paris. When this place is vulgar, it's really vulgar and this is nothing to what this city was like before the war."

"Lead on," Reed-Henry said, clutching the tickets.

They pushed through some red velvet curtains and entered a large, high-ceilinged room. All around the sides were sheepskin-covered couches and to one side a huge wheel of fortune with a large arrow lit by coloured bulbs. Around it, like the numbers of a clock face, swung twelve very pretty naked girls on sheepskin-covered swings. With a raucous fairground fanfare their seats revolved, the arrow spun and when it came to rest the compère shouted out the lucky ticket number that had won the girl. A blue film was showing soundlessly against another wall. Through some bead curtains to the right of the entrance there were blue-lit bathing pools with girls and men splashing around in them. Half-way up was a mezzanine floor furnished with Roman-style couches on which couples were making love. Most of the men were dressed or half-dressed, but the girls were all naked.

"This is the only place in Berlin where I can be damn certain what I'm dancing with," Dade growled. "If they wear clothes, no matter how good they look, I'm suspicious."

The three men found an unoccupied corner and a waiter brought them a drink. Haddad was glad he wasn't paying: the prices were exorbitant. A tall, blonde girl came up and claimed Tom Dade, throwing her arms around him like a long-lost lover, and led him away. Reed-Henry lost interest in the blue film and turned to Haddad.

"I'm sorry about this," he said, "but it's Tom Dade's favourite club and every time we go on the town we always seem to end up here."

One of the girls came up. "I'd like to, my dear," Reed-Henry smiled, "but I can't afford it."

As soon as they heard his accent they moved away.

"Listen," Haddad said impatiently, feeling ridiculous fully dressed and sober in a brothel, "you and that American set me up, now what do you want from me?"

Reed-Henry looked at him for a moment. He spoke quietly: "I hear that you're trying to get Hess out of Spandau, is that true?"

In spite of his reserve, the major kept catching Haddad off-balance and he shrugged, trying to give himself time to think.

"Are you asking me a serious question?" he said.

"Yes," Reed-Henry answered. "Very serious. In certain circumstances I might even be prepared to assist. Don't worry," he continued, "we can speak freely here, with all the noise and naked bodies it's one of the few places in Berlin that's impossible to bug. You've had a good look at Spandau, I take it?"

Haddad nodded.

"I spent some time on guard there as a young subaltern and I would say the place is almost impenetrable," Reed-Henry confirmed. "But in Intelligence a lot of work is routine, and to save myself from total boredom some time ago on night watch outside a Russian barracks, I gave some thought to a way by which Hess could be rescued. Of course it's very much an untested idea but I do have access to inside information, so I could be of use to you."

"Why would you be prepared to help me?" Haddad asked suspiciously.

"Perhaps my actions are semi-official," Reed-Henry said carefully. "You see, detente is breaking down and for as long as Hess remains in Spandau, the Russian Army has access to West Berlin and a right to station soldiers in the heart of the Western sector. The West would like this to stop but Hess stubbornly refuses to die and even if he did," Reed-Henry sounded bitter, "the Russians would probably put a mark up over the man's grave and insist on guarding that. You can imagine the danger represented to our security in West Berlin by having, once every four months, a fortress containing a company of Russian troops controlling the ground between our military barracks. If you remember that eighteen million Russians died in the Second World War then you will understand that the West cannot let him go, the political repercussions would simply be too great. If someone like you got him out, that would be a different matter, providing, of course, it was not the British Army's turn to be on guard."

"Who do you suggest?" Haddad asked drily, distrusting Reed-Henry's motives.

"The French," Reed-Henry said, considering the matter. "Yes, the French, let them take the blame, they're always blaming us these days. Did you know Hess has a weak chest?"

"Yes, I read that."

"Well, if you should happen to be outside Spandau towards mid-morning of the day after tomorrow, you'll see a convoy leave there and convey Hess to the British Military Hospital where he is being admitted for a check-up. In my opinion that's the one flaw in the security net. Hess must be about the most closely guarded man in the world, but occasionally they have to move him and they do so by wheel transport and along public roads. You can count on two factors that will always remain constant. One, because Spandau is in the British sector, Hess is always guarded, when he leaves the fortress, by the British Military Police, and secondly, he is always taken to the British Military Hospital on Dickens Weg, where a whole floor is sealed off and kept in readiness for him. The hospital, I should tell you," Reed-Henry added quickly, "is well guarded and any type of attack there would be extremely embarrassing for us."

"How large is the convoy?" Haddad asked.

"Ah," Reed-Henry smiled slightly. "Now you're on my wavelength. Normally very small, they like to move him inconspicuously. Say two or three R.M.P. Landrovers and two V.W. mini-bus ambulances, one's a decoy and one carries Hess."

"I'll be there the day after tomorrow," Haddad said, finishing his drink and getting ready to leave.

"One last thing," Reed-Henry added. "In return for my assistance I must know and approve each stage of your plans. I'm going into the East tomorrow, I'll be there for some ten days. If you want to reach me before then, contact Tom Dade."

Haddad rose to leave.

"I'll come with you," Reed-Henry said. "I haven't got Tom's American sense of exhibitionism."

"Hey, wait!" Tom shouted from the dance floor. "Gina here says she's going to put on a private show for us." Reed-Henry spoke to Dade who shrugged and went back to his girl.

"I'll give you a lift," Reed-Henry offered as they reached the street. "Tom will make his own way home when the girls have fleeced him, he always does."

Immediately he felt the cold air strike, Reed-Henry raised his gloved hands and tucked them protectively under his arms.

"How are the chilblains?" Haddad asked.

"Much better really," Reed-Henry said gratefully. They drove in silence down the Ku-damm.

"Have you seen anything of Herr Stroebling?" Haddad asked. Reed-Henry knew what was on his mind.

"He's been in the East," he answered, "taking a course of injections. He's got cancer of the bowel, you know, not much longer to live, but we'd like to keep him around for as long as we can. He used to be one of their best operatives but now he's making mistakes and it's affecting his whole organisation. We don't want some younger man to come along and rectify them so we're leaving him a pretty free run at the moment."

The car pulled up. "Will this do you?" They were parked at the end of the street, just a few yards from his hotel. "I would like to think we can work together, Mr Haddad," Reed-Henry said. He paused. "A word of advice. Berlin has so many watchers in the employ of various powers that they spend most of their time watching each other. But even though you came in on the train, amongst the Turks, you can be sure you won't have come in unnoticed. Good night to you."

Haddad watched the exhaust smoke curl as the car moved away. He made sure that he was alone in the street before going into his hotel.

CHAPTER NINE

Haddad was waiting across the street from the entrance to Spandau prison when shortly after 11 a.m. the main gates swung open and a convoy of vehicles, in the British Royal Military Police markings, swung onto Gatow Strasse. Haddad followed them in a hired car. Reed-Henry's information had been accurate. The convoy was a small one, two Landrovers and two mini-buses.

There was no shrieking of sirens. The convoy moved well within speed limits, keeping a low profile, not wanting to attract any more attention to their movements than could be helped. Once clear of Spandau, blue warning lights spun on the roofs of the Landrovers.

The traffic lights were against them as they turned into Heer Strasse. The Landrover in front moved out, blocking a lane, allowing the convoy to proceed across the lights at a continued steady pace. The other Landrover took the lead, the first vehicle swinging in behind. The R.M.P.s had caused almost no disturbance to the general flow of traffic; it was a neatly handled operation.

Haddad beat the lights and swung in behind the convoy, then dropped back as they proceeded down Heer Strasse, one of the broad five-lane autobahns leading into the city. The convoy passed over two bridges that spanned the Havel river, past the British Commonwealth War Cemetery on the right, then swung hard left into Passenheim Strasse. A hundred metres down the road the convoy swung right into Dickens Weg then right again through the gates of the British Military Hospital. Haddad drove on, turned at the end of the road and cruised slowly back.

The hospital was a modern multi-storeyed building with the colours of the Royal Army Medical Corps flying in the car park. Armed British paratroopers in camouflage jackets guarded closed iron grille gates. There were more soldiers in the glass-fronted porter's lodge, scrutinising the passes of even the medical staff; Haddad guessed that snipers had been placed on the roof and other vantage-points. As soon as the convoy carrying Hess had passed through there had been a total security clamp-down. The British Military Hospital might not look as impregnable as Spandau, but it was well guarded.

Haddad returned to Spandau and slowly retraced the route taken by the convoy. Gatow Strasse was built up on either side. He turned left into Heer Strasse. There were no chains or islands to impede a vehicle changing from one lane to another; the autobahn consisted of a great sheet of open tarmac with the traffic controlled by overhead lights.

Further down Heer Strasse Haddad came to the bridges that crossed the Havel. Some two hundred metres on the left, just after the first bridge, there was a sand road almost hidden in the trees. It ran at right angles for some way into a wooded area and then sloped sharply down to a boatyard on the river, a drop of some twenty metres below.

The entrance, apart from the small opening into the sand road, was blocked by railings, trees and traffic signs and then a low wooden stump vehicle barrier. Haddad got out of his car and walked down the small sand road. The boatyard below was virtually deserted, the boats having been frozen in for the winter. A steep wooded slope rose to one side of the road with a sharp drop on the other. He returned to his car and drove on past the second bridge. A cobbled road ran alongside the freeway, giving access to the British Commonwealth War Cemetery. Just before and after the bridge there was a steep drop to the river below. The area was thickly wooded and if an ambulance was pushed over the edge it was just possible that the trees would stop it from falling too far.

Haddad turned into the cobbled side road, left his car and walked up the slope to the British War Cemetery. The noise of the traffic was reduced to a murmur by the screen of trees. Haddad found himself in a large, open space, lined with white gravestones standing above the snow. He passed the grave of a Canadian pilot, aged twenty, who had died in the air over Berlin. Others, the ones who had been too badly burnt to be recognised, stood out like orphan children with the forlorn inscription, "Known to God".

Wherever you went in Berlin it was impossible to get away from memories of the war. What intrigued Haddad, however, was the discovery of a large empty area screened from city buildings and lying parallel to the road. He memorised the layout of the cemetery before returning to his car. He was beginning to realise that Heer Strasse presented the best opportunities. If he could interfere somehow with the convoy coming from Spandau to the British Military Hospital. . . .

Haddad traced several other routes the Royal Military Police could choose but Heer Strasse was the shortest, most direct way, the one in which Hess would be vulnerable for the least possible time. It was also the most likely route they would use in a time of emergency.

Haddad went back to his hotel room and drew a plan of the area around both the bridges and another of the cemetery. He discarded the second bridge: the risks were too great of the ambulance plunging unchecked down the side, through the trees into the river. The cemetery seemed the most suitable place to operate from because of the large area of ground that lay away from the road, but the more he studied his sketches the more Haddad began to see the possibilities that lay in using the sand road by the first bridge. He had realised in Paris that the only time the four powers were vulnerable was when Hess was taken out of Spandau. Now the weak point was confirmed he felt the first faint pulse of excitement stir as the plan began taking shape in his mind.

A small two-way radio receiver lying beside his desk squawked to life. He picked it up and pushed the button.

"Haddad," he said.

"Hey man," Maroun's voice came through clearly; he was probably in an opposite room in the same street. "There's a tail on you. Look outside across the street in a doorway about four blocks down."

Haddad opened the corner of the curtain and looked out. It was a formality; Maroun was a professional. He wouldn't make a mistake. Haddad saw the tail, a big man in a heavy overcoat with a fur-lined collar and fur hat. He was one of Stoebling's street soldiers who had harassed him on the first occasion. Haddad guessed there would be another man in a car somewhere further back, keeping warm, and probably someone else watching from a window in a buidling across the street. He was almost glad they had come. He went back to the radio.

"Maroun," he said, "there's a chance they may decide to kill me this time without bothering to pick me up. I want to make my move first."

"O.K.," Maroun replied. "Lead them onto the street, take them to the place I told you about off Kottbussertor. Follow the route I showed you and you'll find yourself in a courtyard amongst some buidlings. Lead them in there and just keep out of the way, I'll do the rest."

"Maroun," Haddad said, teeth clenched, "if I lead them in you be there, don't let me down."

The voice on the other end of the radio chuckled. It was

an unstable sound that gave the listener no confidence.

"Haddad," Maroun murmured, "you are my brother."

Haddad turned the receiver off.

* * *

Haddad lay on his bed in the darkened room with the glow from the street lights on the ceiling. He waited three hours. He blanked out his mind and stared at the wall, not feeling the cold that was creeping into his bones. When he knew that he had allowed enough time for Maroun to move into position he rose from his bed and checked his weapon, loading and reloading the magazine and spare. He wanted to call up Maroun to make sure he was there; now the time had come, it was taking all his courage to go down into the streets.

Haddad shrugged on his overcoat, put the receiver in his pocket and closed the door. He left a clinically empty room behind him. There was nothing in it, no photographs, no letters, nothing that could be used to trace his identity.

There was a mist, a haze of cold that hung in the air beneath the street lamps, the pavements slippery with ice. Away from the bright neon lights of the Kurfürstendamm, the Berlin that rose out of the rubble of the war was a faceless, stark, sinister city with the winter pressing down on it.

Stroebling's men shadowed Haddad in the familiar pincer pattern. One man in front, one man behind, one following in a car and this time, to ensure they took no chances, a fourth man moving parallel to him on the other side of the street. Haddad made no attempt to get to his car—he knew he would never make it. Instead he led them on across Potsdamer Strasse heading for the Kreuzberg district. In the first quarter of an hour his nerves twisted and his back had crawled waiting for a bullet.

When nothing happened he knew that they were waiting for instructions. They had probably sent for Stroebling. He quickened his pace. The tags closed the distance between them, letting him walk but keeping him boxed in. The new housing development of soulless high-rise flats gave way to the crumbling five- and six-storey buildings, dark alleyways and empty lots of the Turkish quarter in Kreuzberg.

Haddad had been walking for nearly two hours now. He knew the feeling of being hunted, of being totally exposed to his enemies. He was nearing the end of the hunt: the tension made him tired, it was an effort to keep his brain clear, to keep thinking. The tags, if they had been leading him, could not have forced him into a more decrepit, ill-lit, lawless area of Berlin. They knew that he was far from any kind of help and he was relying upon this making them over-confident. Haddad was staking everything on Maroun, that he was lying up faceless and quiet as the dust somewhere. God help the men he was going to kill, for Haddad knew he was a good killer, the best, as long as his mind hadn't snapped.

He walked through the arcade leading from the u-bahn station, down a grubby street with garbage in the sleet-soaked gutters. On either side of him were passages leading into the buildings, open doors, narrow, dark, dirty stairways, inner courtyards with the plaster broken away and the brick crumbling. He passed children's paintings on the bleak walls of the empty lots, slogans sprayed across the advertising hoardings, Turks in leather jackets playing cards in the small, steamy-windowed bars.

Haddad turned off Oraninen Strasse. Maroun had chosen the killing ground and Haddad had no choice but to follow his directions. The tags were growing concerned now, wondering what he was up to. They feared they could lose him in the crowded tenements. The driver of the car was probably radioing urgently for instructions and the rest of the tags had drawn so close to him now that they were almost breathing down his neck. One of the tags caught Haddad's eye. He reached into his overcoat and took out the plastic bag that he had nearly asphyxiated him with on the last occasion. He held it up so that Haddad could see it and grinned at him. He was confident that his victim had no way of escape and he was gloating over what was to follow.

"Soon," he called out across the street, showing Haddad the plastic bag. "Very soon."

Haddad guessed that Stroebling had been letting him walk to see if he would lead them anywhere but was now running out of patience. Haddad glanced up, saw the almost obliterated number sixteen on a building, turned in through the open doors, along a pitch-dark passage that led to an inner courtyard. The squalor of the Turkish quarter was not so evident on the streets, which the Germans tried to keep clean, but inside the sprawling overcrowded slum buidlings, where the ninety thousand Turkish Gastarbeiters of West Berlin lived twelve to a room. Banked-up snow and rubbish lay in the courtyard and the buildings rose up six storeys all around him. Lights still shone from many of the windows and there was a babble of sound, music blaring, women shouting and children crying. Haddad crossed the courtyard and took cover in the shadows thrown by some steep stone steps that led up to one of the buildings. He was trapped now; there was no way out except back through the passage.

Haddad took out the radio. He saw the shadow of one of the tags blend into the wall opposite him.

"Maroun," he whispered, "they're coming through the passage now, can you see them?"

There was no answer.

"Maroun," Haddad whispered again fiercely, "can you see them, they're almost on to me?"

Still there was no answer. Haddad looked despairingly up at the windows in the buildings above him, then he drew his gun.

All three tags were in the courtyard now. They had fanned out, using the shadows against the walls for cover, and were moving towards him. Haddad was too vulnerable in his position by the stairway. He vaulted over the rail and scrambled up the steps, trying to make for the open doorway, but he slipped on the ice and fell, cracking his head, sliding back down the steps. He heard the sound of a gun being cocked behind him and then came three rifle shots. The reports followed one after the other so quickly they sounded like one, but the outburst was almost drowned by the noise from the tenement buildings. Haddad got shakily to his feet, looked for his gun and picked it up.

Someone opened a window above him, looked out, then quickly closed it again, not wanting to get involved. All three tags were lying in the snow. Haddad walked up to one and turned him over with his boot. The bullet had gone straight through, leaving a neat blue hole in his forehead and smashing out through the back of his skull. Haddad checked there was no life in the others, then he reached into his pocket and took out the receiver, shook it to see if it was still working and pressed the botton.

"Maroun, you bastard," he whispered furiously. "Why did you let me think I was alone, why didn't you answer me?"

"You know I don't talk when I'm working," Maroun replied, his husky voice elated after the kill. "It breaks my concentration."

Haddad saw something stir behind a darkened window a couple of storeys up. He thought it was Maroun jeering at him but among the shadows he could not be sure. He walked out of the courtyard and back through the passage. The car was parked across the street; the driver was expecting the other tags. He had no time to move before Haddad wrenched open the door and dragged him out. He spun the driver around, spread him over the bonnet, kicked his legs apart so that he had to use his hands to keep his balance and took away his gun.

"Your friends are dead," Haddad said. "And the only reason that you're going to live is because I want to get a message to Stroebling. Tell him I want to talk to him, tell him to be at that number." Haddad pushed a piece of paper into the driver's pocket. "At eight tomorrow night. I'll phone him there."

Haddad watched the driver speed away. He took out his radio. "Maroun," he said. "It's set for tomorrow night. Ask Pierre Helou to hire some Turkish friends of his and make it look good."

CHAPTER TEN

Haddad phoned Tom Dade. "I want to see Reed-Henry," he said. "O.K.," the deep, friendly voice boomed back at him. "I'll try to make it for this afternoon. Where are you staying? Can you find your way to the Blue Church?"

Haddad visualised the ruined church at the end of the Kurfürstendamm with the modern blue glass tower beside it.

"Yes," he said.

"O.K. Up the street on the right is a pretty good coffee-house called Kranzlers. If the meeting is on I'll pick you up at three."

A battered white Mercedes drew up punctually. Haddad paid his bill and crossed the pavement as the passenger door swung open for him. Dade was in civilian clothes.

"You got a passport on you?" he asked as the car pulled out into the traffic.

"Yes, why?"

"We're meeting Reed-Henry in the East."

This was something Haddad hadn't expected.

"Don't worry," the American major said reassuringly. "You're with me."

They made their way along the Landwehir Canal, across Askanischer Platz, past a grim-looking shell of a building that was once an SS and Gestapo headquarters. The Mercedes turned into Friedrich Strasse and drew up at Checkpoint Charlie just ahead of a convoy of tourist buses.

Dade spotted two Landrovers, filled with British troops, drawing up to the barrier and nipped in smartly behind them.

"Are they going to cross?"

"Sure," the major replied. "That's a flag tour. Allied forces in West Berlin have a right to send mobile contingents into the East and vice versa."

Haddad noticed that soldiers in uniform went through the barriers unchecked and his interest quickened.

"What will they do?" he asked.

"Tour around for a while, see what the Russians and the East Germans are up to and then report back."

He handed his documents to the American Military Police who cleared Haddad.

"Right," Dade said as the traffic moved forward. "Our turn."

The Mercedes left the West and rolled through no man's land to the first East German barrier.

"There's a building on the right beyond the wall," the major told Haddad. "Look three-quarters way up and you'll notice a window with a blind half-drawn; behind that is a high-powered camera. Ahead of you is an observation tower—there's a guy up there now watching us through binoculars. When we stop at the barrier keep your window rolled up, put your passport open on page one against the window."

One of the G.K.M. border guards, wearing a heavy overcoat, a sub-machine gun slung over his shoulder, stared at the passport through the window and signalled for the page to be turned over. The major was holding his military i.d. card up to the guard who was at his side.

"Turn the page over for the guy," he said. "Let him have a good look but you don't have to go beyond page five."

"Can they make us get out and search us?" Haddad asked.

Dade shook his head. "They can search civilians but they cannot touch the military. If there's any trouble you take no notice of these East Germans and demand to see a Russian officer. We don't recognise the East Germans, it's one of the anomalies of this place."

The boom opened and the car went forward, turning through the narrow entrance between the thick walls along which were the walkways and searchrooms for pedestrians. They passed the vehicle search area on the left and came up to another boom operated by the members of the East German Customs Police.

"This is one of the several crossing points between East and West Berlin," the major said as they waited for the boom to lift. "But it's the only one used by Allied Service personnel; the others are for West Berliners."

As they drove under the barrier and out into Friedrich Strasse Haddad felt his stomach unknotting. The experience had brought back memories of the crossing points dividing Beirut during the Civil War. The American had noticed the tension in him.

"It's always the same the first few times you go through the checkpoint," he said.

They made their way down Leipziger Strasse. About seventy per cent of this city had been reduced to rubble but Haddad noticed that the Russians got the best of the old buildings that were left.

It was an overcast, bitterly cold afternoon. The few people on the streets were dressed in winter clothes and bent against the wind. There were fewer and smaller cars, the shops were less brightly lit, but there was not the great contrast that he had been expecting. They passed through Alexander Platz, a large open square, with the big hotel, Stad Berlin, on one side and numerous shops and cafés on the other.

"What you are seeing," the American warned, "is the communist window-dressing. It's all most tourists ever see; behind that are some pretty grim places where the real people live. It takes a man about seven years' salary to buy one of those Wartbug cars with little two-stroke engines. He pays in advance and then joins the waiting list. Same goes when he marries and tries to get accommodation, that's unless he's a communist party member and you can only get to be one of those if your father was there before you or the State has some use for you. Then you are one of the privileged ten per cent who gets to buy in the State-owned shops and live in the State-owned apartments."

They had left the city centre and were travelling towards the outskirts of the city. They crossed a bridge over the river Spree and passed an electrical factory with a large sign proclaiming "East German Soviet Friendship". "And don't take that too seriously," the major added. "Underneath the East Germans and Russians hate each other's guts, you'll see why soon."

He parked the car by Treptow Park. They walked through the entrance to the Russian War Memorial in East Berlin. Above them was a grey, snow-laden, freezing sky and an Arctic wind cut straight through their clothes. The memorial spread over a great distance. Before them was a statue carved from granite of an old peasant woman bowed with sorrow, facing Russia, weeping for her dead sons. On either side of her, stretching down a broad avenue, were lines of weeping silver birches and tall poplar trees, symbolic of the young Russia rising again and mourning its dead. At the end of the avenue, forming a gateway, carved into two enormous red granite triangular structures, was a statue of a young Russian soldier kneeling with his head bared, facing a soldier of the older generation.

They walked past the gates and stood on the parapet. Below them was a small grave wherein were buried, in the upright position, facing Russia, three bodies in the uniform of a Russian private, N.C.O. and officer. There were five large grassed areas containing four thousand eight hundred dead. Placed on top of a mound containing another two hundred bodies was a massive statue of a young Russian soldier. In his right hand he held a naked sword and in his left he cradled a child. On a cold day under a grey sky the whole place spoke of pain and death and suffering.

Haddad was standing at the parapet when Reed-Henry came up beside him. "It's impossible not to be impressed by this place," Reed-Henry said. "That's why I asked Tom to bring you here. I wanted you to understand how the Russians feel about the Germans and vice versa, except you won't find a monumemt anywhere in the East to the German dead. And the Russians still keep twenty divisions of their troops and about eight thousand tanks stationed in East Germany, which is equivalent to military occupation."

Haddad looked around for the American major but he had moved away.

"I want you to understand," Reed-Henry continued, "that to the Russians Hess is the last of the old Nazi leaders and to the Germans he was a crazy patriot, unjustly imprisoned. Even though a new economic giant has risen from the rubble, Hess's continued imprisonment in Spandau reminds most Germans of the bitterness of humiliation and defeat."

"And the British?" Haddad asked.

Reed-Henry smiled. "We just like to see fair play," he said gently. The man seemed so unassuming that it was difficult to doubt him. "But if you begin to understand the international pressures surrounding Hess, then you will realise that we're dealing with a powder keg."

"I understand," Haddad said.

Reed-Henry rested his arms on the stone parapet. "I hear you've had a brush with Stroebling again," he said. "The German police are really quite upset."

"I felt it better to deal ruthlessly with him. I need a clear run in Berlin without Stroebling interfering. If he should harass me again could I look to the British or the Americans for assistance?"

"Negative," Reed-Henry said. "You're on your own, you know that. We're unable to assist you directly in any way and I have to tell you that the Americans are not involved in this at all. Tom's doing me a favour in a private capacity. There's not many people I can trust with something as sensitive as this, even amongst my own unit."

"How much power has Stroebling got?" Haddad asked. "I haven't been sure up to now what I'm up against."

"He has a great deal of power here and a great deal of

influence throughout Europe. Stroebling was once a Gehlen man working with West German and American Intelligence, but towards the end of the cold war he switched sides. The East set him up as an independent and they used him as paymaster/quartermaster to the left-wing terror groups. By the early seventies Stroebling had organised a cell in Europe under Bondia which he used as the main artery of supply—weapons, arms, plastics—for terror organisations including Basques, Bretons, Corsicans and of course the I.R.A.

"The terror network that he helped to build across Western Europe had an inner and an outer circle. The outer circle were the groups I have just mentioned and were considered no more than tribal resistance groups. The inner circle were made up of four small Marxist terror groups: the Japanese Red Army, Stroebling's own controlled terror group here known as the Begwegung-2 Juni Movement, the Turkish People's Liberation Army and the Italian Red Brigade.

"In the period 1971 to 1975, sometimes acting alone and sometimes together, these groups bombed, murdered, kidnapped and hijacked in Italy, Austria, France, Germany, Sweden, Britain, Holland and Ireland. So you see the Eastern bloc's manipulation of the radical left has been extremely successful until the last couple of years, when there have been signs of the tide gradually beginning to turn against them. But Stroebling's position is so secure that even the most ruthless of the Eastern Intelligence agencies can't replace him for fear of losing contact with the extreme left-wing terror groups, so they are stuck with a dying man who refuses, for his own safety, to groom a replacement.

"I've told you his illness is causing him to make serious mistakes which we are acting on. And the Eastern bloc is in a quandary as to what to do about it at the moment. But for all that," Reed-Henry said grimly, "he's still a very dangerous man to cross. It would be almost impossible for you to penetrate his guards—and even if you did, we could not let you kill him."

Haddad was silent for a few moments. It occurred to him that, Hess apart, somehow Reed-Henry intended to use him against Stroebling and the realisation of just how isolated he was in Berlin struck home. They turned, hunched against the cold, and began to walk back through the memorial. The tops of the trees seemed to touch the lowering grey sky.

"It takes weather like this to remind me that we're only forty miles away from Poland as we stand here," Reed-Henry observed. "And beyond that is Russia waiting to swallow us all up. I meant to ask you, did you follow the convoy?"

"Yes."

"Successfully?"

"Yes."

"How will you do it?"

"I think an accident on Heer Strasse."

"That would be the most likely place," Reed-Henry agreed.

"Is it at all possible for me to get access to one of the warders? I need someone inside Spandau who can provide me with information and possibly assistance."

"I think I can help you there. A British N.C.O. from the S.I.B. section of the Military Police joined the Spandau staff recently. He's married to a German girl so he's very keen to stay on in Berlin. I'll see what I can do."

"I've planned on switching the body with that of a dead man of similar age and characteristics. Very few people have actually seen Hess: the deception could last at least until the prisoner reaches the British Military Hospital. How long will it give us?"

"You could have as much as four hours," Reed-Henry answered. "The Russians would demand an autopsy, so would the French and the Americans. It could take that long to assemble the various Allied officers. I know what you're thinking," Reed-Henry said. "The problem is to get the real Hess out of Berlin and then out of East Germany. If you can get Hess clear of the convoy then British Intelligence would actively assist you after that. You can rely on us, we would find it very embarrassing if the real Hess were to suddenly pop up in East Germany."

"How would you do it?" Haddad asked.

"As long as no alarm is given we could lift him out of the British War Cemetery by helicopter."

"Can your helicopters move along the corridor at night?"

"You leave that part of the planning to us, Mr Haddad. The only request I have of you is that you devise an accident in which the least number of people are harmed. I'm finishing a tour of duty at B.R.I.X.M.I.S., I'll be back in the West in a few days. When I return," he scribbled a number, "contact me here, use a call-box and set up a meeting in some public place, make it sound casual and keep your conversation down to a few seconds. There are few telephones in Berlin that aren't bugged by one side or the other."

They had reached the statue of the peasant woman and it was beginning to snow. Tom Dade was waiting for them.

"I'm glad you two are finished," he said bitterly, his overcoat hunched around him and his hands deep in his pockets. "I'm damned near frozen. You owe me for this," he said to Reed-Henry who nodded.

"Tom will take you home," he said to Haddad. "I've got to get back to Potsdam now."

In the car on the way back they passed the Ostbahnhof.

"Did Reed-Henry tell you about the Russian dead?" the major asked. "From that station," he nodded to the Ostbahnhof, "over three million German soldiers left for the Russian front and none of them came back. My mother was German."

He dropped Haddad off in the Kudamm.

"Listen," he said as Haddad got out of the car. "Whoever you are, a man could get to like you. You ever heard of a nineteenth-century German socialist called Johann Most who wrote a book, The *Science of Revolutionary Warfare?* He was credited with inventing terrorism: in his view there are no innocents and ninety per cent of the human race is expendable. I know Herr Stroebling goes along with that philosophy and Reed-Henry doesn't care too much about the welfare of his fellow men if they get in his way. You probably guessed you are swimming amongst the big fish, so take care."

* * *

At 8 p.m. that evening Haddad made the call. A man answered.

"It's Haddad," he said briefly. "Get me Stroebling."

He waited.

"Mr Haddad," Stroebling said tiredly when he lifted the receiver, "I'm not a well man, this is a great inconvenience. What do you want?"

"A meeting."

"Why should I meet with you, Mr Haddad? You have killed three of my men."

"I have something to offer you."

Stroebling paused. "Very well then, where?"

"U-bahn exit on Dresdner Strasse in one hour's time."

"That's too soon, I would have no time to prepare."

"That's why I want you outside the u-bahn in precisely one hour's time, Herr Stroebling," Haddad said.

The Dresdner Strasse u-bahn exit was situated at the edge of a busy, well-lit traffic circle, with garishly decorated high-rise flats on one side and the Turkish quarter sprawled on the other. The big black Mercedes drew up. Haddad was standing well back from the street, close to the protection of the u-bahn exit. The door opened.

"Get inside, Mr Haddad," Stroebling called from the dark interior of the car.

Haddad shook his head. "I would feel more comfortable if we were both on the street," he said.

Before Stroebling could press the issue Haddad indicated the men who, in ones and twos, were appearing out of doorways and at the ends of the streets. Pierre Helou and Maroun had drilled them well; the Turks took up their positions and waited. Stroebling's bodyguards were impressed by the show of force and fidgeted nervously with their weapons.

Stroebling eased himself out of the car. Haddad watched the pale face with its hollow cheeks and glittering sunken eyes approach him.

"Mr Haddad," Stroebling said, barely containing his anger, "you seem to have extraordinary powers of survival. Your return to Berlin surprises me." He looked around at the Turks who were lounging on the street corners and leaning up against posts. "And now you seem to have found yourself some friends," he observed.

"Three of your men have died. It's important that you no longer dismiss me as an amateur. If you send any more of your men after me, I'll kill them as well."

"Mr Haddad," Stroebling snapped, betraying a little of his bitterness for the death of three of his men, "I can tell you that I respect your professionalism enough not to waste any more of my men on you. I have merely to notify the P.F.L.P. and they can send their own operatives to claim the price on your head."

"That's partly my reason for calling you to this meeting," Haddad said quietly. "Herr Stroebling, I think I have found a way to kidnap Hess."

Stroebling was silent for a few moments. He turned and led Haddad away, out of possible earshot from the car.

"If that were so then I would want him," Stroebling said softly, but emphatically. "I would want Hess very badly indeed and I would pay you well if you could deliver him to me." He paused and regarded Haddad suspiciously. "You seem the sort of man who would only work for one master at a time. Why this sudden change of loyalty?"

"If I guarantee to deliver Hess to you then I want a free run, without any interference on your part, in Berlin. Secondly, on the day I hand him over I want to know that the

P.F.L.P. have lifted the price off my head. I can tell you that it will not be an easy favour to deliver."

"Why?"

"Because I killed a lot of their men. The reason that I'm making this deal with you is because I know the extent of their organisation. As I go on now it's only a matter of time before they find and kill me. With regard to my survival I have no masters, I'm working for myself."

Stroebling's own research bore out Haddad's statements. He thought he could see what was driving the man.

"Your life for Hess?" he mused. "It seems a fair exchange. Of course you understand I want Hess alive," Stroebling said. "He would be of no use to me dead."

"Agreed."

"When could you deliver him?"

"I'm not sure yet, I think the first two weeks of February."

"I don't suppose you wish to tell me how it can be done?"

"No, the whole operation must be left entirely up to me. That's one of my conditions."

"Very well. I take it you'll still appear to be working for your liberal academics? It's a good cover."

"Yes."

"I'll see to it that you are left unhindered by any left-wing elements in Berlin. When you deliver Hess to me I'll use my influence with the P.F.L.P., which is considerable, to persuade them that memories of an old war should be allowed to rest."

Stroebling climbed back into the car.

"Good luck, Mr Haddad," he said. "I'll keep in touch."

CHAPTER ELEVEN

Haddad worked in his hotel room, drawing up lists of the material and information he required, the men he still needed to recruit. There was a hesitant knock at the door. It was repeated. Haddad spun round, reaching for his gun. There was only one entrance to the hotel. Maroun should have been watching, should have warned him, but the radio on his desk was silent. He took up position by the door against the wall.

"Who is it?" he shouted, his nerves still raw.

"Kathy," a voice replied.

Haddad let the gun drop to his side and opened the door.

"Hi," Kathy said shyly. "I guess I haven't heard from you in a while and I wasn't doing us any good in Paris."

She tried to smile, her shoulders hunched against rejection. Haddad knew then how much he had missed her: all he wanted to do now was take her in his arms and hug her, but he couldn't risk her being here. She glanced up, hoping for a welcome. There was a stony expression on Haddad's strong face.

"How did you find me?"

"Tom Dade."

He was blocking the doorway. She squeezed past him into the room. "I thought I could be of some use to you," she said defiantly. "I know more about Hess than you do." She knew that Haddad never betrayed any emotion unless he wished to. He was so inhumanly self-controlled, so strong within, and she felt so vulnerable. . . .

She looked around her. The room was small and terribly bare, unlived in. She couldn't see anything of Haddad's there and it frightened her, as though she had lost him.

"Kathy, you shouldn't have come," Haddad said.

"Why should I wait in Paris? I kept thinking that something had happened to you. I'm as much part of this rescue as you and Maroun," she said hotly. "I've a right to be here."

"This isn't Paris, it's not safe for you. I can't let you stay."

She had lost him, he was back to his old unreachable self.

"O.K.," Kathy said bitterly. "You've made your point. Do you want me to leave now or do I get a few more seconds? It's late and I'll have to find some place to stay."

The radio bleeped impatiently, a signal that Maroun

wanted to speak. Haddad cursed the interruption, crossed the room and switched it on.

"Yes," he said shortly.

Maroun ignored him. "Hi, Kathy," he said, his husky voice warm and drowsy with hashish. "How are you, girl? Been watching you in the street."

Kathy felt embarrassed, knowing that he would have seen her walking up and down outside the hotel, trying to pluck up the courage to go in.

"How's the bastard treating you?"

Kathy glanced quickly at Haddad, then pushed down the radio transmitter button.

"Like a bastard," she said, trying to keep the pain out of her voice.

"I should have warned you about him," Maroun said sympathetically. "He needs me to keep him alive and look how he treats me, like a dog." He breathed heavily, sulkily. "I tell you Kathy, one day he'll turn his back on a Moslem or one of the Germans and I won't be there and he'll be dead and it will be his own damned fault."

"Where are you, Maroun?" Kathy asked, warming to him as a fellow-sufferer.

"In a room across the street."

"Can't you come over?"

"No," Haddad interrupted them. "He has to stay where he is, he's working."

Haddad reached across and switched the radio off. Then he steeled himself against all weakness.

"Right," he ordered Kathy, making for the door.

A bullet from the Dragunov sniper's rifle came at such velocity that it made only a neat hole in the window pane and net curtain and went straight through the table to bury itself in the corner between the brickwork and the concrete. It narrowly missed both Kathy and Haddad. The shockwaves set up by its passing stunned them both for a moment. Then Haddad, reacting instinctively, threw Kathy down and switched out the light. He pushed her under the narrow bed and crawled in after her. She clung tightly to him. Silence descended and then the radio bleeped angrily. It had been knocked off the table and fallen to the floor.

Haddad reached out cautiously for it and turned it on.

"Listen, you shithead," Maroun's voice came through, angry and menacing. "Don't you ever switch me out like that again, you hear me?"

"What the hell do you think you're doing, you crazy idiot?"

Haddad yelled back furiously. "You could have killed us."

"I sit up here in the dark all the time, all by myself and when I want to talk you just switch me out," Maroun said sullenly. "Well, let me tell you, you bastard, you do that again and I won't miss, I'll shoot your fucking arse off. Kathy," he went on, "you O.K.?"

"Yes," Kathy said breathlessly, "I'm O.K."

"Good," Maroun said, calming down. "I wouldn't want to hurt you, but if that bastard gives you any more trouble tell me and I'll shoot his fucking arse off."

"Sure," Kathy said happily, still partially in a state of shock.

"Right," Maroun said and the radio went dead.

Kathy turned her head to Haddad, biting her lip to keep from laughing, her grey-blue eyes shining.

"Who's in danger now?" she said. "I've got friends."

Haddad felt himself relax.

"Yeah," he had to agree, and he cursed Maroun. She felt so good lying there next to him that he knew he wasn't going to be able to let her go.

In the morning when Haddad came out of the bathroom he found Kathy dressed and waiting. She knew he had work to do and she wanted to show him that she wouldn't slow him down.

"O.K.," she said, using an efficient businesslike voice. "Where to first?"

"We're not going anywhere," Haddad said. "I've got someone I have to see and I can't take you with me. You go shopping, amuse yourself today, I'll be back late this evening."

Kathy was very hurt. "Look," she flared, "I didn't come all this way just to sleep with you, I came to help rescue Hess. I care about that man, I thought you understood, I want to be involved."

"Listen to me," Haddad said, now coldly angry. "For you and your brother Michael this may be some crazy, romantic crusade, but for me this is business, a business that I have to give my full attention to if I want to stay alive. I don't want you involved, I don't want you getting hurt, I don't want people thinking they can hurt me through you. Do you understand that? I want you out of here before any trouble starts." He took the radio from his pocket and switched it on. "Maroun, is the street clear?"

"Yeah," Maroun answered. "It's clear. There's been no-one in the streets, no smell of their soldiers since the meeting."

"What meeting?" Kathy asked.

"Just a meeting."

"Listen, I'm a partner."

"No, you are not."

"Then I'm your employer. I have rights." She immediately wished she hadn't said that. Haddad was a proud man and she had needled his pride. He took her arm and the pressure of his grip hurt her wrist.

"You hold my contract," he confirmed dangerously, "but in the field I make the decisions. I'll try to rescue Hess from Spandau, beyond that there are no rights, for either of us, just survival."

He walked out of the room.

CHAPTER TWELVE

Haddad found the address he was looking for in a block of flats near Spandau prison. He knocked on the door and it was opened by a military-looking man in his fifties.

"Major Reed-Henry said I could find you here."

"Yes sir, come in, I've been expecting you."

He led the way into a small, pleasantly furnished flat. "Wife's out at work, I'm afraid. Mind you, she won't be working much longer, we're expecting a nipper, you see. Can I get you some coffee?"

Haddad hesitated.

"It's no trouble, I've got it all ready in a vacuum flask."

A life of discipline had given the British N.C.O. a liking for order. Everything in the flat was spotlessly clean and in its proper position, as though laid out for inspection.

"I believe you were recently with the British Military Police?" Haddad said, settling down in a chair.

"Royal Military Police," the N.C.O. corrected him. "Yes, I was sir, W.O. 2 in the S.I.B. section. Then I married a Berliner, this was the second time round for me, army life messed up my last marriage, so when I got the opportunity for a transfer to the prison staff at Spandau I jumped at it, you can see why."

He poured out the coffee and gave Haddad a cup.

"If you help me with Hess you could be doing yourself out of a job."

"Yes sir, but I'll have a German pension as well as my British one. Besides, sir, there are other reasons." He didn't finish the sentence but Haddad knew it was something to do with Reed-Henry. "You know," the British warrant officer went on, "in spite of him being a cantankerous old bastard, in the two years I've been a warder there I've really got to care about him, Hess I mean."

"I understand," Haddad said. He had thought about little other than Hess for months now, and he used an expression of Maroun's to explain. "The old man's beginning to grow into my bones too. Tell me, how is Hess's health, do you expect him to die soon?"

"There's no reason why he should, he's surprisingly fit for

his age. I suppose it's through living all those years like a monk."

"What's he like, describe him to me as he is now?"

"Well, sir." The warrant officer shifted uncomfortably in his chair. "He's a wizened, shrunken old man, he is eighty-four, you know. He's got salt-and-pepper colour hair, plenty of it still, swept off a bulging forehead, dark eyes, gaunt face, but he gives the impression of vigour, very alert. There's still a power, an aura around him. You'd pick him out in a crowd, if that's what you are asking, you'd know him for who he was, even after forty years in a cell."

"I take it," Haddad said, "that the guards, even the Allied guards, would shoot anyone trying to gain access directly to Spandau prison, like going over the wall."

"They would shoot without question, sir, those are their instructions. There have been a number of attempts over the years by right-wing and left-wing groups to get Hess out and they've all failed. They are just not reported if they can be hushed up."

"I really wanted to check that the guards had orders to shoot without question and you have satisfied me on that. I wasn't thinking of approaching him in Spandau."

"Yes, sir, I'd heard that."

"Then you will know that we intend to arrange an accident on Heer Strasse?"

"Yes sir."

"Tell me two things. I'm counting on the fact that very few people have actually seen the real Hess, and much of the identity goes out of a corpse when the face sags and the eyes become glazed. If we were to switch, say the body of a dead man of similar facial characteristics to Hess and keep up the deception until the impostor is taken to the British Military Hospital, how long do you think we'd have before he is discovered?"

The warrant officer considered for some moments.

"You could have as much as four hours," he said at last. "Maybe more, depending on what was happening between the East and West at the time. You can count on the Russians demanding to be present at any autopsy performed on Hess, and the French and the Americans. It could take four hours to assemble the various Allied officers and no one would move without them being present. The whole prison is run like that.

"I can tell you a story that happened just after I got there. Hess was moved to the B.M.H. for his regular medical check-up. Getting the four powers' permission to move him was a performance in itself, but then when he leaves for the hospital the governors, one from each power, go along too and nothing can be done with the prisoner without them all agreeing, a unanimous decision. Of course, I didn't go with him to the hospital but I heard that when he got there, to his specially security-cleared floor, it was a hot day and he asked if a window could be opened. Do you know sir, the doctors, no-one, could make a move without all four governors going into a huddle in the corner of the room to reach agreement on whether or not the window could be opened. When the time comes I expect you could use the sort of interpower bureaucracy that has built up around the prisoner to your advantage."

"I will remember that," Haddad said.

"And the other thing?" the warrant officer enquired.

"We can't just wait around for Hess to be moved," Haddad explained. "It's vital for us that we pick the time and force the escorts to take a route of our choosing. For that we would need to find some drug that would make Hess sufficiently ill so that he would have to be rushed directly to the B.M.H. If the R.M.P.s were convinced it was a real emergency I'm sure they'd use the Heer Strasse route. If we knew when the drug was going to be administered, we could be waiting for them."

"Well lately, sir, Hess has been developing asthmatic-like attacks, he always did have a weak chest, you know, and the only thing he seems to respond to is Ephedrine. If he was to be given Propanolol this would have exactly the reverse effect to Ephedrine. It would bring on an acute attack of asthma. Hess could collapse and if they didn't move quickly enough he could die."

"What procedure would they follow?"

"The medical orderly on duty would put him on oxygen immediately and he might administer an anti-asthmatic injection, but the dramatic effect of the Propanolol would probably confuse him. He'd be worrying about heart attacks and such and he would want Hess in the intensive care unit at the B.M.H. as fast as possible."

"I'm planning it for February when the French are on guard."

"Don't worry, sir, the French wouldn't want Hess dying on them any more than we would. By the time they got the oxygen mask on him the French governor would be calling out the R.M.P.s and trying to get shot of him."

"Propanolol," Haddad said softly. "I take it Reed-Henry

has been talking to you about this?"

"You could say so, sir," the warrant officer agreed. His eyes met Haddad's and there was a flash of understanding between them.

"Will you be prepared to administer it?"

"Yes sir. Give me a couple of days' warning and I'll see to it that the prisoner leaves Spandau within a few minutes either way of the time you want him."

"Could you put some mark on the ambulance which is carrying Hess so that we can identify it?"

"Yes sir. I could use a small luminous strip above the back mudguard. No one would spot it unless they were looking for it. Would that do? Right or left side, sir?"

"Right."

They got to their feet.

"You've been very helpful," Haddad told him.

The warrant officer cleared his throat. "I've no doubt you will be well paid for this, so seeing as I will be working with you. . . ."

"Of course," Haddad said, anticipating his demand. "You can take your share equally with the others."

"How much can we expect, sir?" the warrant officer asked.

"That's being arranged now," Haddad replied.

He drove to Heer Strasse and checked the route taken by the R.M.P. convoy again. He walked the area by the bridge and carefully timed each section of the journey from the prison to the hospital. The plan was beginning to fit together. He was ready to confirm the contract. He phoned the hotel. The concierge told him that Kathy had left a few minutes before. He added respectfully that she was dressed for an evening out.

Kathy had sat in the hotel room. From the high of the previous night she was feeling depressed. She had never been good at waiting. There was no sign of even Maroun. She wandered into the bathroom and looked at her face in the mirror, thought listlessly of taking a bath, then the phone rang. She rushed to pick it up. It was Tom Dade.

"Hi there, Kathy," the cheerful voice boomed down the telephone at her.

It was good to hear him. His big bear warmth and unfailing humour always seemed to cheer her up.

"What are you doing tonight?"

"Nothing."

"Where's Haddad?"

"He's out."

"Look, the Russians have sent us tickets to the opera in the East. My general has decreed that I should be seen in cultured surroundings for a change. I was going to ask you both, but do you think Haddad would kill me if I asked you along to be nice to the Russians?"

"No," she said. "I shouldn't think so." She hesitated for only a moment; the thought of seeing an opera in the East and the Russians intrigued her. "I'd love to go."

"It's formal. Pick you up at about 6.30 then."

"Fine."

Tom Dade arrived in his battered Mercedes. He was in full dress uniform. They crossed the wall at the checkpoint and went down the broad Unter Den Linden, past the enormous Soviet Embassy with the bust of Lenin in the front. Dade parked in a back street beyond some trolleys which were used to store scenery that would not fit backstage. They walked around to the ornate stone main entrance.

The performance was obviously going to be a glamorous occasion. Beautiful women from the Third World embassies and high-ranking Soviet and East German officials, many of them in uniform, thronged the brilliantly lit foyer and there was a scattering of French, British and American officers in full ceremonial dress.

The interior of the theatre had a magnificent chandelier hanging down from a curved dome; the walls were covered in sumptuous baroque decorations of ivory, gold and grey which contrasted with the red velvet of the tiers of seats. Kathy couldn't take her eyes off the people around her.

"This beats even Carnegie Hall on its good days," she gasped.

"You've seen the best part," Tom Dade replied mournfully, adjusting his bulk into his seat, trying to get comfortable. "Now comes a long two hours. I'm tone-deaf and anyway I don't understand a word these Germans are singing."

There were boxes by the stage. In one of them a lone man watched the first act. Tom Dade pointed him out to Kathy. The man had a ravaged, pale face and hunched shoulders. He was wearing a coat, even though the auditorium was warm. He seemed to feel them watching, looked down and nodded.

"Herr Stroebling," Tom Dade remarked casually. "Do you know him?"

"No," Kathy said. "Who is he?"

"A D.D.R. official."

Kathy glanced up at the box at the end of the performance but the man had left before the lights went up.

They hit the cold night air at the bottom of the theatre steps. Kathy's head was still spinning from the glitter and the glamour of the occasion as they walked to the car.

"I never knew the East was like that," she said. "You know, we get so much propaganda about the dreariness of the D.D.R. that you begin to believe it's true."

"All you saw tonight, honey," Dade warned, "was the party officials. Come on, I'll show you something."

They walked past the car and he stopped across the street from a long, blank wall.

"This used to be a Nazi barracks," he told Kathy. He pointed to the wall: it was deeply pitted with bullet marks. "Notice," he said, "they start high on the left and drop down to a couple of feet on the right: German thoroughness. They used to line the Jewish families up against that wall, mothers and fathers on the left, children on the right."

Kathy stared horrified at the lines of bullet marks, imagining the tiny, pitiful figures of children falling bloodied on the pavements. Dade nudged her and pointed a gloved hand upwards.

"There's a Vopo—a member of the People's Police."

Kathy saw the silhouette of a great-coated figure with a sub-machine gun slung over his shoulder, staring down at them through night glasses. The figure above the bullet marks was menacing, evil. Dade took her arm and led her away.

"National Socialists or the German Democratic Republic as they call themselves now, it doesn't make any difference. Other names, but the Germans don't change."

"They do," Kathy said defiantly, thinking of the Germans she knew and loved. "They do change."

They reached the car.

"Listen," said Dade. "This is your night out in the East, I don't want to spoil it. I know a great restaurant, the Ganymed, it's the best in East Berlin."

They found the Ganymed, in all its fading glory, down by the canal five hundred metres off Unter Den Linden. The interior seemed not to have been refurnished since Berlin's heyday in the glorious thirties. Kathy gazed at the worn scarlet curtains, shabby carpets, high-backed chairs and the waiters in long aprons and old-fashioned evening clothes. Two aged musicians, one on the piano and the other on the violin, broke into the theme from *The Sting* as soon as they recognised Tom Dade's uniform. They welcomed him warmly.

"We bring the sheet music over from the West," Dade explained.

They took a table by the wall.

"Interesting place, this," Tom Dade commented quietly. "Quite a few of the people who come here are terrorists, or freedom fighters if you like, who have completed their training and are waiting to go back to their countries."

He indicated a table with a couple of Blacks at it. At another table an Indonesian man sat alone, a plaster across the bridge of his nose, which obviously had been recently broken. He was wearing a dark blue shirt and a dark blue checked sports jacket. Kathy watched him: the way he sat, the deliberate way he poured his wine, the aloneness and the pent-up anger in the man set him apart from the other diners. There was something in him that reminded her of Haddad. Suddenly she wasn't hungry any more—she wanted to go back to Haddad and feel his arms around her. But Tom Dade was holding out the menu, asking her to order. Dade was a perceptive man. He smiled at her. "Don't worry," he said softly. "You won't turn into a pumpkin, we've got to be back across the wall before twelve." He found himself a little jealous of the hold Haddad had over her.

"Well, Kathy," he teased her, "you must like Berlin to be back so soon."

"Yeah, well, you know how it is," Kathy said. She bit her bottom lip and her eyes twinkled.

"The man's exciting company?"

She nodded.

"Haddad's got a friend," Tom Dade said casually. "No one ever gets to see him."

"You mean Maroun?"

"Yeah, that must be him. What's he like?"

"You mean describe him?"

"Yes."

"Well, he's young and impossibly good-looking; he's just a kooky kid," she dismissed him.

"He's the one with the gun, right? Watches Haddad's back?" Dade persevered.

"Yeah."

"Do you know where he lives? I mean which building he's in near Haddad?"

"Why do you want to know?" Kathy's suspicions were alerted.

"It's not important. What's Haddad up to? You said he was off seeing someone."

Kathy realised that Tom Dade had been pumping her all evening ahd she'd been too much of a fool to realise it.

"Tom," she sounded aghast, realisation dawning. "You set me up right from the beginning when you gave me all that information, then you let me go as bait and waited to see who I would bring in. Now you're using me to spy on Haddad. Why should you be helping Reed-Henry, what's your part in all this?"

"I can't tell you much, Kathy," Dade said. "Only that Britain and America have been Allies in this part of the world for a very long time. Oh, and that guy that you dismissed as a kooky kid is one of the best killers in the business. He killed three men right here in Berlin only days before you arrived and if you really were bait, as you think, then, in Haddad, you brought in a real mean shark, one of the meanest in all the ocean."

Tom Dade seemed sincere. His massive hand reached out and covered hers. "Look, Kathy, I know you got involved in this because you're out looking for a crusade, but you'd do best if you drop right out of it. If you're not prepared to do that then join us."

"You mean spy on Haddad?" she asked, bewildered. "I thought he was on your side."

"That's what worries us, he's got contacts with the East and we don't know whose side he's on."

Kathy leaned back in her seat and breathed in deeply. She didn't know what to think. Her mind was racing. Dade appeared genuine but all her instincts trusted Haddad.

"Listen," she played for time. "I should be getting back now."

"Think about it." Tom Dade spoke casually, easing back on the pressure. "Let me know."

He dropped her outside the hotel and refused an invitation to come in for coffee.

"It's late," he said. "And these Arabs have got a reputation for being very jealous."

"He's not an Arab," Kathy corrected him. "He's a Marionite."

"They're all Arabs to me," Tom Dade grinned cheerfully. "I've been with you all evening and I'm not risking him putting a knife in me."

CHAPTER THIRTEEN

Haddad returned to the hotel at 11 p.m. Still there was no sign of Kathy. He lay on his bed in the darkened room and stared up at the ceiling. Normally, at this time he could force himself to relax, to think clearly about his next move, but as he lay there his mind was raging, partly with concern for Kathy and partly with jealousy. He had emptied himself of all emotion after the death of his wife and child, so these feelings were strange to him. He hadn't had to give of himself for more than two years and now he cursed his stupidity for letting Kathy get close enough to hurt him. He was weak, he raged to himself, weak and foolish. If he became deeply involved with her he would make a mistake, be caught unawares: he was living too dangerously to risk that.

Kathy made her way nervously to the bedroom. Haddad was cold, silent, inwardly furious. She climbed quietly into bed beside him without switching on the light. She cuddled up to him, pushing her breasts into his chest, her legs across his, but he remained unresponsive. He lay so still that she thought if he moved his bones would crack. She forgot all about Tom Dade's warnings, pleased that their roles were reversed, that he was jealous, that she had made him show hurt for a change: hurt was close to love. She moved next to him, teasing him drowsily with her body.

Suddenly his still form uncoiled with a surge of power and speed, his hands seized her wrists and she almost cried out in pain. Then he was on top of her, pinning her down so that she was helpless. She felt, even through the darkness, his eyes burning into hers, she felt his barely suppressed rage like a blast of white heat and for a moment she was terribly afraid that he would kill her, use the great strength in his body to snap her neck like a twig. He said nothing but in that moment she understood the extent of his power and ruthlessness, that now she had become part of him she must never cross or betray him.

He lowered his head and kissed her, still angry but no longer wanting to hurt her. Kathy felt his grip relax. She put her arms around him, pulling him down on her, their embrace growing deeper and deeper, their passion surging through all the anger and hurt. Her heart sang because she knew for the first time that he cared and she loved him.

* * *

Kathy woke up and reached for Haddad, but his side of the bed was empty. From behind the closed bathroom door she heard him putting himself through his violent exercise routine. She was beginning to loathe his rigid sense of self-discipline. When he came out he was back to his old withdrawn, dangerous, unreachable self and she knew that last night had only been a small victory. She swung her feet over the edge of the bed.

"Tom Dade was trying to pump me for information," she began carefully.

Haddad was silent, his dark eyes watching her.

"He asked about Maroun," Kathy continued hesitantly.

"What did he ask you?"

"He wanted to know where Maroun was holed up in relation to your hotel. I told him I didn't know." Kathy looked up. "You told me about Reed-Henry, but what's Tom Dade doing in this?" she asked.

Haddad didn't answer. He picked up the radio from the bedside table. "Maroun," he said.

"Yeah," a husky voice replied.

"Some people looking for you."

"Which side?"

"Allies."

"Do they have a lead on me yet?"

Haddad looked at Kathy and she shook her head emphatically.

"No," Haddad said. "But move on to the next safe house anyway. I'll do the same in a day or so."

"O.K."

"Who are the other side?" Kathy asked, remembering Dade's warnings about the East.

"Why do you ask?"

"There was a man alone in one of the theatre boxes during the opera. Tom Dade made sure I would notice him, as though he wanted to gauge my reaction."

"Did he give you a name?"

"I think he called him Stroebling or Stroebler." She shivered. "He was a very ugly, evil-looking man. Do you know him?"

Haddad nodded, wondering how much she knew. "He's a senior official in the Stasis, the East German State Security Service."

Haddad had been growing concerned about the absence of Stroebling's men on the streets. Why weren't they checking on his movements? Accepted, they had made an agreement, but Stroebling had pulled his people too far back to be believable; the German was acting out of character in taking such chances unless he had something stronger to bargain with. A warning note began sounding in Haddad's mind.

"And why should Tom Dade and Reed-Henry be prepared to help you?" Kathy asked, perplexed.

Haddad shrugged. "I don't know, all I can tell you is that without the Allies' help we couldn't begin to rescue Hess."

"But if the British want him out," Kathy was now thoroughly confused, "why don't they just open the prison gates one month when they are on guard? They could make it into a big public relations exercise and a lot of Germans would love them for it."

"It's not that simple," Haddad explained. "If they let Hess out in defiance of the judgement of Nuremberg then the whole four-power agreement over the status of West Berlin would be in jeopardy. In the present political climate, the Russians could even use it as an excuse to take the city."

"Then why are they helping you if so much is at risk?"

"I don't know."

Kathy looked into Haddad's face and was sure he was telling her the truth.

"I really don't know," he repeated.

Reed-Henry's motives were something else he had been considering for some time.

"These men represent the power here; I have no alternative but to accept any help they give me."

"I don't trust Reed-Henry," Kathy said. "He gives me the impression of mildness but he's cunning, like a fox, and he can't be doing this for nothing, he will want some kind of payment."

"I know."

"And Stroebling?"

Haddad shrugged as if a great weight were on his shoulders. "The same."

"What if we all want Hess, then whose side are you on?" Kathy asked.

He realised that he was being harsh with her, that Kathy was seeking reassurance which he couldn't give. "Kathy," he said more gently, "the time will come when you may have to judge me for my actions. I can't hope for your understanding until I explain some of the pressures I'm under, and I can't do that now. Don't ask me any more questions, I can't answer them, and don't expect more of me than I can give. I'm only just one step ahead of the field. I have Maroun to watch my back but they can hurt me through you. Now can you understand why you must leave Berlin?"

He reached out and touched her hair, lifting it off her face. Kathy nodded, realising that she made him vulnerable.

"When do you want me to go?" she asked, trying hard to believe in him.

"Soon," he said. . . . "Meanwhile, I want to keep you close to me, for protection," he added, not wanting her to think he was jealous.

Haddad had been very tense as he spoke to her, choosing his words carefully. Now he relaxed and smiled.

"Do you like racing-cars?"

"I don't know," Kathy answered, trying to match his mood, smiling uncertainly back at him. "I guess I've only seen them on television."

"Well, they're not exactly racing-cars," Haddad said. "They're ugly, dirty stock-cars. Anyway, tonight I want you to meet an old friend of mine."

* * *

After dark Haddad took Kathy into the southern suburbs of Berlin to a crudely built stock-car circuit. They arrived before the start of the first race and found Pierre Helou in the pits, working on his car. He was a small, slim man with brown hair. His face was badly scarred on one side and his left hand was missing: he used a steel claw instead. Pierre was delighted to see them and embraced Haddad warmly.

"I have been expecting you," he said. "Why didn't you get in touch with me again after you phoned?"

"There were people watching me," Haddad replied. "I didn't want to lead them to you."

Pierre's attention had turned to Kathy. Traces of the Orient showed in his large dark eyes. He regarded her approvingly.

"I don't know how Haddad found you," he said, taking in their relationship immediately. "But I'm glad he did."

He turned away again with the cocky, self-assured air that small men sometimes adopt to make up for their lack of size.

Haddad had told her that Pierre had been on his way to becoming one of Lebanon's top racing-car drivers. The injuries that he received were due to the war; a mortar bomb, not a car crash as she might have expected, but it had effectively put him out of first-class racing all the same.

"Hey," Pierre was shouting, looking around him. "Where's my son? I talk a lot about you," he said to Haddad. "You know, of the old days, the boy remembers a little. Hey, Angelo, come here."

A skinny eight-year-old made his way timidly around from the back of the car. He took a few more steps under his father's indignant urging and then stopped, overcome by shyness, unable to go any further. Haddad reached out before the boy could protest and swung him lightly into the air.

"Hey, Angelo," he said. "I remember you small and now you are big like your father. Do you do the driving?"

"Not yet," the boy said proudly, his shyness disappearing fast. He indicated his father. "He won't let me."

"He's my mechanic," Pierre said, his proud love of his son shining in his eyes. "We're a great team."

The hooter sounded.

"Listen, Angelo will look after you, I have to get ready for the race."

"Where's René?" Haddad enquired.

"She doesn't come here, it worries her to watch me driving."

Pierre pulled a yellow silk scarf out of his pocket and wound it around his neck. Then he climbed in through the window of his car, started the engine and set off towards the grid. They saw the yellow scarf fluttering through the open window as they walked with Angelo to the stands.

"René, his wife, gave him that scarf for luck," Haddad told Kathy, "soon after he drove in his first race. He wore it all through the war in Beirut whenever we went into action."

For a moment Haddad saw the white buildings of Beirut gleaming in the Mediterranean sunlight, and then blurred under a pall of smoke. He thought of Pierre and Maroun and of the men who were no longer with him. Kathy saw the sadness in his face for a moment before he could hide it. She wanted to ask him more about Pierre and how he came by his injuries but then she remembered the boy, Angelo, was there.

The V8 beat of enormous motors filled the stand with a rumble like live ammunition exploding, popping and banging and spluttering. Sheets of flame jetted out of exhaust studs that were raised above the roof. Some old racing hand was using Castrol oil and the distinctive racing-car smell of two decades ago hung in the air. The commentator was whipping the crowd to fever pitch when the flag went down and the great cars careered away with an ear-shattering roar. Angelo stood between Haddad and Kathy, clinging grimly to their hands as he watched his father's car hurtle around the track. Pierre had started well back on the grid.

"The others won't let him pass!" Kathy shouted indignantly, getting caught up in the excitement of the race. "They won't let him through!"

The cars were cannoning off each other as they tried to find a gap and the crowd screamed for blood. Pierre came up behind a slower car, into the inside corner of the lead car's tail and gave it a nudge. He backed off fractionally to keep clear while the forward car went wide and missed the corner, then spun off out of control against the wire.

"You see that, you see that!" Angelo screamed as his father took the gap and moved ahead. "Only the very top drivers can do that and my dad's the best!"

Kathy winced. The driver of the front car had stood on his brakes. Pierre had slammed into his tail and bounced back, the car behind smashed into him and shunted him on. There was a noise of rumbling engines and twisting metal, then the cars disengaged, with Pierre racing ahead. No-one could catch him after that and he made it first to the finishing line.

The first race ended. Exhaust fumes and dust hung in the glare of the arc lights. Kathy realised that she had been shouting herself hoarse alongside Angelo and she was weak from the excitement and violence of the race. She saw ambulances standing by some overturned cars.

"Don't they hurt themselves when they crash like that?" she asked Haddad anxiously, picturing Pierre's already damaged body being violently tossed around inside the cab.

"No," he assured her. "These men know what to expect and they are well strapped in. There's hardly ever a serious accident."

They followed Angelo back to the pits as the cars came in, decelerating, shooting sheets of flame through the exhaust pipes to please the crowd. Pierre had unstrapped himself and was climbing out through the window by the time they arrived. The doors were welded shut and the windows had been taken out and replaced with wire mesh. The roof was reinforced with roll bars and the suspension had been lowered so the centre of gravity of the car lay close to the ground. Pierre's cheek was bleeding from a stone that had found its way through the protective wire. Kathy wet a cloth and sponged away the blood. Pierre was pale, more shaken by the three-car crash than he cared to admit.

"I'll give you a hand," Haddad offered. "What do you want me to do?"

"Grab a hammer then," Pierre ordered. "This isn't like the Formula One pits. When you work on a stock-car it's normally with a hammer, straightening it out."

Haddad began working, beating out the fenders.

"What did you think of the race?" Pierre asked.

Kathy looked around at the other cars in the pits, like metal monsters, their drivers beating them back into shape.

"I'm not sure," she shrugged. "So much noise, so much violence—it's like watching gladiators destroy each other."

Pierre nodded. "That's what the crowd comes for, they like to think they're smelling blood. In fact most of the accidents are more spectacular then dangerous, as long as you know what you're doing."

His son came up beside him and he rested his arm on the boy's shoulder. "Once I used to drive Formula Ones." It was important to him that she knew that he hadn't always been just a stock-car racer. "It was like riding a thoroughbred," he said. "The harness, the steering-wheel and the fact that it has four wheels are about Formula One's only similarity with the stock-car."

She knew he was telling her that it was like coming down to earth and playing the clown after having been on the high wire. She didn't know what to say and he didn't seem to expect any words; he was just glad that she understood.

The hooter sounded the start of the second race. As cars peeled off into safety fences or piled up and turned over Kathy clung to the rail beside Angelo, reminding herself of his words: the accidents were supposed to be more spectacular than dangerous. She also began to understand that Pierre was a very good driver. He won his heats all through the evening. At the end of the meeting she realised why there had been so many violent crashes, for the sponsors paid out not only to the fastest drivers but to those who had driven in the most crowd-pleasing manner.

They made their way down to the pits. Pierre had some business with the management, and by the time he came out the lights were going off and most of the crowd had gone. He looked tired but as soon as he saw them he forced a smile.

"Hey," he said, tapping the cheque in his breast pocket, "it was a good evening, now we must celebrate. You have a car? Good, then follow Angelo and me home."

"What about René?" Haddad asked warily.

"René's expecting you, don't worry, it will be alright." Pierre looked into Haddad's face. "Come back with me, old friend," he said. "We haven't spent an evening together in a long time."

CHAPTER FOURTEEN

The Helous lived in a squalid, crumbling, five-storey apartment block behind Kottbusser Tor in the Turkish quarter. Haddad took his time finding somewhere to park in the narrow, garbage-strewn street, letting Pierre go up first. Kathy was amazed that such a sordid area could exist after the almost clinical cleanliness of the rest of Berlin, but Haddad had seen it before. They went through a doorway into a dank, freezing hall and climbed past ragged children playing on the steep steps. Haddad found the apartment and knocked on the door. They heard the noise of voices raised in argument inside and then the door was flung open. A thin blonde woman confronted them, openly hostile.

"So you've come," she snapped at Haddad. "The last time we heard from you my son waited on a u-bahn station for you half the night. You know how the boy hero-worships you. He wouldn't leave, his father had to go and fetch him in the end."

"Not now, René," Pierre tried to remonstrate.

"Yes, now," she answered furiously, shaking off her husband's restraining hand. "I don't want this man here, he brings trouble wherever he goes. We have enough problems, we're illegal Gastarbeiters, they'll deport us if they find us."

Haddad was not prepared to be harangued on a doorstep. He turned to go, but René saw the expression on her husband's face and put out her hand to stop him.

"I'm sorry," she said resignedly, her shoulders sagging in defeat. "It's the memories I fight against, I don't mean to make you so unwelcome. There's food prepared for us all, please come in."

She led them into a tiny apartment. Compared to the rest of the building, she had worked wonders: brightening the dark walls with pictures, some of them carefully cut from magazines and pasted on boards. It was apparent that they had had nothing when they came and that she had skimped and saved and collected and worked her heart out to make her family as warm and as comfortable as she could. She saw that Haddad and Kathy were seated, then quickly made her way to the kitchen. Kathy made an excuse to leave the men: she found René leaning against the sink, weeping silently to herself. She heard Kathy come in and hastily straightened her shoulders and dried her eyes.

"I thought perhaps I could help with something," Kathy offered quietly.

René turned to face her. It was obvious that once she had been a very pretty woman. Some of her looks still remained, but her face was thin now, pinched with the misery and poverty of her existence as an illegal refugee amongst strangers in a land far from her home.

"I don't understand the magic that man has with men," she said angrily, referring to Haddad. "My husband lost a hand and half his face for him in the war, and still he has only to snap his fingers and Pierre would drop everything and follow him." She closed her eyes wearily. "I haven't the strength to start again. He came here for a reason, I know it," she said.

There was a cry from the next room and she put her hands over her ears as if to block out the noise. Then she went out and came back with a small child, now lying quietly in her arms.

"Our youngest," she said, rocking the child. "She is nearly three. Do you know what Haddad wants of my husband?" she asked almost pleadingly of Kathy.

"I don't," Kathy answered. "Really, I don't. He doesn't tell me and I don't know what goes on in his mind." She paused. "Did you know him when he had his wife and child?"

René shook her head. "Pierre met him after that, when he was leading men in the street battles. To me he was always a cold-hearted bastard but the men who followed him loved him, I could never understand why." She pulled herself together. "Come, we'd better serve the men their food."

Angelo sat by his father's side and watched Haddad throughout the meal, which infuriated his mother. She tried repeatedly to send the boy to bed but Pierre wouldn't hear of it. He was gentle but firm. "Tonight we are celebrating," he said. "Let the boy stay."

Kathy helped to clear away the dishes.

"You have done some good," René observed from the safety of the kitchen. "With you at least Haddad is half human." She shot Kathy a shrewd glance. "You're in love with him," she said and Kathy nodded. "You are a fool," René warned, "the man's an outlaw, he brings trouble wherever he goes."

The words came out more sharply than she had intended. She was beginning to like the girl: it was good having another woman to talk to. Her expression softened.

"It's Christmas in a couple of days," she said. "Where will

you be then, will you be alone?"

"I don't know," Kathy shrugged. "Maybe I'll go back to Paris. Haddad wants me to leave here."

They went into the living-room with the coffee.

"You must let her stay for Christmas," René demanded of Haddad. "We'll have a meal here. You remember at home in Beirut?" she turned to her husband. "We always used to have a big Christmas."

"Why can't you go back to Beirut?" Kathy asked, seeing the hunger in the other woman for her home.

"It's Pierre," René sighed, "he won't go back."

"We lost everything," Pierre said. "Now we have to start again. Berlin is one of the most expensive cities in the world but it is also the richest—we can make money here and then one day we can go back."

"If he hasn't killed himself before then," René cut in bitterly. "He works through the day, then drives cars at night. The children and I hardly see him. But it's always Angelo must have this and Angelo must have that. Go to bed," she snapped at the boy. "Don't sit there listening to your parents quarrel, you have school work to do in the morning."

"Did you know Maroun?" Kathy asked as the boy left the room.

René looked up, thoroughly alarmed. "Is Maroun here too? I thought he would have destroyed himself by now. I don't want that madman coming near me or my family."

Haddad caught Kathy's eye in warning.

"Maroun will stay where he is." He spoke firmly. "You won't see him."

Pierre shot Haddad a surreptitious glance, understanding by Maroun's presence in Berlin that Haddad was working on something.

When they were ready to leave Pierre found an excuse to walk with Haddad to the street.

"I could use your help," Haddad said quietly to him.

"To do what?"

"I could show you tomorrow."

"I can slip away from work and meet you around one."

"O.K."

* * *

Haddad drove out and picked Pierre up at the garage where he worked during the day.

"How's it going?" he said as Pierre climbed into the car.

"O.K.," Pierre answered with forced cheerfulness, wiping his hand clean on a piece of cotton waste.

"How do they treat you at this place?" Haddad asked casually as he pulled off the garage forecourt into the main stream of traffic.

Pierre Helou had never been rich but he had lived well in Beirut, where his driving skill had made him something of a hero.

"Perhaps it was a mistake coming here," Pierre said. It was the first time he had ever admitted that, even to himself. "I thought with so much money around I'd get my hands on some. But it's not easy unless you can get papers. The bastard who employs me only pays me half what he pays the other mechanics, the same with the stock-cars. Everyone takes a cut from an illegal Gastarbeiter and if you complain they report you to the authorities and you'll be deported—they've got me by the balls."

"Can't you get back into racing again?"

Pierre held up his steel claw. "Who's going to trust me in an expensive racing-car with this?"

They drove on silently for a while, then Pierre's confidence reasserted itself. "Alright," he said. "What's this job you have in mind for me?"

They had turned east onto Heer Strasse, heading towards the city. Haddad drew up some two hundred metres past the first bridge, in the entrance to the small sand road that led through the trees down to the boatyard on the river.

"I want you to arrange a motor accident," he said.

"Where?"

"Here. Imagine a small convoy of vehicles proceeding along Heer Strasse in this direction. Probably at night, so there would be little other traffic on the autobahn. You are coming the other way. You are going too fast—you hit something—black ice on the road maybe. You spin across the traffic lanes and you hit a certain vehicle, knocking it over on its side so that it ends up over here." Haddad got out of the car and stood in the side road. "It's important that the vehicle you hit ends up here, right against this bank. The whole thing must look like an accident. There will be armed soldiers protecting this convoy and they must not suspect for one moment that anything has occurred other than a traffic accident. Could you do it?"

Pierre looked out across the broad five-lane stretch of tarmac. "What sort of vehicle will I be driving?"

"That's up to you."

"Can I modify it to help me control it in a spin?"

"No, it must be a perfectly normal car. The same goes for you inside, you can't wear a helmet or have any extra protection other than a normal seat-belt. We can't take the risk of some soldier with sharp eyes spotting anything out of the ordinary."

"What sort of vehicle will I have to hit?"

"A V.W. mini-bus."

"They have a high centre of gravity." Pierre pondered. "It shouldn't be too difficult to knock one over, especially if I use a heavy, powerful car like a Mercedes." He looked back again across the autobahn, his brow furrowing. "So you want it to look as though an oncoming car goes out of control on the ice, careers right over here and at this certain point knocks a particular vehicle out of a convoy. That's a very tall order."

"You're a good driver," Haddad reminded him. "And you've had lots of practice at accidents."

Pierre grinned. "I suppose you want the mini-bus not only to end up at the exact spot of your choosing, but also to be knocked over onto a certain side?"

Haddad took him seriously.

"The spot is here," he said, indicating a stretch of ground opposite the steep drop to the river bank. "It must be here or within a very few feet either side, so that it ends up on its right-hand side. That's the normal way it would fall anyway, but most important for us is that the guard in the front will be trapped against the road with the driver on top of him. The steering-wheel will get in their way and we'll see to it that they don't manage to open the driver's door until we're ready. In the back the medical orderly will fall away from the patient so that we can get him out quickly."

"I take it that the patient will be strapped down?"

"Yes, strapped into a stretcher and the stretcher will be secured, that's their normal procedure."

"Who is the patient?"

"Hess."

Pierre whistled softly. "That's a very big fish you're after, my friend. It could get very dangerous."

"I know. But your job will be just to arrange the accident, this one great stunt, if you like. You won't be involved beyond that."

"How much is this 'one great stunt' worth?"

"I thought twenty-five thousand U.S. dollars would be a fair payment."

"That's a lot of money," Pierre said, tempted. "With that

behind me I could break free and maybe start something up on my own."

"Will you do it?"

"First I'll have to see what can be done to achieve what you want without breaking my neck."

Haddad nodded. "Will you build me a scale model of this area including the side road, bridge and this stretch of the autobahn? We can work on it together."

* * *

Haddad contacted Reed-Henry. They met in the deserted boatyard below the bridge. Reed-Henry tested the ice covering the river with his foot. It held firm. He turned back to Haddad.

"It's a good plan," he agreed. "It could work and from this spot it's only a few hundred metres through the trees to the British and Commonwealth War Cemetery. We can take Hess from you there."

"I have one problem," Haddad said. "My men will have to impersonate a unit of the British Military Police."

"That could be a problem." Reed-Henry looked thoughtful. "Each British unit has its own very identifiable traditions in uniform, method of operation, even in rank. The R.M.P.s have a tradition of being a particularly smart unit. It could be very difficult to impersonate them unless your men have had some previous military experience."

"They have no knowledge of regular military matters. That's why I want you to recommend someone to train us, to ensure that we are dressed and behave correctly."

"I see." Reed-Henry considered. "How long would you epxect this impersonation to last?"

"Not more than a few minutes and it would be at night. But even though it will be during a time of great confusion, nothing we do or say must cause suspicion."

"I'll try and find someone to help you," Reed-Henry said. As they walked back through the lines of boats laid up for the winter he asked, "Do you know anything about an exercise we hold here code-named 'Rocking Horse'?"

Haddad shook his head.

"A crash-out alarm is given and all British troops in this city are sent immediately into position to hold back a simulated Russian attack. At the same time the wives and children and all the other military dependants are taken to Gatow, the Royal Air Force base, where they would be flown to safety in the West. These exercises occur quite often and they are made as real as possible. Every British soldier, armoured car and tank in the city would be on the move. If we could combine the night of the exercise with the night that you make your move against Hess, then it would add considerably to the general confusion and few people would challenge an extra military police patrol out on a night such as that."

"How much warning could you give me before the exercise takes place?" Haddad asked.

"Only the British general and a few of his top aides know the date and the time of the exercise. If I could find out I could give you, say, a maximum of thirty-six hours' notice. You must appreciate," Reed-Henry warned, "that my general knows nothing about this; the orders I have to assist you come directly from England. I think that's all until nearer the time. Oh, yes," he added, as though he had almost forgotten, "we have lost track of Stroebling. We suspect that he is out of the country. Have you come up against him or any of his men lately?"

"No," Haddad replied, wondering if Reed-Henry somehow knew of their agreement. "He seems to be leaving me alone at the moment."

"I wouldn't count on that," Reed-Henry said pleasantly. "It's always a worry for us when a man like Stroebling drops out of sight." He climbed into his car and slammed the door. "I'll be in touch over someone to help you with the Military Police."

* * *

Haddad took Kathy out to dinner. She noticed Maroun further down the restaurant, sitting alone with his back against the wall. A couple of very pretty waitresses hovered around him and a girl at the bar was trying to catch his eye. His presence was beginning to rattle Kathy.

"Can't he join us or leave us alone?" she asked. "He makes me uncomfortable watching us all the time."

"I'm afraid he's necessary," Haddad replied. "I'm prepared to accept the contract," he changed the subject. "My price will be 225,000 U.S. dollars. That's a great deal of money. Are you sure you want to go on with this?" He was hoping that she'd back out, but Kathy had no intention of withdrawing.

"We'll pay you," she answered. "Michael will clear up all

the details with you. Can you tell me how you're going to do it?"

Haddad shook his head. "No, but with the help of the British I think I can assure you there will be a minimum of violence."

She was conscious that they were both very tense, their conversation becoming formal and businesslike. "When will you make your move?"

"Early February."

"That long?"

"It's soon enough. You and Michael will have less than five weeks to complete your arrangements to receive Hess," he reminded her.

"Michael's got all that in hand."

"Where do you want him delivered?"

"What choice do we have?"

"Scandinavia, Austria, Holland, Greece—these places suit me best."

"I'll speak to Michael and get back to you, but Greece sounds good to me."

"Very well," Haddad said. Both realised the commitment had been made. "The time has come for you to leave Berlin. Phone Michael tonight, tell him to meet you in Paris tomorrow. It's dangerous for you to stay here any longer."

She looked at his face and didn't argue, though she suspected by now that his hard exterior was mainly a front. She had seen the warmth with Pierre and his family: he was human and vulnerable after all and it gave her hope that he could care for her.

She reached out and touched his hand. He followed her onto the dance floor. Her blue-grey eyes seemed to be searching his. He thought her very beautiful and she moved with a sensuous grace. She felt his arms go around her and she kissed him.

"I'm going to miss you," she whispered, hating the thought of leaving him. "Take care of yourself and Maroun."

CHAPTER FIFTEEN

The big black hired car swept out of Dublin, heading south along the twisting coast road towards Kinsale. The driver was a local man, born in Cobh and lately released by the British from the Maze Prison in Northern Ireland. Beside him sat a silent blonde-haired man with a flat, expressionless face and the cold eyes of a professional killer. Alone on the back seat, wrapped in a heavy coat and scarf, Herr Stroebling stared sightlessly at the Irish countryside. He was no longer sure just how far his own agency had been infiltrated by his superiors in 2 Dzerzhinsky Square—the K.G.B. headquarters in Moscow. They made little secret now of the fact that they were trying to replace him. His associates in the East German state security service would have realised that his power was failing; perhaps they had turned on him already. He could rely on no-one. The course of injections that he had undergone to limit the progress of the disease had failed and the cancer was growing unchecked; he would die soon anyway. What weighed most heavily on him was not the fear of death, but the frustration of having so little time left in which to wreak vengeance on the enemies who defeated and divided his country.

The occupants of the car saw little of the fabled Irish green, for as they went south the storm-driven clouds flowed over the high ground and the grey, dripping stone walls of the villages nestled for protection against the folds of the hills. On the other side of the road a steel-coloured sea under a low, leaden sky surged against the rocky coastline.

The big car ate up the miles. They passed a sign, "Murphy's Pub 300 yards—Good Grub", then came down the long hill towards the town of Kinsale with its boats moored in the estuary. The car surged through the narrow streets and a little way up into the surrounding hills. The driver pulled the car into the walled, gravelled churchyard. The bodyguard got out and opened the door for Stroebling. They had arrived just as the service was ending. A piper tuned his pipes by bouncing a few notes off the grey walls. Then the church doors opened and the pall-bearers, shuffling as they accustomed themselves to the weight of the coffin, came out into the cold rain. The local I.R.A. unit formed up, the Irish tricolour fluttering in the soggy chill of the day. A handful of the faithful trudged behind the piper along the narrow road out of the village.

A man in a long tweed overcoat, leaning on a walking-stick, limped over to Stroebling. He was in his sixties with a battered, broken-veined, ruddy face and bloodshot eyes.

"I am MacBride, Chief of Staff to the Cork Brigade. We haven't met before. I've been in the North."

He was definitely a Cork man: his accent rasped through clearly when he spoke. Stroebling knew he would have no time for the Dublin Command.

"You'll come with us," said MacBride. "It's not more than a short step to see the boy buried."

They followed the procession to a lonely graveyard on the side of a hill. The body was lowered, prayers were said. Stroebling looked into the bitter, hard faces of the young men. All but three were thinly disguised in black berets, dark glasses and camouflage jackets. They stood to attention behind the Irish flag. There were very few women present and no tears were shed: too many of their men had already been buried in this war. A bent old man stepped forward and recited a few prayers in Gaelic. Then the stones rattled down on the coffin and the earth swallowed up another body.

MacBride had been leaning throughout the proceedings on his walking-stick. He limped over to the priest. "It's a grand job you did for him, Father," he said.

"I could do nothing less," the old priest replied vehemently. "The boy was a patriot, he died for us all."

"He did that," MacBride agreed. "Indeed, he did that, and his death won't go unavenged."

The mourners shuffled away. Only the fighting men were left now in the churchyard, standing in the cold mist with the grey sea crashing below. MacBride knew what Stroebling was thinking. There had been scenes like this enacted again and again throughout Ireland's turbulent history, when agents from the Continent came to recruit the Wild Geese, the famous Irish mercenaries, to fight in their wars. To escape the prying eyes of the English agents a ploy was used: the recruiters followed the funeral processions and there by some graveside they made their choice of men. Stroebling had come on a similar mission. He could no longer trust his own organisation.

"You have the people I requested?" Stroebling asked.

"I have," the Irishman replied. He signalled with his stick and three men came forward. "Pat Hourigan," he said, pointing his stick at the chest of the man he had just named.

Hourigan was small, square-jawed, broad-chested, red-haired, with powerful arms too long for his squat body. His thick, muscular neck was almost sunk into his shoulders. He had wicked little eyes and the dark brow of a man with a violent temper. He was in his forties, with ginger beard-stubble on his face, and he moved with the bow-legged, balanced gait of a man who had worked all his life among horses.

"He's one of our best," MacBride told the German. "We've been resting him. They had his face on every wanted poster in the North at one time, but he took a bullet in a gunfight eighteen months ago and the Brits think they killed him then. He isn't known on the Continent, so he'll do for what you want him for. These are the other two." He pointed to two cold-eyed youths not long out of their teens. "David O'Neill, Sean Devenish. They're good lads, trained gunmen from the Belfast Brigade. They'll work well under Hourigan."

MacBride put his arm around Stroebling's shoulders and moved him out of earshot. "Understand me," he said. "Hourigan is one of our best, he's very experienced and he has the devil's own cunning when it comes to killing Brits, but he has a wild temper and he's difficult to control. I want him back alive. Ireland still has use for him. As to the two young pups, well, if anything was to happen to those two I wouldn't be unduly concerned, they are replaceable. Now, you have something for us."

They made their way back to the car. Stroebling's bodyguard opened the boot lid, pulled away the carpeting and unscrewed the floor panel. He lifted it out, revealing a neatly ordered row of brand new Armalite AR18 rifles, their metal barrels gleaming dully through the protective grease coating. "Ah, good," MacBride approved. "I thought it would be Kalashnikovs, we're running short of ammunition for those."

Stroebling knew and had counted on the fact that the Palestinians, particularly the P.F.L.P., had supplied weapons and training to the I.R.A., but were becoming wary of forging too close an association. The I.R.A. was achieving a reputation for wildness that made the Palestinians seem tame. With that, and the noticeable cutting back of support from the United States, the supply of weapons was becoming a problem.

"I've brought you some Dutch V40 Fragmentation Grenades as well and there is ammunition for the rifles under the back seat," Stroebling said. "I'll bring you more when I return your men. And I have my operative for you." He indicated the tall blonde man. "He has been trained in the East to handle virtually all types of explosives."

"Are you sure he isn't known to the British?" MacBride asked. "He'll have to walk right through their security services to kill the man we're after."

"He doesn't appear on any file," Stroebling affirmed. "The British don't know of his existence. He has passports, documents, everything for his cover, but like your Hourigan, if possible I want him back."

"It's a fair exchange then," MacBride replied as his men unloaded the weapons. "Will you stay overnight? The Bristol Hotel in Kinsale is very comfortable—I've reserved you a room."

"No, I want to get back as soon as possible."

MacBride looked into the gaunt face, saw the cold glittering fanatic's eyes that he had known amongst his own people, and didn't argue.

"Are your men ready to leave?" Stroebling said.

"They are."

Stroebling got into the front beside the driver. The three men put their travel-bags into the boot and climbed silently into the back seat. The car headed back towards Dublin as darkness fell.

"Where are we going?" one of the young men asked. He was frightened of Stroebling, of the pale, skull-like face and the smell of death on the man.

"Paris," Stroebling said. "I'll tell you what I require of you when we get there."

Stroebling turned back and watched the headlights gleaming off the rain-slicked tarmac of the empty road. He was ready now to take out insurance on the bargain that he had struck with Haddad.

* * *

Kathy waited for her brother in a café on the Boulevard Saint-Germain. Three days in Paris and already she was missing Haddad terribly. She visualised his strong features and her fingers traced his profile on the steamy window beside her. She compared Haddad to the other men in the café and found the pale, slim Frenchmen wanting. They lacked his authority, his exciting, dangerous aura. Haddad brought her a new vitality, a self-awareness, that she had not had before. She realised that he had never committed himself with words. Even when they parted at Tegel he had been stiff, almost abrupt, with her but she had felt his arms around her. Womanlike, she was convinced he loved her.

She looked up. Michael was making his way to her table. "Hey, Kath," he greeted her fondly, unbuttoning his coat as he sat down. "You been waiting long? I'm sorry, I got held up."

"It's O.K.," she said.

She saw that he was looking at the profile which she had drawn on the window and hastily rubbed it away.

"Kathy," Michael warned, having recognised the drawing, "if you stop to think about it for one minute, you must see there's nothing for you in that relationship. You're getting involved with a guy who has no future."

"I'm not thinking of the future with him," Kathy answered stubbornly. "Just the present." Kathy didn't yet have the courage to examine the areas of her relationship with Haddad that she coudln't understand. And for all her regard for her brother, he had been out of her life too long to come back now and start questioning her.

"O.K.," Michael said, realising this and changing the subject. "The sale of the candlestick is going through. I've arranged with Haddad's Liechtenstein attorney to make two payments. One now and the other half when Hess has been delivered to us. Did you get in touch with Matt?"

"Yes, he's got our foot back in the door. The message from the committee is if we're successful they're interested in being involved."

"Well, we're going to need their support," Michael reasoned. "The kind of publicity we want for Hess is much too big for us to handle alone. Besides, I'll want expert medical help when it comes to conditioning Hess's mind so he can cope with his exposure to the media. After all those years in a cell we'll certainly have a very introverted personality to contend with."

"He won't have to do much more than face the cameras," Kathy said. "It's the fact that we got him out of Spandau, when no-one else could, that's important."

"You told me that Haddad is under a lot of pressure in Berlin." Michael sighed. "I've been getting this feeling that the ability to control events could be taken out of our hands. There were a lot of old wounds left over from that war—perhaps in letting Hess out of Spandau we could be opening Pandora's box."

Kathy could see that her brother was worried. But he had always been cautious while she'd been headstrong.

"Listen," she said. "You've got a lot further ahead with your career than I have with mine. You should drop out of this, but I'm going on. I've thought about it, Michael. It's not just ambition, I'm not looking for fame, it's just that I sincerely believe in what we're doing and the time has come for me to translate this belief into action." She sat back, pushing away the coffee that the waiter had brought.

Michael knew that his sister was being completely open with him.

"Why don't you keep out of harm's reach until this thing breaks?"

Michael shook his head. "I'm staying with you, but you have to promise me that we'll take it step by step and if things look like getting out of hand, you must agree to call it off."

"Alright," Kathy agreed.

Michael glanced at his watch. He was expecting a phone call from Haddad, but he didn't want to tell Kathy that. Now that she was away from him, he wanted to keep them as far apart as possible. "I have to go back to the apartment and see to a couple of things," he said. "What are you going to do now?"

"Well, the bank want my signature on the money transfer and I've got to check on the accommodation you've arranged for us in Athens. When I've finished that, I thought I'd go and see Madame Cela."

"How is she?"

Madame Cela was one of the their mother's oldest friends: she had been part of their childhood.

"She is old and sick, Michael. I guess she needs a visit. Will you come one day?"

"Yes, as soon as this is over. You buy the food on your way home," Michael said, getting up. "I'll cook you a really superior supper."

"By the way, did you see anyone outside the apartment when you left?" Kathy asked.

"No, should I have?"

"It's nothing," she shrugged her shoulders uncertainly. "I just thought I saw someone watching us."

"Berlin really put a scare into you."

Kathy nodded. "Yes, I must have been mistaken."

CHAPTER SIXTEEN

Michael went up the stairs of the rickety old building two at a time. On the second-floor landing he almost collided with the concierge.

"Ah, Monsieur Michael, I have something to tell you."

"Not now," Michael said, pushing past the old man. "I've got to take a phone call, I'll come and see you as soon as I can. We'll talk then."

The Frenchman was persistent. He grabbed Michael's sleeve as he was starting up the steps.

"There was someone here asking after you."

"Who?" Michael asked, impatient to be on his way.

The old man shrugged eloquently, "A stranger. He asked questions and gave me money, but I pretended not to understand. I can be very deaf when I need to be." The concierge had the native Parisian's loathing for all strangers, and he was proud of his cunning.

"Will you warn me if they come again?" Michael was immediately anxious.

"I am warning you now," the old man said, shuffling away. "One of them's outside the building across the street, he's been there all day."

Michael let himself into the apartment. He crossed the living-room and looked down into the street. Sure enough, amidst the bustling people below he picked out one man who was not moving. He was young, fair-haired, wearing a cheap-looking coat and he was leaning half-hidden in a doorway across the street from the entrance to the apartment. Michael was concerned but he didn't yet realise the full implications, he didn't feel the fear—that was to follow. The phone rang. He picked up the receiver.

"It's Haddad," a voice said and Michael felt a moment of relief.

"I wanted to tell you that the money is going through," Michael spoke quickly. "But something else has come up. There's a guy outside my apartment and the concierge says he's been asking questions. I was hoping perhaps he was one of your people."

There was a long silence on the other end of the line.

"Are you alone in the apartment?" Haddad asked.

"Yes."

"Check that the front door is locked then come back to the phone."

Michael did as he was told.

"Alright," Haddad said. "Now look out of the window carefully, don't go right up to the glass, keep your face in the shadow and describe the watcher to me."

Michael took the receiver to the window. "I can't see him too clearly," he said. "He's standing back in a doorway and I'm looking down on him but I guess he's young, very young, fair hair, I can't make out his build too well because he's wearing an overcoat. I mean, hell," Michael tried to be rational, "it's probably all some mistake and this guy's waiting for someone out of the cold. It's just the way that the concierge tipped me off got me worried."

"Look down the street," Haddad ordered. "Tell me if you can see anyone else. There should be a relief man sitting in a car, he won't be there alone."

Michael cautiously craned his head. "The place is full of cars and people, I can't make out anyone else. Who is this guy? You sound as if you half-expect him to be here."

"I wasn't expecting him, Michael," Haddad said. "If I had been I wouldn't have let you and Kathy be at risk. Where *is* Kathy?"

"She's gone to the bank, then she's going on to an old friend of the family. After that she's coming back here."

Like a chess-player Haddad had planned his moves, but so had Stroebling. He thought that he had spotted in Haddad a weakness, a soft spot in his armour and he was poised to strike. Haddad knew what was going to happen now and he couldn't intervene himself, he was too far away. He had to rely on Michael.

"Phone Kathy," Haddad instructed tersely. "Reach her wherever she is and tell her not to come back to the apartment. Tell her to stay with that friend she's going to visit until we contact her. I'm in a call-box," he gave Michael the number, "I'll wait here until I hear from you, come back to me as soon as you can."

Haddad's voice betrayed none of the fury that he felt for his own stupidity but the tension in it infected Michael. He began telephoning and at the same time watching the front door of the apartment, feeling that something was out there about to break in. Kathy had left the bank. He phoned Madame Cela but the number just rang and rang and no-one answered. He feverishly dialled Berlin, heard the number in the call-box connect and Haddad answered.

"I can't get hold of her," he said breathlessly.

"Alright." Haddad sounded calm. He had had a chance to think. "Did Kathy tell you about a man called Stroebling?" he asked.

"A little."

"I think it must be one of his men out there. They're waiting to get you and Kathy together, then they can use you both to blackmail me. Can you get hold of the concierge?"

"I've tried," Michael said. "He's gone out."

"What time are you expecting Kathy home?"

"I don't know. Maybe an hour from now. She was going to do some shopping on her way back."

"Give me the number you have for her," Haddad ordered. "I'll keep trying to reach her there. In the meantime, I want you to leave the apartment. Try and get past the man in the doorway, look scared, make sure he knows that you've spotted him. I want them to think that you have already tipped off Kathy or that you're on your way to do so. Lead them away from the apartment, take them right away from there—buy me time to contact Kathy."

"Where shall I go?" Michael asked, frightened now.

"Choose some area of Paris that you know well, keep to the streets where there are plenty of people. They may just follow you for a while then go back and wait at the apartment: it depends on how many men he has. But if they are still with you at dusk, you'll know they mean to get you. They will start closing in and that's when you have to lose them. Remember, choose some area of the city you know well and keep with the crowds. Oh, and watch out for cars coming up behind you," he added. "Don't go some place where they can just pick you off the pavement."

This was too much for Michael's mind to cope with. "Why don't I just call the police?"

"What are you going to tell them?" Haddad retorted coldly. "You can't arrest a man for standing in a doorway and when they're ready to make their move against you, I can promise you, you won't have the opportunity to call the police. I warned you both it could come to this, Michael. You should have believed me then. Now we've wasted enough time; Kathy could be coming up the stairs at any moment. Get out of that apartment, lead them away from her. I figure that you're safe as long as you aren't together, at least for the next few hours. I'll be waiting by this phone booth, call me back when you can."

The phone went dead and Michael put the receiver down. He went carefully to the window. The man was gone, no he wasn't, he was still there, but in a different doorway further down the street. Michael looked more closely. It wasn't the same man, this one was the same age, much the same build, but he was wearing a different overcoat. Michael looked wildly up and down the street, trying to find the other man. He couldn't see him, he must be inside the building. He could almost hear his footsteps on the stairs. Oh, God, there he was alone with no means of defence. Suddenly he was entering a world of violence that he knew nothing about and the prospect of going out onto the street terrified him.

He left a note for Kathy, then unwillingly he went to the door and drew back the bolts. There was no-one on the landing outside. He went cautiously down the steps, noticing for the first time how gloomy and badly-lit the old building was. At the bottom he knocked on the concierge's door again and again but there was no answer. Michael forced himself through the hallway and onto the street.

The man in the doorway spotted him and Michael didn't have to act out Haddad's instructions, he lived them. He hurried off towards the Pont Sully and turned left along the Boulevard Henri IV. He kept looking back over his shoulder: sure enough the man was following him. Michael was moving so fast that he was almost jogging, he forced himself to slow down, clear his head, work out a route. Haddad had said choose an area of the city he knew well, but at the same time had told him to keep with the crowds.

Michael dodged into a subway entrance and hurried down the steps. He glanced at his watch: he had been on the streets for less than fifteen minutes. Haddad had told him to buy Kathy time but how much did he need? He resolved to get to a phone box and call in, but one of the tags came up just behind him. Michael had felt safer underground, but the fright of seeing the man so close kept him moving on. He came up into the Rue de la Roquette, seething with traffic and pedestrians.

There were two tags, young, fair-haired, almost indistinguishable from the rest of the warmly-clad passers-by except for their cold eyes set in old-young faces, and the fact that whenever he looked back they were there just behind him. Michael glanced at his watch: forty minutes, they were still going up the Rue de la Roquette.

The cold shock that had numbed his mind was lifting. An innate sense of survival was making him totally aware of his position on the street and of the people around him. His perception seemed heightened as never before and now that his brain was functioning again, he began to work out the moves. They crossed over the Boulevard Voltaire and continued on along the Rue de la Roquette.

Michael knew where he was going now, he was heading for Ménilmontant and Père-Lachaise. He slowed his walking pace right down, wasting time, conscious now beyond his own fear that he was doing a good job, drawing them away from Kathy. He looked up at the apartment blocks rising on either side of the street. He had never noticed so many dogs before. He couldn't understand how a nation as civilised as the French could leave their dogs all alone through the day to bark hysterically at the windows of high-rise apartments and then bring them down at night to foul the city's pavements. He glanced at his watch: another half-hour at least before darkness descended. Already he could feel the clammy chill of the oncoming night. The tags were still with him; he quickened his pace again. Ahead of him now were the curving ivy-covered walls and massive wrought-iron gates of the cemetery of Père-Lachaise.

Haddad had said, if they're still with you when dark falls, then you'll know that they're serious about picking you up and that's the time you've got to lose them. Watch out for cars coming up behind you, don't choose a place where they can just pick you off the pavement. If they kept Michael on the streets too long after dark the crowds would thin, and the thought of a car coming up on a pavement after him was more than he could bear.

Michael walked through the gates of Père-Lachaise.

"Monsieur," the uniformed guard shouted a warning after him, "it's only thirty minutes before closing time."

Michael nodded to show that he understood. He followed the Avenue Principale, passing a scattering of cold tourists who were drifting towards the exits ahead of the oncoming evening. The Parisians had designed their mausoleums very much as they pleased, and the cemetery was reputed to house one of the most fabulous collections of necromantic statuary this side of the Pyramids. Michael passed an array of stone, metal and concrete memorabilia lining either side of the avenue with larger than life-size representations, ranging from dogs and nymphs to angels and ballerinas. He turned into Avenue Laterdale South, a narrow, cobbled pedestrian way leading up several flights of steps into the heart of the cemetery.

An air of distinguished yet seedy eroticism seemed to pervade the place. Many of the great mausoleums of the old French families were falling into disrepair. Some had had their ivy-covered doors forced open, and stained glass and broken vases littered the floors before the altars inside. Michael had come here often as a child, but always in summer when the tree-shaded alleys, nooks and crannies had provided ideal adventure playgrounds for boys, trysting-places for lovers and excellent viewing-points for the prowling voyeurs who haunted the cemetery. Now, in the winter's cold, the stark snow-covered gravestones lay beneath leafless trees: the cemetery was left to a few tourists and the hobos and stray animals of Paris.

At one time many of the great names of France had been buried here and the ground beneath their sarcophagi had been tunnelled out into burial vaults of up to ten metres deep, where, resting on slabs, one on top of the other, lay generation after succeeding generation of Parisians. In the case of families who had died out and left no one to renew the lease, workmen would disinter their bodies. Beside a memorial with massive, spreading angels' wings or similar ornament would be a deep dark hole, choked with rubbish.

As the last of the tourists disappeared an intensely gloomy feeling settled over the cemetery. Michael headed, in the failing light, for a small exit on the far side of the cemetery leading into the Rue de la Réunion. Before he reached there he intended to lose his tags in the narrow paths that led through the mausoleums. He dodged in and out amongst the great stone tombs and by the time he heard the whistles blowing, the guards warning that only ten minutes remained before they closed the gates for the night, he had convinced himself that he had evaded his pursuers.

Michael made his way ahead cautiously, looking back again and again, checking that there was no movement behind him. He dashed across a gravelled alley and hid behind a marble tomb. He made himself wait, counting the seconds. No-one was following: he would have heard their footsteps across the gravel. He felt as if a great weight had been lifted off his shoulders. Never before had he known such a terror of being hunted, the suspicion of every man's hand against him. He had only minutes remaining now to reach the exit. He began to move on quickly. The guard, blowing impatiently on his whistle, had already half-closed the gate.

Michael was about to break from his cover among the tombstones and race down the steps when he spotted the figure of a man just in front of him, crouching behind a mausoleum, out of sight of the guard, covering the only possible way to the gate. The light was fading fast, but there was still enough of it left for Michael to see that the man had a gun in his hand, and he felt again the panic of being trapped. The guard looked at his watch for the last time, let his whistle drop, and walked out, pulling the ten-foot iron-spiked gate closed behind him and locking it. There were two more exits but it would have taken Michael twenty minutes to reach either of them. The whole cemetery was enclosed by a high brick wall and the occupants were locked in for the night.

CHAPTER SEVENTEEN

Darkness came swiftly, and with it silence and the cold, chill smell of the dank earth. Michael moved cautiously backwards away from the man with the gun, deeper into the tangled area of statues and tombstones and empty graves. He knew that he had to move not only silently but very carefully, for the sides of the empty graves were brick-lined and sheer. If he fell into one of those he could break his legs. In the distance, beyond the walls, there was a glow of lights against the sky and the subdued traffic roar of Paris.

The cemetery, after nightfall, held at first an uncanny quiet, a stillness, as though it were a world apart from the surrounding city, with nothing stirring—everything dead. Then came a sound, a human whistle, one of the tags attracting the other's attention. "Did you see him?" the tag whispered hoarsely and either the sound of his voice travelled well after dark or he was very close to Michael.

"No," came the reply. "But he didn't leave by the exit, he must be still in here."

Michael noticed the Irish accent but didn't have time to reflect on it, because the men were moving towards him, circling the sepulchres, methodically clearing each sector. Michael moved back, looking for a place to hide. There was a beat of wings, then a screech—an owl passed overhead. It gave a scream, a piercing cry that sounded like a lost soul tumbling down into a bottomless pit.

"Jesus Christ!" came a startled exclamation from one of the tags. "Sean, did you hear that?"

"Shut up!" came the hoarse reply. "Or you'll still be talking when we're on him."

Michael tried the door to a mausoleum: it was rusted half-open. When he put pressure on it, it gave way with a rasp of grating hinges. The tags moved towards the sound and Michael backed quickly away into the darkness. It was freezing cold but he was sweating, panting, so filled with terror that it was all he could do not to cry out. And now after the silence—the total stillness that came with nightfall—the cemetery was coming alive, filled with the sound of dogs and cats and owls and rats. A guttural, hoarse cry was followed by snorts and wheezes, hawking, gasping, choking, sobbing.

Then suddenly there came the shrill cry of some animal in terrible pain, the beat of wings, and the scream of an owl again.

The cemetery occupied an area of one hundred and six acres. It was too dark to see the direction signs. Michael knew that if he left the black silhouette of the wall he would lose his way completely. He kept moving back. He tried the door to another mausoleum which opened without too much noise. He made enough space to get his head and shoulders around and was met by the most terrible stench of festering, unwashed humanity. The snoring changed to a choking wheeze as the hobo, swathed in sacks, came awake and kicked at the door to close it.

"Get out," he shouted in gutter French. "This is taken."

The sudden movement from the darkness, the shout when he least expected it, had nearly stopped Michael's heart from beating. He sank down against the base of the mausoleum with his face in his frozen hands, ready to give up. He had been hunted long enough. The cold and the fear had sapped all his will-power; he felt he couldn't go on. The tags had heard the sound: they were trying to establish which mausoleum it had come from. They were coming closer but Michael no longer had the strength to move. Beside him was a wrought-iron railing and then a cobbled path. On the other side of the path was a small arched tombstone and there was a gap about half a metre wide between the roof of the tombstone and the ground: a narrow tunnel leading to an underground burial vault. The entrance to the tomb was almost invisible in the darkness.

The tags were nearly on him when the sense of survival took urgent hold of Michael again. He crossed the pathway, fell on his stomach, wormed his way over the half-frozen mud into the entrance, put out his hand and felt nothing. He dislodged a stone and it seemed to rattle down forever. There was nothing below, just the sweet, sickly smell of death and darkness. He felt around and found the top of a rusted ladder. He shook it and it creaked but seemed as if it would bear his weight. He squeezed the rest of his body through the narrow archway, wrapped his hands and feet around the rungs of the ladder and began to descend, not knowing if the ladder would hold or how deep was the void below him. He went cautiously down and down, a rung at a time. He put his hand out in the pitch dark, felt a stone shelf running along the wall. His fingers moved on and found the crumbling wood of some

She caught sight of the hollow glittering eyes and the pale wasted face of the man she knew was Herr Stroebling. She couldn't turn her head to see who was holding her. Her sleeve was pulled up. She felt the needle sink into the vein of her forearm and then darkness as the walls of the apartment seemed to collapse in on her.

* * *

Michael had the taxi drop him by a call-box. He phoned Madame Cela's. Still there was no reply. He dialled the number Haddad had given him in Berlin. A voice answered.

"Haddad," Michael said urgently.

"No," the voice answered. "I'll get him. Call this number back in twenty minutes."

Michael waited and rang again. Haddad answered.

"Kathy," Michael said. "Did you reach her in time?"

"No," Haddad said. Michael sensed a great weariness in his voice.

Haddad had phoned Kathy's apartment again and again until someone had lifted the receiver. When they heard his voice the person at the other end had just put the receiver down.

"I think they've got her," Haddad told Michael.

Michael was almost crying with rage and frustration and worry for his sister.

"You bastard," he shouted. "How could you let this happen? You're supposed to know about these things. Why didn't you protect her?"

Haddad ignored his outburst.

"They won't hurt her as long as they need her. I'm waiting for them to contact me now," he said.

"What do you want me to do?" Michael asked helplessly.

Haddad knew that no matter how much he had wanted to avoid it before, he had to bring Michael in now to where he and Maroun could protect him.

"Have you got money on you?"

"Some and some credit cards."

"Alright, don't try and go back to the apartment, leave everything there as it is. Take a plane tomorrow to Frankfurt, meet the Middle Eastern Airways flight that comes in from Beirut in the afternoon. Two of my men will be on it. Stand by the exit gate. They'll be looking for you and they'll take you with them to Berlin."

CHAPTER EIGHTEEN

Haddad made his way to the hotel where he and Kathy had stayed. He found a message for him there telling him to wait by the phone, that was all, it specified no time. Haddad sat in the hotel lobby as hour after hour dragged by, waiting for them to contact him. On the surface he appeared icy calm but his mind was in turmoil.

After the death of his wife and child he had sworn that he would never let himself care about anyone so deeply again, but now he was aching for Kathy. He heard the porter calling his name and he quickly crossed to the phone booth by the reception desk.

"It is Stroebling here," the voice said and it was clear that he had enjoyed making Haddad sweat.

* * *

Pat Hourigan sat in the kitchen of a house on the outskirts of Paris. He was leaning back in his chair with his legs resting on the table.

"Ah," he said, "those were the days, before the bastard British were hunting me. I may not have been much to look at but I had a way with the women then. It was these hands." He held out his hands. For all his ugly, squat appearance and ape-like long arms Hourigan's hands were indeed beautiful, with the long, powerful, sensuous fingers that should have belonged to an artist or a musician. "I could work wonders with these hands," he said proudly, "but the real secret is to treat a woman like a filly. You hold them tight between your knees now and ease them into the bit." Hourigan barked out a laugh, pleased with the image that he had created in the mind of the boy across the table from him.

They heard a noise in the room above, the sound of a struggle and the crash of broken crockery.

"What's that?" Hourigan said sharply.

"It's nothing," the cold-eyed youth answered uncomfortably. "Just Sean taking the girl up some food."

"That's what he's doing, is it?" Hourigan snapped. He swung his feet off the table and went up the stairs. He paused outside the door for a moment, listening to the noise, then he twisted the handle and kicked the door, sending it crashing open. The sallow-faced youth called Sean, startled by the noise, lost his grip of Kathy for a moment and she broke away from him.

"What are you doing?" Hourigan demanded menacingly.

The youth was terrified of Hourigan, of the power coiled in his squat body and the sadistic, violent streak that he knew was in the man.

"It was nothing," he stammered. "I was just bringing . . ."

"Get out of here, you bastard," Hourigan cursed him, cutting him short. "If someone's to have her it's grown men, not boys. Get out!" he spat and the youth fled.

"Don't you ever let that boy come in here again," Kathy said angrily.

She was standing silhouetted in the light streaming in from the high barred window, her hair and clothes dishevelled. Hourigan watched her, his hot little eyes burning away her clothes. He kicked the door closed and came slowly towards her, then he stopped.

"That's as far as I go," he said. His voice had gone silky soft and cruel, savouring her impending humiliation. "Now you come to me, my lovely, come," he commanded her.

He knew that he had more than enough physical power to take her, but that was not enough, he wanted to break her will, to make her come meekly to him. He kept talking to her, bidding her obey him in soothing, silken phrases. The promise of sadistic violence showed in his wicked eyes if she refused. Kathy was mesmerised. The squat, unshaven little man terrified her. Without touching her he had filled her with a dread of the consequences if she disobeyed him. He held out his hand to her.

"Come," he ordered. His voice could be both cruel and caressing at the same time. "Come to me now."

Kathy moved slowly towards him. He waited until she was standing in front of him, then he reached up and put his fingers on her temple and ran them lightly down behind her ears to the pulses in her neck. His touch was so light she hardly felt it. His hands went on down, touching her, caressing her, stroking her. When he thought she was ready he brought his hand up, grasped her hair and forced her head down to make her kiss him. Instead she bit him, savagely sinking her teeth deep into his cheek, drawing blood. He cursed and slapped her hard across the face. He let the pain of the blow sink in, then he slapped her again. She backed away and he raised his hand and touched his bleeding cheek.

"Now, that was foolish of you, my lovely," he said calmly, his voice betraying none of the anger he was feeling, but he would punish her now until she broke, he would make her pay for the blood on his cheek.

Hourigan realised that he was still a long way from winning, but he didn't care, he relished what lay ahead. Kathy had backed away into the corner of the room, looking around wildly for a weapon. Hourigan was moving towards her again. "We are going to have to gentle you down, my lovely. Gentle you down." He was addressing her as though she was a mare trapped in a stable. He spoke so softly that he was almost whispering to her. "Have you heard of the twitch now, my lovely? That will bring you to your senses. The bottom lip on a horse is soft and smooth and very sensitive, see?" He was undoing his belt. "Now you take the twitch, slip the noose over and drag it up tight and the mare feels the pain so greatly that she just stands there quivering and you can run your hands all over her, everywhere, anywhere you want and she's glad to let you if you will only stop the pain. That's just one way, there are several more. Now, what shall we do with you, my lovely?"

His hand flashed out and caught her before she could squirm away. They heard footsteps running up the stairs and the door burst open. Sean Devenish stood there, sour-faced and nervous.

"Get out, damn you," Hourigan shouted at him.

"I've got a message for you from Herr Stroebling, he's just come back."

"I don't care who you've got a message from," Hourigan shouted, the last vestiges of his self-control going. "Get out."

But the youth wavered in the doorway. "Stroebling says you're to come now," he said defiantly. "And bring the girl. We're moving."

Hourigan heard footsteps painfully climbing the stairs and he let Kathy go. Stroebling entered the room. His cold, glittering eyes took in the scene immediately.

"Has he hurt you?" he said quietly to Kathy.

She moved away from Hourigan and shook her head, trying to hold back her tears.

"She will be of no use to me if she is damaged," Stroebling told Hourigan. "No-one may touch her until she has served my purpose."

* * *

Michael Lakas made his way through Customs at Tegel airport, escorted between the two massively built, competent men who had met him at Frankfurt. He had learned that they were brothers who had worked in the Beirut docks before a civil war had discovered their other talents, which led them to follow Haddad.

Pierre Helou was waiting for them, leaning against a glass wall near the exit. He gave one of the brothers an almost imperceptible nod, then left, making his way to the car park. The brothers gave no sign of recognising him and moved on with the crowd, turning off into the snow-banked car park. Michael had no idea what to expect as he hurried after them. They zig-zagged amongst the cars until they heard an engine start, then a car without lights pulled up beside them. One of the brothers kept Michael in the cover of a parked car while the other checked the identity of the driver.

The two men operated as a perfect team, seeming to understand each other without need of words. It took only seconds before Michael was bundled into the back of the car and it pulled away. The driver kept looking into the rear mirror.

"Did you spot anyone following you?" he asked.

The big man beside him shook his head. The driver relaxed a little and turned to Michael, offering him a steel claw to shake. In the lights of the oncoming cars Michael saw the scars on his face.

"Welcome to Berlin," he said. He had a pleasant, friendly manner. "My name's Pierre Helou. I take it you have already been introduced to these two, Joseph and Jamil Khoury."

Michael nodded impatiently. "Where's Haddad?" he asked. "Has he heard any news of my sister?"

"I believe he's trying to arrange a meeting," Pierre said carefully. "That's all I know."

Michael could tell by the glow of lights against the sky that they were heading into the city. The precautions that they had taken at the airport, the wall and the historical implications of the city itself served to increase the spine-crawling sense of unease that he felt. He was entering Berlin for the first time in his life. For all his communist leanings, his father had died a devout Jew, but Michael scoffed at all recognised religions. He had always felt secure in simply being American, that was enough. But in Berlin, gazing out of the car windows at the glistening wet streets, he felt all the half-forgotten insecurity of being a Jew return to him. He could almost hear the jackboots of forty years ago pounding along the pavements beside him, the screams from the inmates of concentration camps. He could not forget that it was from this city the orders had gone out that led to the death of six million Jews.

Pierre glanced into the mirror once more, then he swung the car around. Eventually they were headed west out of the city again. He took the autobahn route over the bridges, then swung right into Gatow Strasse. As the car sped up the incline towards the junction of Wilhelm Strasse the men in the back saw the tall, thin steeple of Melauchton church. Looming out of the darkness on the left appeared the red brick turrets with the solid double doors below, like the entrance to a fort, and beyond that the massive, austere towers and ramparts and small barred windows. The whole mighty, seemingly inpenetrable edifice was surrounded by a seven-metre wall and protected by concrete and glass goon towers and flickering searchlights. Spandau prison! Michael had seen it many times in photographs but now, close to it, he was awed.

"Dear God," he breathed. "We're never going to get him out of there."

"We don't have to," Pierre answered. "Haddad will tell you how when he is ready."

Haddad was waiting for them as the car pulled into the safe house that had been set up near Neustadt in the Spandau district. The brothers, Jamil and Joseph, went to greet him. One put his arms around Haddad and hugged him while the other simply reached out and laid his hand on his shoulder. Little was said, but it was the manner of the greeting that impressed Michael. These men shared many memories: they were united by bonds of loyalty, born out of hard times, that went deeper than friendship.

"You must be tired," Haddad said, turning to Michael. "I'll show you to your quarters."

The house, reminiscent of a barracks, was sparsely furnished. Haddad opened the door to a narrow room with a metal camp bed pushed against the wall.

"You can sleep here," he said. "You'll find a sleeping-bag under the stretcher; use your coat as a pillow. The kitchen is at the end of the passage on the right. You'll take it in turns with the others to cook and keep the place clean. Do you want a weapon while you're here?"

"Good God, no." Michael was aghast, loathing all firearms. "I'd never use one."

"Well then," Haddad said unsympathetically, "you'd better keep close to Jamil and Joseph."

"What have you done about my sister?" Michael asked.

"A meeting has been arranged for tomorrow night. I can do nothing but wait until then."

"With Stroebling?"

"Yes."

"I'll come with you," Michael offered.

Haddad shook his head. "I have to go alone."

* * *

Haddad walked along Bernauerstrasse, a West-East border area of Berlin where the wall had been rammed straight through a row of houses. The front doors were simply closed and bricked up behind. The night was pitch black with a freezing mist forming halos around the arc lights which illuminated the wall. He walked over the memorials set into the pavement for those who had jumped to their deaths from the upstairs windows of their houses as the Vopos moved in. The row of houses had long since been demolished; just the wall remained, with the sagging front doors inset to serve as a reminder. On the opposite pavement life in West Berlin went on as usual.

Haddad had been instructed to wait outside a church. It was a disused building looming up behind the wall, stranded in a no man's land of patrol lanes and tank traps. He paused by a slogan that had been painted on the blocked entrance to the church: "In Tyrannos". It was the sub-title of an eighteenth-century German play that had become a watchword for those opposed to tyranny. In the distance Haddad heard a clock striking the hours. He was the only man on his side of the street, standing in a pool of light that illuminated the wall. Stroebling had chosen the meeting-place well: even Maroun couldn't cover him here.

Haddad felt himself being watched: it was the sixth sense of the hunted man, the instinct that kept him alive. He looked up above the wall to the decaying church that towered over him, its broken windows like empty eyes with a sniper behind any one of them. High above the nave Haddad saw a statue: Christ with an arc lamp at his feet, staring out over the barbed wire and the wall to the West. Perhaps it was a trick of the light or just the way Haddad was feeling, but that Christ-figure on the decaying church had the saddest face he had ever seen.

He heard a car come quietly to a stop by the pavement, and he spun round. The door opened. Stroebling climbed out and straightened up painfully. The car moved on a little way and parked. Haddad was conscious that men had positioned themselves in the shadows on either side of the street.

"Long before the wall was built," Stroebling said to Haddad by way of greeting, "this was known as the Church of Reconciliation. I thought it an apt place for our discussion. You see, a different situation exists now from when you last demanded a meeting. I have the men to command the streets and I have the girl."

"Why go to all that trouble?" Haddad asked. "I have already agreed to give you Hess."

"You agreed when you had too many cards left in your hand still to play, Mr Haddad," Stroebling replied bitingly. "From now on I want to be sure that you are working for me and no one else."

Haddad shrugged. "What more do you want me to do?"

"For a start," Stroebling said, "there's the assassin called Maroun. I want you to bring him out into the open so that we can kill him."

Haddad knew he could be blackmailed into a position where he would have to obey Stroebling's instructions, but Maroun was so unstable that no opponent could guess what he would do. At all costs Maroun had to be kept alive: he was Haddad's ace in the pack.

"I can't do that," Haddad answered finally. "I can undertake to give you Hess, that means nothing to me, but I cannot let you kill Maroun. We have owed too much over too long to each other."

"You have sentimental reasons," Stroebling scoffed, mocking him. "I cannot believe that. What if I was to say to you that it's the life of Maroun against the girl?"

"Then you must kill the girl," Haddad said quietly.

Stroebling had not been expecting that. Haddad was too controlled, too self-assured; perhaps he was mistaken in thinking he could control him through Kathy. Stroebling turned and signalled with his hand.

"Would you like to see her?" he said. "It might serve to refresh your memory as to how you feel about her."

A car loomed out of the darkness. As it crawled slowly past them Haddad saw Kathy's white face straining against the sealed window. Her lips were moving, she was calling out his name. The car stopped. Haddad took a couple of paces after it, then the car moved on again, keeping just in front of him. Haddad knew that Stroebling was waiting for him to break and run after it, to try and wrench the door open to get to Kathy—it would have been a natural reaction. The image of her pale, exhausted face at the window was in his mind as he turned his back on her and rejoined Stroebling.

"Take the girl away," he said. "If this is a game you're playing, then there's no reason behind it."

"I have heard that women who associate themselves with you don't live very long," Stroebling remarked.

"That's true," Haddad answered, his cold dark eyes burning into Stroebling's face. "I've become accustomed to death."

The car reversed. Haddad watched Kathy pass him. He knew that she would be terrified, that she was begging for some gesture of reassurance from him, some sign, but he gave her none. He stared fixedly after her as the car disappeared and if anything his eyes burned a little colder.

"So," Stroebling said, understanding that he was inflexible on this point, "no Maroun."

Haddad shook his head. "No Maroun," he confirmed.

"And the girl, what shall I do with her?"

Haddad laughed. It was a terrible laugh, so intense and yet controlled that Stroebling did not doubt him when he said, "If you harm her in any way then I will kill you."

"That is no great threat," Stroebling answered mockingly. "I will die shortly anyway."

"Then I will kill anyone you ever loved, Herr Stroebling, and Hess, I will surely kill Hess. Remember what I did to the Palestinians. But we waste time talking of killing, you want Hess and I can get him for you. You suspect me of disloyalty so you hold the girl. When I return Hess to you then you can give me the girl. Surely that is acceptable to both of us?"

Stroebling was beginning to respect Haddad. He thought he had been misled over Kathy until he heard the terrible laugh that told him beyond any doubt that Haddad loved her and that Stroebling could control him through her. Other than that one slip he had hidden his weakness well. Stroebling was satisfied now.

"Very well," he said. "Your man Maroun remains alive but I want you to bring him in where I can watch him. From now on he stays with the others. I have someone for you, an Irishman: you are to make him part of your team. He will be your lieutenant and he will see that you honour your part of the bargain."

Haddad agreed; he had no choice.

"How are your plans progressing?" Stroebling asked.

"They're coming on well; we should be ready to move within the first or second week in February. Where do I deliver Hess to you? I would prefer it to be in the West because I know of no way to get him across the border into the East."

"The West will suit me perfectly. I'll collect him from you here."

"Do the Russians know what you're doing?" Haddad asked.

"No, Mr Haddad," Stroebling's thin lips cracked into a bitter smile. "This is a personal matter. I have no cause to love the Russians even though they are my masters." His car drew up. "Where did you leave your vehicle?"

"At the end of the street."

"Get in, I'll take you to it."

Stroebling sat beside Haddad in the luxurious dark warmth of the car, leant back and closed his eyes. He was weak from being on his feet too long and it cost him an effort to speak. "When I was a boy of little more than twelve," he said, "I and the rest of my brigade in the Hitler Youth fought against the Russians in the last battles for Berlin. We dug in in the Grunewald not far from here. Behind us the city was being reduced to rubble by constant shell-fire. All that was left of its population were the old and the women, our mothers and sisters, hiding in the cellars.

Many of the boys in my brigade were children no taller than their weapons, but we held the whole might of the Russian Army back in those forests for two long days. We had no food and little ammunition. Those of us who survived the battle fell back and we held the Pichelsdorf Bridge until we were wiped out almost to the last child.

I was wounded, I remember, so frightened that I was going to bleed to death, and I made my way back through the flames and the rubble into the heart of the city. The Russians took Berlin and raped and pillaged and looted as they had done throughout the rest of Germany, and I hid in the cellars, listening to the shrieks of the women and the crash of the artillery barrages. But the peace was the worst part because then the Russians starved us. I think more Germans died in the year after the war than during the occupation of the country."

Haddad could imagine the scars left by that experience on a twelve-year-old's mind.

"No," Stroebling said softly, more to himself than to Haddad, "I have no cause to love the Russians, or the British and their American Allies, for the defeat and destruction of my country twice in two world wars. I have received information through my sources that your attempt to rescue Hess is aided indirectly by the British. I have long suspected that they have good reasons for wanting Hess removed from Spandau. And here, at the last minute, I have this God-sent opportunity to intervene, to use Hess to strike back at both the British and the Russians. Whatever happens to me after this is not important. My health is failing fast, I have not much longer to live, but I still have the power to take Hess and place him in the hands of people who will know how to deal out the most damage to both those nations. Hess must remember many of their secrets. Deliver him to me and I will reward you well."

They drew up at the end of the street. The car carrying Kathy pulled in behind them and a squat red-haired man got out.

"Pat Hourigan, your new lieutenant," Stroebling announced as the the Irishman came over and stood on the pavement.

"The girl," Haddad said quietly. "I shall want to know that you're treating her well."

"Alright," Stroebling assented. "She will be brought to a telephone where you can speak with her once in every seven days. Hourigan will be supplied with the number. But please, don't waste your efforts in trying to find her, Mr Haddad. She will be very well guarded and if you were fortunate enough to locate her, she would be dead before you came through the door—is that clear?"

Haddad climbed out of the car.

"I want a daily report," Stroebling said sharply to Hourigan. "Good luck, Mr Haddad," he called as the cars pulled away.

CHAPTER NINETEEN

8.00 a.m. The men in the safe house assembled in the dining-room which had been converted into an operations room. There were maps of Berlin, West and East, and of the districts surrounding Spandau pinned to the walls. On the table was a detailed model of a section of the Heer Strasse autobahn with its bridges, side roads and steeply dropping ground to the river all carefully constructed from papier-mâché. Haddad took up his position behind the table: the others gathered around him.

"Where's Maroun?" he asked, looking up.

"He's coming in now," Pierre replied.

"Maroun gets a room on his own," Haddad ordered. "He's used to it being that way. Pierre is sleeping at home, the rest of you take the big room at the end and mess in together."

Jamil was muttering something.

"What is he saying?" Michael asked the other brother.

"He doesn't like having to work with Maroun," Joseph answered. "He says that Maroun is so crazy it increases the risk."

Maroun wandered almost shyly through the door and nodded a greeting to the assembled men. He didn't apologise for being late and Haddad didn't expect it.

"Before I start," Haddad said, "the old rules apply. Each man's responsible for his weapons and we keep a dry house while we're here, no liquor. Is that clear?"

"Wait a minute," Hourigan broke in. "I've got something to say. I'm not sharing a room with those wogs," he indicated Jamil and Joseph.

"Why not?"

"Because I don't like wogs, that's why," he glowered.

"Hey man, who are you?" Maroun asked good-naturedly.

"Hourigan, Pat Hourigan," the squat Irishman said.

"Don't offend those good people man, you can move in with me if you like."

The others were watching them, afraid of Maroun.

"Alright," Hourigan agreed grudgingly.

"But I have to tell you I'm a wog," Maroun added cheerfully. "Born in the same place as them," he indicated Jamil and Joseph.

"At least you've got a whiter skin," Hourigan answered, as offensively as possible.

Maroun looked around. He had been popping tabs and was so laid-back that he appeared only half-conscious. "People, this short man means no offence," he said fondly of Hourigan.

Haddad was not going to let himself be drawn by Hourigan. He turned impatiently to the wall map behind him.

"To begin by orientating you," he said. "Berlin is divided into four sectors. We will be operating in the British sector which runs from north to south following the river Havel. This river also separates Spandau from the other districts of this sector. Beyond Spandau is the border of Soviet-occupied East Germany. The French sector lies to the north, the American to the south and all beyond here," he pointed to the border marked in red, "the wall of East Berlin. Our object in being here, gentlemen, is to capture Hess. The method is as follows. Hess will leave Spandau prison," he pointed to a mark on the map, "on his way to the British Military Hospital and he will be conveyed in a British military police convoy along here," he moved across to the scale model. "This is a section of Heer Strasse on which we can expect Hess to travel. You can see a five-lane highway here," he pointed, "and there are two bridges, both with banks sloping sharply down to the river Havel. Further along the road on the right-hand side, this green space indicates the area of the British and Commonwealth War Cemetery. The plan is to intercept the convoy at this point." Haddad indicated the area by the first bridge.

Pierre helped Haddad move forward two model Landrovers and two V.W. mini-buses painted with the British Royal Military Police insignia. "The convoy will be making its way from West to East along here," Haddad said. "Pierre will be coming along the autobahn in the opposite direction. At this point," Haddad indicated again, "his car will go into a spin. Pierre will tell you what happens next."

"Well," Pierre said, taking a model of the vehicle he was to use, "the idea is to make it look as though it's an accident. The car goes out of control, I start to spin, I correct about here, which is the only hope I have of keeping on line with the vehicle I want to hit. The British will see that, like most amateurs who aren't accustomed to driving on ice, I hold the wheel too hard over, the car spins again and again, three times, which will bring me to here."

He positioned the Mercedes by the second V.W. mini-bus. "The car will be skidding, apparently out of control, as it side-swipes the mini-bus here. The mini-bus has a high centre of gravity: if the accident is staged correctly it will topple onto its side and end up here." Pierre pointed to just within the entrance to the side road marked on the model.

"Can you do all that?" Michael asked in disbelief.

Pierre looked up and smiled. "In theory, yes. Haddad and I have gone over this many times. It should be possible to control three spins with enough precision to strike the vehicle I am aiming for, but in practice, it depends on the weather and the conditions of the road at the time we make the attempt—if conditions are against us there could be as little as a fifty-fifty chance."

"Pierre will keep practising," Haddad said, "until he makes the odds better than that. In the meantime, for insurance, we'll have Maroun positioned here," he marked a spot on the opposite bank to the side road. "If Pierre misses, he will shoot out the tyres of the mini-bus. We can still make it look like the accident has taken place and no one's going to go looking for bullet holes in the tyres after they've seen a car spin across four lanes at them."

"That's a hell of a long shot to make in bad light, at a moving vehicle," Jamil commented dubiously, gauging the distance.

"Man," Maroun said simply, "I don't miss."

"What're the rest of us going to be doing?" Hourigan asked.

"We will be here." Haddad pointed to a Landrover placed in some trees a little way from the entrance to the side road. "We impersonate a British military police patrol. As soon as the accident occurs we move forward and take charge of the scene. We'll have only a few seconds with the ambulance to ourselves while the rest of the convoy are regrouping and coming back for it. In that time we have to make the accident look as bad as possible: light fires, cause confusion, while the real Hess is removed from the back of the ambulance and another body is substituted."

"Surely there will be guards in the back with him?" Joseph queried.

"No, we expect there to be only one, a medical orderly, who'll be attending to the patient. The orderly will be rendered unconscious if necessary, and drugged. The main force of guards will be in the Landrover at the back and the front of the convoy. Before they can reach the scene of the accident the real Hess must have been moved out of sight, and we will be seen rescuing the substitute on a stretcher from the back.

We believe that the R.M.P.s responsible for Hess's safety will be glad to leave us to take charge of the traffic around the accident, while they rush with what they suppose to be Hess to the hospital."

"What happens to Hess after that?"

"Once Hess is rescued," Haddad's gaze lingered on Michael for a moment, "he becomes no further concern of ours. We'll go into fuller detail later but are there any questions at this stage?" he asked.

"You can't be serious," Hourigan said scornfully to Haddad. "With some good I.R.A. boys to back me I might just be able to carry out a plan like that, but with a bunch of bloody wogs you're just begging for disaster. For a start, how do you propose to impersonate the Royal Military Police? I served my time with the British Army – I know those bastard M.P.s and though I hate their guts, I know you're never going to get a scruffy wog like him," he pointed jeeringly to Jamil, "to look like one, much less act like one."

"Unlike you, Mr Hourigan, none of us here have received a formal military training," Haddad told him coldly. "I accept that we have a problem in disguising our identity. We intend to use a retired member of the Royal Military Police to turn us into a body of men smart enough to pass muster for one of their units. He'll be reporting tomorrow. Also, for your own good, I would advise you not to keep referring to Jamil as a wog. He is a patient man and I can control him up to a point, but if you keep up your jibes then I have to warn you that I cannot guarantee your safety. Do you understand me?"

Hourigan was grudgingly prepared to recognise Haddad's authority. There was something very dangerous about him: a ruthless, deadly quality that made it wiser not to cross him.

"Very good," Haddad said. "We have three weeks left in which to prepare ourselves for this operation. Over the next few days each man will be given his role to play and we'll practise it again and again until we have it perfect. I have one word of advice to you all: think about this operation the whole time, live, eat, and sleep your particular role and as we train, watch that the others carry out their parts correctly. Remember that we are foreign nationals with different customs in a strange country—no detail is too small to be overlooked. You have the rest of today to attend to your personal affairs. Tomorrow we start training in earnest and from that time on no-one leaves this house."

* * *

Michael woke up shortly after midnight to find the house shaking to the distant thunder of heavy-calibre gunfire. The noise went on and on and he couldn't get back to sleep. Across the room from him the brothers, Jamil and Joseph, slept on unperturbed. Around his camp bed, laid out on the floor in such a way as to create his own private space, were the toilet articles and few clothes that Michael had bought to replace the ones he'd left in Paris. He had not yet grown used to living off the floor of a barren room and he missed his privacy bitterly. He got up, made his way down the passage to the living-room and switched on the lights. Haddad had been sitting there alone in the darkness.

"What's the noise?" Michael asked.

"Russian tanks—we're very near the border here and most of their manoeuvres take place at night."

The rumble of gunfire unnerved Michael. "Does this happen often?"

"Yes, but one of these nights they're not going to stop at the border—they're going to come straight through and there's nothing here to prevent them."

Michael sat down. He was worried about his sister, and still badly scared after being hunted by Stroebling's men in Paris. He was floundering out of his depth amongst these violent men in a Berlin safe house, but worst of all he wasn't sure how to handle Haddad. He could never tell what the man was thinking, and that made him nervous. Knowing he had to be firm, he summoned up his courage and said, "This is about the first chance I've had to talk to you alone since I got here, Haddad, and I want to make this clear. Since I'm paying you I want to know and approve all your plans from now on before you pass them on to the others, but most of all I want to know what the hell you're doing about my sister. You've told me hardly anything about the meeting with Stroebling."

Haddad sat silent for a moment or two before he spoke. "I have a contract to deliver Hess to you; beyond that you don't approve plans and you don't give orders." Haddad's cold dark eyes seemed to pierce right into Michael and he saw again the cruel, ruthless side to the man. "You have a choice," Haddad told him. "If you remain in Berlin, then for your own safety you will have to obey me at all times without question. If you feel you can't do that then tomorrow you must return to Paris, or safer still, America."

"What about Kathy?" Michael asked.

"You'll have to trust me to do the best I can for her."

Michael thought for a moment, then he took off his glasses and rubbed at the weariness in his eyes. "I'm too involved to leave now, you know that, but is there any way that I could call off this contract? I don't mind losing the money but I've got in too deep and so has Kathy, and Hess doesn't seem so important any more."

"We've left it too late for that. Don't you see?" Haddad said. "We're no different from any of the others who tried to rescue Hess. We never had a chance until the British stepped in and made it possible. Now we're caught in the middle. Whatever we offer, Stroebling will continue to use Kathy to blackmail me in order to get Hess, and, knowing as much as we do, the British and Americans aren't about to let us leave Berlin. We can be manipulated like pawns in a game of chess, and now there's no way of dropping out until the game is over."

"So, it's that bad," Michael said. "No wonder you were sitting here alone in the dark."

Haddad understood Michael better than he realised. "You were lying when you said Hess wasn't important any more," he challenged.

Michael nodded. In his own way he could be as ruthless as Haddad. "Kathy and I have put too much of ourselves into winning Hess's freedom to give it up now, but if calling it off meant Kathy was safe, I was ready to give it a try." He looked up at Haddad. "Is there any way we can get Kathy back and keep Hess at the same time?"

Haddad seemed to relax. He smiled at Michael and suddenly Michael understood why men followed him. He was accustomed to giving orders and almost impossible to get to know, yet he possessed a magnetism, an extraordinary power of leadership.

"I want Kathy," Haddad said. "With your brain and my ability perhaps we can bring them both to freedom. Shall we work as a team?"

Michael nodded. "What do you want me to do?" he asked.

"What you're trained for," Haddad answered. "Study the men we're up against, look for their weaknesses and their motives and, more mundane but equally important, study the social calendar for both East and West Berlin for the month of February. I want to know about every public occasion, from visiting dignitaries to football matches and religious processions. I'll brief you as to what I'm looking for nearer the time."

CHAPTER TWENTY

Haddad woke the men early, well before dawn. They were standing in the operations room, drinking from steaming mugs of coffee, when a vehicle drew up outside. Maroun was by the window.

"It's Pierre," he said.

"All right," Haddad ordered, "everyone embus."

"Does that include me?" Michael asked.

Haddad nodded. "Everyone takes part in the initial training, then if one man drops out we can replace him with another."

The men climbed aboard the mini-bus, Haddad beside Pierre.

"She's not bad considering the price," Pierre said, referring to the mini-bus, as they moved on. "I picked her up last night and I spotted a Mercedes that will suit us, a 1974 230 taxi."

"I thought you needed a 280?"

"This one will do. The difference in value between the two cars goes towards my new business, O.K.?" Pierre asked. Haddad didn't like it. "It's your neck that's at risk," he said coldly. "Choose what you want."

In fifteen minutes they arrived at a large single-storey warehouse surrounded by a ten-foot fence.

"How long can we use this place for?" Haddad asked.

"The agents have slotted us in for six weeks while it's between tenants."

"Did you make it clear that we don't want to be disturbed?"

"Yes," Pierre confirmed.

A V.W. Passat stationwagon was parked by the fence. Haddad got out and opened the padlocked gate; Pierre was already unlocking the main doors. The Passat and mini-bus drove into the warehouse, one behind the other, their lights shining over a vast expanse of space some four hundred metres by two hundred. The doors rumbled shut and Haddad switched on the overhead lights.

"Pull the cars in over there," he shouted, pointing to the far corner.

The man in the Passat got out and opened the boot of the stationwagon. Haddad walked over to him. The man turned.

"Morning, sir." It was the British warrant officer guard

at Spandau whom Reed-Henry had sent Haddad to see.

"It was good of you to come," Haddad told him.

The warrant officer was lifting some boxes out of the back. "Well, sir, in for a penny," he said lightly, then his expression became serious. "When the major put it to me it seemed fair that I should earn my money."

Haddad lifted the top off one of the cardboard boxes. "Uniforms?"

The warrant officer nodded. "How long have I got to turn you into soldiers?"

"Less than twenty days, and a couple of my men don't even speak English very well."

"Well then, sir," the warrant officer said purposefully, "we'd better start as soon as possible."

Together they walked over to the waiting men. "This is Sergeant-Major James Cooksley," Haddad introduced him.

"Don't worry about giving me their names," the warrant officer said, "I'll get to know them soon enough."

He stood before the assembled men, lifted his head and squared his shoulders. He was tall and, in spite of his years, still a powerful man, with deep-set eyes in a strong, raw-boned face and a prominent jaw. Everything about him was disciplined, purposeful, accustomed to authority.

"You have heard my name," he said. "I spent twenty-five years in the Royal Military Police before I retired and I have to tell you that if pride is a sin then I am a sinful man, because I'm proud of having served as a warrant officer in one of the finest Corps in the British Army. I've only got twenty days, but by the time I've finished with you, you're going to feel the same way because it's not going to be enough to dress like a R.M.P., you've got to feel like one." He kicked open one of the boxes at his feet. "Right then, put your uniforms on." His words were growing more and more clipped as he settled back into a familiar role of training men. It was bitterly cold in the warehouse but he had no mercy on them. "Strip down," he ordered. "Jump to it."

Cooksley moved amongst them, helping them adjust their gaiters and webbing.

"Pull the laces flat. You'll have to use some spit and polish on those boots to shine them up. Who's going to be the W.O.1?" he asked. "He'll be doing most of the talking."

"It'll have to be Hourigan," Haddad told him. "He's had experience in the British Army and he's the only one of us who speaks the language fluently."

The warrant officer tossed Hourigan a jacket with the royal

ciphers on the cuffs. "You're a staff sergeant then," he said, handing Haddad a jacket. "The rest of you are corporals."

"Don't we need an officer?" Haddad asked. "What happens if we come up against one at the accident and he starts countermanding Hourigan's orders?"

"This Corps relies on very few officers, sir. It's mostly run by the N.C.O.s, so it's very unlikely that you'll come up against an R.M.P. officer at the scene of the accident. I have specially chosen a regimental sergeant-major to lead your patrol because he would be a man of enormous experience with more than enough authority to take charge. Nobody, sir," Warrant Officer Cooksley assured Haddad firmly, "below the rank of major is going to argue with a British R.S.M., much less one from the Corps of the Royal Military Police."

He paraded the group in front of him. "You will notice," he said, "that you are all N.C.O.s. That's because a recruit in this Corps starts out as a probationer and when he's finished his training goes straight to a non-commissioned officer. Officers and regimental sergeant-majors don't wear scarlet cap covers, the rest of you do. You'll find that we are known as the 'The Bloody Red Caps': it's a derogatory term, but we're the first in and last out of every battle. We're respected, even feared, by the other soldiers because we're the disciplinarians of the British Army, but we've taken more men safely back to their barracks than we've ever thrown into the cells. When you wear this uniform you have a lot to be proud of.

"Now, all ranks up to W.O.2s wear a whistle and chain, in exactly the same way as the British police, which is from the top button-hole to the top left pocket. The W.O.1s and commissioned officers wear a lanyard on the left shoulder. N.C.O.s wear pistols on the left hip in the white webbing holster you have there with the white brace coming over the shoulder.

"Everyone on duty wears this," he passed out an armband with the letters M.P. in blue on a scarlet background. "Put it on," he instructed. "That's called a brassard, never refer to it as an armband. From now on, whenever any of you enter this training area, the first thing you do is put on your uniforms—you haven't long to get used to them. Hold yourselves upright like soldiers, as though you had spent time on a parade square," he barked.

"For your own good I'm going to drill you until you think like an R.M.P., until military behaviour is second nature to you. That way, in the heat of the moment, you won't make mistakes. When I summon you from now on, you don't walk, you double. You'll get away with murder if your action looks sharp. Now, one of the first things you have to learn is how to come to attention and salute properly. Like this," he showed them. "Now you do it. Don't wave your arms around like a wet rag, snap into position. That's the secret, look smart and soldierly in all things and no-one's going to question you. Again. Again. That's better. All right, stand at ease."

Cooksley looked at his watch. "I'll have to go now. Tonight work on your uniforms, make sure they fit, polish up your boots and clean your webbing. Tomorrow we'll start off with a kit inspection and then we'll try a little foot drill to get your blood moving in the early morning."

"Thank you, Mr Cooksley," Haddad said.

The warrant officer saluted and strode to his car. Haddad signalled to Joseph to open the doors. It was still pitch dark outside. As the car drove out of the warehouse the others broke ranks and moved around to get warm.

"Shit, I'm freezing," Michael said, stamping his new boots on the concrete floor, feeling ridiculous in his uniform with his beard and glasses.

"You won't be for much longer," Pierre answered him unsympathetically, watching Haddad making his way towards them. "He's going to work us now."

Jamil threw Hourigan a mock salute as he passed him. It was a jeering gesture that stung the Irishman. "Get off, will you," he said furiously, unable to control himself any longer. "I hate those bastard red Red Caps. When I was in the Paras I kicked more of their bloody heads in than any others. They threw me in the glass-house trying to break me, but they never did—all it gave me was more good reason to hate them. You watch, I'll get that bastard Cooksley before this is out. So help me, if I don't kill him I'll beat him bloody."

"Little man," Jamil answered him, weary of his outbursts, "why are you always looking for trouble? Leave him alone, he's working with us."

"What I do is none of your bloody business, wog," Hourigan said savagely.

Jamil shrugged and moved away, but Pierre had overheard their exchange.

"Why did you bring Hourigan into this group?" he asked Haddad. "That poisonous bastard isn't one of us, he just causes trouble. Get rid of him," he urged.

"I can't," Haddad answered. "We need someone with a

British Army background to act as the warrant officer. Gather round," he shouted to the men. "All right, now the real training begins. For a start we have to create a mock-up of the Heer Strasse autobahn."

At the end of the day Michael made his way, exhausted, back to the safe house. He took off his boots and crept miserably into his sleeping-bag. A hand shook him roughly by the shoulder. It was Joseph. "Get up," the big man said. "You and I have to cook tonight."

Michael followed him down the corridor to the kitchen. Haddad passed them. He looked Michael up and down.

"If I need you in the Landrover, you're going to have to get rid of that beard," he said.

"What's the matter?" Joseph asked as they entered the kitchen.

"I've had this beard a long time," Michael told him, stroking it protectively. "It hides a weak chin."

"One of us lays out the plates and washes up and the other cooks," Joseph replied, unmoved.

"I'll cook," Michael volunteered. "Joseph," he asked, banging the pots down on the stove, "what brings a man like you all the way from your home in Beirut to Berlin?"

"What would you expect?" Joseph answered. "The money, excitement of action, the smell of blood. What brings any of us to this place?" He sent the plates he was carrying clattering onto the kitchen table and smiled at Michael. "Besides," he said, "I love your cooking."

* * *

They were up long before dawn again the next morning. Warrant Officer Cooksley drilled them until the sweat ran freely, in spite of the fact that the temperature was well below freezing in the warehouse. As before, when Cooksley left to go on duty at Spandau, Haddad took over.

The section of the autobahn that they were going to use had been chalked out on the floor. They had discovered sacking and timber stacked against one wall and this was used to mark the bridges and the side road.

"Can we turn the mini-bus on its side?" Haddad asked.

"If you don't mind spilling some fuel it won't do any harm," Pierre told him.

"All right, put it over," Haddad ordered. "The men who'll be waiting in the Landrover, that's myself, Hourigan, Joseph and Jamil, take your positions. We're going to run through this slowly one more time. If you have questions, if you aren't sure of what you're doing, stop and ask me."

Maroun went to his firing point. Pierre took the two-way radio and called out the sequence of events as they occurred.

"Convoy in sight. Convoy approaching, seven hundred metres, six, five."

"All right, hit it," Haddad called. He counted the seconds off on the stopwatch. "There goes the crash," he shouted. "The mini-bus is on its side. All right, the Landrover moves forward, stops, everyone out. Joseph, you've got to get around to the front and jam that door so the driver and the guard can't get out. Jamil, you and I open the back of the ambulance. Hourigan, the guards bringing up the rear of the convoy will be on us within fifty seconds from now—you've got to warn them of the danger of the ambulance burning, keep them away from us."

"What about the back door of the ambulance?" Jamil asked. "Surely it will be locked from the inside if they're carrying an important patient?"

"We'll open it with a small charge of plastic explosive," Haddad answered. "That's my job."

Pierre came up.

"I've been thinking," he said, "if you don't want to use fire and you still want to create a diversion, then after I've side-swiped the ambulance, I can roll the Mercedes over. I estimate that I'll be coming out of the last spin and side-swiping the ambulance at just over sixty kilometres an hour. My speed will have reduced right down, I figure I'd roll once or twice, not more. Mercedes reinforce the roof as standard and the doors are burst-proof. I should be safe enough, and it will look spectacular. I've been worrying about that rear R.M.P. Landrover," Pierre added. "If I don't manage to block them with my car they'll turn right into the side road on you after the ambulance. So this way Hourigan can send them to pull me out of my car."

"Can you decide whether you're going to let your car roll or not after the side-swipe?"

"I think I should have enough control left," Pierre said.

"O.K. It's all going to have to depend on which ambulance they put Hess in."

"How far away do you think we'll be able to spot the markings that Cooksley's going to put on it?" Pierre asked.

"About five hundred metres."

"That's too short a distance. We'll need a man in a car outside Spandau to spot the ambulance for us as it comes out, and then he'll have to follow it down Heer Strasse to make sure the R.M.P.s don't change its position."

"It's a simple enough job for a man with a two-way radio," Haddad said. "I'll find someone."

"Perhaps Michael could handle that," Pierre suggested.

The men gathered round. "That was a good day," Haddad told them. "You did well, but keep thinking, keep going over your part of the plan. If you have any questions or ideas tell me, we'll work them out together. Everyone O.K. for the moment?"

They nodded tiredly.

"Right," Haddad said. "The slow run-throughs are over, we start speeding it up tomorrow."

CHAPTER TWENTY-ONE

Pierre climbed the dimly-lit stairway of the tenement block to his apartment. He unlocked the door and slipped inside, checked that his children were sleeping, then went quietly into his bedroom and began to undress.

René reached out and switched on the bedside light. "Do you know what time it is?" she demanded angrily. "How long is this nonsense going on for?"

"Hush, René," Pierre tried to quieten her. "You'll wake the children."

René propped herself up in bed so that she could face him. "The children," she shouted, losing her temper. "What do you care about the children? You never see them."

"If you wake them Angelo will be tired for school."

"So what if he is tired, at least he still has a father! If I don't try to stop you, next week or the week after that he'll have no father at all. Pierre," she pleaded with him, "you've given up your job to risk your life, your family, everything, for this one crazy gamble. It can't be just the money—what does Haddad offer you that makes it worth more than me and the children?"

Pierre climbed into bed. She turned away but he reached out, put his arm around her and pulled her rigid, protesting body towards his.

"Nothing is worth more to me than you and the children," he said. "You know that. But each day at the garage I was just a drone. I changed people's spark plugs, I changed their oil. I didn't even have to be a good mechanic, they have machines that can tune engines now. I brought money home but that was all, there was nothing for myself. Now the risk I face brings its own excitement—I feel a man again. My talent is vital to the success or failure of the plan: everything depends on me. René, when I could no longer drive a racing-car I lost more than my hand. This way, if only for a short time, let me feel important to myself again."

He felt her softening and went on talking, holding her tightly to him.

"With the money I earn from this we can buy our freedom—no more tenement flats."

"Could we go home?" René asked. "I miss my home more

and more now." She sighed. "I miss the souks and the narrow streets, I miss the harsh, bright sunlight on the sea. And the people, all our people, I miss them most of all."

"René," Pierre said hopelessly, "whatever happens, I can't go back, I hate too much."

"But why?" René protested. "We live among Moslems here. The Turks are our friends, they have helped us, they have been kind to us."

"They aren't our Moslems, René, they aren't Arab. They were never part of our war and I have no quarrel with them. In any case, the war in the Lebanon goes on in the south. If we went back, before long I would have to take sides and fight again. No, we aren't going back to open old wounds. We're going to go to America. René, I have it all planned, we're going to open our own business, we'll make money, enough to maybe buy you your own house. It will be a good life for you and the children if we can get to America."

It was hard for René to surrender completely to his enthusiasm.

"You said that when you wanted to come here," she pointed out dubiously.

"This time it's going to be different," Pierre told her. He was kissing her neck and behind her ears to arouse her. She let him pull her towards him until her body pressed against his.

"Oh, Pierre," she whispered, "I get so frightened. When you aren't here I feel so helpless. I'm far from home and things that I know, I don't want I'd do if anything happened to you. The children and I, we need you so much, please be careful for us."

"There's no danger," Pierre whispered, reassuring her. "I promise, there's no danger."

He remembered sadly the girl he had married, so rounded and beautiful and bursting with the joy of life. Now she was a worn, tired woman pining for the sunlight of her home. She lay within his arms, so thin that when he felt for her flesh he touched only bone. Pierre felt guilty at what he had done to her. His plans for Berlin had not worked out but they could try again and this time, with the extra money, they would make it. He kissed her on the lips, his mouth pressing urgently on hers. She turned her body to face him, clinging desperately to him, and he whispered, "Sometimes I am a very selfish man, but I love you, René, I really love you."

* * *

"A word with you before I go, sir," the warrant officer said to Haddad at the end of the next early morning training session.

Their footsteps echoed as they walked across the warehouse to his car.

"The men are pulling together well as a team, sir," he went on. "I'm pleased with them, but I've got trouble brewing with Hourigan. I don't know if you've spotted it yet but I've enough experience to know that he's going to try something on me soon."

"I haven't noticed anything, Mr Cooksley, but I'll keep my eyes open," Haddad answered.

"Thank you, sir, he could be a dangerous bastard if he came up from behind." Cooksley opened the door of his car. "I've seen that face of his somewhere before and he knows me, which is why I rile him so much, but I can't place him. Maybe I got him sent down to Colchester. Do you know if he's done any time in a military detention barracks?"

Haddad shrugged. "I employed him on a recommendation for this operation, other than that I know very little about him."

Cooksley drove out of the warehouse to return to duty at Spandau and Haddad went back to his men.

"Alright," he said, beating his arms across his chest to keep his circulation moving. "Now we're going to practise switching the bodies in the ambulance again."

The mini-bus was already on its side. In a far corner of the warehouse, behind a screen of sacking, Pierre was spray-painting the Royal Military Police colours onto a Landrover.

"Is it ready yet?" Haddad shouted.

"No," Pierre yelled back, angered by the added pressure. "Tomorrow. Use the other Landrover, I haven't started on that one yet."

Haddad signalled to Hourigan to drive the second Landrover into position.

"Michael," he called, "on this run-through take the stop-watch. We'll try the new way. Joseph, when the Landrover stops you make for the driver's side door and jam it. Jamil, you and I open the back. Hourigan, as the door opens we'll pull the medical orderly out first and you take care of him. If he's already unconscious, drug him with morphine to see he stays that way—if he isn't unconscious, then knock him out but see that his concussion appears to have been caused by the accident."

"How much morphine do I give him?" Hourigan asked.

"The orderly will have to remain unconscious for at least four hours. I'm told one c.c. will do it—don't give him any more or you'll kill him."

"That doesn't matter," Hourigan said callously.

"It does to me—this operation relies on brains and skill, not brawn. I want no deaths if I can help it."

Haddad took up his position in the Landrover with the others. "Shout out the seconds," he called to Michael. "Here comes the crash. . . . The ambulance is over. Go!"

The Landrover roared out from its supposedly sheltered position in the side road and stopped by the stricken ambulance. Everyone leaped out and raced to their positions. Joseph was first.

"In position," he yelled; the others' shouts followed a few seconds later.

"Eighteen seconds," Michael called.

"Good," Haddad said. "Now phase two. Go!"

Joseph jammed shut the upturned ambulance driver's door, slapped the panel, then raised his hand to show Michael that it was done. He raced back to the Landrover to lift out the substitute body, represented by a bundle of sacks. He was a big man, capable, with the aid of the device he had rigged, of carrying a corpse and a stretcher on his own. Haddad had placed small plastic explosive charges on the top and bottom of the ambulance doors where the rods locked into the roof and floor. He pulled back around the side of the vehicle, unravelling a fuse wire, and connected the circuit to the detonator caps.

"Doors open," Haddad yelled.

"Fourteen seconds," Michael called.

The two men dived into the back of the ambulance, grabbing the orderly the split second after the doors opened, pulling him out. They unclipped the stretcher which would be carrying Hess from its supports. Hess would have been well strapped in and should have suffered little or no harm from the accident. Haddad and Jamil lifted out the stretcher and gave it to Joseph who carried it back, past the first Landrover, to where the second Landrover would have been parked unseen in the shelter of some trees. The two men lifted in the "corpse" to take the place of Hess and placed the oxygen mask over its face.

"Forty-seven seconds," Michael shouted.

Haddad jumped down from the ambulance. "We have to do better than that," he said.

Jamil shrugged. "It's difficult working with the stretcher

in the ambulance when it's on its side."

"It'll be worse when there's some weight on it," Haddad warned. "We'll have to allow for that. Joseph, don't forget, as soon as you get Hess to the second Landrover you must inject the antidote to the Ephedrine. We'll try again. This time we need a medical orderly. We'll practise getting him out of the back when he's unconscious and again when he's shaken, but still with some fight in him. If he's in that state, we have to let him see our uniforms—he has to think we're friends, at least for the first few seconds. Michael, you be the medical orderly, Maroun can take over with the stopwatch."

Michael climbed into the back of the mini-bus.

"Right," Haddad said. "I want this run-through to be as realistic as possible."

The assault on the ambulance went smoothly but as Michael was pulled out Hourigan was waiting for him. He kneed Michael in the groin and punched him in the solar plexus, not hard enough to fell him but enough to hurt and wind him. The others laughed, expecting that Michael would know how to protect himself, but the last time Michael had fought anyone in earnest was back in his boyhood. They ran through again and this time Hourigan chopped Michael in the kidneys. Again there was laughter as Michael spun round: it relieved the tension and Hourigan was too quick with his punches for them to see that it was anything other than horseplay. But Michael knew from the Irishman's face that he was relishing more and more the pain and humiliation he was inflicting on him.

"Michael," Haddad called, "you're too limp, this time put up some fight when we take you out, make it difficult for us."

"It's a practice, right. You got that?" Michael warned Hourigan before he climbed back into the ambulance.

Hourigan didn't reply, he just nodded. Michael already felt a gulf dividing himself from the others: for a long time he had been a stranger to physical violence. Intellectually he could understand that, but his maleness wouldn't admit weakness. This time Hourigan threw off all pretence. Again he kneed Michael in the groin. As Michael clutched at himself Hourigan stepped smartly around him and chopped him in the kidneys, then drove his knuckles into his spine. None of the blows were very heavy but they were administered with such speed and precision that they brought agonising pain. Michael pitched forward, cutting his cheek and his nose on the concrete floor.

"Alright, you bastard," Michael shouted, spitting out the

blood that was running from his nose into his mouth as he struggled to get up off the floor. His only thought now was to land one punch, just one good punch in Hourigan's jeering face, but before he got to his knees a boot in the ribs kicked him over.

"You lie there until I tell you you can get up, you fucking university professor," Hourigan said menacingly. "You see my boot," he put the toe-cap next to Michael's nose, "you make one move and I'll kick your face in. Go on," Hourigan breathed. "Move, try it." But Michael accepted his humiliation and stayed where he was until Haddad came up.

"Why did you hit him?" Haddad asked Hourigan as he helped Michael to his feet.

The sadistic gleam in Hourigan's eyes disappeared and he stepped back, afraid of Haddad's anger. "You said to make it realistic this time," he glowered.

"He's no use to us hurt," Haddad said. "Go clean yourself up," he ordered Michael.

He walked Hourigan out of earshot of the others. The Irishman was cunning as well as vicious. Before Haddad had a chance to speak he whined, "Sure now, don't you go threatening me and telling me what a bad fellow I am. We've got your girl, see, don't forget what we can do to her."

Haddad controlled his anger and appeared to ignore the incident. All the same, when he glanced at Michael, he knew that life on a university campus was no training for company such as this. He needed a break.

"Take over the stopwatch," he told Michael.

* * *

Michael went to see Haddad a night later. He was alone in the operations room, staring down at the model of the autobahn.

"Can I see you a moment?" Michael asked. "I've got a problem. It's not what happened with Hourigan, I could learn to handle that. You said the other day you might need me in the Landrover team at the accident: I've been going over and over it in my mind and I know I couldn't do it. If things went wrong, and we got involved in a shoot-out with the British guards, I wouldn't be able to use a weapon. I just couldn't kill anyone. I'm sorry, but I thought I'd better tell you now before you come to rely on me and I crack when it's actually happening."

Haddad looked at him. The cold dark eyes bored into

Michael and Michael shifted uncomfortably. In his mind's eye he had gone over the details of the accident time and time again until he had made himself almost physically sick with fear at the possibility of having to maim or kill someone, or be maimed or killed himself. All forms of violence terrified him.

"No one knows what they're going to do or how they're going to behave in a violent situation without a lot of experience," Haddad said. "But if you feel that way, the other's won't want to have to rely on you in a tight spot, so you're off the hook. You can ease up on the training. Tomorrow start work on the social calendar for East and West Berlin. Then I've got something else for you to do."

"O.K." Michael sounded relieved.

Haddad turned back to examining the model.

"Michael," he said, his mind already half-distracted by the problems confronting him, "I think you should know something. If the accident doesn't pass off absolutely smoothly and a gun-fight does break out, then all of us have little chance of leaving Berlin alive. The British will see to that."

Maroun came to Haddad's room late that night. He didn't bother to switch on the light – he knew Haddad was expecting him. He refused to sit down and it was obvious that he was feeling strung-out. He was shifting about as though his skin felt uncomfortable, as though it was itching and crawling under his clothes.

"I can't take being cooped up in here much longer," he muttered. "Pissing about being a soldier and living with all these people, it's driving me out of my mind. When can I go back on the outside again?"

"You won't have to wait much longer. Just hold on, Maroun," Haddad begged, unsure of what forces were at work in his friend's mind. "Don't crack up on me now, not when I need you so badly."

Maroun shot him a triumphant look. To Haddad it meant: I told you you'd need me one day, you bastard.

"How're you managing with Hourigan?" Haddad asked.

"He's O.K. That guy's so nasty I find him fascinating. He keeps feeding me with orange-blossom tabs and when he thinks I'm too spaced out to notice he goes out through the window, doesn't come back for maybe two or three hours."

"That's when he'll be reporting to Stroebling," Haddad said thoughtfully.

"When do you want me to kill him?" Maroun asked.

"I'll let you know when it's time," Haddad replied.

CHAPTER TWENTY-TWO

The following morning Michael remained behind as the others were leaving for the training area.

"Why isn't he coming?" Hourigan demanded.

"I told him to stay," Haddad said.

Hourigan understood. "O.K., chickenshit professor," he jeered. "If you're scared of getting hurt with the men then you do my share of the cooking tonight." He blew Michael a kiss as the vehicle moved off. "Make something tasty."

Michael worked through the day on the papers that Haddad had provided.

In the evening, when the others returned cold and tired from the day's training, they found supper waiting for them.

"Now, university boy," Hourigan said as he sat down at the table, "you're doing something to justify your living here, just when I was beginning to think you were useless."

"In our type of life it's not good to interfere in another man's affairs," Joseph said to Michael afterwards. "But if it gets too bad let me know."

The others avoided Hourigan. The only person who seemed to get on with him was Maroun.

That night Haddad waited until the rest of the men were asleep, then he went to Michael's room and woke him. "Put your clothes on and come with me," he ordered. Michael obeyed. They went to the garage and pushed the little hired Golf out of earshot along the street before Haddad started it.

"Where are we going?" Michael asked, climbing in beside Haddad.

"To the Kottbussertor. A cunning old Turk lives there. He's reputed to be the best fixer in Berlin. We need his help."

Haddad drove in silence for a while, weighing something up in his mind.

"Michael," he said at last, "I can take care of Hess and everything relating to that up to the time of the accident, but I need your help to plan our escape from Berlin. I've thought most of it through but I'm going to need you to attend to the details. It's very important for us all that you make no mistakes. Can I trust you for that?"

Michael nodded. Haddad, when he wished, could make a man feel special, important to himself. In those few words he restored some of Michael's self-respect.

They parked the car in Gorlitzer Strasse and walked to a small, steamy-windowed ground-floor bar. Haddad pushed open the door. After the freezing air of the street it was like entering a hothouse. A small of spilt alcohol, rich tobacco and spicy food struck Michael with an almost physical force. At first he didn't think his stomach could take it, but after a few moments he managed to will it to quieten down. Turks, many of them small thin men, with brown eyes and sharp, work-worn faces, hunched on hard-backed chairs over small tables. A few were spending the hours away from their overcrowded tenements playing cards, others were engaged in "Favli", a game similar to backgammon.

Haddad walked through the haze of cigarette smoke and oily cooking fumes to an empty table by the wall. Soon after he was seated a small, hunched man in his sixties with close-cropped salt-and-papper hair and beard-stubble sprouting from his hollow cheeks, left his place by the bar and joined them. His left eye was covered by a patch.

"It's some time since we made that train journey into Berlin," he said to Haddad. "Until you contacted me yesterday I was hurt to think that you had no use for a man of my talents." He clapped his hands for the barman. "You are my guests here. Relax, drink, tell me what you want, we can discuss the fee later."

"What happened to your eye?" Haddad asked. "You didn't have that patch on the train."

"A little matter," the Turk replied, making light of the injury. "Unfortunately I moved too slowly and an enemy was able to introduce the point of his knife to my eye. I'm told that I'll never see out of it again."

"What little matter could cause a thing like that?" Michael asked, horrified.

The Turk was amused. He smiled and showed his yellow, broken teeth. "It's no longer important," he said. "The man who cost me my eye died a short while later and I don't wish to speak ill of the dead." He changed the subject. "Is this the man you want me to work with?" he asked Haddad.

When Haddad nodded the Turk ran his remaining shrewd, bright eye over Michael's face and seemed doubtful.

"Have you been involved with this sort of work before?"

"No," Michael said. "But I learn fast."

"We'll see," the Turk reserved judgement. "Your name?" he asked.

"Michael Lakas."

"I have so many names that I sometimes forget which to use, but you call me Mustapha Jumblatt, I'll answer to that."

"There's a football match at the Olympic Stadium on Saturday, 3rd February," Haddad said. "The West Berlin football club, Hertha Berlin, will be playing the Greek club, Athens Panathinaikos."

"That's correct," the Turk confirmed.

"Do they expect big crowds?"

"Football is very popular here, I follow it myself."

"I'm told," Haddad said, "that the package tours carrying supporters sometimes use the East Berlin airport at Schönefeld."

"It depends on which country they come from, but the Greeks would probably use Schönefeld. There's a tour operator on the Kudamm who handles all the package tours that come through from the East. Our colleague," the Turk indicated Michael, "could easily check that out with them, but be careful how you do it," he warned. "The tour company is believed to have connections with the East Germans."

"Very good," Haddad said. "Next we will need seven passports."

"What nationality?"

Haddad looked at him. "Greek—we'll supply you with photographs."

"Of course," Jumblatt was angry with himself for not having understood more quickly.

"We'll need passport entry stamps from Schönefeld, East Berlin, dated on the day of the football match."

The Turk nodded.

"Will you have any problems with our requirements so far?" Haddad asked.

Jumblatt shook his head. "None, as long as you can pay the price. Ever since the Berlin wall was made almost impossible to cross, this city has become a centre for forged documents. I can get you almost anything you want, the finest quality."

The liquor was burning its way down to Michael's stomach and the Turk ordered more.

"Seven Greeks who come on the tour to watch the match will have to be persuaded to stay in Berlin and later make their own way home. You may have to visit Athens to interview them and secure their co-operation. We'll need their documents and airline tickets to match the names on our passports."

"Of course," Jumblatt said. "But a visit to Athens will not be necessary. I have friends there who will attend to that.

Now, if that's all we can discuss. . . ."

"I have one last favour to ask you," Haddad interrupted him. "I want you to find me the body of a man in his eighties. I know that in death very old people grow to look much alike, but find me a man with the same hair colour and physical characteristics as this one." Haddad handed the Turk a description sheet.

"What about teeth, identifying marks?"

"You'll find it all in there. Give the description to a mortician that you trust and tell him to find me as clean a corpse as possible; if we need a particular mark he can put it on for us. The corpse won't have to pass a very intense scrutiny," Haddad said. "We just want to avoid dissimilarities."

"In that case, why bother with a mortician? For a few Deutsche marks more I'll pick out an old man who'll suit you and wring his neck like a scrawny chicken just before you need him. When a man has reached that age he is no use to his family, it will be a service to him."

"Just do as I say," Haddad ordered. "Give the description to a mortician and tell him to let us know as soon as he has a body that will suit us. I want him to keep it frozen until I see it. That's all for the moment," Haddad said, getting up. "Michael will discuss your fees when you contact him."

"How much do you pay for a body?" Michael asked as they drove back to the safe house.

Haddad shrugged. "Not much, bodies are cheap. It's the forged papers that are expensive."

"What did you mean when you said that the body wouldn't have to pass a very close scrutiny?"

"Once Hess is pronounced dead on arrival at hospital, no one is going to touch that body until the pathologists are ready to do the post-mortem, and when that happens nothing is going to disguise the fact that the corpse isn't Hess."

Michael leaned back in his seat, staring out at the icy streets.

"What about Kathy?" he reminded Haddad. "The telephone call is due soon. Which one of us is going to speak to her?"

"You do it," Haddad said. "The men have to have absolute trust in me if this is going to work and it's important that they think I've nothing on my mind other than the operation. But when you speak to her," he added, "I want you to listen carefully to her voice, tell me if she seems very scared, as though someone's holding a gun on her. You'll be able to tell from the way she speaks if she's reading from a prepared speech. Make sure you ask her questions, listen carefully to how she responds, I want to know everything she says and how she says it."

Haddad stopped the car and switched off the engine some distance before the safe house.

"There is something else I want you to do for me," he said.

* * *

Michael dialled the number Haddad had given him from a call-box on Theodor Heuss Platz. The phone at the other end rang a couple of times, then someone lifted the receiver.

"I want to speak with my sister," Michael said. "My name is Michael Lakas."

"Wait," a voice replied.

Michael heard the sound of a door slamming in the distance, footsteps drawing closer, then a muffled command and the receiver was picked up.

"Kathy," he said, "Kathy, is that you?"

"You have two minutes," the voice cut in.

"Are you O.K., sis?" Michael asked worriedly. "How are they treating you? Tell me, we haven't got much time."

"I guess I'm alright," Kathy said, struggling to keep any fear she felt out of her voice. "They've put me in a little room and I'm going crazy there all by myself not knowing what's going on, but they leave me alone and treat me well, Stroebling sees to that. How's Haddad?" she asked.

"He's O.K."

"Is he still going ahead with getting Hess out?"

"Yes."

"Tell him not to worry about me."

They both knew that they didn't have much time left.

"Michael," Kathy asked hesitantly, "It's going to be alright, isn't it?"

All along she had sounded defiant, but Michael guessed that she was scared half to death.

"Yes," he said, putting as much conviction into his voice as he could. "Kathy, trust me, we've got a deal with Stroebling, everything's going to be alright." Then in the seconds remaining Michael tried a stupid gamble. "Where are you, Kathy?" he asked. "Do you know?"

Before Kathy could reply she was cut off. An icy voice said, "No, Mr Lakas, that was foolish of you to attempt to break our agreement," and then the line went dead.

Michael had never heard Stroebling speak, otherwise he would have recognised the voice.

Michael made another call to Major Tom Dade, identified himself as Kathy's brother and demanded a meeting. He waited in Kranzlers until the big man showed up. Dade had forgotten his gloves: he came through the doors and up to Michael's table rubbing the warmth back into his hands.

"Lakas?" he asked, recognising the description.

Michael nodded. "Can I get you some coffee?"

"Hell, no," Dade boomed. He had a bluff, honest, instantly likeable face. "I'm going to drink. Beer and Schnapps," he called to the waitress. "Make that a double. It's taken me a long time to get used to that stuff," he said. "But by God it helps keep out the cold. Now, tell me, what can I do for you?"

"Remember Kathy?"

"Sure I do."

"A man called Stroebling has kidnapped her. What are you going to do about it?"

"Hell, what do you expect me to do?" Dade said, surprised. "I dated her a couple of times, that's all. If you've got evidence go tell the police, don't come to me, I'm just a lowly major attached to my general's staff."

"Stop giving me that line of bullshit," Michael said tiredly. "Listen, the Russians know you're in our Intelligence, so do the Germans and the British and French, everyone knows here, so why hide it from me? I'm an American like you, I need help. We're supposed to be on the same side, remember?" He brought the subject back to Kathy. "I've just spoken to her, she's scared and alone, you've got to help her."

The major was suddenly uncomfortable in Kranzlers. It was too crowded and Michael had no concept of security. He got rapidly to his feet.

"Let's take a walk," he said.

They left the coffee-house and made their way along the broad pavements of the Kudamm past Kempinski's, the best hotel in Berlin.

"You got us into this, you let the British use us," Michael began again. "Now you've got to get Kathy out."

"Listen to me, sonny." All the bluff good-naturedness had gone out of Dade's face and suddenly it was hard and bleak. "You and your sister are up to your necks in a pile of shit of your own making. You despised your own country's enforcement and Intelligence agencies, but now you're in trouble you're the first to holler help. But why bring me in? You've got your friend Haddad to help you."

"That's why I've come to you," Michael said wretchedly. "Haddad doesn't give a damn. He's got the money, we're no use to him any more. Stroebling thinks he can control Haddad with Kathy and Haddad's encouraging him to believe that, but when the time comes he'll hand Hess over to Reed-Henry and to hell with Kathy. I know he will. He thinks his future work lies with the West."

"Well, he's right in that," Dade said. "The East have all the battalions of Cubans they need, we can use any good mercenary we can get."

They walked on in silence for a couple of paces. Dade sighed. "I guess I'll help you all I can but you're going to have to help me in return. You tell *me*, not the British, nor anyone else, just me, everything that goes on amongst those men you're with, right up to the time they strike. Keep close to Haddad, I want to know his every move, hell, I want to know what he's thinking even before he does."

Michael shook his head. "No-one can tell you that. Haddad talks to no-one, he just gives the orders when he's ready, but if you'll protect Kathy, I'll pass on everything I can."

"Tell me," the major asked as they turned back and walked towards his car, "what in hell were you going to do with Hess if you did get hold of him?"

"Start a human rights revolution," Michael said.

"Oh, dear God!" Dade exclaimed, shaking his head in exasperation at Michael's naïvety. "Did you really think you could do that with him? Just across the wall from here, in the East, if the parents are caught trying to escape, the State judges them politically unsound and takes their kids away from them and puts them in institutions. Do you really think Hess would have made that much difference?"

"What do you want him for?" Michael asked.

"The pressure is building to have Hess released, right? Everyone thought his mind was wiped out but he's been writing a book three months out of four. No one can touch him in Spandau but once he's out, if the right people were able to question Hess, he might start remembering some old double-crosses that are best left forgotten."

"That's a problem for the Brits," Michael protested. "Why are we interfering?"

"They know as much about our dirty secrets as we know of theirs," Dade said drily. "And they have a way of appealing for help that's just about irresistible. More than that, they've come up with an idea of killing two birds with one stone that's almost brilliant. Stroebling's half-crazy with pain and going down and they're going to use Hess as bait to collapse the whole of the East German Intelligence around him. That will severely disrupt the supply of weapons and money and safe houses to the left-wing terror groups operating in Europe and it'll give us the chance to break them up. The stakes are high," Dade said as he opened his car door. "The British aren't going to concern themselves with Kathy, and they'll stop you if you get in their way. If Haddad's no use then I'm about the only hope you have of getting her out alive, so you just keep the information coming."

CHAPTER TWENTY-THREE

Warrant Officer Cooksley passed slowly along the small rank of men at the 5.30 a.m. inspection. They were standing to attention under the harsh glare from the warehouse lights in full dress and webbing, and the sharp eyes of the warrant officer missed nothing. He pulled the peaks of their caps down over their eyes until they looked like guardsmen, adjusted a lanyard, checked a buckle on a gaiter, commenting, criticising all the time, demanding as close as he could get to perfection. He stopped opposite Hourigan, resplendent as a regimental sergeant major with the royal cipher on his sleeves.

"Smarten up that man," Cooksley commanded sharply. "Stand up straight, get your shoulders back! God made you small but he didn't want you to act like a dwarf. I hear you were in the Second Paras."

"I was," Hourigan said, hate blazing from his little eyes.

"That regiment always was an undisciplined shower of shit and it shows in its men," Cooksley said dismissively.

Hourigan was stuck for an answer; he would never defend his old regiment but at the same time he wanted no "bloody Red Cap" insulting them.

"That goes for the whole British Army," he jeered after Cooksley, but the warrant officer had moved on to the next man and ignored him.

"Their bearing and movement are getting better, sir, more like regular soldiers," Cooksley told Haddad after the parade.

"Good," Haddad answered. "But aren't you looking for trouble with the way you're pushing Hourigan?"

"Don't worry, sir," the warrant officer replied. "I've got the measure of that man now. By the way you're stepping up the training I gather it must be getting near the time. When are you thinking of staging the accident, sir?"

"I haven't made a final decision," Haddad told him. "But I'm working towards February 3rd. Would that be alright for you?"

"I'd have to check the prison duty roster, sir, but I can't see any problems. I'm due a few days occasional leave and I thought I'd spend the time with the men. I could watch the final run-throughs and spot any faults."

"I'd be glad to have you with us."
"Right, I'll move my things across."

* * *

Michael knocked on the door of Haddad's room. He found Maroun inside, leaning against the wall. Haddad was sitting on the bed.

"I wanted to see you for a moment," Michael hesitated.

"Come in," Haddad said. "Don't worry about Maroun." He glanced into Michael's face, then he reached into a drawer and took out a bottle of scotch.

"I thought this was a dry house?" Michael queried.

"This is for medicinal purposes," Haddad answered. "Pour yourself a drink, you look as though you need one."

Michael poured himself a stiff scotch.

"I'll join you," Haddad said, passing over another glass.

"You?" Michael asked of Maroun, but Maroun shook his head disparagingly. "Never touch the stuff."

"What happened with Kathy?" Haddad asked.

"She's O.K.," Michael answered. "She's not being badly treated, I believed that from the way she spoke, but she's lonely and scared."

"And Dade?"

"The arrogant bastard behaved as we expected him to." Michael raised his glass and peered through the crystal. "You've got another spy in your camp," he said quietly. "Me."

"That's O.K.. Lead him along, but watch out for Reed-Henry, he'll see straight through you."

Michael nodded. The whisky felt good in his stomach. He lifted up the bottle. "Do you mind if I get drunk?" he asked. Haddad shook his head. "Not as long as you're prepared to sleep it off here."

Maroun pushed himself away from the wall. "I guess I'll leave you guys," he said. "I've got to check on Hourigan."

After Maroun had gone, Michael continued, unable to hide his hurt, "When I told Dade what we wanted to do with Hess, the bastard just laughed at me. But those guys don't understand how a cause is made. People are denied their human rights all the time, but one man alone in a cell for forty years can shake the public's conscience enough to make them start listening to the message on both sides of the wall. Especially here in Germany, Hess means a lot to them. Do you think I'm crazy too?" Michael asked.

Haddad shrugged his shoulders. He could see that Michael

was down and he needed all the support he could get. Courage was something that Michael had to work at all the time.

"Karl Marx and Darwin were crazy, so were all the great religious prophets, you're in good company."

Michael smiled at him over the rim of his glass. "Hey," he said, warming to Haddad, "maybe you aren't such a black-hearted bastard after all. You want some?" He was going to push the bottle across but Haddad shook his head.

"You know, Dade gave me a lead though," Michael went on, splashing more liquor into his glass. "The Hess that landed in England was a big, very fit specimen of a man, capable of flying a Messerschmitt alone eight hundred miles across enemy territory and baling out at night within ten miles of the place he wanted to be. That took a great deal of concentration and a hell of a lot of nerve, and yet the man who was placed on trial at Nuremberg four years later was a dithering physical wreck. Stranger than that, within six weeks of the Deputy Führer of Germany landing in war-time England, Hitler pulls back from mounting his invasion on England and goes and attacks his ally, Russia.

"The diverting of all those war planes, men and ammunition to the Russian front, that must have saved England's bacon, rather than that strip of water they call the Channel. Somewhere in there the greatest double-cross of all time took place. The Russians have always suspected this. If they got their hands on any proof they might want to lay the blame on someone other than the Germans for their eighteen million war dead. And so I figure that in order to protect themselves the British, using chemicals and then deep hypnosis, scrambled up that man's mind, removing all the information that would be dangerous to them.

"Remember that a fit man, at least judged so by his family and friends before he left them, sat most of the war years out in comparative comfort in England in a country house staffed with guards and doctors. And yet by the time he reached Nuremberg in 1945 he looked a wreck, he complained of imaginary pains in his body and he had total memory blackouts in which he failed to recognise the secretaries who had worked for him for seven years and many others on his staff. Then he started remembering some things and not others and the things he remembered don't matter, but there are always gaps in his memory."

"What use is he going to be to you if he's crazy?" Haddad asked.

"He isn't crazy," Michael said. "He never lost the use of

his conscious mind and I think over the years he's been getting his memory back. Dade slipped me that by mistake. He's been writing a book three months out of four. The British must be watching him, which is why I think they would want him dead rather than let him leave Spandau a free man. But they can't touch him in Spandau, no-one can, he's too closely guarded and the Russians would be instantly suspicious if they thought he had died of anything other than natural causes. So they're going to use us to bring him out into the open."

"I'd already figured that," Haddad said.

* * *

Hourigan came up to Maroun, crouched in the corner of their room.

"How are you feeling?"

"Good, man, good," Maroun said. "These tabs you gave me are the best, I'm really flying."

Hourigan studied Maroun's face, saw the dilated pupils, the filmy, far-away look in his eyes. "So you are, you crazy bastard," he agreed softly. "So you are."

Hourigan sank down against the opposite wall and waited as the L.S.D. took effect.

"How are you, man?" Maroun asked, his concentration slipping out of focus. "You flying too?"

"Sure I am," the Irishman said. "Just like you."

Maroun let out a deep breath through his clenched teeth. "Wheeeeeu! You sure you gave me the right stuff? It must have been double strength. I don't think I can handle it," Maroun giggled. "Man, I'm stepping right out of my mind."

Hourigan watched Maroun's head start to droop, his shoulders sag. "Did you know Haddad's girl?" he asked, raising his voice to penetrate Maroun's consciousness.

"Kathy, sure," Maroun replied hesitantly. "I know her."

"Now, there was a girl," Hourigan reminisced, "with a good, soft body. I trained her to my hand, I brought her trembling and sweating to me like a frightened mare. Shall I tell you how I did it?" Hourigan gloated. "You liked her, didn't you? Well, you'll enjoy this." He was using the hallucinations induced by the drug to upset the fragile balance of Maroun's mind.

"No," Maroun said, shaking his head, beginning to comprehend what Hourigan was doing to him. He wanted to throw himself at Hourigan, to tear his throat out, but it was too late, he couldn't get his body gathered together enough to move it. Crazy patterns began forming in his mind, objects flying at him like moons out of a science-fiction movie. He felt his mind coming apart with the terror of a bad trip. Hourigan had left his place against the opposite wall. He held Maroun by the hair, pulling his head back.

"You are in a room," he said, loudly enough for Maroun to hear him. "Upstairs alone in the pitch dark. You've got a gun but you can't use it because you can't see, you are blind, do you hear me, you are blind and there's men coming in through the doors and windows of the ground floor and they are going to kill you. You can hear them coming and they can see you but you can't see them." Hourigan let go of Maroun and scratched the wall. "Listen," he said urgently. "You hear a knife, they are going to use a knife, you can't escape, they are going to rip it through your guts."

Maroun's face was covered in sweat, the veins on his neck and forehead stood out like cords. He cowered in a corner of the room, death masks flashing in front of his eyes, then he felt the knife go in and he began to scream and scream, trying to climb out of the dream.

Hourigan sat back against the wall, his wicked little eyes fixed on Maroun. "Go on, you crazy bastard," he said. "Go mad, kill yourself."

The whole house awoke to the sound of Maroun's screams. Haddad burst through the door first, followed closely by Jamil and Joseph.

"What have you done?" Haddad demanded of Hourigan.

"It wasn't me," Hourigan answered defensively. "He took himself on a bad trip—I've been trying to help." But Hourigan was satisfied that help had come too late: Maroun's mind was breaking up.

"Catch him," Haddad ordered the brothers. "Hold him down."

The two big men caught Maroun and pinned him, struggling and screaming, to the floor. Michael appeared in the doorway, rudely awoken and still groggy from the effects of the whisky.

"Get some Valium," Haddad shouted to him. "It's in the first-aid chest under my bed. Move." His voice cut like a whiplash.

Michael sobered up instantly, spun around and dashed for Haddad's room. He came back with the tranquilliser to find Haddad kneeling, holding Maroun's head.

"What dosage are the capsules?"

"Ten milligrams."

"Give him two, no, three," Haddad instructed him. He held Maroun's jaws apart while Michael forced the Valium down Maroun's throat.

"Shall I get a doctor?" Michael asked.

Haddad shook his head. "No, there's nothing he could do now. Maroun's mind is so far away it's almost out of reach. We've got to talk him down, he needs voices that he knows. Maroun," Haddad began. "It's me, John, it's John, I've got you safe. Listen to me, trust me, I want you to do what I say." But it took Haddad five minutes before he even reached Maroun, then, gently, carefully, he began to bring him down, step by step.

"John! John!" Maroun cried, clinging to him. "They've got a knife and I'm blind."

"Where are you?"

"I'm in a room."

"O.K., O.K.," Haddad said. "I'm your eyes, I'll see for you. Lift your rifle, draw a bead ninety degrees from where you're facing, a little to your right, a little more, that's it, now you've got the door covered, no-one's going to get through there."

"The windows!"

"I'm watching the windows. No-one can get in. O.K., now rest up a little then I'm going to take you out of that room and pretty soon you're going to see again."

It took another twenty long minutes before the Valium became effective and Maroun passed out.

"Is he going to make it?" Michael asked.

"I think so," Haddad answered. He was mentally exhausted, every inch of his willpower and concentration had been exerted in the battle to save Maroun's mind. He got to his feet.

"Right," he said to Jamil and Joseph. "Take Maroun to my room, he'll sleep twelve, maybe fifteen hours. We'll take it in turns to watch him. Not you," he said to Hourigan, who was making for the door. "You stay here, I want to talk to you."

The others left, the door closed. Hourigan was alone with Haddad and the fear showed in his face. There was great strength in Hourigan's squat body but he had nothing to match the terrifying power of Haddad. Without prior warning and almost in a blur of speed, Haddad flung Hourigan face-on against the wall. Hourigan felt his arm nearly wrenched from the socket and forced up over his back. A hand took the back of his head and smashed his face into the wall again, then it settled like a steel band around his throat. The pain was so great that he was powerless to resist.

"Who told you to do that to Maroun?" Haddad's voice whispered savagely in his ear.

"Stroebling, Stroebling did," Hourigan gasped. "You know he wants him dead. Maroun's so crazy that you can't even look in the bastard's eyes. He's a mad dog, not even you know what he's going to do next."

He felt his neck being bent remorselessly back. He could do nothing to stop it and within a minute or less it was going to break.

"The girl," he screamed, in terror for his life. "We've got the girl."

The pressure remained for a split second more, then Haddad let him drop.

"If Maroun survives," Haddad said coldly, "you'd better pray that I can stop him from killing you."

* * *

Michael found Haddad in the living-room, sitting alone in the darkness. He had left orders to be called but he was already awake. He seemed to be allowing himself less and less sleep.

"I think Maroun's regaining consciousness," Michael said. Haddad followed him to Maroun's bedside. Maroun's eyelids were twitching, he was muttering to himself, tossing restlessly about on the bed. Haddad put his hand out and felt Maroun's forehead. It was hot, clammy, his face was sweating.

"Get me some water and a cloth," Haddad said. Gently he began to sponge down Maroun's face, neck and hands. The feel of the warm cloth soothed Maroun.

"You want me to bring some more Valium?" Michael asked.

Haddad shook his head. "Go and get some sleep," he said. "I'll look after him, it won't be long now."

Shortly after Michael left Maroun seemed to fall into a peaceful sleep. Haddad sat in the darkness beside him. He must have dozed because suddenly he heard Maroun's voice calling.

"Is that you John?"

"Yes, I'm here."

"Don't turn on the light."

"I wasn't going to."

"I like the darkness, I find it soothing."

Haddad said, "You and I are going to have to learn to live without sleep. We can't afford the nightmares, old friend."

Maroun was silent for a moment, then he spoke. "You know, it was weird, I was like a pilot letting down through the fog. I was coming down, down, down, but I couldn't see where to land, I couldn't see a thing. I knew I had to find the way back into my mind and if I missed it I would crash and that would be for ever."

"What else do you remember?"

"Enough to know that Hourigan did it."

"I had hoped that the Valium would have wiped that out."

"No way. John, I'm going to kill him now and nothing you can do or say is going to stop me."

"I know I can't stop you," Haddad agreed. "But if you kill him before I'm ready then I'll lose Kathy."

Maroun was silent.

"How are you feeling?"

"Like I've been kicked around inside a bucket for a week. There's not one part of me that isn't hurting. I can't believe that I let Hourigan do that to me." Maroun's voice was filled with shame. "That I could have been so shit-stupid. I'm vulnerable among people, I'm better on the outside working alone. John, you should never have brought me into the open."

"I had to."

They were silent for a while.

"Yeah, I guess I knew that," Maroun said tiredly. "I've been thinking, they're squeezing Michael, they're squeezing you through Kathy. I don't trust that Brit Cooksley, he's supposed to have a young wife and yet he's sticking his neck right out for us. John, don't you see, they're squeezing so tight from all sides that they're choking us to death. We've got no room left to move, you must let me fight back now while we still can."

"Wait," Haddad said urgently. "Wait, Maroun, be patient, our time will come."

CHAPTER TWENTY-FOUR

"Stop the car here," Mustapha Jumblatt ordered. He was leaning over from the back seat—Michael had to endure his foul-smelling breath as best he could.

Haddad pulled the car into the curb and the three of them walked a few metres along Dresdner Strasse. Behind them ultra-modern high-rise apartment blocks towered over the ghetto.

"It's just what you've been looking for," Jumblatt said, unable to resist trying to sell them the body. "This man I'm taking you to buries everyone, not just the Moslems but all the Gastarbeiters, the poor who live in this part of the city."

The one-eyed Turk pushed open the door of a run-down flower shop. The bell jangled. There was a pause. Then a very tall man with a long, thin face, dressed in an age-shiny black suit, appeared from behind an office fronted by a two-way mirror. He bowed his head to his visitors; he had been expecting them.

"Come with me," he said. "I think I have what you want."

They followed the mortician into the rear of the building, and then down a short ramp to where part of the basement had been extended into a mortuary. As a gesture towards the health regulations the area had been painted white and was harshly lit by neon-fluorescent lights. There were two tile-topped embalming tables in the foreground, then a refrigerated bank of body boxes lining the whole of one wall. The mortician leaned forward and pulled the handle of a body box in the second row. It glided smoothly out on its rollers. He lifted back the shroud covering the contents. Michael was having trouble making himself look at the corpse. Haddad was standing back, checking the facial characteristics with the photograph that he carried. They appeared similar enough to pass a cursory examination.

"The hair colour matches," the mortician said. "I have cut it to fit your description." He was soft-voiced, as befitted his years of dealing with the dead and bereaved, and he must have worked in England at some time because he spoke the language with hardly any accent.

Haddad took the description sheet out of Michael's hands. "Start at the top," he said, "and we'll work down."

"In death, as you know," the mortician began, "the lines and creases fall away from the face and the eyes become vacant. The lack of expression helps to confuse the identity, especially among the aged where their sinuses have collapsed and their figures have shrunk."

"I know," Haddad answered briefly. "Michael, check the feet, make sure there are no obvious marks."

Michael went gingerly to the corpse's feet. There was an identity label tied to the big toe. "Oh Jesus," he said quietly, steeling himself.

Haddad was checking the torso, hands and arms.

"It's O.K. my end," Michael said, stepping back hastily.

"Can you do anything about the two scars on the chest that the description sheet called for?" Haddad asked. The mortician shook his head. "If I tried to draw them in they would be noticed immediately. The description says they are very faint. Unless you think that someone's going to actually look for them it's best to leave them."

Haddad thought quickly. The only person who would be in a position to identify the real Hess after the accident would be the medical orderly travelling with him, and he would already have been taken care of.

"You will see that the height and bone structure are very similar," the mortician said.

"What do you think?" Haddad asked.

Michael was gazing, white-faced, at the corpse. "Good, I guess," he offered hesitantly. "You'd fool me."

"Alright," Haddad said. "Will you be able to persuade the family to part with this old man?"

The mortician shrugged his narrow shoulders. "Why bother the family? I'll bury a dog instead, they won't know."

"Surely the family should receive some money," Michael protested.

"Why create suspicion?" Jumblatt sounded impatient.

"How long can you keep this body in perfect condition?" Haddad enquired.

"If I keep it frozen, as much as eight days."

"You know that we'll want to exchange him with another body and when that happens he must pass for newly dead. Is that possible?"

"Yes, I can arrange that. When you're ready to exchange bodies let me know. I'll require at least eight hours' notice to thaw this one and dry it off for you, then I'll hand him over to you at body temperature. You'll have to transfer him to his destination either very well insulated or in a heated vehicle in order to maintain the body temperature, that is very important."

"How long will we have before rigor mortis sets in?"

"Three to four hours, if you maintain the body temperature. How will you want him dressed?" the mortician enquired.

Haddad made a mental note to ask Cooksley how Hess would be dressed. "We'll send you the clothes when we get them," he said.

They left the shop and made their way back to the car.

"I take it that mortician is entirely reliable?" Haddad asked.

"He is very professional," the Turk replied earnestly. "I have dealt with him on several occasions myself and I trust him, otherwise I wouldn't have recommended his services."

Haddad had no doubt that Mustapha Jumblatt was taking a large percentage of the money that they were paying the mortician.

"I hope you're right," he said. "Because if there's any mistake your head will be on the block as well as his. What's the position with our papers?"

"They will be ready within the next two days."

"Was your photographer able to make the changes to the girl's photograph?"

"Yes, I have seen his work myself, it's perfect. Gentlemen, I'll leave you now," the Turk said when they reached the car. "I'm only a short walk away from my home."

"I've checked on the Panathinaikos football club supporters' package tour. Our people are organised and the tour leader has been bribed," Michael said as they drove back to the safe house. "Once the match is over and the supporters are accounted for, the coaches are locked and leave directly from the Olympic Stadium for Schönefeld. By the way," he added, "Panathinaikos colours are green shirts and white shorts. Since 1946 they have won the league eleven times and in 1977 they completed the double, winning the league and the cup, so it's a hot side we'll be supporting."

"Make sure you brief the others on that." Haddad leaned back. "We're nearly ready to go," he told Michael.

As soon as they reached the house Haddad went to see Maroun.

Jamil moved his huge bulk out of the doorway. "No trouble," he said to Haddad.

Haddad nodded and went into the room. The curtains

were closed, the room was in semi-darkness. Maroun was sitting up with his back propped against the wall.

"This house is no longer secure," Haddad said. "Tomorrow I'm moving everyone out of here—we'll camp in the training area for the last few days before the operation. As soon as you feel strong enough to move I want you to lose yourself, go on the outside again, but stay in touch, O.K.?"

"I'm glad you said that, John," Maroun answered. Again there was that crazy look in his tawny eyes, that flickering mad light. "Sitting here thinking about it, I've become so filled with anger that you're going to have to let me go to war soon."

"I'll let you know when I need you," Haddad said. "It won't be long."

* * *

Haddad met Reed-Henry by the entrance off Heer Strasse to the British and Commonwealth Berlin War Cemetery. They parked their cars in a side road and walked up the incline.

"Do you think you'll be able to bring the vehicle carrying Hess up here?" Reed-Henry asked.

Haddad tested the ground underfoot. "If I use one of the Landrovers I don't see a problem."

"Good," said Reed-Henry. "There's no lighting here and we're out of sight of the autobahn."

At the end of the snow-banked incline on the right were stone-pillared archways, seven in all, leading into the main area of the cemetery. A similar series of archways stood at the opposite end, with a tall white cross surrounded by gravestones in the centre of an unbroken snow-covered area. The remainder of the graves lay in neatly ordered rows, fifty metres to either side of the central cross. A helicopter could have operated easily from there, but Reed-Henry was past pretending that he had any intention of flying Hess to freedom.

"Bring the Landrover up here," Reed-Henry said, marking the spot before the cemetery entrance. "We'll be waiting for you."

Haddad's first thought was that the stone pillars would make an ideal ambush site but he nodded, to indicate his agreement.

"You're determined to go ahead for the evening of Saturday 3rd February?"

"Yes," Haddad said. "The French will have just taken

over the guard at Spandau and the senior officers of the four powers will be relaxing at the weekend. My men are ready—this seems the best time."

"I can't guarantee that my general will decide to stage the 'Rocking Horse Crash Out' then. But I suppose that if someone in Intelligence were to suggest to him that such an exercise on that particular night would catch the Russians off-guard, it might be accepted."

"Any extra confusion would be helpful."

Reed-Henry gave Haddad a thoughtful glance. "How's Stroebling?"

"I can handle him."

Reed-Henry nodded. "So I've heard. I'm glad that you're professional enough not to involve yourself too deeply with that girl. I must say your infatuation over her caused me concern for a while. I was becoming uneasy about on whose side you stood."

Haddad knew that Tom Dade would have reassured him, and he was grateful to Michael.

"What will happen to the girl?" he asked.

Reed-Henry shrugged. "Stroebling's a ruthless man. It's unfortunate that she became implicated, but the stakes are now too high for us to concern ourselves with individuals. That goes for you too, Mr Haddad. I may as well tell you now that unless this operation proceeds smoothly, you and your men will have no chance whatsoever of getting out of Berlin. All the exits to the West are being watched."

"Those are risks I'm paid to undertake," Haddad said. "I understand."

They turned and began to walk down the incline towards their cars.

"Be careful of Stroebling," Reed-Henry warned. "He's planted one of his men on you, and he may still have a sting left in his tail."

"I'll be watching for that," Haddad confirmed. "But I've never been able to understand why you should be so vitally concerned in this. I don't believe it can be just a matter of trying to get the Russian military presence out of West Berlin. What do you want with Hess?"

"Why," Reed-Henry answered innocently, "we're going to give Hess to Stroebling. We've marked a trail for him to the West German right-wing and left it to others to follow. They'll find evidence that Stroebling and some of his colleagues schemed to use Hess to further the old dream of a united Germany. Remember, Hess stood next to Hitler,"

Reed-Henry explained. "There's no one of that stature left in Germany today. He was present when Hitler agreed the pact of steel with Stalin and knew of the secret codicils they entered into to divide Northern Europe. I imagine the Russians would not want to be reminded of that. He was also one of the least culpable of the Nazis in that he tried to stop the war and, properly exploited, he could still evoke an enormous emotional response from a generation who knew a united Germany. The Russians distrust their powerful satellite at the best of times. If we were able to bring the Russians' wrath down upon the East Germans, forcing a purge and a complete re-organisation of their security organisation, then in the confusion, while their links with the urban terror groups are cut, the West could mount a very effective operation to destroy those terror cells."

Reed-Henry made using Hess as bait for Stroebling sound part of the on-going cold war battle between East and West. That was all he was prepared to tell him, but Haddad knew he was still only being given part of the answer.

CHAPTER TWENTY-FIVE

The final run-down began for the operation. The mini-bus brought the last of the equipment and the men's possessions across from the safe house and offloaded it at the warehouse. It was bitterly cold in there; the banks of lights along the centre roof supports blazed ceaselessly down, voices echoed. In the far corner, camp beds with sleeping-bags on top had been set up in rows against the wall. Michael found that sleeping there, inches above the concrete, seemed to draw all the body heat out of him and, adding to the general discomfort, all the food had to be prepared on primus stoves so nothing could be kept warm. The men were tired, their nerves rubbed raw under the increasing pressure, tempers began flaring, but Haddad drove them on ruthlessly.

"Today is Wednesday, the 31st. The operation commences on Saturday 3rd February. We have little more than seventy-hours remaining," he told them urgently. "We've got to get it right, there can be no mistakes. Joseph, remember, as soon as you've carried Hess to the second Landrover you must return, unjam the escort's door and pull both the driver and him out."

"Do we start the fire then?"

"I still haven't decided. If the operation is running smoothly up to that time then I may want to draw as little outside attention as possible to the accident. Wait for my orders on that. Alright," he said to the men, "you can break, get some sleep, we'll start again early in the morning."

Pierre came over to Haddad. "I've been trying to find the time to tell you: the new tenants have contacted me, they want to look over this place."

"Who are they?"

"Some big furniture removal company."

"Stall them until the end of the week, we'll be gone by then. Now go home, old friend, your wife will be worried about you."

Hourigan approached. "Where's Maroun?" he demanded, watching Haddad warily. "Stroebling wants to know."

"Tell your master," Haddad said, "that in order to save your miserable life, I've had to send Maroun away until the night of the accident. Stroebling knows we're going to need him then—after that he's your concern."

* * *

Thursday 1st February.

"It's been confirmed that the British will be holding their military exercise, code-named 'Rocking Horse', commencing at 15.00 hours on the 3rd. Dusk should be at 4.30 p.m.," Haddad said to the men gathered round the wall maps of the accident site at the evening briefing. "Dark, depending on weather conditions, within fifteen minutes of that time. The accident is set for 5.15. Mr Cooksley, do you have everything under control at Spandau?"

"Yes sir, I'll make my move at 16.40 hours but you're going to have to allow me fifteen minutes either way; the problem's to get to Hess while there's no other warder watching."

"Pierre, what's the weather report like?"

"The temperature is expected to remain below freezing—plenty of black ice on the roads."

"Good," Haddad said.

* * *

Friday 2nd February, 6.00 a.m.

Haddad sought Michael out as the others prepared to start the last rehearsals.

"Work with Pierre on the skid-pan this morning," he said. "He needs someone to help him."

The large circular concrete skid-pan was situated near the stock-car arena. In summertime oil was spread over the surface to enable drivers to practise controlling their cars in a skid, but in the winter it was enough to let the snow cover it and freeze into ice. Pierre was waiting for him, working under the bonnet of the Mercedes, assisted by young Angelo.

"Hey," he accused Michael cheerfully, "you're late."

"I'm sorry, I had trouble finding this place."

"No problem, it's just Haddad and I worry about you after what happened to Kathy. This is my mechanic," Pierre said to Michael. He grabbed the child by the scruff of his neck and pulled him from under the bonnet. "Angelo, say hello," Pierre ordered.

Shyly the small boy nodded from behind his father.

"What are you doing to the car?" Michael asked.

"Tell him," Pierre said, pulling his son forward. He was trying to help him to overcome his chronic shyness. "We are a team; I drive, he's the mechanic. That right?"

"That's right," Angelo agreed. "We've checked the cables, wheels and bodywork all round, tuned the motor and adjusted the brakes, especially the handbrake. That's all Mr Haddad would let us do."

"I take it you can drive?" Pierre asked.

Michael nodded.

"Good, get in. I'll show you what I'm trying to do, then I'll tell you how you can help me."

Michael climbed into the Mercedes beside Pierre.

"Buckle yourself in," Pierre ordered.

The boy let down the bonnet and slapped the grille to show that it was fastened.

Pierre pointed to a line of tyres that stretched across the far end of the skid-pan. "That's the convoy," he said, "coming down Heer Strasse."

He gunned the engine and the car moved off along the ramp. Michael felt himself being pressed back against the seat. "I have to accelerate to approximately 150 kilometres an hour to gain enough forward velocity before I can break into the spins," Pierre shouted above the noise of the engine.

They came off the good surface of the ramp onto the skid-pan and now Pierre was fighting for control of the car, the wheel bucking in his hands. As the needle on the speedometer touched 150 kilometres, Pierre swung the wheel slightly to the right, then left. Michael was pinned to the seat as the car came round in a fast three hundred and sixty degree turn. Pierre brought the car out of the spin and repeated the manoeuvre. They careered round, moving towards the tyres that represented the ambulance. The noise inside the car and the effect of the horizon spinning past the windscreen was terrifying. The Mercedes scattered the tyres and came to a stop at the far edge of the skid-pan.

Michael lay back in his seat. He felt a pumping sensation in his chest, his head was full of blood from the "G" force and his eyes were red. "Dear God," he said weakly, "how often have you practised that?"

"All the time," Pierre answered cheerfully. "The Mercedes is low, the centre of gravity of the ambulance is high. If I can hit the tail of the Mercedes against the rear wheel arch of the ambulance, the ambulance will topple and the Mercedes will continue to spin and effectively block the second R.M.P. Landrover."

Michael shook his head to clear the blood from his eyes. "You hit those tyres without any trouble. What do you want me to do?" he asked fearfully.

"Those tyres aren't moving," Pierre replied. "I'll be approaching the convoy at 150 kilometres an hour, they'll be coming towards me at approximately 80, our combined speeds will total 230 kilometres an hour. I've tried timing myself to gauge the speed in which to close the distance but that's not effective."

Pierre pulled the Mercedes up to where Angelo was waiting beside two garishly painted stock-cars. They were massive, fitted with roll bars and wire mesh screens. Pierre got out and patted one of them on the side.

"This is the ambulance, the one I want you to drive." He pointed to the other one, "And that's the Mercedes. Do you think you could hold a steady eighty kilometres an hour in a straight line over the skid-pan?"

Michael nodded dumbly. "Are you going to crash into me?" he asked.

Pierre grinned. "Don't worry, you won't go over. In fact, in this monster, you'll hardly feel a thing."

There was only one seat. They strapped Michael in. Pierre put his head to the wire screen and shouted above the beat of the engine, "Hold the line, when you see me coming don't let yourself swerve."

At the first two attempts Pierre missed Michael altogether, but then he got the knack and with a tearing crash of metal he struck Michael solidly in the side.

"Shit," Michael shouted to himself above the roar of the engine when he saw Pierre coming at him again, bitterly regretting that he had ever let himself get talked into this. "Oh, shit, shit, shit!"

When Michael thought that his teeth were coming loose from his gums, that every bone in his body had been shaken apart, Pierre called a halt.

"That's good," he said. "I feel much more confident. Now no matter what the other driver does I'll get him, because if I miss him with the side-swipe I'll get him with my tail." Pierre glanced at his watch. "Go and park the car—Haddad wants us back at the training area at 18.00 hours for the final dress-rehearsal."

Michael parked and climbed out shakily through the window.

Angelo was waiting for him. "Do you think my father's going to be alright?" he asked, trying to hide his concern.

"Sure," Michael answered feelingly. "He knows what he's doing."

"Yes, he's the best driver in the country," Angelo told him proudly.

* * *

Friday, 8.00 p.m.

The men were tired now, almost to the point of exhaustion: even Haddad was showing the strain. At the end of the run-through he drew the men around him. To one side the waiting Landrovers gleamed under the warehouse lights. They were painted in the British Royal Military Police colours with the red stripe down the sides, and correct to the last detail of the Martin horn and the blue beacon light on the roof.

"That was pretty good," Haddad said. The men deserved their praise: the final rehearsal had gone almost without a hitch.

"Mustapha Jumblatt," Haddad indicated the Turk who had joined them on that last day, "will be waiting outside Spandau. He'll be in contact with us over the two-way radio and he'll let us know which ambulance is carrying Hess. The ambulance will be marked and Jumblatt will follow the convoy to check that the R.M.P.s don't change its position. Anybody want to ask anything?"

"Yes," Pierre said. "Could Jumblatt give me a commentary on the speed of the convoy as it approaches along Heer Strasse? If he lets me know when he passes Pichelsdorf, I'll time my run from that."

"Very good," the Turk said.

"Anything else? Mr Cooksley, have you anything to say?"

"Yes sir. You've shaken down well," he told the men. "No one's going to mistake you for a scruffy shower like the 2nd Paras now." The jibe was intended for Hourigan and it found its mark. "Remember," Cooksley continued, "the accident will take place after dark tomorrow, it will be bitterly cold and you'll be in great-coats with the peaks of your caps pulled well down over your eyes, so only a few inches of your face will be exposed. You'll be too busy getting on with the job to talk, but if one of the other R.M.P.s should approach you just swear horribly about the cold and move out of his way. And that reminds me, while I've been putting you through your paces these last few days, I've heard some of you swearing. God knows what language you were using, it sounded like Arabic to me. If you do that on the day, you're finished, so remember, swear in English. Get Hourigan here to teach you. If you can swear like a bog Irishman then no-one's going to bother trying to understand you."

Hourigan had a short-fused temper at the best of times; by now he'd been baited into a fury by Cooksley's jibes.

"Fuck you, Cooksley," Hourigan swore at him. "Let me tell you, good Irishmen have killed plenty of your bloody British soldiers. Derry, Bogside, Bloody Friday, I was there. What's your darling British Army coming to? You're putting young boys on the streets but that doesn't stop me shooting them and watching them go down kicking."

Cooksley's face had gone pale with the memory of men in his unit struck down and bleeding their lives out on the rubble-strewn slum streets of Belfast. "I know you," he whispered murderously. "I've known you all along, you I.R.A. bastard, you fucking murderer, hiding behind your women, using children to carry your guns."

Hourigan advanced menacingly from the ranks, his little eyes glowing with savage delight. "I'm going to take you now, Cooksley," he gloated sadistically. "You may think you've still got the strength but you're too old now to stop me."

"Get back, Hourigan," Haddad ordered.

"Leave him, sir," Cooksley said calmly. "He's got this lesson coming."

"You two can settle your feud after tomorrow," Haddad said. "Until then I can't allow either of you to be damaged. Hourigan, break off now or I'll stop you myself!" The voice cut like a lash and Haddad moved swiftly to intervene. That threat was effective: Hourigan stopped closing in on Cooksley and raging, turned back to rejoin the others.

The Irishman had thought to use his fists and his boots and his bullet-shaped head to reduce Cooksley to a bloody pulp, but Cooksley had other ideas. All attention had been riveted on the confrontation between Haddad and Hourigan: noone had been watching the warrant officer. Now he lifted his hand from his side. He was holding a revolver.

"Hourigan!" he called sharply.

As the Irishman turned, the report from the heavy-calibre revolver crashed across the empty warehouse and echoed in the rafters. The bullet ripped into Hourigan's stomach. He was knocked backwards by the impact, then he sank onto his knees. With no-one close enough to stop him, Cooksley calmly thumbed back the hammer and the second bullet exploded in Hourigan's chest just above his heart. Hourigan went down, writhing on the ground, clutching his stomach wound, screaming with pain. Cooksley quickly crossed the few paces between them and cold-bloodedly, to make sure there was no doubt, put the gun barrel to Hourigan's temple and blew out his brains.

Haddad looked at the body, then at Cooksley. "What have you done to us?" he said, stunned.

"You can get by without him, sir," the warrant officer answered him steadily. "Major Reed-Henry's compliments. He wanted the pressure taken off you. He didn't want Hourigan at the scene of the accident with his gun at your back, it would have given the major reason to doubt your loyalty—and it's too late for Stroebling to bring in another man."

"What happens to the girl?" Haddad asked bitterly, knowing that he had been trapped.

"The major says she's expendable," Cooksley replied. "He said you had accepted that."

"He's a very ruthless man, your major," Haddad said calmly.

"Yes sir." Cooksley recognised the controlled, deadly anger in Haddad's voice. "People are fooled by his appearance but, as you say, he's a very ruthless, very clever man. It would be best to follow his orders. Well, sir, my work is done, I'll say goodbye now. You won't want me around any more and I'm due back on duty at Spandau." He turned to the men whom he had trained and lived with. He had grown to care about them and the strain of leaving them showed in his angular, raw-boned face. "Good luck for tomorrow night," he said.

Haddad walked Cooksley to the door of the warehouse.

"It never was the money with you, was it?" Haddad asked.

The warrant officer shook his head. "No, sir, call it old-fashioned if you like but my loyalty's to my Queen and country, it always has been. You'll manage without Hourigan," he added reassuringly. "I've been watching the rehearsals. With men as strong as Jamil and Joseph to help you, you can take on Hourigan's job as well as your own. Your English is good enough to see you through and the authority accorded by the royal ciphers of a British regimental sergeant-major will sit well on your shoulders, sir. Just remember, the British Army's full of colonels and generals and relations of the Queen but the R.S.M. stands next to God. If an officer from another unit should interfere at the scene of the accident, don't actually tell him to bugger off, just recommend that he does and he'll get the message quick enough."

They reached the door. Cooksley turned and held out his hand, "No hard feelings, sir," he said as Haddad took it, "It's a pity that you aren't British, it would have been a pleasure to serve with you."

Haddad closed the door, turned and went back to the others.

"Get the badges of rank and the buttons changed to my uniform," he said to Joseph. "Then dispose of the body."

"What are we going to do?" Michael asked, his mind paralysed by the implications of Hourigan's death. The other men were just beginning to understand fully the forces weighed against them.

"Nothing changes," Haddad said, his dark eyes blazing, his extraordinary willpower dominating his men. "We continue with the plan except that now I take over as the R.S.M."

CHAPTER TWENTY-SIX

Friday night, 2nd February.

As the last hours ticked away before the operation a feeling of tension pervaded the warehouse. None of the men could sleep. Haddad summoned Michael to him in the middle of the night. Michael knew what was on Haddad's mind.

"Kathy?" he asked.

Haddad nodded.

"How long before Stroebling finds out?"

"Hourigan should have reported in tonight. I'll have to contact Stroebling in the morning, it'll be dangerous to stall longer than that."

"Oh Christ," Michael muttered, sick at heart and scared. "He's going to kill Kathy."

Haddad was silent for a few moments, then he said, "There's a way we can turn Hourigan's death to our advantage, but it would involve considerable risk to you."

"What do you have in mind?" Michael asked cautiously.

"I want to offer you to Stroebling to hold as a second hostage, as a gesture of my good faith. Your life will then be equally at risk with Kathy's. Do you accept this?"

"Will it keep Kathy alive any longer?"

"Maybe the extra few hours that we need."

"Well, then," Michael said, summoning all his courage, "what choice have I got? I'll do it."

"When I've made the deal with Stroebling I'll put you on the streets where Stroebling's men can take you. Maroun will be watching, we'll use you to lead him to their safe house."

"So I'm to be the decoy." Michael was thinking fast.

"They'll be moving her around—there's no other way we can find that safe house," Haddad said. "I'm gambling on the fact that Stroebling will hold you and Kathy in the same house in the West that he intends to bring Hess back to after the accident."

Michael took off his glasses and began to polish them. "You've been planning this all along," he accused hesitantly. "I remember now noticing that you were understudying Hourigan's role—you intended to take his place from the start. If Cooksley hadn't killed Hourigan you or Maroun would have done it tonight."

Haddad shrugged. He saw no point in lying to Michael.

"I couldn't allow Stroebling to have his man at our backs after we'd recovered Hess from the accident. None of us would have survived that. As it is, Reed-Henry has assisted me by using his own man to kill Hourigan. He's kept us uninvolved and at the same time convinced himself that we have no option but to accept his control over us."

"You made sure all along that there would be no role for me in the operation, that I would be expendable at this time," Michael said with a shock of realisation. "Haddad, you ruthless bastard, I was just beginning to relax and like you and you were planning to put my head in a noose all the time."

"I didn't ask you to come here," Haddad answered coldly. "I would have given anything to keep Kathy uninvolved, but now we've all got to take risks in order to survive. Michael," he said, unbending a little, "do you think it's been easy for me to let Stroebling taunt me with Kathy, to lie still while both sides chew over our bones? They manoeuvre us this way, they manoeuvre us that way, they think they have all the power while we have none. Well, that's good," Haddad said harshly, his dark eyes gleaming. "Let them think that, because I've waited and waited and laid my plans and tomorrow is our day."

* * *

Saturday 3rd February.

Haddad raised the men early that last morning. With Hourigan dead and Cooksley gone there seemed pitifully few of them remaining to undertake such a vastly complicated operation, but Haddad gave them no time to consider the odds mounted against them.

"Check through all the kit and equipment, that includes the Landrovers," he ordered. "Then Jamil, Joseph, I want the three of us to run over our part in the accident without Hourigan."

Haddad glanced at Michael whose imagination had been running riot half the night. His nerves were stretched tight, he looked a wreck.

"Michael, go help Pierre on the skid-pan," Haddad told him, wanting to keep his mind occupied. "I'll come for you when I've made the arrangements with Stroebling."

* * *

"The death of this man will have serious consequences both for you and for me," Stroebling said threateningly when Haddad managed to contact him on the telephone.

"I kept to my bargain," Haddad protested. "It was through no fault of mine. You know Hourigan looked for trouble."

"This man Cooksley who killed him," Stroebling was violently suspicious, "he works for Reed-Henry?"

"Yes."

"Where is he now?"

"Back at Spandau."

"Mr Haddad, what security do I have now that my man is dead?" Stroebling asked coldly.

"You still hold the girl."

"That's not enough. Who else can you give me as a guarantee of your good faith?"

"I need all my men—we have to do Hourigan's work as well as our own."

"Then I must send one of my men to watch over you," Stroebling said.

"I can't accept that, there's no time to train him. We'll be working right under the noses of the British Army—one false move from your man and he'll destroy us all." Haddad paused. "I will give you Michael Lakas," he said. "You know that he's my principal, the man who holds my contract."

"What does a man like Michael Lakas mean to you?" Stroebling scoffed.

Haddad laughed. It was the same laugh Stroebling had heard once before, near the Church of Reconciliation: intense, controlled and terrible. He understood when Haddad said, "He's the girl's brother, now you'll have both of them."

"Very well," Stroebling agreed. "How soon can you deliver him to me?"

"Not immediately, because we're making our final preparations," Haddad stalled. "Do you know the AEG-Telefunken building on the Ernest Reuter-Platz?"

"Of course."

"I'll leave him there for you shortly after 3 p.m."

"Make sure that he's well exposed on the pavement, we don't want to have to go into the building to get him."

"Have any of our other arrangements changed?"

"None, everything remains the same as Hourigan last briefed you."

"The operation commences at approximately 5.15 p.m. this evening. Look for our signal, we'll want you at the scene of the accident to collect the patient from us as soon as possible after that."

"And the British?"

"They'll be waiting to receive him at Tegel airport, that's forty minutes away. Herr Stroebling, if for any reason we can't make the transfer to you at the scene of the accident then five hundred metres further up the road is the British and Commonwealth War Cemetery. The entrance is set back well clear of any specatators. We'll meet you there—one of my men will direct you."

"Very good," Stroebling said.

Haddad wasn't certain but he thought he detected a tension, an excitement creep into Stroebling's voice.

"When do I get my hostages back?" he asked.

"When I have Hess."

"That's not good enough," Haddad argued. "What guarantees do I have?"

"Mr Haddad, you are in no position to bargain or even ask for guarantees, you never were," Stroebling reminded him.

"Then I must speak to the girl. I have no wish to hand Michael Lakas over to you unless I'm certain she's alright."

Stroebling thought for a moment. "Very well," he said.

"Is she there?"

"Yes."

Haddad waited while Kathy was brought to the phone.

"Oh John, John, John," she said, when she heard his voice. All her thoughts in her terrible isolation had been centred around him. "I love you, John."

Haddad made his words sound warm; he wanted to give her some of his strength. "Kathy, hold on, it's nearly over. We're going in tonight and it's going to be alright, I promise you, everything's going to be alright."

Kathy was strained and emotionally overwrought from her long periods of confinement in a small dark room. She was having trouble answering him and in his mind's eye Haddad could see her clutching the receiver, needing desperately now all the reassurance he was trying to give her.

"Michael's coming, he'll stay with you a little while," Haddad broke the news to her gently. "It's not serious, Stroebling wants to hold more security, but you're going to be alright, Kathy," Haddad said sharply. There was a steely quality in his voice now that made her take note of his words. "Michael will be coming in some time after 4 p.m., now get yourself together so you can expect him. You don't want him to see you a wreck."

"No," Kathy said wryly, getting a grip on herself. "No, of course not."

"Alright, Mr Haddad, finish now," Stroebling cut in. "You've had more than enough time to trace this number."

Stroebling took the receiver from her and replaced it. Kathy found it hard to look at him. The ghastly, unhealthy pale face and glittering eyes, and the smell of death about the man frightened her and she turned her head away.

"Collect what possessions you have," Stroebling said to her. "We're moving on to another house now."

* * *

Twelve noon, Saturday.

"He's here," Pierre said.

Michael withdrew his head from under the bonnet of the Mercedes and looked up. Across the snow-covered skid-pan was the black-coated figure of Haddad, waiting for him like the angel of death.

"Well, I guess I'd better be going," Michael muttered. He fumbled with the tools he had been using, trying to put them back in the box.

"Leave it," Pierre said. "You've already dropped a screw-driver and two spanners into the engine."

Michael had used his time with Pierre to try to control his fear. He told himself that he was ready now, but Pierre saw the effort it took for him to square his shoulders and lift his head and his heart went out to the stocky little man. He went up to Michael and took his hand between his good one and the steel claw.

"Good luck," he said sincerely.

"Hell, it's nothing," Michael replied. "I'm just going for a ride—it's you that needs the luck. Take care of yourself with that car, don't do anything crazy."

"After your help it will be a piece of cake," Pierre told him cheerfully.

Haddad, waiting in the car, was becoming impatient. Michael made his way towards him through the snow.

"Did you speak to Stroebling?" he asked as he climbed in.

"Yes," Haddad said as the car moved forward. "His men

will pick you up shortly after 3 p.m. You've got a lot of work to get through before then."

Michael followed Haddad into the warehouse. Camp beds and sleeping-bags, together with all other signs of human occupation, had been cleared away, the wall plans of the accident and the scale model burned. All that remained now were the waiting Landrovers, still and gleaming under the lights. In the far corner of the warehouse the hunched figures of Jamil, Joseph and Maroun worked over packing-crates left by the previous tenants; around them were scattered little piles of empty shotgun cartridge cases.

Maroun stood up as they approached. He was looking a lot better than when Michael had last seen him. He had gathered strength from his time alone.

"How's it coming on?" Haddad asked.

"We're nearly finished," Maroun answered.

He signalled Michael to him and fitted on the heavy black cloth overcoat that they had been working on. Maroun stood back and looked it over critically.

"Button it up," he ordered Michael.

Bewildered, Michael did as he was told.

"It looks good," Maroun said at last. "Nothing shows."

"What have you done with it?" Michael asked.

"We've put a layer of fluffed-up cottonwool under the lining," Maroun explained. "It's been coated with double-base nitro cellulose."

Michael glanced down and saw the grey flakes from the shotgun cartridge charges on the packing-case tops.

"Around the hem of the coat," Maroun continued, "we've put plastic explosives rolled as thin as pancake strips. I'm going to need a diversion to get into the house where they'll be holding you and Kathy, and this is it. The first thing this coat is going to do is burn like hell and then hopefully, as Stroebling's men rush to put it out, it's going to explode. To set it off we need some form of igniter and this is it," Maroun said, holding up a fountain-pen. "In the rubber tube where the ink would normally be stored we've put in a tiny glass ampoule of sulphuric acid. The remainder of the barrel has been filled with a fifty per cent potassium chlorate and sugar solution. A fine piece of celluloid has been glued under the filler-lever to stop any fluid leaking through here. Just before they take you into the house pull the filler-lever back hard—you've got to feel the ampoule break—then replace the pen in your inside pocket. There's a piece of fuse wire connecting the pocket to the plastic explosive in the hem. Now," Maroun continued before Michael could speak, "Hourigan will have made a full report on you. They know how badly you react to violence, they'll have searched you for weapons and found nothing. We've left enough ink with the sulphuric acid ampoule in the rubber tube for some suspicious bastard to be able to write his name."

"We're counting on Stroebling's men to be lax," Haddad cut in. "They know we'll be fully occupied by the accident—the last thing they'll be expecting is Maroun to follow you in."

"Once you pull that lever," Maroun said, "you're a walking bomb. We tried to fit the thickest tube we could and time the acid eating through it. I reckon you've got ten minutes, so get rid of that coat when you reach the house. It shouldn't be hard. If you have to, go to the lavatory and leave it there. But if you're stuck in the same room as that coat then count the minutes in your mind, get back from it as far as you can, but whatever you do, don't let yourself keep looking at it."

"Michael, we've purposely insured that they'll have very little time to settle down," Haddad said. "The guards won't be expecting an explosion inside the house. During the confusion, if you're with Kathy, just hold her flat on the ground, don't make a move until Maroun comes for you. If you aren't with her, but she's near enough to hear you, shout to her to stay down. Maroun's got a few scores to settle, there's going to be a lot of shrapnel flying around that house."

"One last thing," Maroun said. "When Haddad leaves you on that street keep your eyes down, don't look for me. I'll be there, but don't look for me because the opposition, unless they are complete fools, will be watching before they move in to pick you up. And the coat, remember not to watch the coat."

Michael noticed that Maroun wasn't relaxed any more: there was an underlying tension growing in him now like a spring coiling. He was breathing just a little faster, his nostrils flaring—in his eyes you could see nothing except the madness of a killer. Michael was scared half to death of Maroun like this: at least, he thought, they were on the same side.

"That's all," Maroun said. "I'll go now. I want plenty of time to take up my position."

"Has Jumblatt provided you with the men to help as he promised?" Haddad asked.

"Yeah," Maroun's gold earring flashed as he tossed his head, impatient to be off. "They're waiting for me. I'll use their help to tag Michael but once we've found where he is I'm going in alone. O.K.?"

"O.K.," Haddad agreed.

Maroun glanced across at Michael and shrugged: he didn't like greetings or farewells. "I'll see you," he said.

An hour later Haddad led Michael to the car. As they crossed the Havel river at Schulenburg Strasse they passed a convoy of British army lorries rumbling in the opposite direction: the "Rocking Horse" exercise had started. The infantry, armoured cars and tanks would be on their way to take up defensive positions against a simulated Russian attack. The families of the soldiers would be being picked up from their homes and taken to the Royal Air Force base in Gatow for evacuation. No matter how often they practised it, the first couple of hours of the operation were always pretty confused.

"Give me a run-down one more time on what happens before and after the accident," Haddad said.

Michael answered, sitting stiffly back in his seat, forcing himself to think clearly. "4.30 p.m.—the match is over and the crowds are still coming out of the Olympic Football Stadium. 4.50 p.m.—dark. 5.15 approximately—the accident. 6.00 p.m.—the buses take on the supporters at the Olympic Stadium. They'll have had to wait for the team. 8.15 p.m.—the plane takes off from Schönefeld."

"O.K.," Haddad said. "Then you understand that you and Maroun and Kathy have to make it back to the stadium by 6.00 p.m., not later than that?"

"What are you going to do if Stroebling has outsmarted you and decides to hold us in the East?" Michael asked.

"I've told Maroun to stop the car before it crosses the wall."

"That will mean Kathy's finished."

"Perhaps," Haddad answered. "She'll have to take her chances with Stroebling, I have no other choice. If you cross the wall I'll lose you both." Haddad spoke with his eyes fixed on the road ahead. "But I don't think it will come to that. Each time either of us have spoken to Stroebling it's been in the West, he's got plenty of contacts and he seems to feel safer over here."

"Well, if we lose we lose," Michael said stubbornly. "Tell Maroun to let the car go through and get yourselves out of Berlin. We started all this and if it's got to end bloody then I guess I'd like to be with Kathy when it does, but there's something important you can do for me. If I don't make it,

I want you to contact the committee on human rights that Kathy and I were part of. We've been in touch with them and they've agreed to help. I've listed their names here." Michael gave Haddad an envelope which he slipped into his pocket. "Get Hess to them," he said. "They'll know what to do and at least something good will come out of this mess."

They were nearing the Ernest Reuter-Platz. Michael was acutely conscious of the inflammable material used to fill the lining of the bulky black coat he was wearing so uncomfortably. His fingers kept stealing to his inside pocket to feel the top of the pen.

Haddad drew up outside the A.E.G. building. Michael fought down the fear that swamped him now they had arrived.

"Remember," Haddad told him, "stand at the edge of the pavement and don't look for Maroun."

Before Michael opened the car door, he said bitterly: "Kathy and I were used as the fall guys right from the start, weren't we? You realised that but we never did. We never understood the politics, we just cared about the ideal." He shrugged wretchedly.

Haddad reached across and took Michael's face between his hands. Throughout that day Haddad had shown no emotion, coldly, deliberately following each step of the plan, but now, to Michael's amazement, he saw in Haddad's face—concern for him.

"Michael," Haddad said urgently, "you remember you once told me that you could never pull the trigger. Well, you aren't an academic any more, forget your civilisation. You're one of us now—if you get the chance to save Kathy or yourself, pull that trigger." Haddad was embarrassed by his display of emotion. He removed his hands and in doing so touched Michael on the shoulder.

"Take care of yourself," he said.

Haddad pulled away, leaving Michael standing on the pavement. It was 3 o'clock on a winter's afternoon and the cold grey dusk was settling down over the city. Michael, as he waited for the car that was coming to collect him, knew that he had never felt so frightened or so alone.

CHAPTER TWENTY-SEVEN

A large black Mercedes pulled up against the pavement some thirty metres from where Michael was standing. He had been watching the passing traffic, and now instinct warned him that this was the car. He couldn't see any of the occupants through the tinted glass windows and, when they waited without making any effort to contact him, Michael wondered nervously if he was supposed to walk towards it. He was still debating with himself when an arm from behind went through his, forcing it away from his side.

"Herr Lakas?" a voice asked softly over his shoulder.

Michael nodded. The back door of the Mercedes opened and he was hurried towards it and forced into the back seat. The man slid in beside him, closed the door and the Mercedes glided smoothly away. The street lights hadn't yet been turned on and it was almost dark inside the car. A large man in the front passenger seat leaned silently across, grasped Michael by either hand and wrenched him violently forward so that his neck was pinned over the top of the front seat, his arms stretched painfully out in front of him. The man who had pulled Michael off the pavement began to search him. He checked the underarms and pockets, then felt along the collar of the coat, over the shoulder pads and down the sides. He found the pen, took it out and unscrewed the cap. Michael twisted his head to see what he was doing.

"That pen is valuable to me," he gasped painfully. "For my work. Please don't break it."

It was an old, well-used, battered pen. The man shook it by his ear and heard the liquid swirl in the barrel, then he scratched the nib along the back of his hand, noting the broad ink mark it left. He put the pen back in Michael's pocket and continued with the body search.

"Alright," he pronounced himself satisfied at last in German. "It's good."

The big man in the front passenger seat let Michael's hands go and he felt the numbing pain as the blood flowed into them again. The driver had been weaving the Mercedes in and out of the streets. He glanced in the mirror, checked the road one last time.

"It's clear," he announced and everyone in the car relaxed except Michael.

* * *

4.00 p.m.

Pierre dressed quietly in the bedroom. René had said that she wanted to rest after he had left, and she was lying under the bedcovers with her face turned away from him. She knew that there was nothing more to be said and yet there was so much suddenly that she wanted to tell him. Pierre's suffering, as a result of his injuries, had seemed to strengthen his character, making him warmer, kinder, more tolerant and, until now, less ambitious. It had drawn them closer together, even through the misery of being stateless menials in Berlin, and she loved him, dear God, how she loved him. She heard Pierre making his way around to her side of the bed. He lifted away the cover to kiss her and found her face wet with tears.

"This is a small thing I have to do," he said reassuringly. "I'll be back within two hours, three at the most, and by then we'll have won our freedom from all this."

"I told the children to stay in their room," René said, knowing that he would want to see them.

Pierre nodded. He went softly down the passage and opened their door. Angelo was amusing his sister with some crayons on the floor. Pierre lifted the child up and kissed her, then he kissed Angelo. The boy had been waiting for him all afternoon in that room.

"Aren't you going to need your mechanic?" he asked, his enormous brown eyes pleading to be allowed to go too.

Pierre shook his head. "No," he answered gently. "Thanks to my mechanic the car is tuned perfectly. I'll have to manage without you tonight."

He closed the door, stood outside for a moment, then he picked up his coat. René, from her room, heard the front door close.

* * *

The mini-bus swung into the warehouse. Haddad and Jumblatt were waiting for it. Haddad was dressed in the greatcoat and uniform of a British regimental sergeant-major. Joseph lifted out the corpse that he and Jamil had just collected from the mortician.

"It's in perfect condition," he told Haddad as he carried it to the second Landrover.

Haddad helped him strap the corpse into the stretcher and place it under a thermal sleeping-bag with heating pads inside it. The brothers changed into their uniforms. Jumblatt collected their civilian clothes and placed them in the mini-bus, then he swung into the driver's seat.

"Have you got all the entry visas, tickets, passports and clothes?" Haddad asked, checking again.

"I have everything," the Turk assured him.

"Go to your position then," Haddad said.

Jumblatt drove the mini-bus out of the warehouse. Haddad brought the brothers to attention and inspected them carefully. The afternoon was freezing under the snowy winter sky. The time as 4.15: it would be dark within twenty minutes. The warehouse doors were thrown open, the Landrovers came through, one following the other. Joseph ran after them, closing the doors and locking the outside gates, then he climbed into the first Landrover beside Haddad.

They drove down Gatow Strasse, past military trucks and convoys swarming in and out of the nearby British Army barracks. They passed that test—no one gave their vehicles a second glance. On they drove past Spandau fortress with its massive towers, dark and bleak in the fading light. They turned into Heer Strasse at the road junction. It was a short run from there to take up position in the side road at Pichelsdorf. Haddad directed Jamil as he backed the second Landrover out of sight amongst the trees and banked-up snow. He left it there and took over the wheel of the first Landrover. Haddad sat beside him, Joseph moved into the back. The time was 4.35.

* * *

Michael couldn't make out where they were going, but the car seemed to have travelled only a short distance from the centre of West Berlin when it stopped and he was hustled out and up the steps of a suburban house. The front door opened as they reached it. Michael was taken straight through the hall to a well-furnished living-room and made to sit in a chair before a writing-desk. He had hardly time to take in his surroundings before another car drew up. The front door was flung open again, he heard a voice which he began to recognise and then Stroebling came into the room. Kathy followed him between two young, blonde-haired, cold-eyed youths. Stroebling glanced at Michael.

"Have you searched him thoroughly?" he said to the guard.

The guard nodded.

"Very good, put them together."

Michael was pulled to his feet. He disregarded the guard's arm on his shoulders—all his attention was on Kathy. Her face was pale and drawn and her eyes almost without hope.

"They are going to kill us, Michael," she said.

"They can't," Michael protested. "We're hostages, Haddad won't give up Hess without us."

"They're going to take him anyway."

"That's not the agreement!" Michael shouted.

"Don't be stupid," Stroebling answered in English, impatiently looking up from the message he was reading. "I can't allow you to live. If not myself, you could incriminate my men."

"But Haddad promised!"

"He can do nothing. If you choose to put your faith in some half-caste Arab then I'm afraid that's your affair," Stroebling said coldly. "When this is finished none of you will be left."

* * *

In his Landrover, parked unobtrusively in the snow-covered side road some 150 metres in from Heer Strasse, Haddad lifted his two-way radio and extended the aerial.

"Maroun," Haddad said into the receiver, "Maroun."

"I hear you man," Maroun's voice came back.

"Have you found them?"

"I'm there," Maroun breathed triumphantly. "I followed them in."

Maroun had come in over the back fence, broken through the kitchen door, was was now in the second-storey front bedroom of the house across the street from Michael. The owners, fortunately, were out and one of Jumblatt's men waited downstairs to pacify them should they return unexpectedly. The sight of Maroun in their bedroom would probably have killed them with fright. His hair was swept back and his face painted up for night ambushing. On the quilt he had laid out his weapons for their final check.

"Do you know where you are?"

"Some suburb called Wedding, it's close to the city. Stroebling arrived less than five minutes ago, he's got Kathy with him."

"Guards?"

"Plenty—I'm still trying to figure out how many."

* * *

Warrant Officer Cooksley left the medical room at Spandau and closed the door behind him. The whole prison was silent, except for the echo of his footsteps as he walked past the closed cells on either side to the cell door at the end. He opened the locks with keys he carried on his belt and went inside. A wizened, grey-haired old man turned guiltily from the narrow desk where he had been writing. It was with relief that he recognised Cooksley. The old man had a suspicious nature and Cooksley, with his bluff, honest face, had put a great deal of effort into trying to win his confidence.

"It's setting in for a bitter cold night," Cooksley said. "And your chest's been playing up lately. Doctor says you should breathe into this, it'll ease any congestion." He held out a simple plastic inhaler of the type used by asthmatics.

The time as 4.40 p.m.

* * *

Haddad called up Jumblatt. "Are you in position?" he asked.

"Yes," Jumblatt replied. He was in the mini-bus parked in Adam Srasse directly across from the entrance to Spandau.

"Pierre?" Haddad called.

"I'm in position," Pierre confirmed. He had parked the Mercedes in a cobbled access lane parallel to Heer Strasse, opposite the British and Commonwealth War Cemetery.

"Remember, Pierre," Haddad said, "there's no Maroun now to back you up if you miss, so the accident's got to come off perfectly."

"I know," Pierre replied. He settled back in his seat and waited.

* * *

Maroun stripped and carefully checked his weapons, then he began to arm himself. On the bandoliers that he wore crossed over his chest he hooked three olive-green M.26 fragmentation grenades down one side. On the other side he hooked three equally lethal but lighter RGD 5 anti-personnel hand-grenades. Under his jacket, in a holster fitted into the small of his back, he placed a black-handled Browning high-power automatic. Then from the bed he lifted a squat, evil-looking Uzi sub-machine-gun. He snapped the thirty-round magazine home with the palm of his hand, set the safety catch and slung the Uzi over his shoulder to keep his arms free. The four spare magazines he fitted into their slings on the bandolier. By the window rested the heavy Dragunov sniper's rifle, the first weapon he would use. He went to it and picked it up. Two of Stroebling's guards were patrolling the street in front of the safe house.

* * *

It was another warder who raised the alarm at Spandau. Hess had collapsed, his face had taken on a dusty blue colour, he was in shock and gasping for breath. The effect was so sudden and severe, so dramatic, that it confused the mind of the medical orderly on duty. The French governor was summoned. He was a short fat man and he arrived in a muck sweat, having run the length of the jail.

"What is it?" he demanded, barging into the cell.

The orderly looked down at Hess's face. "Diagnosing from the general stressed appearance, noting the blue around his lips, I think he's having a heart attack, sir," he said.

"Mon dieu!" the Frenchman yelled in alarm. "Not in my prison, not in the month we're on guard!" The Russians would be suspicious—they would make accusations. "Get him out of here," the French governor spluttered, shedding the responsibility fast. "I want him out of here—call the British."

* * *

The call went through to the British Military Police operations room, which was attached to Military Headquarters at the Olympic Stadium. It was close enough to the sports stadium for the men to have heard, all afternoon, the roar of the football crowds. A German police liaison officer passed the call on to a British M.P. warrant officer. Controlled chaos was reigning as reports were constantly coming in from units in the field on the progress of the "Rocking Horse" exercise. The British Military Hospital was alerted and an M.P. unit which was held permanently on standby was dispatched to Spandau. The time was 4.54 p.m. The distance to Spandau was just under five kilometres—it took them eight minutes and thirty-two seconds. Jumblatt informed Haddad of the arrival of the M.P. unit at Spandau.

* * *

The phone rang in the safe house and the big guard, Hans, answered it. He passed a message, in German, on to Stroebling who immediately made preparations to leave.

"It must have started," Kathy said helplessly. "Stroebling's going to kill Haddad when he hands Hess over to him."

"Maybe," Michael answered her distractedly.

He and Kathy had been placed together on the sofa against the wall. While the attention in the room was focussed on the phone call, Michael, summoning up all his courage, had slowly reached into his overcoat pocket and wrenched back the filler-lever. He felt the ampoule crack and some liquid, sticky with the sugar content, came away in his fingers. He was suddenly seized with panic: he had to get rid of that coat before he went up like a funeral pyre, but he made himself wait until Stroebling left the room. He closed his eyes and tried to count the seconds in his head. At last the front door slammed—that would be Stroebling leaving. Two guards remained in the room, one more in the passage and perhaps one at the back, but Michael couldn't be sure about him. Hans got up from the table and came towards them. He expected little trouble from Michael and Kathy, but, even so, he was taking no chances. He held a pair of handcuffs. When Michael saw them he shot up from the sofa.

"Not when I'm wearing my coat," he protested in a strangled voice. Handcuffed to Kathy, he would never get that coat off. "I don't mind cuffs, handcuffs, O.K.," he shouted to the bewildered German guard who understood only a few words of English. "But not in my coat, it's too hot in here, too hot!" He mouthed and made motions, trying to make the guard understand, as he struggled furiously to get out of the heavy coat.

"I'll take it," Kathy offered. "I could use some extra warmth."

"No," Michael turned on her fiercely. "No, it's too hot in here, you don't want this coat."

The guard grabbed at Michael's wrist, trying to fasten the handcuff on to it, but Michael tore his arm away. Kathy was looking at him in amazement.

"Have you gone crazy?" she said.

Michael had got one arm out of the coat and he was trying to free the other arm, but the guard had had enough. Using the edge of his hand he hit the side of Michael's neck: not a vicious blow, just enough to stun him. Michael collapsed on the floor. The guard picked him up, placed him on the sofa and slipped the handcuffs over his and Kathy's wrists. He picked up the coat that was crumpled at Michael's feet. The pain was shooting through Michael's shoulder.

"That's a good coat," he said groggily to the guard. "You can have it, I guess I won't be needing it."

The guard didn't want any gifts from Michael. He carried the coat across the room and contemptuously tossed it over the writing-desk.

"What in hell are you doing?" Kathy asked, irritated by her brother's behaviour.

Michael ignored her. He was trying to measure the distance between them and the coat: it wasn't much more than five metres. As far as Michael was concerned that wasn't enough. The coat was only supposed to be a diversion but he remembered that Maroun had been responsible for placing the explosives in the lining, and a man like Maroun would think nothing of knocking down walls. There was a clock on the mantelpiece above the fireplace—he couldn't look at that or the coat, so he gripped Kathy's hand tightly and closed his eyes.

* * *

Maroun had moved up close to the window.

"Stroebling's leaving for your position now," he spoke over the two-way radio to Haddad. "He's taking four men in the car with him and there's an ambulance following him down the street. That must be the way he intends to take Hess out."

"Do you know where they're holding Michael and Kathy?" Haddad asked.

Although the curtains were drawn Maroun had been able to make out enough comings and goings to be convinced. "I'm pretty certain they're in the living-room, ground floor on the right."

"How many guards remaining?" Haddad asked.

"Two on the street and I make it three or four in the house," Maroun replied.

The glow of light showing through the living-room curtains

suddenly became more intense.

"There it goes," Maroun said. "There goes the diversion."

Haddad could tell from the husky tone of his voice that he was ready to be let off the leash.

"O.K. Maroun," Haddad ordered calmly, "go to war."

Maroun waited out the seconds for the fuse in the inside pocket of the coat to detonate the plastic explosive in the hem. He heard the front windows shatter and the explosion rip clear across the street. As one man the guards outside turned and raced towards the house. Maroun was waiting with the rifle. He killed the first guard on the steps and the second one at the door. He wrenched the sash window fully open: there was a small tiled roof providing protection over the entrance below. He jumped, using it to break his fall; and landed on his feet on the grass. He dropped the rifle. Jumblatt's man appeared from the house and picked it up to cover him as Maroun raced across the street.

He jumped the gate, unhooking a ten-second-delay fused fragmentation grenade as he did so, and flung it against the safe house door. He paused for a moment, a grenade in either hand. With a powerful overarm swing he lobbed one grenade through the second-storey bedroom window, the other he threw through the ground-floor window on the opposite side of the front door from the living-room. He hurled himself down behind the side wall as the grenades went up one after the other. Anyone in those rooms would have been killed instantly.

The windows and great chunks of masonry blew out as the interior walls caved in and the ceilings collapsed. Since the first explosion Maroun had been in action for less than fifty seconds. He unslung the sub-machine-gun and ran up the steps. The front door and part of the entrance hall were blown away, the walls pitted with shrapnel. Maroun saw a man staggering towards him from the end of the passage and he fired a burst that cut him down. In the confined spaces of house-fighting everything depended on speed and the savagery of the attack: the man who kept moving stood the best chance of survival. Maroun had no time to clear the upstairs of the house. He lobbed a grenade up onto the first-floor landing, then turned through the smoke and swirling dust from the crumbling, shrapnel-blasted plaster and kicked open the living-room door.

There was one guard left alive in there and he was waiting for Maroun. As the door crashed off its hinges the guard fired blindly, spraying the opening with bullets, but no-one was there. Then Maroun hurtled in low and hit the floor, rolling out of the way. The guard, gun in hand, peered over the upturned chair trying to see where Maroun was hiding.

Behind him the whole room was burning. As the guard left his cover Maroun shot him. The bullets stitched across the guard's chest, the impact spinning him away from the chair. Maroun got up and checked that both guards were dead and then he moved quickly across to Kathy. The room was lit by flames. Kathy was crouching behind the sofa, holding Michael's head in her lap, and she was crying.

"Is it bad?" Maroun asked, kneeling down beside her.

Kathy didn't know who it was for a moment then she saw the moustache, the hooded, tawny eyes, and she relaxed.

"I don't know," she said helplessly. "He's still breathing." Blood was oozing from a bullet wound in Michael's stomach. The flames were raging through the room—the alarm would have been raised by now.

"There's no time to doctor him here," Maroun said. "We've got to get him out." He lifted Michael up and laid him over his shoulder, then he noticed the handcuffs.

"Get the key," he ordered Kathy.

Kathy scrabbled in the pockets of the dead guard and found the key.

"Who got that one?" Maroun asked as she unlocked her brother's handcuffs.

"Michael did," she said. "That man was going to kill me."

"Keep close behind me," Maroun told her. He carried Michael carefully through the burning room and out into the street. A car was drawn up waiting for them.

"How much time have we got to reach the Olympic Stadium?" he asked the driver as he climbed in.

"Twenty-three minutes," Jumblatt's man replied, accelerating down the street.

"O.K.," Maroun said, cleaning the camouflage paint off his face. "Make time to stop on the way, I need to buy some bandages."

CHAPTER TWENTY-EIGHT

Warrant Officer Cooksley followed the stretcher bearers into the main courtyard of Spandau prison. The convoy was drawn up, waiting for them.

"Which ambulance do you want Hess in?" he asked the convoy commander, who he noted with satisfaction was a warrant officer, second class: an experienced soldier but one rank lower than that assumed by Haddad.

"Put him in the second one," the convoy commander ordered. Hess's stretcher was lifted into the back and the medical orderly climbed in with him, strapping Hess down and adjusting the drip and the oxygen mask that covered his face. The door slammed and the orderly locked it from the inside. The convoy commander signed for the patient then ran his eye quickly over his vehicles, checking that the armed soldiers were in place in the Landrovers and that each ambulance driver had an armed escort beside him. Satisfied, he made his way quickly to the lead vehicle.

The engines of the convoy started up and the great fortress gates swung open. Just as they pulled away Cooksley leaned across and slapped his hand against the rear door of the ambulance carrying Hess. He made it seem like an innocent gesture of parting but when he withdrew his hand a thin luminous strip was fixed above the rear door hinge.

Cooksley watched the convoy roar through the prison gates, then he turned and made his way up the steps. Safe in his pocket was a plastic inhaler. Once all evidence of the Propanolol was removed, it would be returned to the medical room.

Jumblatt watched the convoy turn into Gatow Strasse and swung the mini-bus in behind it.

"Convoy on the way," he reported into his two-way radio. "Two Landrovers and two ambulances." He raised his night-glasses and picked out the small luminous strip. "Hess is in the second ambulance, they are taking the Heer Strasse route."

Haddad, listening in, felt a moment of relief, though he had never really doubted that in a genuine emergency the convoy commander would choose the autobahn as the shortest and fastest route to the British Military Hospital.

"Convoy turning on the autobahn," Jumblatt reported. "They are spacing out, picking up speed to 80 kilometres an hour, 50 metres between each vehicle."

Pierre was listening in from his car. The distance from Spandau to the accident site was 2.25 kilometres: it would take only a couple of minutes for the convoy to reach them at their present speed. He checked his safety-belt, started his car and let it move forward along the cobbled side road towards the entrance to the autobahn.

"Convoy speed constant, 80 to 85 kilometres," Jumblatt began his commentary.

Pierre turned onto the autobahn. The traffic was light and the surface was icy, the autobahn brightly lit by the shadowy glare of street lights.

"Coming up to Pichelsdorf," Jumblatt reported.

Pierre moved onto the outside lane and began his run.

"They're changing position," Jumblatt suddenly said urgently. "The ambulance carrying Hess is moving up to the front."

It was obviously a routine manoeuvre but Haddad had been willing it otherwise and the convoy commander nearly caught them off-guard. Haddad reached for his radio but he knew it was too late to say anything to Pierre now. Pierre had heard, he needed both hands on the wheel, the radio lay beside him. He grimaced wryly to himself. The ambulance moving forward was sheer bad luck. He pushed the accelerator pedal to the floor. The speedometer needle climbed to 90, 110, 130, 145, 150 kilometres an hour. Pierre was gripping the wheel, holding the car steady on the icy surface, his eyes searching ahead for signs of the convoy. The autobahn was straight and level, visibility good except for a halo of freezing mist forming under the street lamps.

"We are coming up to the bridge," Jumblatt reported. "The convoy is on the inside lane."

He moved his mini-bus onto the outer lane to block any oncoming traffic and provide Pierre with a clear field to cross the autobahn. For a moment Pierre thought he had mistimed his run and that he was going too fast. He saw ahead the side road where Haddad was waiting, then he spotted the convoy bearing down on him. The vehicles were closing the distance from each other at 230 kilometres an hour. There was no room for error: the lead Landrover flashed across the bridge. Pierre waited until the ambulance carrying Hess entered the area he had marked on the crash ground. He had no time for fear—his concentration was intense. The others were watching, he had an audience—people who believed in his skill and his nerve—it was like his racing days again.

Pierre swung the wheel slightly to the right to break the Mercedes's line of travel, then three-quarter lock left. As the car responded he tapped the foot brake and the tail end broke away. The car came around in a fast 360°, the "G" force pinning Pierre to his seat. Pierre pulled the car out of the spin, steering to the right to maintain direction for the impact with the ambulance. The ambulance driver spotted him careering, apparently out of control, across the traffic lanes. The driver tried to take avoiding action but he was on the inside lane and he had little room for manoeuvre. Pierre threw on three-quarter lock left, over-correcting from the skid as any novice driver would be expected to do. He maintained a steady pressure on the accelerator and the wheel. The Mercedes careered around, spinning and bearing down on the helpless ambulance. Pierre felt the blood from the "G" force pounding in his head, he was half-deafened by the engine roar, the tyre slick on the ice. The noise inside the car and the effects of the ambulance and the autobahn spinning across the windscreen erased all room for thought, he controlled the car by instinct.

The ambulance driver caught sight of the side road and pointed his vehicle towards it. For a second or so it looked as though he might make it, but then the spinning Mercedes side-swiped his vehicle above its rear wheel axle and the ambulance went over with a shattering crash. It skidded for some ten metres into the gap in the side road, tearing the metal along its side, before coming to rest. Pierre had hit the ambulance at a speed of some 60 kilometres an hour. The heavy Mercedes rocked back on its suspension, continuing to slide in the direction of travel, successfully blocking the path of the second ambulance. But the driver of the rear escort Landrover was well practised in the art of defensive driving, and he was already pulling out to avoid the accident site and follow the ambulance carrying Hess into the side road.

Pierre wrenched the wheel over in a hard left lock and hit the brakes. He felt the side wheels lift off the surface of the road, the back wheels came up and the nose went down. He felt the car going over and tried to brace himself. The Mercedes rolled down on the second ambulance. The driver, to avoid it, spun his wheel and crashed into the railings just after the bridge, the Mercedes and the ambulance blocking and pinning the rear escort Landrover inside them. The vehicles had been halted well back from the side road. The Mercedes lay on its roof with its wheel spinning. Pierre had been more successful than he could have possibly hoped. The ambulance driver and his escort leapt out and ran towards the Mercedes. There was no movement from inside.

* * *

Haddad watched the Mercedes knock the ambulance over, saw it sliding into the side road.

"Go!" he shouted.

The Landrover roared out of its sheltered position and drew up by the stricken ambulance. The doors opened before it stopped. The three of them leapt out and raced to their positions. Joseph jammed the upturned escort's door closed, then turned and raced towards the second Landrover hidden further back in the side road. Haddad tried the doors of the ambulance—they were locked. He placed a small plastic explosive charge on the top and the bottom of the ambulance doors, then he pulled back around the side of the vehicle unravelling the fuse wire and connected the circuit to the detonator cap. There came a small explosive crack and the doors flew open.

Both men dived into the back of the ambulance. They grabbed the medical orderly who was dazedly trying to get to his feet and pulled him out. Haddad hit him over the head with a pistol butt. The orderly collapsed. Haddad knelt beside him and injected morphine straight through his trouser leg into his thigh. Jamil was unclipping Hess's stretcher from its supports. The shock of the accident hadn't killed the old man: he was still breathing and seemed unharmed. Haddad had seen the lead Landrover pull up onto the side of the autobahn. The traffic was snarling up, it was dangerous to reverse, but the soldiers would be running back to them now. Haddad helped Jamil lift out the stretcher. Jamil jumped out of the ambulance. He gathered up the stretcher single-handed, put one of the poles over the hooks specially placed on his belt, and using that and both his hands to steady it raced off towards the second Landrover.

Haddad was left alone at the accident site for a moment. He heard the escort kicking up at his jammed door trying to get out. "Wait!" Haddad shouted. "We'll get to you in a minute." He heard the shouts of the British soldiers as they raced back along the autobahn. He heard the lead Landrover reversing, the escort commander having decided to risk the oncoming traffic. He saw its spotlight shining along the top of the embankment. The pitch darkness beyond the glare of the autobahn's street lights, the trees and the snow banks lining the side road provided shelter, but at any moment the British soldiers were going to be on them.

Joseph loomed out of the darkness, carrying the corpse on its stretcher. He was panting and sweating profusely with the effort of carrying its weight over the slippery, snow-covered ground. Haddad helped Joseph load the stretcher into the ambulance. He left Joseph to insert the drip and place the oxygen mask over the corpse's face and dashed around to the front of the ambulance. The escort was trying to kick out the windscreen. Still dazed with the shock of the accident, he was having difficulty finding leverage for his legs without standing on the driver, who was crumpled unconscious beneath the steering-wheel.

"I'll give you a hand," Haddad said.

He gripped the edge of the windscreen as it came loose and wrenched it away, then he helped the escort out.

"About bloody time," the escort swore bitterly as he struggled to his feet and then he saw the royal ciphers on Haddad's sleeve and came stiffly to attention. "Sir," he added.

"You are in no danger," Haddad said. He kept his words clipped and the tone harsh as a man giving orders under stress would do. "I'll attend to the driver. Now double around the back there, the medical orderly is out cold and my corporal needs help with Hess."

The escort dashed to the back of the ambulance. Haddad pulled the driver out. There was blood on his face from a cut on his head and he seemed quite badly concussed. The British soldiers were arriving now. Haddad marched up to meet them. One of the Landrovers roared into the side road, its spotlight shining on the wrecked ambulance.

"Who's in charge here?" Haddad demanded.

"I am," the escort commander said, dismounting from the Landrover. "Who are you?" Then he saw that Haddad outranked him.

Some of his soldiers were hastily taking up positions of all-round defence, while others were helping to lift the corpse out of the ambulance, one man holding the oxygen, another the drip.

"I don't think he's breathing, sir," a soldier called.

"Right," Haddad barked. "Bring that other ambulance up here quick and a couple of you men get a stretcher to the driver, he's badly hurt."

The rear escort Landrover and the second ambulance had managed to extricate themselves from behind the Mercedes and were racing up to the entrance of the side road. Out of the corner of his eye Haddad saw Joseph unobtrusively leave the wreck site and make his way to Haddad's Landrover where he could pretend to be manning the radio. Jamil was hidden in the Landrover further down the side road with Hess, leaving Haddad to control the British soldiers on his own.

"I don't know you, sir," the convoy commander said to Haddad, his suspicions aroused as he had time to think. "You aren't with the 247 Provost Company. What are you doing here?"

Cooksley had briefed Haddad against this. The 247 Provost Company were a small, tightly-knit unit of the R.M.P. that had been stationed in Berlin since the war. They would spot a stranger in their ranks immediately.

"Name's Robinson, initial F.R. 102 Provost Company, stationed at the Army H.Q. Rheindahlen. You'll need that for your report," Haddad said tauntly, indicating that it was going to be a pleasure giving evidence at the convoy commander's court-martial. "I'm here on special duties for the 'Rocking Horse' exercise."

The soldiers were guiding the second ambulance up alongside the wreck. Haddad saw that it had sustained some damage from its collision with the railings.

"Is your vehicle fit to travel?" Haddad demanded.

"Yes sir," the ambulance driver replied. "We'll make it as far as the B.M.H. anyway."

"Right," Haddad ordered the convoy commander. "Load Hess and the rest of the injured on board and get them to the B.M.H. as fast as you can. Hurry."

The convoy commander let Haddad take charge, glad to be relieved of the responsibility. He spun on his heel and hurried off to supervise the loading.

Haddad walked back to the ambulance driver and his escort.

"Did either of you see what happened to the driver of the Mercedes?" he asked, making his voice sound casual.

"He's dead, sir," the ambulance driver said. "The poor bastard must have been so scared when his car went out of control that he couldn't get his foot off the accelerator. A few inches either way would have made all the difference, but there's a vehicle barrier of wooden stumps just up from the bridge and his car rolled right over one of them. It punctured the roof, crushing his chest. The only good thing is he must have died quickly."

The terrible manner of Pierre's death had done more to convince the British that they were the victims of a genuine accident than Haddad's uniform and obvious authority could have done. Haddad nodded, his face showing no expression, but he felt the cold, numbing, sick hurt strike in the pit of his stomach at the death of his friend.

"The injured are on board, sir," the convoy commander reported. The vehicle engines were throbbing: his Landrover was edging forward to collect him.

"Have you notified the operations room?"

"Yes sir."

A series of blue flashing lights appeared at the entrance to the side road.

"The civil police have arrived, sir," someone called out.

"Tell them to get down to the Mercedes and set up hazard lights," Haddad ordered. "Right then, on your way," he said to the company commander. "I'll take care of things here."

Haddad stood alone by the wrecked ambulance, watching the convoy roar out of the side road onto the autobahn. Joseph came up behind him.

"What happened to Pierre?" he asked.

"He's dead," Haddad said harshly.

Joseph knew that Pierre had been as close as any man could be to Haddad.

"Do you want me to go and get his body?" he asked.

Haddad shook his head. "The civil police are with him now, they'll take care of him. Make the signal," he said. He had estimated that it would take the operations room a minimum of sixteen minutes to bring army units up from the exercise area. They had just under eight minutes left.

Joseph ran back toward the Landrover and drove towards the autobahn, flashing his headlights on and off. Moments later a large black Mercedes glided into the side road and stopped. Joseph jumped out of the Landrover and ran towards it. An electric window wound down. Stroebling was seated beside the driver and to protect his failing body from the cold he was muffled in a heavy overcoat, scarf and hat. He turned his ashen face towards Joseph.

"Where is Hess?" he asked.

Joseph caught the glint of metal as one of the bodyguards in the back seat raised his gun and aimed at Joseph's stomach.

"The civil police have arrived and the British reinforcements are expected at any moment," Joseph reported. "Haddad instructed me to tell you that he would make the delivery at the War Cemetery. He said you must take this Landrover. You know that the British are staging a military exercise—it will help you to get through their road blocks and up the slope of the War Cemetery where there is no road."

There was nothing behind Joseph but the wreck of the ambulance. Stroebling signalled to his men. They climbed out of their car and made for the Landrover.

"There's some Military Police caps and British Army overcoats inside," Joseph told them. "Put them on."

Stroebling turned to the driver of his car. "Get rid of him," he ordered, indicating Joseph. "Then follow me. Wait for us in the road below the cemetery."

The driver climbed out of his car with the gun levelled at Joseph. He indicated to him to raise his arms from his sides. Stroebling's Landrover was turning into the autobahn. The driver pointed to the edge of the side road where the banks fell away in a steep drop to the river below. He wanted Joseph to walk towards it. Joseph took two unwilling steps. Then came the low phutt from the silenced gun that he had been waiting for. A neat bullet hole pierced the driver's head and he slumped against the fender of his car. Haddad climbed out from the back of the wrecked ambulance. Wordlessly he and Joseph gathered up the dead driver and threw him over the edge. The body tumbled a few metres towards the frozen river, then disappeared into the snow bank.

"What about the car?" Joseph panted. He was ready to send it over the edge after its driver but Haddad shook his head.

"Reverse it back out of sight," he ordered. "The police won't find it until morning."

Joseph leapt into the driver's seat and the wheels spun in the snow as he reversed the car with Haddad running after him. They left it in the trees beyond the bend in the side road. Joseph took the keys out of the ignition and threw them away. Jamil was at the wheel of the second Landrover. He started the engine, moving it forward out of its hiding-place. Haddad caught up with the moving Landrover and jumped into the passenger's seat. Joseph followed him in and climbed over the seat to the back.

"How is Hess?" Haddad asked, glancing into the back. "Were you in time?"

Jamil nodded. "The Ephedrine Cooksley told us to inject

him with reduced the symptoms almost immediately. His colour is better and his breathing is regular and deep."

"Did you drug him?"

"Yes, he's sleeping now."

Jamil switched on the Landrover lights and set the blue hazard light on the roof flashing as they turned into the autobahn. They passed the wreck of the Mercedes with the police cars parked around it and am ambulance reversing up to collect Pierre's body.

"Wait a minute," Haddad said. "Jamil, stop the Landrover." A policeman standing nearby came up to Haddad's window and saluted.

Haddad indicated the wrecked vehicle. "Do you know who the driver is?" he asked.

The policeman shook his head. "No sir, not yet. The body is pinned into its seat, we can't get to it until the wreckers arrive."

"There's a military vehicle in that side road," Haddad said. "Put a guard on it please and when my colleagues arrive, tell them that I've been called away. I'll make my report as soon as I can." Haddad turned to Jamil who was staring at the overturned Mercedes. "Move on," he ordered. "We're running late."

* * *

Hidden behind the arches that formed the entrance to the British and Commonwealth War Cemetery, Reed-Henry listened to the Landrover engine labouring up the slope towards him.

"Alright," he said to Dade who was lying beside him, his eye resting against the rubber socket of the infra-red sight attached to his rifle. "Make sure you kill him cleanly and then we'll make Stroebling a present of a corpse that will collapse his Intelligence organisation like a house of cards."

"Why aren't you doing this?" Tom Dade complained.

"Because I was promised full American co-operation," Reed-Henry replied. "Besides," he added, "I'm a lousy shot."

The arches to the entrance of the cemetery looked over a small snow-covered clearing: on either side was a wall of dark trees. Reed-Henry had positioned two more of his men with sniper's rifles amongst them. The entrance formed a perfect killing ground. The shadowy silhouette of the Landrover, moving cautiously forward with its lights off, came into the killing ground. The front passenger door opened and an old man climbed painfully out. The other doors were opening: men in British Army great-coats were climbing out and they were armed. Reed-Henry should have realised that Haddad would be expecting trouble.

"I've got him," Dade breathed, fixing his sights on the frail figure bundled up in heavy clothes. The overcoat and hat and scarf left only the eyes and nose visible.

"Fire," Reed-Henry said.

Dade squeezed the trigger, the rifle kicked against his shoulder. The slight form was almost lifted off its feet by the impact of the bullet that smashed into his chest. Stroebling was dead before he hit the ground. The other snipers had chosen their targets. At the signal of the first shot, from perfect ambush positions at close range, they dropped all three bodyguards before a shot could be fired back at them. The snow-covered trees seemed to absorb the echoing crash of the rifle shots.

Reed-Henry walked cautiously out to the crumpled figures sprawled in the snow by the Landrover. Dade followed him. He shone a flashlight into the face of the old man. The small, straight-shouldered figure would have fitted any description of Hess perfectly, but there was something indefinably wrong. Reed-Henry quickly knelt down beside the body, pulled away the scarf and wiped the snow from his face.

"Shit," he said, horrified. "It's not Hess."

"What do you mean?" Tom Dade said, coming up behind him and looking over his shoulder. "It's got to be." Then he recognised the face in the flashlight. "Dear God, it's Stroebling. That bastard Haddad has crossed us."

"What are we going to do now?"

Reed-Henry kept his head. "We've got to get these bodies out of here," he said. "Then if we can't find Hess in the next couple of hours we can make sure that no-one's left around to implicate us. I warned Haddad I'd have people watching all the exits to the West," Reed-Henry said furiously, getting to his feet. "I never thought he had the guts to cross us. But I can tell you this, he's not going to leave this city alive."

CHAPTER TWENTY-NINE

Jamil turned the Landrover, hazard lights flashing, across the traffic on Heer Strasse. On the other side of the autobahn, opposite the entrance to the side road they had been using, was another side road which formed a short cut between Heer Strasse and the Charlottenburger Highway. Jamil drove into it. The road was little used in winter and very isolated. On the one side lay the frozen river, the other was thickly forested. In the beam of the headlights Jamil picked up freshly-made tyre tracks and followed them. The tracks turned off into a small summertime picnic area in the trees. The lights of the mini-bus which was parked there flashed as the Landrover drew up beside it. Jumblatt climbed out.

"Did it go alright?" he asked as he stumbled through the snow towards them.

"Yes," Haddad replied. "So far."

"And Hess?"

"We've got him."

"Maroun's on his way," Jumblatt gave them the good news. The one-eyed Turk was almost beside himself with excitement. The Turks had been underdogs a long time in Berlin, and the thought of cocking his leg on the combined Allied powers filled him with glee.

Joseph and Jamil transferred Hess to the mini-bus. Haddad knelt beside the old man, checking for himself that his heart-beat was returning to normal and his breathing was regular. The three of them hurriedly changed into civilian clothes while Jumblatt worked feverishly to strip the Military Police number plates and markings. He removed the blue hazard light from the roof, restoring the Landrover to its former civilian appearance.

Haddad stepped out of the mini-bus, the two-way radio clasped in his hand. "Where are they?" he asked impatiently. "I can't raise them."

Jumblatt shrugged. "I don't know. They said they were on their way—that's all."

Haddad looked at his watch. The time was 5.40. They had twenty minutes left before the buses were due to depart from the Olympic Sports Stadium. Jumblatt collected up the uniforms for disposal later and joined the others waiting tensely in front of the mini-bus. Maroun would be coming in from the Charlottenburger Highway. The minutes ticked away. They were going into emergency time.

Then Jamil said hoarsely, "There they are, I can hear them." A car was making difficult progress over the bumpy, treacherous surface towards them, the driver using only his parking lights to find the way. He picked up the tyre tracks and swung into the clearing. The doors opened; Maroun jumped out first.

"Michael's hurt," he said.

"Where?"

"Bullet wound in the stomach."

"How bad?"

"I can't tell, but I think it looks worse than it is."

"Get him into the mini-bus, Jamil can look at him there."

As the others took Michael from her, Kathy came straight out of the car into Haddad's arms.

"Oh God," she said, her eyes swimming with tears, "I thought I'd never see you again." She saw over Haddad's shoulder Michael's limp body being carried to the mini-bus. "We've got to get him to a doctor," she said urgently. Her clothes were bloodstained and her fingernails bit into Haddad's arm. "I kept telling Maroun but he wouldn't listen to me. Tell them to get him to a doctor. The bullet's still in him and he's losing a lot of blood."

"There's no time for a doctor," Haddad said. "Jamil's had a lot of experience with bullet wounds, he'll look after him."

"You mean you're still going to try and take him with you?" Kathy asked aghast.

"Yes."

"That's crazy."

"Kathy," Haddad tried to explain. "Even if I wanted to I couldn't leave Michael here because either Stroebling or Reed-Henry will kill him. He comes with us," Haddad said with finality.

"No," Kathy shouted, almost hysterical with worry for her brother. "I'll get him to a doctor and I'll stay with him here. You and your men can go."

She wrenched herself away from him. Haddad hit her an open-handed blow across her face. The hurt that he had struck her was much greater than the pain from the blow and it stunned her into silence. She let Haddad lead her to the mini-bus. Jumblatt had taken over the driver's seat, leaving his men to dispose of the Landrover and car. Haddad and Kathy climbed into the back with the others. Maroun passed Kathy a bundle of clothes to change into.

"Hurry," Haddad said to Jumblatt. "We've already wasted too much time."

"I know, I know," Jumblatt nodded feverishly.

He let in the clutch but the vehicle wheels bogged down in the snow. The men leapt out and pushed it along the side road until the wheels found traction, then they scrambled inside.

"How is he?" Haddad asked.

Jamil was on his knees beside Michael, rebandaging the wound.

"The stomach is not a good place to be hit but we've got the bleeding under control."

"Can you keep him alive without help from a doctor for another eight hours?"

Jamil ran his eye over Michael, trying to gauge the man's physical strength and his will to live. "I think with luck we'll get him through."

"O.K.," Haddad said. "Keep him with you, look after him. Have you got anything you can give him for the pain when he regains consciousness?"

"Yes, I've already given him a shot of the Valium we're using on Hess."

The mini-bus left the bumpy snow-surfaced side road and turned onto the brightly lit Charlottenburger Highway. Haddad moved to the back of the vehicle where Kathy was sitting passively letting Maroun work with make-up on her face. He had rigged lights from the roof, one to shine on an enlargement of her passport photograph, the other to shine on her. He was concentrating hard and every time the vehicle swerved or braked he swore with frustration.

Lights flashed through the darkened glass windows into the back of the mini-bus. They turned off Charlottenburger Highway into the smaller streets leading to the Olympic Sports Stadium.

"We'll be there in seven minutes," Jamil called into the back.

The men were pulling on knitted caps, winding scarves round their necks, fitting huge rosettes into the buttonholes of their coats and adjusting banners, all in the colours of the Athens Panathinaikos football team. Haddad opened a couple of bottles of cheap German schnapps.

"Drink enough to get the taste on your breath," he ordered the men. "Pour some of it onto their clothes," he indicated Michael and Hess. "Then Maroun, you and I carry what's left in the bottles. They'll take it off us as we get onto the bus but it will have created the impression we want."

Maroun had finished with Kathy. The change he had wrought in her was startling. He had coarsened her features, tanned and roughened her skin so that she looked like a young man who worked all day in the open. She was dressed in a cheap, ill-fitting black suit with a wide knotted tie below an open shirt collar: this struck the right casual note and at the same time disguised her slender neck. Maroun and Haddad helped her into an overcoat with a huge rosette on it, wrapped a football supporter's scarf round her neck and placed a wide felt hat on her head. Haddad checked her passport photograph, satisfying himself that she would pass all but the closest scrutiny, then he looked again at Kathy. She seemed listless. The long days in confinement, the constant fear and her anxiety for Haddad and her brother had taken their toll of her spirit. She glanced around at the men in the back of the van.

"Where's Pierre?" she asked.

"He's dead," Haddad answered, unwilling to lie to her.

"Oh my God," Kathy gasped, her eyes filling with tears. Was any of this worth Pierre's or Michael's life? Haddad drew her, sobbing, into his arms. "Later you can cry," he said, understanding how she felt, "but not now." He lifted her head so that she had to look at him. "There are seven seats waiting for us on the bus—we have to fill them. If so much as one seat is left empty then the East Germans' suspicions will be alerted and they'll search all the buses. Everything must be absolutely normal. Michael—me—each man here depends on you tonight because what we have to do now is the most dangerous part of all. You see that old man," Haddad indicated and her heart skipped a beat when she realised the frail figure was Hess. "You're his grandson. He's been a supporter of the Panathinaikos club team since the thirties. He's attended every match he could. You've followed in his support for the team. He's had a good day and he's drunk now, and this could be his last trip. You've come along to look after him. Sit by him on the coach, let him sleep against you, handle all his papers. When he has to be moved we'll help you carry him. Can you do that?"

Kathy nodded.

"We're there," Jumblatt shouted.

He brought the mini-bus to a brake-squealing halt at the back of an enormous parking area. The crowds had nearly all departed. Even the few more ardent fans who had braved the cold by the players' exits hoping for autographs were drifting away. Across from the mini-bus, towards the centre of the nearly deserted car park, waited three Panathinaikos supporters' buses. Most of the Greeks were already on board.

"You're in the last bus," Jumblatt said. "You're travelling with the team and the club supporters' leader is in the same bus as you."

The others got out of the vehicle, carrying the half-conscious Michael and Hess over their shoulders, and began to weave their way drunkenly towards the buses. Haddad remained behind for a moment.

"Tell Pierre's wife what's happened," he instructed Jumblatt. "Look after her until I can contact her. And telephone your friends in Athens—ask them to have a discreet doctor who knows his way around gunshot wounds to meet the plane."

Jumblatt nodded, then reached across the back seat and took Haddad's hand in parting. "May Allah protect you," he said warmly. "Make those Allied generals see their asses."

The lead bus departed, the others had their engines ticking over. The German tour hostess manning the last bus was frantically trying to keep the Greeks she had on board seated and at the same time round the others up. She was in her late thirties and not nearly as attractive as her uniform. She had a square-jawed, almost masculine face and a strong sense of her own importance. Her bus was delaying the others and this would reflect badly on her efficiency, and besides, she didn't like Greeks.

"Departing time was 6 p.m.," she said furiously to Haddad's party as they came stumbling up. "Where have you been?"

The men made obscene gestures to her, indicating that they had been offloading some of the vast quantities of liquor they had consumed against the wheels of the nearby parked cars. She glanced disgustedly at the old man who was being dragged onto the coach over the shoulders of a massive,foul-smelling Greek and a boyish-looking young man. She snatched the half-empty liquor bottles from Maroun and Haddad and then barred their way. Though they had done their best to disguise it, both of them had very distinctive faces.

"I don't know you," she said hastily, her suspicions aroused. "You didn't come in on my bus."

Haddad shrugged his shoulders sheepishly. "We came on the other bus," he admitted in hesitant English. "But our friends here have friends there," he indicated the second bus which was impatiently rolling forward to join the lead vehicle waiting by the exit. "They wanted to be together to drink, play some cards—we didn't mind changing."

"It's against regulations," the hostess bristled angrily. "You were told when you came in that you have to return to the same bus and the same seats, otherwise the East Germans will open the bus."

Haddad shrugged belligerently, as if to say stuff all Germans and their regulations. "We were on the other bus," he said, "ask them."

No one seemed to be taking any notice of the argument. The coach was filled with drunken, cheering, happy supporters of the winning side, moving between the seats and replaying the match at the top of their voices. The Panathinaikos supporters' club leader rose hesitantly from his seat near the front of the bus. He had hoped that he wouldn't be called upon to do this, but the time had come for him to earn his bribe.

"I know these men," he assured the hostess. "They came with my tour."

"What's the matter?" the hostess in the second bus called impatiently across the car park. "What's delaying you?"

The hostess pushed past Haddad and down the steps. "Do you have all your passengers?" she called.

"Yes," came the reply.

One of the Greek supporters, unable to hold a bellyful of German beer any longer, was relieving himself out of the window just above the hostess's head. She hurried up the steps.

"Sit down," she yelled at her passengers.

The tour leader assisted her in restoring order and she quickly counted heads.

"Alright," she said, feeling her duty done when the numbers tallied. She tapped the driver on his shoulder. "Go."

The interior lights dimmed and the bus rumbled across the car park to join the others. Jamil sat with Michael, Kathy with Hess, Maroun sat with Joseph and Haddad sat with the tour leader just behind Kathy.

* * *

The coaches, in convoy, roared across West Berlin. As they neared the checkpoint on the wall the hostess lifted her microphone and her strident voice came barking over the tannoy.

"When the bus stops for checking by the border guards, all passengers are to hold their passports open at the photograph page against the window. Pages should be turned over as indicated by the border guards. No one may get on or off the bus, and, while in East Berlin, there must be no photography of official, military or government establishments," she ordered.

The supporters' tour leader rose and began to translate her instructions into Greek. The buses drew up at the checkpoint. It was a bitterly cold wet night; there was little traffic ahead of them. Kathy, if she turned her head, could catch Haddad's profile reflected in the window beside her. She could see the strain in his face—it was here that he expected trouble. His mind raced, checking the alternatives. He thought that if the deception had been discovered when the Hess double reached the Britith Military Hospital, then the Allies would surely have closed the borders. The fact that they were still open must mean that the deception was holding, unless they were waiting for Hess at the border itself.

The bus moved forward and stopped. The hostess gave their papers to an Allied guard. They were returned to her within a few minutes and the bus waved on. Haddad relaxed for a moment: the deception held so far. He knew that Reed-Henry or Stroebling, whoever survived, would have to remain silent and protect themselves as best they could. And whichever one survived would be looking for him in the West, not in the East; they'd know only a fool or a madman would walk right into the lion's jaws with Hess.

Kathy saw a large sign on the right warning, "You are now leaving the American sector!" She saw the guard towers and the glow of searchlights over the wall ahead and her stomach knotted with fear. The boom lifted and the bus drove over the border line. Kathy wanted to get off and run back into the West but she knew she had no friends left there now. The old man was sleeping peacefully on her shoulder; she reminded herself not to try to support his head on her breast. She wished she was closer to Haddad, she needed his strength.

* * *

The bus rumbled into the East. The high-booted, winter-coated guards came up to the windows. They would make no attempt to enter the coaches unless something aroused their suspicions. The East German government were trying to encourage the use of Schönefeld airport—they needed the hard currency brought in by the tours and the landing fees. Each passenger held his passport to the window. The guards checked the photographs against their faces with flashlights and signalled impatiently for the pages to be turned over, noting the entry stamp made at Schönefeld that morning.

Kathy held her and the old man's passport against the window. Jamil did the same for Michael. Hess was leaning against her shoulder, she felt him falling forward. The guard was watching, she panicked, she had no free arm to hold him. Then she felt Haddad's arm reach around the seat and hold up Hess. The guard gave an angry shout to attract her attention: she had lowered the passports. She lifted them up again. The guard shone his flashlight in her face. He stared for several long seconds at her passport photograph. Kathy pressed both passports against the window to keep her hands from shaking.

At last the guard signalled her to turn over. After the third page he lost interest in her. He signalled that he wanted a better look at Hess's face. Kathy held the old man close to the window. She pointed to his age in the passport, made a gesture of drinking and shrugged her shoulders. The guard had seen enough of the alcoholic stupor that afflicted most of the supporters on the bus to understand. He had already noted the blood relationship between them and, satisfied, he moved on to the next window. Kathy collapsed back into her seat, she was shaking so violently with relief that she could hear her teeth chattering. Haddad's hand found hers and squeezed it in thanks.

The bus moved on through the crash barriers to the Customs Police checkpoint. Eventually the last boom lifted and the bus rumbled through into East Berlin. Haddad glanced at his watch. The coaches were catching up on time.

CHAPTER THIRTY

A British soldier checked Reed-Henry's identification, then lifted the boom and let him drive into the grounds of the British Military Hospital. Reed-Henry parked his car and went in through the glass doors. The foyer was patrolled by paratroopers and there was an armed Royal Military Police sergeant on duty in the porter's lodge. Reed-Henry went up to him and produced his identification.

"What happened?" he asked.

"Accident, as I hear it, sir," the N.C.O. replied, keeping his voice down. "Hess was given as dead on arrival."

"Where is he now?"

"In the mortuary."

"Have the doctors seen him?"

"No sir, only the doctor on duty who certified him dead. There's a hell of a flap on. No one's going near him until the Russians arrive for the post-mortem."

"I want to see him," Reed-Henry said. "On the quiet," he added, making sure the N.C.O. understood.

"The mortuary attendant will show you where he is, sir," the N.C.O. replied.

An aluminium body box slid smoothly out from the wall. Reed-Henry pulled the shroud away and looked down. The old man he saw there was a good double, but not good enough to deceive him. He dropped the shroud over the corpse's face. Until then Reed-Henry could not be sure that Haddad had managed to switch the bodies. But there was no doubt remaining now that Hess was running free, and the four powers would know that in a very short time.

"Thank you," he said harshly to the mortuary attendant who stood respectfully aside, and walked out of the hospital to his car.

* * *

Warrant Officer Cooksley finished his duty shift at Spandau. He had replaced the inhaler without difficulty and so far as he knew no-one suspected anything. It was all proceeding very smoothly, according to plan. That's why he liked working for Reed-Henry: he was a man who got things right.

* * *

The French guards let Cooksley out through the side gate. From Spandau prison it was just a short walk to his apartment where his wife would be waiting up with supper for him. Cooksley heard a car accelerate down the street as he crossed the road to his house. He had nearly reached the pavement and he didn't look round, thinking there was plenty of room on the empty road for the car to pass by. Only moments before the car struck him did he turn, screaming, to face it. The car hit him squarely with the bonnet. Both his legs were snapped at the thighs. He was tossed head-first into the air, striking the roof and the boot, his pelvis and one arm shattered. His vision began to leave his eyes. He heard the car stop, then it reversed back, the wheels spinning over his body. The driver seemed to be making certain that Cooksley was dead.

* * *

The coaches ran into fog a mile from Schönefeld airport. Haddad anxiously watched it swirling past his window. By the time the vehicles reached the airfield the fog blanket was so dense that all the drivers had for guidance was the faint glow of lights from the terminal ahead. The football team and their supporters disembarked and, chivvied on by the hostesses, formed a boisterous, disorderly queue at Passport Control. Michael had regained consciousness. Walking upright and unaided, he took his place in the queue under the steely gaze of the sub-machine-gun-toting Vopos. Hess still had to be carried, but as several of the other supporters had drunk themselves into a similar semi-conscious condition, no-one took much notice. The queue didn't move. Maroun pushed forward to find out why and returned with the news that Passport Control were refusing to let anyone through. Haddad saw the hostess from their coach, who had been talking earnestly with an official, approach the tour leader. They spoke within earshot of Haddad's party.

"The airport has been closed due to fog," she reported.

"How long before it lifts?" the tour leader asked.

The hostess shrugged her shoulders. "Who knows? All planes are indefinitely delayed."

Kathy knew it meant they were trapped in the East. She caught Haddad's eye and made a resigned grimace. The blood had left Haddad's face but Kathy felt it made his eyes glow all the more fiercely. He wasn't ready to give up yet.

"The buses have to go back to West Berlin," the hostess said. "We can take you with us and try to find somewhere for your people to spend the night, otherwise, if you wish, you can go through Passport Control, but then you'll have to remain within the departure lounge for however long it takes until the planes can begin flying again. The authorities will not let your tour spend the night in transit in East Berlin."

The tour leader hesitated, then he said, "We'll go through and take our chances with the fog lifting."

Haddad silently blessed him. The queue began to move forward. Maroun went first, followed by Michael who could not stand unsupported for much longer. He was beginning to sway: Jamil tried to help him but Michael brushed him away. Michael's papers were in order—the passport officials processed them quickly and passed him through. Jamil went next, then Kathy and Joseph with Hess between them. Haddad went through last. They were halted again at Customs Control. Haddad saw Michael swaying.

"Hold him up," he said softly to Jamil. "He's going to faint." Jamil caught Michael just before his legs buckled. Haddad came forward and slipped under his other arm. They made it seem like a game and shouting and laughing, with Michael hanging between them, they barged through into the departure lounge.

The lounge was a large modern utilitarian area, in keeping with the rest of the building, and it was already half-full of delayed passengers, some Swedes and Finns, but most of them from the Iron Curtain countries. The Greeks, understanding they could be in for a long night, immediately fought their way to the bar and traded their money at the ruinous East German exchange rates for as much liquor as they could carry.

Haddad and Jamil laid Michael down on a vinyl-covered bench. Kathy moved in beside him.

"Jesus, the pain," Michael gasped, white-faced and trembling. "It feels like my whole stomach's burning up."

Kathy put her hand on his forehead: he was sweating with fever.

"A little bleeding has started again," Jamil said. He went off to the lavatory and returned with some paper towels. "Lie still," he told Michael.

The others formed a screen round him as Jamil began to re-dress the wound.

"What can we give him for the pain?" Kathy asked helplessly.

"Nothing," Jamil said. The little Valium remaining had to be kept for Hess. "Let him lie there, it won't be long now."

Haddad drew Kathy away; her concern for her brother was too obvious.

"Go back to the old man," he ordered. "Look after him, we'll look after Michael."

Haddad looked up at the clock on the wall. It was nearly 8.p.m. The Hess double would have reached the British Military Hospital shortly after 5.30. When he had run over the plan with Reed-Henry they had agreed that the maximum time limit of four hours was all they could hope for before the deception was discovered. Haddad walked to the windows and stared out, praying for a wind, anything that would cause the fog to lift. He could just make out the silhouette of the aeroplanes waiting on the apron only metres beyond the glass. Freedom was as near as that. . . .

Haddad checked the departure lounge: all the exits were patrolled by armed police. There was nothing they could do but wait. The Greek supporters had taken over all the free space in the lounge, good-naturedly elbowing the other passengers out of the way. Now they were beginning a boisterous game of fifty-man-a-side football, using a rolled-up scarf as a ball.

* * *

A fleet of Russian Army staff cars, carrying the Commandant of East Berlin, his aides and top medical advisers, swept through the Eastern checkpoint of the wall. As a formality they drew up briefly in the West and produced their identity to the Allied M.P.s on duty, then drove on. A military policeman, watching from the Nissen hut control room, phoned ahead of them. The American general, along with his French and British counterparts, had already been alerted and their medical officers were waiting at the British Military Hospital.

"The Russians are on their way now, sir," the policeman said.

* * *

Haddad looked at the clock. 8.50: the time was dragging by. He walked to the windows and back. It was difficult to gauge at night, but the fog seemed to be lifting. He passed Kathy: the strain had told on her at last and she was slumped forward asleep by the old man. Michael was awake, but getting weaker. Jamil left him and took Haddad aside.

"He can't go on much longer," he said of Michael, "unless he has proper medical help."

"Jumblatt will have a doctor waiting for us at the other end," Haddad replied. "Until then there's nothing any of us can do but pray."

Haddad realised that he had been pacing up and down and he forced himself to sit still. An announcement came over the tannoy, momentarily silencing the passengers in the departure lounge. Someone nearby translated it into English. "There appears to be a gap in the fog. The authorities are going to try to get as many planes as they can away before it closes down again. Listen for your flight number."

* * *

The Russian staff cars were joined by an American military police escort shortly after they crossed the checkpoint. The vehicles turned into the 17th Juni Strasse and picked up speed.

* * *

The East Germans wanted the drunken football club supporters out before they wrecked the lounge. The tour leader fought his way into the centre of a scrummage and hollered for silence.

"They are going to board us next," he said.

Hadded went up to Michael. "Can you make it to the gate?" he asked.

Michael nodded. "How much time do you think we have left?"

"I don't know." Haddad shrugged. "Just keep praying."

He went to Kathy and woke her up. "We're leaving now," he told her. "Help the old man."

The airport authorities hurried them through the departure doors and onto the aircraft. It was obvious that they weren't expecting the break in the fog to last long. Haddad found his seat and leaned back against the headrest, his eyes closed. He heard the engines start, the plane was wheeled back, then it began to taxi under its own power to the end of the runway. Haddad and the others listened to the note of the engines, knowing that at any moment the plane could be called back. They stopped. Haddad peered out of the window and realised that they were queueing up behind two other planes.

* * *

The Russian staff cars were sweeping along Heer Strasse. They turned into Passenheimer Strasse, then right into Dickensweg. Seventy-five metres further down on the right they swept past the raised barrier and drew up before the steps of the British Military Hospital. Aides sprang out to open the car doors as the British guards came stiffly to attention.

* * *

The Greek supporters' plane, a chartered 727, moved into first position for take-off. It swung round, pointing down the runway, visibility now only fractionally within the safety limits. The engines screamed, the plane shuddering momentarily against its brakes, then it ran foward, the passengers pressed back against their seats as it accelerated hard down the runway, then seemed to stand on its tail as it took off and climbed up through the fog bank. The No Smoking lights went off, the plane banked and the passengers could see through the cloud the glow of the lights of West Berlin.

* * *

The British and American pathologists waited in an office next to the autopsy room with the French medical observer.

The phone rang and the Englishman answered it.

"The Russians are here, they're on their way down now."

The American glanced at his watch. "It's about goddamn time," he said. "My wife and I had tickets for the ballet tonight."

The Russian pathologist appeared.

"At last," the American complained. "You took your time getting here, Dobrynin."

The orderlies were helping the Russian out of his coat and into a medical gown.

"It couldn't be helped," Dobrynin replied. "My general had to speak with his superiors – they are very concerned. They feel that the British and the French have been negligent in allowing Hess to die. I take it you haven't touched the body?" he asked suspiciously.

"No one's gone near him," the American said warily. "We were waiting for you."

The Russian scrubbed up, held up his hands for the rubber gloves.

"Do you want to cut him up or should we?" the British pathologist asked.

"If you have no objections," Dobrynin answered, "I will do it."

The mortuary attendants pushed the body, on a trolley, through the double doors into the laboratory and lifted it onto the table. The pathologists filed into the room. The operating lights were switched on over the body and they gathered around. The shroud was pulled away, leaving the body naked. The Russian pathologist ran his eyes up and down the corpse, then he peered intently into the face.

"Gentlemen," he announced, "this man is not Hess. Call the general," he said urgently to his aide.

* * *

The captain on board the 727 was talking to his engineer but the second officer was listening intently to his earphones.

"They are recalling all planes in the East German airspace," he reported. "We are supposed to turn back."

The pilot was anxious to get home and he didn't want to spend the night in East Berlin if he could help it.

"How much longer until we are into the West?" he asked.

The second officer did a quick calculation. "Less than two minutes."

"Keep on course," the captain ordered. "Pretend you haven't heard anything and don't answer them."

The hostesses switched down the lights and the passengers lay sprawled in their seats in drunken slumber. Haddad had changed places with Jamil and he was tending Michael.

Kathy came up to them. "How is he?" she asked.

Michael's eyes were closed, his seat was back and Haddad had used the pillows to make him as comfortable as possible.

"He's going to be O.K.," he said. He looked into Kathy's eyes as she knelt beside him and marvelled that, even in spite of the clothes and make-up, anyone could ever have taken her for a man.

"The old man is conscious," Kathy said quietly.

"Has he said anything?"

"No, he's pretending to be asleep but when he thinks I'm not watching him he stares out of the window."

Michael had heard Kathy and he beckoned her close to him.

"This aeroplane and everything in it is completely new to him," Michael whispered painfully. "He won't have been this close to strangers for forty years, the whole effect could be terrifying, so don't try to talk to him, just let him absorb it all in his own time and pray to God he doesn't crack."

Kathy went back to her seat.

* * *

The flying time to Athens was approximately three hours and forty minutes. Due to the delay the plane landed well after midnight and the supporters staggered out onto the gangway, clutching their hangovers. No alert had reached Athens yet and they passed through Customs and Immigration without difficulty.

The ambulance, belonging to a private clinic, was waiting for Michael outside.

"Well," Michael said weakly as Haddad helped him into the vehicle, "we made it. Take good care of him," he indicated Hess.

"I will," Haddad told him, "until your friends come."

Kathy climbed into the ambulance with Michael.

"Go with them," Haddad ordered Maroun. "Watch over them for me."

As the ambulance disappeared Haddad turned back to Hess who was standing unsupported on the steps, with Jamil and Joseph behind. He was taking in the airport lights, the swirling traffic, the different air, the different smells.

"Who are you?" he asked as Haddad turned to him.

"I work for a friend of yours," Haddad answered.

The old man looked up at the night sky, filled with blazing stars.

"Am I free?" he asked suspiciously.

"You are free," Haddad confirmed.

EPILOGUE

I

The taxi drew up. Kathy climbed out.

"Wait for me," she told the driver. She went into the reception area of a very modern, white-tiled clinic. A nursing sister was waiting for her.

"How is he?" Kathy asked.

"Much better," the nurse said. "He's gaining strength rapidly after his successful operation. We can expect to release him within the next two or three days." The nurse opened the door and Kathy walked into a small single ward. Michael was sitting up in bed, propped on pillows.

"Where have you been?" he asked at once. Being confined to a hospital bed was making him impatient.

"I've had things to do," Kathy replied evenly, refusing to let her brother ruffle her. The nurse went out and closed the door.

"Have they come?" Michael asked urgently.

"Five of the committee members arrived last night," Kathy affirmed. "They're with Hess now."

Michael grew excited. "They've got to handle him very carefully," he warned. "Did you explain to them what happened when you and Joseph tried to take him out onto the streets, how he nearly died of fright in the traffic?"

"I've told them what I could," Kathy said tiredly, "but to understand the workings of the old man's mind is a job for you and Matt and Blake, not for me."

"Just as soon as I'm out of here," Michael told his sister passionately, "we'll introduce Hess to the world in a blaze of publicity. It's going to collapse the walls of Spandau and all other jails like it. We did it, Kathy," he exulted. "I can't believe we did it."

But Kathy wasn't listening to him. "Where's Haddad?" she asked. Joseph and Jamil had left the previous day, Maroun last night. She had looked for Haddad all that morning without success.

Michael's first instinct was to protect his sister by trying to stall, but he knew Kathy well enough to sense the concern she was hiding and he couldn't do it. "He's at the airport," he said. "He's on his way to Paris. If you move quickly enough you may still catch him."

Kathy left the clinic and climbed into the waiting taxi.

"Airport," she ordered the driver, "hurry."

"Which terminal do you want?" the driver shouted over his shoulder as the car raced along. "International or Olympic?"

"International."

The taxi stopped at the terminal building and Kathy jumped out. She saw from the departure board that Haddad's flight was not due to be called for another twenty minutes, and she searched the building for him. To her relief she found him sitting alone at a table in the cafeteria.

"Michael told me I'd find you here," she said as she sat down at his table.

"How is he?" Haddad asked.

"He's coming along fine. The operation's been very successful. They'll let him out of hospital in a couple of days." She glanced up at him and her face could no longer hide the hurt she felt. "Why?" she asked. "Why leave like this? Why didn't you tell me you were going?"

Haddad shrugged; he hated goodbyes. "My contract is finished. And," he added drily, "you've been very busy these last few days."

"We've all had our work cut out in trying to condition Hess's mind before his presentation to the media," Kathy answered defensively.

"How's he coming on?"

Kathy sighed. "I'm not sure – it's hard to know what's going on in that old man's mind. Anyway, Michael and the other members of the committee have taken over and they can manage well enough without me. I keep on thinking," Kathy began hesitantly, "I always felt that I could defend the methods we were prepared to use by what we hoped to achieve for the future—not mine—everyone's. But lately," she admitted, "I've been asking myself if Pierre's death made it all worth it."

Haddad studied Kathy. "You believed so strongly in your cause that you had no choice but to go through with it," he told her. "Don't blame yourself for Pierre, he knew the risks he was taking and René will be well taken care of. We achieved the impossible. Success," Haddad said, trying to cheer her. He looked around but he could find nothing to toast her with.

"Success," she answered, her eyes shining with tears. "I came to thank you for making it possible."

The airport intercom system was calling Haddad's flight.

Kathy looked into his face, trying to see what lay behind his dark eyes. It was crazy: now that she had found him, she wanted him so badly that she ached inside and she couldn't bear to lose him. A light began flashing impatiently beside his flight number on the departure board. Haddad gathered up his case, turned to say goodbye but Kathy was gone.

He searched for her in the crowd, but there was no sign of her. He told himself that was how he had wanted it in the first place; with a P.F.L.P. price still on his head he could not ask her to share the risk, it was better this way.

He presented his passport and clutching his bag, began the long lonely walk towards the aircraft departure point. He heard footsteps coming up behind him, but he kept his head down, not wanting anyone to see the pain in his face. A hand reached out and touched his. He was forced to look up. It was Kathy. She must have used another passport checkpoint.

"Where are you going?" he asked tensely, unable to believe she was there.

Kathy shrugged her shoulders, trying to appear noncommittal. "Paris."

"Where's your luggage?" Haddad asked, still not daring to believe her.

Kathy smiled at him. "I haven't carried any personal baggage for a long time," she said, and he understood what she meant. "Besides," she added warmly, seeing him relax and smile at her, "you've got all my money and I figure staying with you is the only way to get it back."

Haddad reached out and took her arm. "So it's Paris," he said. She nodded. The city held good memories for both of them.

* * *

The old man made his way through the crowded streets of Athens. The journey he undertook now was more frightening than any he had ever made in his life before. The blaring noise, the rushing cars and milling pedestrians so crowded his mind with new and shattering sensations that he thought he would go mad. He stood wavering on the pavement until a kindly lady helped him across the street and guided him to the address he was looking for. He made his way past the security checks and was presented to an efficient-looking secretary.

"I want to see your Ambassador, please," the old man said.

"Do you have an appointment?" the secretary asked.

"No," he replied. "But if you tell him that I have information on Hess then I think he will see me."

The secretary looked up. She saw a very small, emaciated figure with stooping shoulders, a gaunt face and sunken dark eyes. She was going to tell him that no one could see the Ambassador without an appointment, but there was an authority in that old man, something about him that made her change her mind. She led him into a waiting-room.

"I'll call you when the Ambassador can see you," she said.

* * *

Michael received a telephone call at the hospital. It was from Matt who represented the hastily reformed Committee of Human Rights.

"Hess has gone," he said in a strangled voice. "We can't find him anywhere."

"How could you let him do a thing like that?" Michael yelled.

"How were we to know?" Matt replied. "We thought he was terrified of going out on the streets. He slipped out of the apartment when we weren't watching and then the crazy lunatic went to the pet-shop below us and let all the birds go free. The shop-owner's called the police and he's threatening to sue us, but Hess has disappeared. Can you call in Haddad?"

"I can't, he's gone. You find him," Michael said furiously, struggling out of his bed and searching for his clothes. "I got him out of Spandau," he shouted into the phone. "Don't you lose him in Athens."

* * *

The secretary summoned the old man to the Ambassador's office. It was a large room with a great polished desk at one end and behind it a huge star of David. The old man hesitantly crossed the room towards the Ambassador, staring at the star.

"I hear that you have your own State now," he said. "I wasn't sure whether to believe it."

"Yes," the Ambassador answered, rising from his desk, staring curiously at the old man. "We struggled to make it and now we have to fight to keep it. What can I do for you?" he asked. "I'm afraid I have another appointment soon."

"Sir," the old man said, "my name is Rudolf Hess." He shrugged his shoulders wearily. "I have spent too long in a cell to be free. I would very much like to return to my home in Spandau."

* * *

Tom Dade entered Reed-Henry's office, which was on the second floor of the British Military Headquarters in the old Olympic Stadium in West Berlin.

He drew up a chair. "You know," he said drily, "that was a pretty rough way to treat an old ally."

"I'm sorry," Reed-Henry apologised, "but there were pressures on us. I'm sure you understand." He moved anxiously around his desk to reassure Dade. "It would have been neater for all concerned if Hess had died," Reed-Henry admitted, "but he's no use to them, they'll never be able to prove he's Hess."

"Why not?"

"Because the real Hess was murdered years ago. We conditioned a double to take his place. Britain was on her knees at that time in the war. We had to find something to take the Germans' pressure off us." Reed-Henry shrugged. "Unfortunately, the Second Front cost the Russians nineteen million dead. The deception would have held except that a medical report confirmed that the old man is going to die soon, and the real Hess had wounds from the First World War on his upper arm and left lung. Though we took care to hide everything else, we were unable to disguise the internal damage made by the bullets. If this man was to die in Spandau, then the Russians' pathologists attending the post-mortem would have found out the truth. We couldn't touch Hess in Spandau while the other three powers are watching us constantly and we couldn't afford to leave his body behind, so it had to be this way."

"And Stroebling?" Dade enquired.

"Both his and the Russians' suspicions had been aroused by a book published by a prison doctor called *The Murder of Rudolf Hess*. The Russians decided they could do little without upsetting the present bureaucracy at Spandau and were content to wait for the post-mortem, but Stroebling decided to take matters into his own hands. . . . We can still pin the blame on him providing we eliminate the pseudo Hess," Reed-Henry said persuasively. "They have to surface with Hess somewhere, and when they do, it will take us no more than forty-eight hours to trace them."

"Well, I've got news for you," Dade said. "We just heard

from the Israelis that they've got Hess and he wants to come back." He looked at Reed-Henry's stricken face without pity. "My friend," he said quietly, "it seems you have a problem."

"You have influence with the Israelis," Reed-Henry protested. "Tell them to put Hess away quietly. They'll do it for you."

Dade shook his head, heaved his heavy frame out of his chair and made for the door. "The U.S. isn't involved," he reminded his ally grimly. "You'd better reach an accommodation with the Russians."

* * *

From the London *Daily Telegraph* dated 10th February 1981.

> "Rudolf Hess, one-time deputy to Hitler, is to be returned today from the British Military Hospital in West Berlin, where he has been undergoing observation for an asthmatic condition, to his cell in Spandau. Rumours reaching the outside world in the last week concerning attempts to rescue Hess appear to have no substance. . . ."

With a grimace Reed-Henry carefully folded his paper, laid it on his desk and leaned back in his chair pondering . . . then his phone began to ring. He had been waiting for this summons and the bell sounded a warning note.

* * *

The convoy drew up in the courtyard of Spandau prison. A medical orderly helped Hess down from the ambulance and led him to the steps where the Russian governor and escort of armed soldiers were waiting to receive him. The escort party fell in around Hess. They made their way through the massive doors into the fortress and on along the dark echoing cell passage. Security had been tightened, accustomed warders were missing from their posts.

"Where's Cooksley?" Hess asked.

"Cooksley's dead," came the reply. "Killed in a road accident."

"Welcome home, No. 7," the Russian governor said, standing aside as the bent old man shuffled into his cell. The heavy door slammed on him, the bolts slid home. Alone at last, he shuffled across the cramped cell to the barred window. The prisoner squeezed his hands through the bars and tapped on the glass to tell the birds he was back.

THE END

LET A SOLDIER DIE by WILLIAM E. HOLLAND

'Whether avenging angels or angels of mercy, helicopters are what made Vietnam's tactics so different from every previous war's . . . LET A SOLDIER DIE is the best and most thought-provoking book so far about a chopper pilot's life over there. Holland's book flies'
C D B Bryan, author of FRIENDLY FIRE and BEAUTIFUL WOMEN, UGLY SCENES

LET A SOLDIER DIE is a searing story of war, of war machines and the men who fly them, and of one brilliant young flier grown old before his time in the valleys of death. Sitting in his helicopter above Vietnam's green fields, the man known to his friends as the Bear never has to touch the people he's killing, or even think of them as human. Never, that is, until the day a group of GIs wander into a fire zone, and find themselves on the wrong end of the awesome firepower of US gunships.

Bear and his companions have to retrieve the wounded and the dead. Because of that day, Bear begins to hesitate. And in a war where nothing is ever certain, that hesitation can – and eventually does – kill men and women Bear knows, loves and respects.

LET A SOLDIER DIE is a novel that takes the war on its own terms – the sights and sounds, the unending fear, the awful beauty and the enormous and instantaneous cruelty and violence. It is a novel that ranks with the very best war novels of any time, and which will take its place alongside CHICKENHAWK, THE 13TH VALLEY, FIELDS OF FIRE and GOING AFTER CACCIATO as the finest writing to have ever been produced by the Vietnam war.